THE WEIRD WEST DOUBLE

PETER BRANDVOLD

WOLFPACK
PUBLISHING
EST 2013

The Weird West Double
Print Edition

Wolfpack Publishing
5130 S. Fort Apache Rd. 215-380
Las Vegas, NV 89148

wolfpackpublishing.com

Paperback ISBN 978-1-63977-201-8

THE WEIRD WEST DOUBLE

DUST OF THE DAMNED

With a tip of the hat
to the cross-genre pulpsters of old
who published their yarns in the pages of the great
Weird Tales.

And in memory of cover artist
Margaret Brundage
1900–1976

1

DEVIL'S LAIR

"SUN'LL BE DOWN in an hour, Uriah." The old prospector's voice had a tremor in it.

The big man riding the rangy palomino stallion he called General Lee slanted a hazel eye at the sky vaulting over the towering canyon walls. "An hour and a half, I 'spect."

"That ain't enough time," said the prospector, Junius Webb, riding a mouse-brown burro along a narrow trail meandering through a deep, high-mountain, stream-threaded canyon in the Sawatch Range of central Colorado Territory.

The big man, ex-Confederate ghoul hunter Uriah Zane, glanced at him skeptically. "You said the cave was just over the next rise."

"We still don't got enough time. It's too damn late in the day, Uriah."

"Stop whizzin' down your leg, Junius," Zane said, his voice low and gravelly and pitched with the soft, rolling vowels of his North Carolina origins. "This ain't my first spin on the ole merry-go-round."

"You ever spin on it so late in the day?"

"Later," Zane said as they topped the rise. "Keeps the

fear up, and that's a good thing in this business." He drew back on General's reins.

Zane was a tall, dark, powerfully built man with thick arms and shoulders. A little past thirty but with a hard wiliness that made him appear older than his years, he wore smoke-stained buckskin pants and a tunic, a long, charcoal-colored wolf vest, and knee-high wolf fur moccasins. He had a handsome but rough, square face that from a distance appeared hand-hewn from knotted oak. Closer up the lines and planes looked finer, less severe, but the eyes, not without tenderness, gave the impression of great age.

His cheeks and jaws were carpeted in a thick, black beard. His long, hazel eyes, slightly slanted and owning a wry intelligence, turned color throughout the day—green, gold, yellow, brown, sometimes the blue of a high mountain lake. His hair was long and nearly black as an Indian's though he himself was of Scotch-Irish and French Huguenot descent. He'd been born and raised in the red-dirt heartland of North Carolina. He'd been born into the Southern gentry, his people having arrived on the New World's shores in the 1750s, then traveling to the savage, Indian-teeming North Carolina wilderness via the Pioneer Road. His family had grown wealthy raising bright-leaf tobacco, a skill handed down from father to son.

Even as a young man, Uriah Zane had betrayed his singular, solitary nature. He had preferred stalking the surrounding mountains, hunting bears and panthers and fishing remote streams alone for sometimes days or weeks at a time. He found such activities far more fulfilling and exhilarating than bedding down in the tobacco barn to gauge the furnace temperature during the long, painstaking process of preparing the rich golden leaves for market.

Neither had he cared for the debutantes' coming-out balls and large gatherings so characteristic of his moneyed, socially conscious class. Early on, he'd acquired a reputation for taciturnity and reclusiveness but also one as a formidable backwoodsmen acquiring hunting and survival skills equal to those of the Amerindians he often found himself fighting and killing, though he felt nothing but respect for the natives, knowing he and his kind were the interlopers on their territory.

A necklace of wolf claws dangled from a rawhide thong down the hunter's broad chest, which was clad in buckskin that a Ute woman he'd holed up with one winter had beaded in sun, moon, and star designs across both breasts.

Horn-handled bowie knives jutted from sheaths strapped inside the tops of his moccasins, and on his shell belt he wore two Colt Navy pistols while a stout, savage-looking LeMat pepperbox revolver jutted from a shoulder holster under his vest. He wore two cartridge belts, one appointed with lead slugs, the other with silver. Down his back hung a quiver and a heavy wooden crossbow that Zane had fashioned himself not long after the War, when he'd headed west to hunt ghouls for his personal satisfaction as well as for a living.

Ghouls ran amok on the western frontier, and a man who could bring in a few werewolves or blood-swillers or the infernal living devils known as hobgobbies and collect on the bounty the U.S. government was offering could make a fair living for himself. If he lived, that was. Or wasn't transformed into the very beast he hunted, which was always a risk.

Zane knew that risk better than anyone.

The same curse had befallen a few friends of Uriah Zane, and Zane himself had undertaken the unenviable task of running them down. He'd thought that was only right. In their places, he'd have hated being taken down by a lucky shot from a thirty-a-month-and-found local badge toter, say, or, worse, allowed to live forever in a form they'd once shunned. Cursed for all eternity.

All in all, a man like Zane, broken by the civil strife and the ghastly tools that Lincoln had used to win the War at Gettysburg, could do worse for himself.

He had no home, no family. The plantation at Rose Hill had long since been taken over by carpetbaggers, and those of his family who hadn't fallen under tooth and claw at Gettysburg were battered and broken husks of their proud former selves, defeated not only by the deaths of so many of their own but by the way those soldiers had died . . . or been cursed to live forever like those who'd cursed them.

Now Zane stared out from beneath the brim of his black, bullet-crowned sombrero banded with woven eagle feathers. His eyes, set deep in leathery sockets, narrowed slightly at the corners as he surveyed the canyon before him with the keenness of a raptor's gaze.

He sniffed the breeze, wolflike, listened closely to every weed rustle and branch squawk, to every tumbling pinecone. It was hard even for his keen ears, however, to hear much above the river rollicking down its rocky bed to his left, chugging, churning, and spitting white foam over its pine-clad banks.

But he hadn't made it nearly ten years in the ghoul-haunted West by striding wildly into swiller-haunted canyons. His friend Junius Webb, who'd been prospecting here in Colorado for nearly thirty years, had informed Zane of the swillers holed up here high in the Sawatch Range. Webb had stumbled on the lair when, picking and shoveling along the banks of the Taylor River, he'd sought refuge from a violent summer thunderstorm in a cave at the base of the northern ridge wall. He'd shared knowledge of his grisly find with the stipulation that once the swillers were sent back to the hell they hailed from, Zane would pay his old friend half of the money doled out by the nearest government bounty office.

Detecting no sign of danger—though one never knew

what besides swillers was lurking in these dark canyons—Zane touched his heels to the palomino's flanks and continued on down the rise. His makeshift wagon clattered along behind him, and Junius Webb found himself eyeing the contraption grimly, for it was far from your usual buckboard or spring wagon. In fact, it wasn't really a wagon at all but a coffin, of all things, on wheels!

Yessir, a pine coffin showing the wear and tear of many ghoul-hunting jaunts, with a heavy hinged lid with a stout cross carved into its top. Webb shivered and looked away, saw the sun hovering near the crest of a distant western ridge wall, angling dark shadows down the steep, pine-clad canyon walls, and shivered again.

"Yep, gettin' damn late," he muttered, though he was well aware his protestations were falling on deaf ears.

Zane glanced over a bulky shoulder at his unwilling partner. "Lead the way, Junius."

"You sure know how to torture a feller, Uriah," Webb said, batting his heels against his burro's sides and riding on ahead down the narrowing, darkening path between ridge walls that bulged and knobbed and sometimes leaned inward, sometimes backward.

Ten minutes later, Zane followed Webb off the trail to the right, and climbed the steep slope spongy with forest duff and fragrant with balsam and spruce. The cave appeared at the base of a bulge in the granite cliff that jutted two thousand feet straight up into the slowly darkening sky. The cavern's ragged opening was just high enough for a man of Zane's height of six and a half feet to enter bent forward at the waist.

Zane halted General Lee and, patting the palomino's long, gold neck soothingly—the General always got his blood up around swillers—slung his two-hundred-and-thirty-odd pounds out of the saddle, walked over to the cavern mouth, and dropped to his knees to get a look inside, one gloved hand on the edge of the opening. The darkness was too dense to penetrate much farther than a few yards.

He sniffed. Cool smells of damp stone, mushrooms, and the fetor of bird shit. A bear had investigated the cave's opening some time ago—Zane could still smell its rank sweetness. But it hadn't ventured far inside. The faint tracks led away from the opening.

He turned to where Junius Webb stood in front of his burro, holding the beast's bridle up close to the bit. "How far does this go into the mountain?" Zane asked him.

"Deep. About sixty yards to the swillers' lair."

"What compelled you to venture that far in, Junius? I never would have suspected you of bravery."

"I'm a prospector, Uriah. Might be a mother lode of silver in there . . . though I'd never mine it now, after what I seen in there. Got some good color in the walls, though. I reckon that's what lured me in so far."

Webb's Adam's apple bounced in his turkey neck as he slanted another cautious eye to the west. "You sure you wouldn't rather we got an early start tomorrow?"

"It's ten miles back to your cabin." The big ghoul hunter strode resolutely toward his wheeled coffin. "And I for one don't cotton to bivouacking in swiller country after dark. Nope, we'll take care of this situation right here an' now. Why don't you hold these torches?" He pulled a couple of relatively straight cedar branches, their ends wrapped in burlap and soaked in coal oil, out from the storage rack beneath the casket, and tossed both to his sallow, patch-bearded, weak-kneed partner.

He flipped the hasp on the casket lid and opened it to reveal a brass-canistered Gatling gun nestling among its wooden tripod and other tools of the ghoul hunter's trade —wooden arrows, steaks, hammers, a spare LeMat, a shuriken that Zane was still learning to throw and that worked well against the nasty hordes of hobgobbies that roamed certain regions of the West. There were several coiled bandoliers containing .45-caliber shells for the Gatling gun, which Zane had managed to swipe one night, drunk, his pockets emptied by a run of hard luck at craps and red dog, from an Army paymaster's storage shed.

He'd chewed himself out the next morning for resorting to common, albeit federal, thievery, but the shed was open, and after he'd stumbled into it and passed out on a pile of flour sacks, the gun was there in all its potential ghoul-killing glory—glistening and attainable—so he'd appropriated it and hadn't looked back. He needed the gun worse than the Army did, as they'd proved next to worthless at running ghouls to ground. Mostly, the blue bellies turned at the first sign of a yellow fang or wolf snarl, and ran like hell back to their fort, soiling their drawers.

Junius whistled. "Whoo-ee, look at all them silver bullets. Good Lord, Uriah, you must have a couple thousand dollars there, with silver prices as high as they've climbed in the past few years!"

"I got a secret source. And sometimes Uncle Sam pays my bounties in silver and I have it melted down for bullets."

Zane slid a few stakes aside and lifted the Gatling gun from its grisly housing. As he did, a burlap sack spilled its contents into the nest the gun had occupied. Junius gasped at the head with its ragged, bloody neck staring up at him, pale blue eyes glassy in death, fangs bared beneath a curled upper lip. The ears were large and porcelain blue.

"Christ!"

"Ah, shit. Here—hold this."

Zane handed Junius the Gatling gun, which the old prospector accepted after he'd dropped the torches. The vampire head was already beginning to smoke where the sun touched it, the flour-white skin turning waxy and ready to melt, as Zane opened the bag and nudged the head back inside with his fist, saying, "Get back in there where you belong, Mortimer."

"Nasty damn business," Junius said, scowling down at the bloody sack.

"Tell me about it. Gotta keep the damn swillers' heads covered good till you haul 'em in for bounty, because Uncle Sam don't pay for ashes." Zane scowled and shook his head, and then grabbed the Gatling back from Junius.

"Wasn't that Mortimer Quinn?" asked Junius.

Zane nodded as he rested the Gatling on one shoulder, slung a sack of arrows over the other one with his crossbow, and headed for the cave. "Caught him in Leadville some days ago, cavortin' after dark with fallen women in back alleys. That old stage robber died nasty, but I got him."

He ducked into the cave, then dropped to one knee and lit a match. He glanced out the entrance at Junius, who stood there holding the two unlit torches in his arms, looking stricken. "Come on. You started this thing; now we gotta finish it. And if we dillydally much longer, we'll have to wait till morning, and I don't think you want to camp out here with the beasts in here huntin' out *there*."

Junius gave an agonized groan and lurched into the cave. While Zane lit one of the torches, the prospector said, "I been wonderin' why I been losin' cattle of late. I bet it's these swillers in here been takin' 'em. Thievin' bastards."

"Yeah, well, I reckon swillers livin' this remote have a hard time keepin' their larders filled. Usually live close to towns like that coven they found livin' in that old whorehouse in Aurora near Denver."

"Uriah?"

Zane had begun moving back into the cavern as Junius walked along beside him, holding up the flaming torch. Zane kept his voice down.

"What is it?"

"My Bonnie's one of 'em."

Zane jerked a look at him. "You sure?"

"She disappeared a couple months back. She done me that way before, but I think she musta got bit one night when she was out skinny-dippin' in the creek by moonlight, and they took her. She was always fascinated by 'em, always talkin' about how manly the males were."

"I'm sorry, Junius." Zane wanted to say that Bonnie had been a good woman, but he knew Junius would see the lie. Bonnie was twenty years Junius's junior and had taken up with the man when he'd been flush with gold and silver and bought a herd of cattle with which to start his own small ranch. But she was wild—anyone could have seen that. She'd have slept with a billy goat if he'd been flush with poker chips and had flexed his biceps at her.

The prospector shook his head, smacked his thin lips, which were cracked and stained from tobacco chew, the wind and sun of the mountains, and camp smoke. "If we run into her, let me drill the arrow through that bottom-dealing bitch's heart my ownself, all right, Uriah?"

Zane continued on into the cavern, hiking a shoulder. "I reckon it's the least I could do, partner."

2

BLESSED BULLETS

"We're gettin' close," said Junius, his voice echoing faintly off the stone walls.

Zane could hear water dripping and a faint vibration in the ceiling, feel it in the stone floor beneath his boots. The cave smelled of pent-up air, bat guano, and a bitter, coppery substance that Zane recognized as blood. Even after all these years chasing ghouls, his heart quickened, and the short hairs stirred faintly along the back of his neck.

The floor dropped suddenly, and the vibration grew to a dull roar that then bounded into a louder cacophony until he could feel the moisture in the air against his face and smell the mineral aroma of underground water. Junius walked a little ahead of Zane, sort of sidestepping, holding the torch aloft and sliding the flickering illumination farther and farther into the corridor, pushing shadows back and away and to each side, angling his and Zane's own silhouettes onto the wall to their right and behind them.

"River ahead," the prospector said. "With a bridge acrosst it. I figured some old prospector built it, so I ventured on across."

The floor continued to drop steeply until the torchlight showed the walls falling away to each side and a large, cold, dank area opening ahead. The roar here was almost deafening, and Zane could feel water droplets spitting at him.

"Easy, now," Junius said loudly enough to be heard above the tumult.

He stopped and extended the torch out over a deep, narrow ravine, water coursing through it—white and wild and chugging over submerged boulders. The river's trench was about twelve feet deep and twice again that wide. Straight out from Zane and Junius stretched a bridge constructed of rope and pine planks. The planks were well worn, varnished by countless crossings.

"I crossed it once," Junius said, his voice trembling in earnest now as he nearly shouted above the water's roar. "It's sound. We'd best get a move on, huh? Them swillers'll be wakin' up soon."

"They are in a ways, ain't they?" Zane said, feeling Junius's apprehension at the lateness of the day. Last he'd seen the sun, though, it had just been starting to dip down behind the western ridges. They likely had a good half hour before it fell beneath the horizon.

Zane lowered his Gatling gun to the floor, wincing as the blood flowed back into his shoulder, reawakening numbed nerves, and nodded for Junius to continue. The prospector stepped onto the worn planks and, holding the torch high with one hand, held on to the other torch as well as one side of the rope bridge with the other. He took mincing steps until he was on the opposite bank, and Zane was right behind him.

"Just beyond here," Junius said, walking ahead more slowly now between the cave's narrowing walls, his eyes fairly glittering with terror.

They came to an opening in the left side wall. Junius stopped, holding the torch high. Zane stopped beside him and stared into what appeared to be a library or smoking parlor outfitted by folks of class and culture. There was a red plush fainting couch, heavy, deep chairs upholstered in wine-red and lime-green crinoline, a large scrolled liquor cabinet, and several heavy bookshelves stuffed with well-worn tomes. There were several small tables where drink glasses and ashtrays sat. A Tiffany lamp glowed on one, its wick turned low.

By far the largest chunk of furniture in the room was a shiny black grand piano over which a Union flag was draped.

"This job just got a whole lot easier," Zane said.

"Wonder how long they been holed up here," Junius muttered.

"What I wonder is how they got that piano in here."

"Not the way we came—that's for sure. Must be another way in." Junius nodded at a low door on the room's far side, flanking the piano. "They're back in there. You think we could pick up the pace a little, Uriah?" The prospector made a gulping sound as he breathed heavily through his nose.

He continued forward, crossing the room. Zane followed him, glancing down as he passed the piano to see an ashtray in which a half-smoked cigar rested, its coal cleanly removed, saving the stogie for later. Zane wasn't sure why, but the image made the nerves along his spine twang as he ducked through the doorway to find himself in a long room, even danker than the others, in which seven mahogany coffins sat on pedestals draped in red, purple, or pink velvet with gold tassels.

"Let's set to it," Zane said, moving to the first coffin and unslinging his crossbow from his shoulder.

The coffin had varnished wooden handles carved in the shapes of lions' feet. Zane grabbed one of the feet and raised the lid to stare down at a pale, silk-suited man with gray hair and a carefully trimmed gray beard and handlebar mustache. He slept with his thin-lipped mouth closed. Wrinkles at the corners of his eyes made it look as though he were smiling. A leather-bound copy of *Ivanhoe* lay open on his chest, as though he'd been reading just before he turned out the lamp on the table beside him, and drew the coffin lid closed.

Zane lowered the crossbow in both hands and triggered an arrow through the swiller's chest, just above the book. The eyes and mouth snapped open. The large, powder-white, beringed hands jerked as though to grab the arrow but they didn't come up even halfway before they relaxed, and the light left the swiller's eyes.

Blood oozed out around Zane's arrow, which he'd bought from some Hunkpappa Sioux up in eastern Wyoming—he preferred Sioux arrows because they used the tough, reliable wood of the chokecherry shrub—to stain the silk shirt behind the black silk double-breasted jacket. That was a lot of blood for a swiller, which meant he must have drunk recently—a bedtime snack, perchance?

Zane moved to the next casket, Junius following him closely, wringing his hands. As Zane opened the next lid, the prospector plucked a battered, old railroad watch from a pocket of his baggy duck trousers, and flipped the lid.

"Oh, Jesus . . . damn near six, Uriah. The sun sets around six in these parts this time o' the year!"

"Don't get your bloomers in a twist," Zane said, as he fired another arrow, mortalizing the immortal, red-haired gent in his crossbow's sites. As the beast's jade eyes opened in shock, Zane said, "Nighty-night, pard," and hurried over to the next casket.

Knocking his crossbow again, he opened the lid. His eyes widened in surprise. The female's eyes were already open and staring up at him, fear trickling into them and causing the pupils to widen. Her red-painted lips began to spread, as though she were preparing to scream. Zane quickly aimed the crossbow straight down at her chest, and thumped an arrow between her breasts that were all but revealed by her low-cut, green velvet gown.

"Oh!" she cried, lifting her head sharply and closing both slender hands around the arrow, groaning and grimacing. "Oh, you dirty . . . *shit*!"

"Holy hobgobbies!" Junius exclaimed, leaping back. "Your fear up now, Uriah?"

Quickly plucking another silver-tipped arrow from the quiver down his back, and nocking the crossbow, Zane hurried to the next casket, finding another swiller coming to life before he hastily killed it forever. The next two were also beginning to awaken before Zane drilled arrows through their hearts, then turned to the final coffin.

Junius stood beside the casket, facing Zane, who yelled, "Look out!"

Too late. The suited, black-haired beast leaped out of the open casket and kicked Junius hard in the side of the head. Junius yelped and flew sideways into one of the other coffins, he and the casket tumbling in a heap from the pedestal and hitting the floor with crunching thuds.

The black-haired beast—a young man in shiny black cowboy boots that had never been near a cow pie, and an Indian-beaded, fringed elk-skin jacket stained snow-white and fancily trimmed with whang strings along its arms—bolted, snarling, toward Zane.

The beast's fangs were fully extended, its eyes red as it sprung off its shiny black boots. Zane triggered the crossbow a half second before the beast slammed into his chest. Zane flew straight back into another casket, knocking the casket off its platform and following it down to the cave floor, the snarling, slithering, red-eyed beast on top of him clawing at his throat and trying to bury its jaws in Zane's neck.

Zane released the crossbow, managed to snake his arms up and close his hands around the beast's throat. He wasn't trying to kill the thing—he knew strangulation wouldn't work—but only to keep those damn fangs from tearing into his neck.

No need. The beast's jaws stopped snapping. His body relaxed. The pale lids did not close down over the red eyes, but the eyes lost their savage light.

Wincing at the pain of the casket under his back, Zane shoved the swiller off him and lay there against the coffin, catching his breath. Junius was on all fours, breathing hard and groaning and shaking his head as if to clear the cobwebs. Blood dribbled down from a cut on his earlobe.

Zane heaved himself to his feet and grabbed his hat and crossbow. "You all right there, partner?"

"Ah, hell, Uriah." Junius winced and cupped a hand to his ear. "I don't know how you do this for a livin'. Let's get outta here. I need a drink. I need a drink bad, hoss!"

Zane grinned and was about to inform Junius of the bottle he had in his saddlebags outside the cave, but closed his mouth and frowned. He heard a distant squawking sound, as though of creaky hinges, and the scuffs of shoes across the cave floor behind him. There were groans and what could only be described as muffled, savage snarls.

Junius's torch was almost out. Uriah scooped up the second one and touched it to the first. Fire caught the kerosene-coated burlap with a *whoosh*, and Uriah swung around to face the direction the sounds were coming from, fear making his heart skip beats.

It skipped more beats when he saw that this anteroom of sorts led to others, and from those others, more well-dressed swillers were stumbling, bleary-eyed and a little disheveled, still waking up from their naps, but, realizing the lair had been invaded, were hissing and starting to run toward Zane.

The ghoul hunter swung around and grabbed the prospector's arm, pulling the man to his feet. "Let's pull our picket pins, Junius!"

"What the hell is that?"

"More!" Zane shoved the torch into Junius's hand and pushed him toward the door. "Run—I'm right behind you!"

He swung around as the first swiller sprinted, snarling and cursing in some language Zane didn't recognize, and Zane quickly knocked his crossbow and buried an arrow in the center of the beast's paisley vest. That slowed the throngs of others that were jostling shadows behind him, but not by much. There were too many for Zane's crossbow.

Cursing under his breath, he dropped the crossbow down his back and grabbed the stout LeMat snugged into his shoulder holster. He triggered the shotgun shell under the main barrel. The shell was filled with crushed silver dimes and nickels, and it laid out two or three of the oncoming horde, before Zane, striding awkwardly backward, flicked the LeMat's lever toward the main cylinder, and squeezed off a silver .44 round, dropping a fat, blue-fanged woman in a gaudy pink dress. He bolted out of the room behind Junius, who was sprinting as fast as his old, bowed legs and creaky ankles as well as his heavy hobnailed boots would allow, the torch flaring above his head and showing his long, thin hair bouncing across his shoulders as he ran.

"You're a dead man, Uriah Zane!" one of the swillers shrieked behind him.

"Damn," Zane said, not breaking stride as he headed toward the rush of the underground river. "I didn't realize I was famous in these parts."

"Oh, you're famous in all parts, Uriah!" a male swiller shrieked behind him.

Through his moccasins, he could feel the vibration of the stream as well as the pounding of running feet behind him, and just a glance over his shoulder showed the jostling shadows of the horde catching up to him—at least a few. One made a dive for his feet, tripping Zane, who nearly went down but regained his balance and momentum after firing the LeMat into the swiller's head, and continued chasing Junius.

Ahead, the torch dropped, and Zane saw Junius's crumpled frame on the cave floor beside it, about ten feet in front of the bridge.

"Goddamnit, Junius!" Zane shouted above the river's roar. "Get up an' *run*!"

"Twisted my ankle," the old prospector grated out.

Zane grabbed the old man's arm, and Junius tried putting weight on one ankle. He cursed as it gave out beneath him.

The ghouls were too close, their shadows lurching across the floor around the torch. The hissing sounded like an awakened rattlesnake nest. Zane aimed the LeMat and fired, the report sounding like a hammer rapping an empty rain barrel in the close confines. That gave the running horde momentary pause. Ten or fifteen of them were behind him. Except for their blazing eyes and bared fangs, they could have been a moneyed, well-read group of civic boosters just now leaving a natty opera house on Larimer Street in Denver. Despite their slight dishevelment upon waking, the ladies were immaculately coifed and gowned, the men suited and well-groomed, pomade glistening atop several combed black or sandy heads.

Zane shoved the LeMat at them, and they lurched back. He triggered a silver round into the chest of one who looked especially determined, and then, as the dead, snarling swiller fell back against several of the others, Zane reached down and pulled Junius up and over his shoulder, leaving the torch where it lay, heading for the bridge.

Not to be thwarted, the howling vampire horde jerked back to life behind Zane. As he gained the bridge's other side, he could feel the jostling of the bridge. He set Junius down near the Gatling gun, palmed his Colt Navy from the cross-draw holster on his left hip, and drilled the first swiller on the bridge in the chest while triggering his LeMat into the swiller behind the first.

The swiller yelped indignantly and clutched his breast, from which blood issued as well as several white smoke tendrils.

"Well, I'll be goddamned," Zane said, his face brightening. "I believe Father Alejandro's blessing gives these slugs an extra pop!"

"Huh?" Junius asked, incredulous.

"Never mind."

Zane emptied both the LeMat and the Colt, then holstered both pieces. He scooped up the Gatling gun, quickly spread its three legs, and directed the canister toward the nattily dressed figures once again making a dash, Indian-file, across the bridge. The first one was ten inches from the end of the Gatling's six-mawed barrel when Zane began twisting the wooden crank.

Bam-bam-bam-bam-bam-bam-bam-bam!

The first slug tore a big hole in the belly of the nearest ghoul, who stumbled back and down while the next slug tore into the gent he'd fallen into. That gent screamed and fell sideways over the bridge and into the raging river.

As the Gatling gun continued roaring, the shots sounded like massive empty barrels tumbling down a rocky ridge, causing Junius to drop to his knees and clamp his hands over his ears. The other ghouls on the bridge were blown back onto the planks or thrown over the sides and into the stream.

Junius whooped and hollered as the blasts continued, cutting into the hordes still coming, so enraged at the invasion of their lair that they'd sacrifice themselves to the Gatling gun in an attempt to get at the big man in wolf furs crouched over it, cranking the flashing, hammering cylinder.

Three rounds ripped through a stringy-haired woman

in a plain muslin dress, and Junius whooped louder. "There's Bonnie. Woo-hoo! You drilled her good, Uriah!"

Suddenly, the torch on the other side of the bridge sputtered out, probably under a swiller's boot, but Zane kept cranking the Gatling gun, hearing the screams and the splashes as the bodies dropped into the river and were washed on out of the cave. He'd fashioned his own cartridge belt, which held a hundred rounds of ammunition, so it took a while to empty it.

When the crank clicked on an empty chamber, Zane unsheathed his second Colt Navy and aimed it out over the dancing bridge. He listened as the Gatling's roars faded beneath the rush of the river.

In the inky darkness he could spy no movement. He wished he had another torch. Suddenly, the stygian blackness before him moved, and he heard the bridge squawk on its worn ropes. A persistent ghoul was marching toward him. He triggered the Colt. There was a squeal, but he could smell a sickly sweet perfume as the bitch continued toward him.

He emptied the Colt. The squeal came sharper this time, and there was the thud of a body slamming down on the bridge.

He waited, listening, quickly reloading the smoking Colt from the shell belt around his waist. Finally, he fished a match out of his shirt pocket, scratched it to life on his thumbnail. The glow spread well enough that he could see no more ghouls heading toward him. Four or five lay twisted atop the bridge. Several more lay with their heads and arms dangling off the opposite bank. He couldn't see any farther than the bank beyond, but he could detect no other movement.

He heard nothing but the river.

Junius lit a match, too. He held it up and looked around warily. Finally, he cast his glassy gaze to Zane. "That was a fine mess o' Yankee swillers, Uriah."

"Yeah, we cleaned up," Zane said after a while. "Sorry about Bonnie."

"No need." The prospector paused. "I sure am glad you came loaded fer bear, Uriah."

"Blessed bullets."

"Huh?"

"I had an old friend bless the silver bullets. Gives 'em a little extra punch." Zane gave the old prospector a wolfish grin. "Don't tell no one, Junius. I want it to be my own special secret."

"Blessed bullets. Whatever you say, Uriah."

Zane dismantled the Gatling tripod, hefted the gun onto his shoulder, and rose. "Come on—I'll buy you a drink."

3

GHOUL HUNTER'S LAMENT

ZANE AND JUNIUS WEBB spent the night in the canyon, on the other side of the river from the cave, drinking coffee liberally laced with busthead from the bottle in the ghoul hunter's saddlebags, and roasting a jackrabbit buck that Junius had shot earlier in the day, near the start of their excursion.

Junius had no liking for bivouacking this close to the swillers' cave, and Zane had to admit, if only to himself, to a buzzing along his own nerve endings. He'd never encountered so many swillers shacked up in the same place before. He and Junius had come close to being torn to shreds, the blood sucked out of their bones, in the cave over yonder.

Worse yet, they might have been transformed, though he couldn't imagine himself and Junius fitting in among that crew of fancy swillers.

Good to know the blessed silver bullets worked so efficiently, however. Next time he ran into a sky pilot, he'd be sure to have him bless a few more boxes of .44s for his Colts and LeMat and his Henry repeating rifle.

Zane and Junius took turns throughout the night keeping watch, though it wasn't really necessary. Neither slept except in short spurts, awakened by every owl hoot and falling pinecone, expecting to see a flour-faced demon glaring down at them, saber fangs flashing in the firelight.

They rose early the next morning and returned to the cave, where Zane set to work cutting the heads off as many dead swillers as he could find with a hand ax. As each head dropped away from the ragged neck, Junius gathered them up by their hair and dropped them into a croaker sack, muttering sour lamentations under his breath. When he'd filled four sacks, and Zane had accounted for twenty-three heads, they tied the tops tight, making sure no sunlight could get in and spoil their work.

"Nasty damn business," Junius complained once more as he and Zane draped the four croaker sacks across the wheeled casket in which the trusty Gatling gun nestled.

"Yeah, well, someone's gotta do it," Zane said for the seventh time that morning, doffing his hat and running a big hand through his thick mane of tangled black hair. "You're glad to have them swillers gone, ain't ya? Might have turned you into one of 'em."

"I doubt a swiller'd care for the white lightnin' I got runnin' through these old veins, but I'm damned tired of 'em feedin' on my cows. The neighbors cows, too. And I been wonderin' why all the game disappeared from this neck of the Sawatch."

They had a last cup of coffee, then broke camp, and, Zane straddling General Lee and Junius Webb in the saddle of his burro, they headed back to the main trail and began following it west along Taylor Canyon, the wheeled coffin rattling along behind, the croaker sacks swaying to and fro down both sides. It was a nice day in the high country this late in the year, the sun a warm caress, the leaves of the aspens well on their way to turning their vibrant yellows and golds.

They stopped to rest and water their horses in a horse-shoe of Taylor River, and Zane stepped into the trees to evacuate his bladder. He took a deep breath, leaned back a little on his hips, and glanced at the sky. He glanced away, then lifted his eyes once more to the rim of the granite and sandstone ridge rising on the opposite side of the river.

A bird was winging around up there, likely hunting the ridge crest for jackrabbits or cottontails. Zane squinted. One hell of a big bird.

As he watched the raptor, or whatever it was, wing out over the canyon from the ridge crest, he vaguely detected a slight tightening in his shoulder blades and a thinning of his piss stream. He lifted a gloved hand to shade his eyes and scrutinized the winged beast just now flying over him, about two thousand feet in the air and beginning to bank as it gradually headed back toward the ridge. Massive lime and gold wings, like giant bat wings, swatted against the air while a long tail, spiked on its top side, curled like a ship's tiller. The head owned the shape of the alligators Zane had once seen on a tobacco-selling journey to southern Georgia, only this head had large triangular ears, like a dog's ears.

Green and gold scales along the winged beast's reptilian body flashed in the sunlight as the beast careened back over the top of the ridge and disappeared behind it.

Zane stood staring, incredulous. He blinked his eyes as if to clear them, wondering if what he had spied was really only a large hawk or eagle but a trick of the light had given it the shape of a dragon.

He stared at the sky over the ridge, hoping the beast would appear once more. After a time, Junius called from behind him, "Uriah, if you're havin' trouble in the peein' department, I know a fella in Gunnison. Sells an elixir that'll have you streamin' like a Belgian plow horse!"

"Did you see that?" Zane said, buttoning his pants and striding back toward the prospector.

Junius was holding the burro's halter and waving

blackflies away from his own long, wart-stippled nose. "See what?"

"That bird up yonder?"

The prospector lifted his gaze. "What bird?"

"Ain't sure it was a bird." Zane brushed past the man and grabbed General Lee's reins. "Do me a favor. The rest of the way to Gunnison, keep an eye on the sky for me, will you? Don't laugh or spread it around the saloons till I know for sure, but I think I seen a dragon."

Junius had turned, wincing a little on his twisted ankle, to follow Zane with his gaze. He arched a skeptical brow. "A what?"

The ghoul hunter swung into the leather and felt his bearded cheeks warm with chagrin. Was he going mad? "Just keep an eye skinned upward and let me know if you see anything you ain't used to seein'. Now, come on, goddamnit. We don't have all day to burn out here. I wanna turn these heads in before we start attracting mountain lions!"

He neck-reined General Lee around and, the casket wheeling along behind him and the croaker sacks swishing like grisly ornaments down its sides, headed back up the western trail. They wound around through the canyon until the steep walls gradually lowered and they were on a broad open flat, the river to their left now, distant mountains jutting like storm clouds in all directions, several peaks already snow mantled.

They crossed the river, wide and shallow here on the sage flats, and entered the cow and mining town of Gunnison. The rough little prairie oasis was so high in altitude that the sun literally appeared to be raining gold out of a vast cerulean sky upon the log shacks and shanties and tent saloons and corrals and leaning privies and stock pens.

Gunnison had a broad main street, its crown jewel a turreted sandstone opera house at a hitch in the road. The log and frame false-fronted businesses around it were more than humbled by its gaudy opulence, though there was a three-story brothel painted red and deep purple, with balconies on the upper two stories, that tried its damndest to compete.

Gunnison was bustling, as it always was this time of the year, with drovers driving beeves to be shipped out on the railroad to Denver or Salt Lake City and prospectors making their gradual way out of the extreme high country around Crested Butte and Tincup to lower altitudes for the winter. And since Gunnison was sandwiched between two known ghoul hideouts—one of hobgobbies, the other of werebeasts, of which there were several known varieties including bobcats and pumas—there was the ever-present and generally unheeled bounty-hunting crowd as well.

A couple of pianos were being hammered in saloons up and down the street. Cutting through the patter as well as the rumble of conversations rising from clumps of waddies and frontiersmen of all shapes and sizes all over the street, a man's angry voice shouted, "Goddamn your vermin hide, McCreedy! I want you outta here *now*!"

Boots clomped. A man yelled. Spurs rang. The batwings of the Wolf's Howl Saloon on the street's left side belched out a burly gent in a short bearskin coat, duck trousers, and brown bowler hat. He stumbled across the gallery, arms akimbo, and continued on down the three steps to the street where he fell and rolled, kicking up a sand-colored dust cloud, and lost his hat.

A dapper-dressed, mustached gent wearing a five-pointed copper star and a ten-gallon Stetson stomped out the batwings, descended the gallery steps, and drove the point of his right, black, hand-tooled boot into the ass of the man in the street. His victim yowled and leapfrogged forward, cursing bitterly and holding one hand against his ass. The badge toter kicked the pilgrim's ass again, through his hand, and again his victim leapfrogged forward and twisted around, red-faced, blond hair hanging in his pain- and fury-pinched eyes. One hand flew to the six-shooter on his right hip.

The mustached badge toter laughed and stood with his boots spread, both hands on his hips shoving back the tails of his charcoal-colored frock coat. "Go ahead, McCreedy. Jerk that toad, if you've a mind. Never know; you just might be as fast as you *think* you are!"

McCreedy stayed his hand but kept it on his pistol butt, glaring up at the tall gent with the badge who dared McCreedy with his mocking blue eyes. Men had come out of the saloon behind the town marshal, holding beer mugs or shot glasses, some smoking, eyes glittering their appreciation of the show before them. McCreedy cut his wounded gaze to the onlookers, then shuttled them back to the town marshal, veins bulging in his forehead as he jerked his Schofield out of its holster.

The lawman slapped leather, his hand a blur as the steel-blue Schofield came up in a flash, and roared, smoke and flames stabbing from the barrel. McCreedy's head jerked back as the .44 round drilled through his temple and plunked into the dust about two feet behind him, spraying blood, brains, and bone into the grit.

McCreedy's quivering hand opened. His six-shooter tumbled into the street by his right knee, and he sagged back in the dirt, shivering as though he'd been struck by lightning.

The crowd fell silent.

Zane and Junius Webb had stopped in the street about thirty feet before the saloon from which the ruckus had erupted. Zane clucked as the lawman, whose name was Wayne Lomax, strode toward the still-shaking carcass.

"That's a mighty fast draw you got there, Marshal," the ghoul hunter said.

Lomax stood over McCreedy but turned his head toward Zane and Junius and grimaced. "Oh, Christ. Not you, Uriah. As if I don't have enough trouble." He picked up McCreedy's gun and turned to Zane once more. "This son of a sow been leadin' up a gang sellin' busthead to the hobgobbies out on Eagle River. You ever confront a drunken hobgobbie, Uriah?"

"A time or two. Like takin' down a bear with a slingshot. I see now why you were so contrary, Wayne."

Lomax beckoned toward the saloon veranda, and three men came down and started to pick up the dead McCreedy and haul him off to the undertaker's. The lawman shoved the dead man's pistol behind his black cartridge belt and sauntered over to Zane and Junius, canting a skeptical eye to appraise the wheeled casket behind the bounty man.

"That's some outfit you got there, Uriah."

"Thanks."

"What's in the sacks?"

"Swiller heads. Ran into a cave teemin' with the vermin, like bedbugs in a Mexican brothel, about ten miles up canyon." Zane arched an admonishing brow. "Ain't that your jurisdiction, Marshal Lomax?"

Lomax's nostrils flared, and he hardened his jaws. "Sundown."

"What's that?"

"That's your deadline for hauling your crazy ass, your crazy friend, and your ghastly casket the hell out of my town, Zane. Sundown!"

Zane's broad, bearded face darkened. His voice was pitched low with an almost affable menace. Darkly, he smiled. "Now, you know better than to tell *me* what to do, Wayne." He splayed his right hand across his thigh, near the Colt Navy jutting on his right hip.

4

U.S. BOUNTY OFFICE

TOWN MARSHAL WAYNE LOMAX looked pained and frustrated.

He cut his eyes from side to side to see who, if anyone, was witnessing his confrontation with the notorious ghoul hunter Uriah Zane. Since most of the onlookers had drifted off after Lomax had killed McCreedy, Lomax looked vaguely relieved.

But he kept his voice low as he said in defeat, "Goddamnit, Uriah. You bust up any more saloons in my town, I'm liable to get voted out of office. Now, will you "—he paused to look around once more, then stepped up so close to General Lee that the horse nickered nervously, and said quietly through gritted teeth—"kindly finish whatever business you have here, stock up on the supplies you need, and all the firewater you can hold, and move on out? Plenty of ghouls up in them mountains yonder. You have a way, Uriah, every time you're here, of makin' me look bad. Weak. And it ain't a good thing for a lawman to look weak in the eyes of those he serves."

"Ah, shit, Wayne—you're fast enough. Why don't you just go ahead and shoot me? You been wantin' to since we was six years old."

Lomax ran a frustrated hand across his mouth, and rattled a sigh. "You know I can't shoot my own blood. 'Specially since there's so few of us Lomaxes and Zanes left in the world. But believe me, if we weren't kin, they'd be hauling you off to where they're taking Lyle McCreedy even as we speak."

"I'll be damned," Junius said with awe, raking a hand across his patch-bearded face. "I didn't know you two was kin."

Lomax turned his agonized eyes on the wizened prospector. "Hold your tongue, Mr. Webb, or I will fabricate a reason for incarcerating your rock-breaking ass!"

"Double cousins," Zane told the prospector. "We're *real* close, Wayne an' me. Least we were till I won a turkey shoot when we was tit-high to a sow's belly, and Wayne had to take my turns in the tobacco barn that summer 'stead o' sparkin' Constance Summerfield, who ended up my brother's betrothed."

"So help me, Uriah, if this ever gets out . . ."

"Ah, don't worry. I won't ruin your reputation," Zane said, touching heels to General Lee's flanks and starting forward, his indignant cousin scrambling aside. "Just don't go thinkin' you can tell me what to do. Gravels me, and you know how we Zanes get when we're graveled."

As he and Junius rode forward through the blood splotch that Lyle McCreedy had left in the street, Lomax called behind him, "Marshal Angel Coffin was in town earlier . . . inquiring about you." His voice owned a faintly mocking tone.

Zane sawed back on General Lee's reins and looked over his shoulder. The marshal stood grinning at him, a fist on his hip, one boot cocked with self-satisfaction. Zane worked a corner of his broad mouth pensively and said with a wolfish growl, "Have I ever been tied to lace panties or apron strings, cousin?"

Undefeated, Lomax chuckled. "Just passin' along a little news, is all."

The marshal turned and started to stroll away.

Zane burned. "What'd she want?"

Lomax stopped, turned back toward him, his cheeks above the upswept ends of his mustache dimpling in delight. "She was goin' after a gang of train-robbin' hobgobbies down around Montrose; was hopin' she'd find you here, since you're familiar with the area, an' all. I told her I hadn't see you in a month of Sundays, thank the good Lord, so she rode on toward Montrose." His mocking grin broadened. "Alone."

Zane's brows furrowed.

"Hope she don't run into no trouble out there. Me, I woulda backed her play, but I got no deputy, so of course it wouldn't be right to desert my post here in Gunnison. Oh, she'll probably be fine. I hear the girl can take care of herself."

"That's right—she can," Zane said and heeled General Lee ahead once more.

Riding off his right stirrup as they continued along the street, meeting broad-wheeled mountain wagons and horseback riders, some of whom Zane nodded to, Junius said, "Who's that your cousin was talkin' about, Uriah?"

"No one," Zane said curtly and began angling the palomino toward the right side of the street, where the low-slung, shake-roofed U.S. Bounty Office hunched beneath the glaring sun. Smoke issued from the place's tin chimney pipe and slithered forward over the brush-roofed gallery.

He dismounted General Lee, wanting to keep his mind off Marshal Coffin. Not that he figured he could. He and the redheaded marshal from Denver had thrown in together a few times to hunt ghouls—once in the Indian Nations and once in Dakota Territory, another in eastern Wyoming. She was the daughter of a famed senior U.S.

marshal, and Zane, who didn't normally cotton to badge toters, had found himself liking the young woman's sand. She was pretty as a desert dusk, an Amazon straight out of a boy's fairy tale with her straight, rose-red hair that fell to the middle of her back, and her curvy, high-busted figure decked out in black leather and a soft, butternut, doeskin vest.

Somehow Angel managed to wear the scar she'd incurred from a wolf's claw at an angle across her right cheek as well as any man would. It not only didn't mar her beauty but somehow heightened it by adding a touch of danger to complement the smoldering green eyes that were in heart-skipping contrast to her hair.

She was a few years younger than Zane, who was older than his years, and they'd ended up sharing each other's blankets a few times, here and there in camps about the frontier. It had seemed a natural thing, them both being alone and naturally hot-blooded. They'd kicked up quite a storm, those nights. Kept the coyotes quiet, as the saying went.

The only problem was, after sharing the woman's hot roll, she'd somehow gotten stuck in the back of Zane's mind. He wasn't used to women staying with him long—in his mind or anywhere else. Such a distraction wasn't safe out here, where it served a man to keep his mind clear.

Besides, Angel Coffin was as much her own woman as he was his own man. Hell, she was a deputy U.S. marshal. She could take care of herself even in known ghoul country.

But she had asked about him. . . .

Zane tossed General Lee's reins over one of the two hitchracks fronting the bounty office, and mounted the front gallery, Junius Webb falling into step behind him and batting dust from his buckskin shirt and baggy trousers with his hat. Zane punched the latch and stepped inside.

"Pete?"

There was no one in the office, though Zane could hear a man and woman laughing together behind a door in the opposite wall. The woman gave a little squeal, and leather bedsprings squawked raucously.

"Sounds like Pete's bein' entertained," Zane told Junius. "Come on in." He glanced at the bullet-shaped stove in the middle of the room, fronting the cluttered desk of the local U.S. bounty distribution agent, Lieutenant Pete Borgland. A battered black coffeepot chugged quietly atop the warming rack. Zane headed toward a crude wooden cupboard near the stove and grabbed a couple of relatively clean coffee mugs off a shelf.

"I've learned not to disturb Pete when he's doin' the mattress dance. He can get surly as an old squaw and find a reason to short your bounty money." He filled both cups from the pot and thrust one at Junius. "Might as well enjoy his mud while we wait. Hasn't killed me yet."

Zane sagged down in one of the two visitors' chairs fronting the desk. Junius sat in the second one, his eyes glittering, lips quirking a devilish half grin as the sounds of lovemaking continued emanating from behind the closed door that directly flanked the desk.

"Oh . . . oh, God . . . !" said the woman.

"Shut up, Dixie—I'm tryin' to concentrate here," said the man.

The woman laughed throatily. "Relax," she said just loudly enough for Zane and Junius to hear through the door. "You're doin' just fine, hon. Much better than last time."

"Goddamnit, Dixie—you gotta talk so much?"

Leather springs sighed. The headboard of Pete Borgland's bed slammed against the wall with the regularity of a metronome.

Beside Zane, Junius snickered. He tried to sip his coffee but ended up choking on it for laughing.

Uninterested—even a little revolted—Zane sipped his

own coffee and stared at a large map of the western territories to the left of the door behind the desk. It had been printed by the government offices in Washington several years ago, and it delineated the Ghoul Lands, the scattered chunks of the western frontier where the main ghoul populations were known to reside throughout the West.

The swillers' main territory occupied a good portion of western Utah and southern Idaho—though any hunter worth his salt knew they could be found in and around any major town or city—while the hobgobbies dominated a large, egg-shaped portion of western Colorado Territory starting just outside of Montrose, where, according to Lomax, Angel was headed. The main packs of werewolves had spread onto two smaller chunks of land, one in the Anvil Mountains around Tombstone, Arizona, the other west of Laramie, Wyoming—though they, like the swillers, were known to haunt portions of every territory west of the Mississippi. According to untrustworthy Washington reports, their numbers were supposedly dwindling.

That was merely propaganda meant to keep President Sherman in office. Zane didn't believe a word of it.

The ghoul hunter sighed and turned away from the map. He knew better than any map where the ghouls resided. He'd just been trying to keep his mind off what Deputy U.S. Marshal Angel Coffin was up to, because he wasn't her damn keeper, and even if he started out after her now—which he couldn't do until General Lee had had several hours of good rest and plenty of oats and water—he likely wouldn't catch up to her before she caught up to the train-robbing hobgobbies she was after.

What plucked at him, however, was the fact that she was asking around for him. She was a proud woman, and she rarely asked for help even when she needed it. That must mean she really thought she needed it now.

"Ah, hell," Zane said as the seemingly never-ending love cries continued behind the closed door.

Beneath the ruckus, he'd been hearing a rat scratching around in the room's rear corner, behind Pete's desk. The rat was still there, scuttling along the wall and munching up what looked to be the remains of a venison sandwich.

Zane's heart thudding impatiently, he wrapped his right hand around the big Colt Navy conversion revolver holstered high on his left hip and raked the hammer back. "Stick your fingers in your ears, Junius."

"How come?"

Zane answered with a thunderous blast of the .44. The rat disappeared in a spray of blood and fur, then landed in two quivering halves.

5

VERMIN CONTROL

BEHIND THE DOOR, the woman screamed.

"What in God's name . . . ?" came Borgland's indignant cry from behind the door.

Zane let a devilish glint spark in his eyes as he holstered the hogleg. Bare feet slapped the bedroom floor. The door jerked open and Pete Borgland poked his wide-eyed, unshaven, double-jowled head into the room. He didn't have a stitch on, and his pale belly curved forward like a big water bladder carpeted in curly black hair.

"Sorry, Pete," Zane said. "Just doin' a little vermin control. Hope I didn't disturb you and Dixie back there!"

Borgland followed Zane's glance to the dead rat that had fallen still amid its own spilled blood and innards against the wall. His eyes popped wide in his broad, round face. "Goddamn you, Uriah!" Then he slammed the door and, cursing and stumbling around, started dressing.

He and Dixie spoke a few words in hushed voices, and then the door opened again, and Pete Borgland was stomping into one boot, his blue cavalry bib-front tunic half-buttoned, as he stumbled into the main office and slammed the door behind him.

Borgland, a rotund man with thinning, curly dark brown hair and bulging blue eyes, stopped and pointed. "You've gone too far this time, Uriah!"

"Ah, sit down and have a cup of your rotgut mud, Pete. Besides, you said the same thing last time."

Borgland scowled, his breathing slowing gradually, and pressed his hair against the sides of his head with both hands. He glanced at Junius. "What's this drunkard doing here?"

"I bet I don't drink no more than you do, Lieutenant." Junius grinned, showing about four discolored, misshapen teeth. "I threw in with Uriah. Showed 'im where a devil's lair of swillers was holed up. We got us over twenty heads out yonder—don't we, Uriah?"

Borgland scowled as he drew up the suspenders of his cavalry trousers. "Where in the hell did you find that many swillers all in one place?"

"There were more than that," said Zane, taking another sip of the bitter coffee. "Lost a whole passel in a river."

Borgland continued to stare skeptically at Zane. Finally, he said, "Let me see these heads, so I know you two ain't been on a bender the last few months."

Zane led Borgland and Junius outside. He slid the staghorn-handled bowie knife out of his right moccasin, and cut into one of the four bags draped over the casket holding his Gatling gun. One of the severed heads spilled out, hit the street with a thud, and immediately started to smoke and sizzle until the skin melted and curled away from the bone. Flames licked out of the growing black hole in the head's temple, where the sun hit it directly.

The fire exploded with a *whoosh!*, and almost instantly the head was turned to a pile of gray ash from which a few lingering flames licked before dying.

The head hadn't completely burned up before Zane was holding the cut bag up by its bottom and shaking out the four other heads in it, all of which hit the ground and rolled and burst into flame.

"That's five there."

Zane summarily cut into and emptied the rest of the heads while Pete Borgland watched ruefully from the veranda. Junius stood one step down from Borgland, letting his injured ankle hang lightly over the step's edge, thumbs hooked behind the cartridge belt wrapped around his concave waist and bony hips, grinning gleefully.

When all twenty-one heads had hit the street and flared up like Mexican fireworks, quickly turning to dust, Borgland swung around and headed back into his office. "All right, all right. Quit showin' off. Get in here and I'll see if I got enough cash to cover the bounty."

"He'll come up short," Zane said with a fateful sigh, cleaning the blade of his bowie on Junius's ragged shirt as he mounted the veranda.

As he ducked through the door and into the office, Borgland was crouched over the safe abutting the back wall, to the right of the door, which just now opened. A pretty though tired- and disheveled-looking redhead with sandy eyebrows appeared. Borgland looked up as Dixie came out and started toward the front of the room.

"Hey, where you goin', honey?" Borgland said, spreading his arms. "I done told ya—I'll be back in a minute."

"You paid for an hour, Pete. That hour was up pret' near two hours ago."

Dixie, dressed in a low-cut, cheap, pleated dress with a red sash to match her hair, and taffeta flowers pinned to one thin shoulder strap, rolled her hips as she approached Zane, who stepped to one side, making room. She blinked slowly and spread her thin lips in a smoky smile. "Hi, there, Uriah. Long time, no see."

Zane removed his hat and dipped his chin. "How you been, Miss Dixie?"

At the door, she swung around and slid a slender lock of hair behind her ear, caressing the doorframe with her rump as she raked her eyes across the big ghoul hunter's tall, brawny frame. "Come on over to the Wildcat later, and we'll discuss it." She cut a wry glance at Borgland. "I'll give you a good deal."

She rolled on out the door and pulled Junius's battered canvas hat down over his eyes as she stepped down off the veranda and headed out into the street.

Borgland sighed as he removed a small canvas sack from the safe, whose only other content was an old Civil War–model Colt Army, straightened his back with a slight crunching sound, and, wincing, tossed the sack onto his desk.

"Twenty-one ghouls," he muttered, shaking his head and tipping up the sack to allow a mess of gold coins to spill out onto the blotter half covering the scarred top of his desk. "And here I thought we were runnin' them ghouls to ground, cleanin' 'em out good. Ain't that what the Army's been tellin' us—that we're winnin' the goddamn war against those creatures?"

"That's what the Army says," Zane said, digging a small hide makings sack out of an inside pocket of his wolfskin vest. "But I been out there in them mountains and canyons as much or more than any Army patrol, and I can tell you, you can't ride from Bozeman City up Montaway to Denver without runnin' into more than I got bullets and arrows for. Everywhere you go, settlers are havin' a time of it—losin' stock to the swillers' and werewolves' night raids and bein' attacked right out in open ground by the hobgobbies."

Thoughtfully, Zane dribbled chopped Mexican tobacco onto a sheaf of wheat paper troughed between the first two fingers of his left hand. "And I don't know if the altitude's gettin' to me, or what, but I think I saw a dragon on the way into town."

The government paymaster stopped counting and sliding coins around with his index finger to glance up at the bounty hunter skeptically. "What'd you say?"

Zane rolled the wheat paper closed around the quirley and stuck the cylinder in his mouth to seal it with spit. "You heard me right."

Borglund studied him for a time, then went back to sliding gold coins away from the scattered group on his blotter. He laughed and shook his head, as though Zane had told him an especially funny joke. But his expression soured suddenly, and, still counting under his breath, he said, "I just hope you're as mad as you must be. The swillers, werebeasts, and hobgobbies are all the monsters I need. Don't need no more."

He reached into a desk drawer and pulled out a small canvas pouch, which he held open beside his desk while he slid the counted coins into it. "At least Charlie Hondo's all sealed up tighter'n a tick on a dog's ear in Hellsgarde Pen."

Zane frowned over the match he'd lit to fire his cigarette. "Hondo's in Hellsgarde?"

"Sure as shit in the hogpen." Lomax smiled though he had only two gold coins left on his blotter. The rest were in the burlap sack he now set down hard on Zane's side of his desk. "They run him to ground two weeks ago in Denver, playin' faro if you can believe it. Drunk as a damn English lord. A barman recognized him from a wanted dodger, sent over to the federal building for marshals, and eight of 'em came in, snugged their rifle barrels up against Charlie's neck, and dragged him away, howlin' like a fork-tailed devil, in chains. They had a quick trial and, since it was obvious they really did have the fearsome leader of the infamous Hell's Angels in custody, hauled him out to Hellsgarde in one o' them armor-plated jail wagons accompanied by an entire company of federal soldiers, three cannons, and four Gatling guns."

"What the hell they go to all that work for?" Zane said, anger burning in him as he remembered that horrific night in the green hills around Gettysburg, when he lost not only a brother, three cousins, and an uncle, but nearly every Confederate soldier bivouacked in the area that night excepting a few wise and desperate enough to throw up a white flag with General Lee's own tearful blessing.

Lee had been mangled and would later take his own life with a silver bullet, just as Abraham Lincoln did a few weeks later, disgraced by his unforgivable sin.

"Shoulda taken his murderous hide out and shot 'im! Course, they shoulda shot Abe right alongside him—if he wasn't already dead, that is—but the least they coulda done is killed the sonofabitch!"

Zane's face was swollen with rage, veins standing out on his forehead. He clenched both fists tightly at his sides until his knuckles nearly popped. Tobacco from his crushed quirley sifted between his fingers. Lomax backed away from the enraged hunter, genuine fear bleaching his pasty features.

"Christ almighty, Uriah—I myself personally had nothin' to do with it. You know what the policy is—those ghouls they think might be more dangerous dead than alive, they lock up in Hellsgarde and throw away the key. They don't want none of 'em comin' back even stronger than they was when they was alive."

Jaws hard, eyes blazing, Zane said, "The superstitions of foolish old men. You kill a werewolf, he's dead. That's all there is to it." He oughta know as well as anyone, Zane vaguely reflected with a moment's feeling of dread.

"Well, some Europeans more experienced with them vermin than even we are seem to think the most powerful of 'em gain more strength if they're killed by humans. Takes a werewolf to kill the most powerful werewolf and keep him dead." Lomax shook his head. "I reckon after the big mistake they made at Gettysburg, trusting those devils *who just seemed so honest and sincere*, they ain't takin' no more chances. It's Hellsgarde for the worst."

"Ah, hell, Uriah," Junius said, standing near Zane, looking apprehensively up at the big man towering over him and Lomax. "It ain't like Hellsgarde's a Sunday picnic along the river. They don't treat 'em none too well there. I hear they cage the werebeasts up tight in stone-walled cells without windows and with stone, iron-banded doors that need to be opened with three keys."

The prospector whistled his appreciation of the government's thoroughness. "I say it's a fate worth than death."

Zane drew a deep breath but he still looked swollen up and ready to rain. "They get the rest of 'em—the other three still on the loose?"

The original band of Hell's Angels had been comprised of forty-five mercenaries, most of whom had been run down and killed by bounty hunters, including Zane himself, who'd personally taken care of a half dozen. Last he'd heard, four remained on the run somewhere in the West, keeping low profiles, including Hondo himself.

"Ain't heard nothin' about them." Borglund sagged down in his chair and pocketed the remaining two coins on his desk. "All I got to say is folks everywhere is gonna be sleepin' a whole lot sounder now that old Charlie Hondo's been run to ground and locked away at Hellsgarde on a diet of cornpone and piss water."

Lomax blew a deep sigh of genuine relief.

"Well, that's somethin', anyway." Zane, calmer now, stuffed the coin pouch into a pocket of his wolf vest and cuffed Junius lightly on the shoulder with his hat. "Let's get us a drink and split the winnin's."

As Junius followed Zane to the door, Borglund said, "Ain't you gonna count it?"

“Why?” Zane said, not looking back but striding on out of the office, the little man limping along behind him. “I’d feel cheated if you didn’t short me.”

6

WELCOME TO HELLSGARDE

"HEY, CURLY JOE!" summoned the uniformed driver of the prison wagon making its way along the scruffy, two-track Hog Wollop Trail in the shadow of the snow-dusted San Juan Mountains in southern Colorado Territory. "You know what smells worse than you and your amigos, Lucky and One-Eye?"

"No, what's that?" yelled Curly Joe Panabaker above the jail wagon's incessant rattling and clattering. He slouched in the modicum of shade provided by a bobcat hide tied over the cage's top.

The driver winked at the man riding shotgun beside him and glanced over his shoulder at Curly Joe and the other two men riding in the cage, their hands cuffed, their ankles shackled to the strap-iron bars. "Nothing stinks worse than you boys. *Nothin'!*"

The driver threw his head back and laughed. The shotgun rider laughed as well.

Curly Joe looked at his cohort riding directly across from him. One-Eye Langtry returned the dull stare as he jerked and lurched with the wagon's pitch and sway. The other man—the third prisoner in the wagon—rode with his back against the rear door.

Lucky Snodgrass was a tall, rangy redhead with a face nearly covered with tan freckles, and a braided ponytail that slithered down his back before it coiled up from the wagon's hard, plank floor to slither onto his buckskin-clad lap, showing the diamondback rattle wrapped into it with cracked rawhide.

"Is that right?" Lucky said to the driver, bunching his broad nose, his pale blue eyes searing into the driver's back, which was clad in a dark blue cavalry tunic, the shoulders of which were mantled in clay-colored dust. "When's the last time you had a bath, Murphy?"

"Me?" said the driver. "I had me a bath last night in Sapinero. Me and Jimbo here both did; didn't we, Jimbo?" He grinned over at the shotgun rider beside him—Sergeant James "Jimbo" Schwartz. "Us and the two whores we bought for ourselves in Missus Dyer's House of Unbridled Badness!"

Murphy and Schwartz elbowed each other and giggled like schoolgirls, both men staring straight ahead toward a high sandstone ridge standing up tall in the desert, a steep arm of the San Juans looming cool and blue behind it.

"You sure there was girls present?" asked One-Eye Langtry, blinking his one brown eye against the dust roiling up from the wagon's right front wheel.

Schwartz looked over his shoulder. "What's that s'posed to mean?"

"It means," said Curly Joe, flexing his right forearm and staring down at the naked dragon-girl tattoo dancing through the thin curtain of fine, light brown hairs, "we think you two Nancy boys mighta been entertainin' each other in that washtub. No girls present at all!" He grinned wickedly. "Accordin' to the rumors we been hearing across the whole Southwest, you two wouldn't know how to please a woman even in the unlikely event you was fortunate enough to bed one!"

"So, instead of women, you boys prefer to play grabbypants with each other." Lucky Snodgrass squirmed around on the wagon floor, lifting one buttock and then the other, and mocking, "Oh, Jimbo, reach down there for the soap, would you, please? Oh, you naughty rascal, that wasn't the soap and you *know* it!"

The three prisoners laughed and yipped like wolves.

Murphy and Schwartz looked at each other, their faces flushing behind the dust and windburn on their bearded cheeks. Finally, Schwartz flexed his fingers on the shotgun he held in both hands before him. "Tough talk for doomed men, eh, Murphy?"

"It is, at that," said Murphy, loudly enough for the men behind him to hear above the wagon's clattering. "We'll see how tough these fellas are once they get to Hellsgarde."

"Hellsgarde won't hold us," announced Lucky Snodgrass. "No, sir—I'd bet the seed bull me and my pards'll be bustin' outta there in a few days. Maybe a week, since the layout's new, an' all. But a week at the most."

Murphy and Schwartz looked over their shoulders at Lucky, as though the man had just sprouted horns and a forked tail and roared in exasperation. Murphy slapped his thigh.

"Son," he said as the ridge wall grew higher and sheerer before them, so that the men in the wagon could make out the pits and fissures in its towering face, "ain't you never heard of Hellsgarde before? No one—and I mean *no one*—breaks out of Hellsgarde. Not even the *ghouls*!"

Schwartz was still looking incredulously back at the three scruffy, dusty prisoners, the long, curly, seed-flecked hair falling from the man's tan cavalry kepi blowing in the breeze. "No, sir, not even the spooks the place was built for even try it!"

"Hey, you know what, Schwartz?" said Murphy. "I wonder if they'll house these fellas with ole Charlie Hondo himself. Hah! Wouldn't that be *fun*?"

"Charlie Hondo'd have these three for a saloon-sized meat plate, first full moon." Schwartz winked at Curly, One-Eye, and Lucky.

Curly Joe feigned a puzzled air, and said, "Who's Charlie Hondo?"

"You mean you ain't never heard of Charlie Hondo?" asked Murphy, staring straight ahead over the backs and bobbing heads of his four-mule hitch.

"Don't recollect I have," Curly Joe said, shrugging a shoulder and looking around at his partners. "You boys?"

One-Eye and Lucky also feigned befuddled expressions and shook their heads.

"Charlie Hondo's the meanest goddamn son of a shape-shiftin' demon son of a bitch in all the West," said Schwartz. "How could you never hear o' Charlie Hondo? Why, he was the leader of that pack of werewolves those two geniuses, Lincoln and Grant, brought over from Russian or Prussia, or wherever the hell they found 'em. You know, the leader of the pack those crazy Yankee bastards used to win the War with." He narrowed a skeptical eye. "You fellas sure you never heard of Charlie Hondo?"

"He only became Charlie Hondo when he came west," said Murphy, flicking his reins over the mules' backs and turning off the main road onto the secondary trail that rose gently toward a dark oval in the sandstone cliff wall. "I believe his name over the big water was Ludwig somethin' or other. Three or four names strung together like freight cars." He gave a mocking snort. "Who the fuck needs more than two names? Someone please inform me."

"Oh, that's right," Schwartz said, nodding. "When this Hondo feller—his real name I can't pronounce—and his yellow-fanged werewolf amigos came west, they took American names, don't ya know? So they'd fit in, you see? And lost their accents, and dressed like us normal folks so they could wreak all sorts of blasphemous, ass-ripping havoc."

Schwartz gave a shudder.

"Well, I'll be damned," said One-Eye, shifting his lone eye toward Curly Joe and quirking his mouth corners ever so slightly. "Learn somethin' new every day, don't we, Curly Joe?"

"I'll say we do," said Curly Joe, glancing at Lucky Snodgrass sitting at the rear of the jail cage, showing a gap-toothed, tobacco-brown grin.

As the wagon approached the cliff wall, Curly Joe saw that the black oval he'd seen was in fact a tunnel mouth. One just large enough to fit a wagon the size of the one he and his compadres were riding in.

As the wagon drew to a stop while a man walked out away from the ridge, Curly Joe saw the blue steel bars over the tunnel mouth. They winked darkly in the late-afternoon sunlight that was touched with salmon and saffron hues, pulling dark pools out from cedars and clumps of rabbit brush.

To each side of the tunnel mouth was a high, wooden, brush-roofed platform. On each platform, a guard in infantry blues sat behind a brass-canistered Gatling gun, which together looked like twin giant, golden mosquitoes. The muzzles were turned toward the wagon, both guards flexing their gloved hands over the guns' wood-handled firing cranks. Long cartridge belts draped down from the gun's brass barrels.

The man walking toward the wagon was large and hairy and sporting a striped serape instead of the customary government-issue tunic. A long, stout cigar protruded from one corner of his mouth. He wore bandoliers crisscrossed on his chest, two pistols in hip holsters, and a third in a shoulder holster.

"Hello, Pablo," hailed Schwartz. "You wouldn't spare another one o' them stogies for an old friend, would you?"

Pablo scowled at Murphy and Schwartz as he sauntered back to the jail cage, the dust just now catching up to the rig and making the big Mexican blink and swipe at the air with one thick, brown hand. He told Schwartz to go fuck his mother. Then, "Who you got here?"

Schwartz reached into his tunic and extracted a bulging manila envelope. "Here's the orders. Bringin' one Curly Joe Panabaker, One-Eye Langtry, and Lucky Snodgrass to Hellsgarde for incarceration under order of the—"

"They spooks?" Pablo asked, ignoring the envelope, standing well back of the cage and cocking his head to one side as he inspected the contents of the jail wagon.

"Nah, hell, they ain't spooks," said Murphy, leaning forward with his elbows on his knees, lightly holding the reins of the stamping, blowing team. "They killed a coupla federals down in Arkansas. You know what happens when federal marshals get beefed."

"Might be against the law to jail humans with spooks," Schwartz said, hungrily eyeing Pablo's big cigar, "but I reckon we won't tell on ole Judge Parker if you boys don't. Besides . . ." He gave a devilish leer to the three slouched, bored-looking prisoners. "We think it'd be kinda fun to see how long these fellas'll last at Hellsgarde, jailed with the likes of Charlie Hondo. Or maybe they'll feed 'em to Avril Wiggins or that crazy blood-swiller Hannibal James." He blinked slowly and held his narrow-eyed gaze on Curly Joe.

"Damn!" Curly Joe feigned a look of bald horror. "You didn't tell me you not only got ole Charlie Hondo housed here, but Hannibal James, too! Law, law, pards, I think I just pissed down my leg!"

The prisoners hissed through their teeth and hammered their backs against the cage walls, making a racket.

Scowling, Pablo turned and walked back to a small, brush-roofed shed that abutted the cliff wall, just right of the steel-banded door over the mouth of the cave. He threw up a hand. "Take 'em in!"

He ducked into the hut. A cranking sounded along with the clinks of large lings looping around a winch, and slowly the steel door rose and disappeared into the cliff face over the cave. When Murphy had flicked the reins over the mules, and the team and wagon had disappeared into the cave, heading toward the light on the other side, Pablo shouted, "You three amigos have a nice time in our fair little prison, now, you hear?"

Pablo and the two men manning the Gatling guns grinned at one another.

From inside the tunnel, above the wagon's loud rattling and the mules' clomping hooves, Curly Joe shouted, "Thanks for the warm welcome, Pablo. But we ain't fixin' on stayin' all that long!"

The prisoners' echoing wolflike yips and howls dwindled slowly. Pablo rolled his cigar from one corner of his mouth to the other and scowled darkly into the tunnel.

7

THERE BE DRAGONS

"House o' ghouls—that's what this place is," Curly Joe said as the wagon rattled out of the hundred-foot tunnel and into the light of the canyon beyond.

Curly Joe, Lucky, and One-Eye stared up at the giant, castle-like dwelling that must have occupied a half square mile of the canyon floor. There was a moat around the place, complete with a drawbridge, and American flags buffeting from the six or seven tower turrets. The castle had been fashioned after the medieval castles in Europe, because not only were they impregnable from the outside; they were damned hard to escape from once you'd been locked up inside.

"What's that?" Schwartz asked as Murphy headed the mule team toward the castle's giant wooden door constructed of complete red oak logs and which, drawn up tight against its casement, appeared wide enough for at least two broad wagons to safely enter in tandem.

"I said this place is a damn house of ghouls," repeated Curly Joe.

"You got that right," barked Murphy, waving to one of the several blue-clad guards standing sentinel in one of the two turreted towers on each side of the drawbridge. "This house o' ghouls is you boys' last resting place. Don't worry, though. There's more like you here. The warden likes to keep a good supply of blood for the swillers—don't ya know? President Sherman says out of one side of his mouth that the swillers ain't s'posed to dine on nothin' but chicken and hog blood, thus the barns way on the back side of the canyon. But out the other side, he says we can do as we see fit, 'cause nothin' quiets a howlin' swiller like human blood."

"Yeah," added Schwartz, widening his eyes in mocking delight. "Fresher, the better." He glanced at the greenish sky arcing over the canyon and the giant hunk of carved granite housing more than two hundred spooks of all known varieties—from werecats to witches—and whistled. "Gonna be a full moon tonight, too. Charlie Hondo, he loves nothin' more than a human thrown into his cage on the night of a full moon." Schwartz elbowed Murphy. "Don't he, Murph?"

"Sure 'nuff," the driver said, having stopped the team and now watching the drawbridge slowly drop down toward the moat. "Keeps him busy for a while. Keeps him from howlin' all night. There's a ranch a coupla miles from here, and we get complaints the day after every full moon. The Chain Link's foreman says Charlie's caterwaulin' stampedes his cattle!"

"Hell," said Murphy. "I hear him down in the quarters by the creek; wakes me up of a night dripping in a cold sweat and streakin' my drawers. Sounds like a hundred million ghouls all howlin' at once. But I reckon it's only Charlie Hondo himself and the two or three other hairy bastards housed here. And the swillers. Plenty of them here, and thank God they don't raise the racket the shapeshifters do."

Lucky Snodgrass curled his nose as he sat inspecting the giant castle from which ribbons of smoke curled through two separate chimneys visible from this vantage. "Smells worse than we do. Even worse than Schwartz."

Murphy chuckled. "You house a few hundred ghouls together, and that's the smell you get. Nothin' stinks worse than a blood-swiller's shit. Like blood sausage left out in the sun—oh, *Lord*!"

"You got that right," said Schwartz as the drawbridge dropped lower, the great ratcheting sounds from a winch inside the castle sounding like the rumble of near thunder. "Some say a werewolf smells worse, but I say hog scat to that. A werewolf's a werewolf, and I have no love for the breed—even though they did help us win the War, by God—but a vampire's shit smells like a whole privy full of well-seasoned dead rats with a couple of dead skunks and adders thrown in to really make you sick!"

The drawbridge dropped to the turf, and the mules brayed and jerked in their harnesses as dust wafted from the platform's impact with the ground on the near side of the moat. The giant chains squawked like the heavy timbers of clipper ships moored to harbor wharves.

"Well, what you fellas might think of doin'," said One-Eye, wrinkling his nose against the almost palpable stench, "is *haul* the shit *outside* and bury it *deep.*"

"Done thought of that," said Murphy, shaking the ribbons over the backs of the mules and putting them up the ramp. He cackled and cut a cunning glance at Schwartz. "Why you think you boys are here?"

He cackled some more as the wagon lurched and thumped onto the drawbridge and headed on over the deep, black water of the moat from which sharpened silver blades protruded at irregular intervals. Schwartz said, "Charlie'll probably feed on one of ya tonight, but that leaves two of you to haul his shit out of the place . . . at least until the next full moon! Charlie's shit ain't as bad as the swillers' shit . . . less'n he's been feedin' on human flesh. Oh, gawd!"

Both men tipped their chins back and laughed as the wagon clattered between the castle's four-foot-thick stone walls. Once inside a broad, open area littered with straw and horse shit, where several cook fires added the smells of roasted meat to the latrine and rancid sweat smell of the place, Murphy halted the wagon.

Soldiers clad in Army blues and fur coats—the sun had fallen behind the western ridges now, and the autumn chill was fast descending—sat around on benches with bored, lazy expressions. Some were playing poker while others whittled or cleaned rifles or, in one case, fed strips of jerky to a three-legged cur that rose on its one back leg, dancing in a circle and howling for dried bits of parched beef or venison.

There were women here, too—broad-bottomed wives or whores of the noncommissioned officers, likely—clad in shapeless skirts and jackets or animal skins, stirring clothes in black kettles suspended over dancing fires. From somewhere unseen came the clangs of a blacksmith's hammer. From a long row of stables to the left of the wagon came the whinnies and brays of horses and mules while a limping soldier in a bobcat skin forked hay into a small corral abutting the stable, where an empty jail wagon sat, tongue drooping.

While the drawbridge began rising back toward the castle's outer wall, Gatling guns atop the twin towers on either side of it were swung around, the soldiers behind them hunkered low and aiming, menacing looks in their eyes beneath their kepi brims. A man moved down the steps from the left tower—a portly, middle-aged man clad in a long bear coat and wearing a blue cavalry hat. The bear coat was open to reveal his blue wool cavalry trousers, a single yellow stripe running down the outside. He puffed a meerschaum pipe, and his tall, black boots flashed in the waning light, the heels clicking on the stone steps.

"Who do we have here?" he asked, removing the pipe

from his thin lips and scowling at Murphy and Schwartz, who'd climbed down out of the wagon's driver's box to walk around to the cage's rear door. Murphy pulled a key threaded on a rawhide thong out of his coat.

"Three prize turkeys, Major Mondrick. Sent out here from Arkansas by Judge Parker with President Sherman's signed blessing."

"Spooks?" asked Mondrick as he neared the bottom of the steps, scrutinizing the men through frosty blue eyes set deep in suety sockets. His nose was long and stitched with crinkled veins like knots of blue thread.

"Not these three. Killed a coupla U.S. marshals out Arkansas way. For non-spooks, they're a savage bunch; I'll give 'em that. They had the choice of being hanged last week in Fort Smith or getting hauled out here." Murphy gave a cockeyed smile.

"Good, good," said Major Mondrick, the warden of Hellsgarde Penitentiary. He slipped the stem of his pipe between his lips and puffed as he approached the jail wagon. "Maybe I shall pit them next Sunday against a couple of the feistier ghouls in our boxing league."

"Maybe oughta feed one o' 'em to the blood-swillers tonight. Or . . ." Murphy grinned at the warden. "Maybe you oughta throw him in ole Charlie Hondo's cage."

"Why?" The warden bunched his wiry brows and loosed a couple more smoke puffs as he gave a condescending gaze to the jail wagon driver. "So you and your lowly ilk can watch the bloodletting, hear the screaming, bet on how long it takes Charlie to clean up his mess?"

"Well, hell, Warden," said Schwartz, his features creasing indignantly. "Ain't that what we'll all be doin' come Sunday?"

Mondrick stretched his lips back in a faintly abashed smile. "Touché." He looked into the wagon where Curly Joe, Lucky, and One-Eye slouched as before, returning the warden's glare. "Oh, well, I suppose I could let you boys have one for this evening. But save the other two for Sunday. You know how Mrs. Mondrick and I and the Considines from the Chain Link Ranch enjoy our Sunday festivities."

"Warden Mondrick!" an English-accented voice called from high above. "Come on up here, Warden. I wish to speak to you about your bathing facilities! Not quite up to the Freeman-Johnson Regulatory Agreement Regarding the Incarceration of Non-Humans, are they?"

Mondrick lifted his head to one of the casement windows in a tower high overhead, in the main part of the castle.

"Shut up, Hannibal. You just got here two weeks ago, and you're already getting on my nerves!"

"Send up one of your big-breasted peasant bitches, will you?" Poking his head out the one-foot-by-one-foot window casement, the swiller named Hannibal James jerked his round, pale face toward where the washerwomen were boiling clothes. "I'm thirsty—and *horny*!"

He snapped his fangs, snarling.

Several of the washerwomen looked up at the castle wall with expressions of great revulsion.

Warden Mondrick glanced at one of the men crouched behind a Gatling gun in the tower to the right of the closed drawbridge He jerked his chin toward the swiller, and the Gatling gun belched, spitting smoke and flames from the end of its six-barreled canister. The bullets hammered the stone wall around the swiller's window a quarter second after the immortal beast had pulled his head inside. The rocketing lead blew up rock slivers and dust.

The Gatling's swivel squawked as the gun was again aimed down at the jail wagon. Warden Mondrick turned his attention back to the new prisoners then, too, and the pipe fell out of his hands to bounce off his right boot, gray tobacco ash smoking.

"Holy shit!" cried Murphy and Schwartz at nearly the

same time, widening their eyes at the jail wagon in which all three prisoners continued to slouch as before.

But, unlike before, they were no longer men slouching with their hands cuffed and ankles shackled.

They were wolves.

The blazing wolf-red eyes and the fangs curving down like sharp, miniature sabers from their upper jaws set the warden's heart to pounding so hard he thought it would literally explode from his chest.

All three sets of pulsating red eyes and grinning teeth were focused on him.

Murphy was slapping the covered holster on his right hip, trying to get his gun out, and screaming, "Holy Christ, they're *spooks*! They're spooks, Schwartz—*shoot 'em!*"

As the warden stumbled backward, swinging his gaze toward the Gatling guns in the guard towers and trying to find the words to the orders he was trying to shout, Schwartz fumbled his Henry rifle up.

Wolves? he was thinking beneath the thundering of the blood in his ears. *It ain't even dark yet!*

Levering a shell into the chamber, he pressed the butt to his shoulder and took aim at the wolf you could still recognize as Curly even if you didn't know where he'd been riding in the wagon—something about the facial features and eyes.

Schwartz fired too quickly, and the first slug ricocheted off one of the iron straps on the door and hammered Murphy's right shoulder, tearing his coat and squirting blood from the driver's back. As Murphy stumbled backward, grabbing his shoulder and grunting, Schwartz fired two more shots into Curly Joe, merely puffing dust from the outlaw werewolf's shirt and pin-striped vest but not appearing to penetrate the tough, hairy hide.

In fact, the lead bullets merely seemed to tickle Curly Joe, for the outlaw tipped his wolf head back and loosed a near-deafening howl, kicking his wolf legs and hammering his paws against the wagon's wooden floor in jubilation.

The others were howling and doing the same, kicking up a tornado in the warden's head. Mondrick finally found the words he'd been searching for and shouted at the Gatling gunners, "Shoot! For Christ's sakes, shoo—"

The air was sucked out of his throat as a weirdly shaped shadow swept over him. A half second later there was a roar like that of a hundred steam valves being released at once.

Varoooooosssshhhhhhhh!

The tower right of the drawbridge, and the man and the Gatling gun on top of it, were suddenly consumed by a great ball of black-stitched, red-orange flames. As the gunner in the other tower turned his head toward the conflagration, he disappeared, too, in a second ball of fire that licked down over the sides of the tower, leaving charred rock in its wake.

The burning gunners' horrific screams were barely audible above the fire's roar and the great creaking of enormous, flapping wings.

Mondrick, who had fallen on his butt at the base of the steps rising to the guard tower, now lifted his eyes to the sky. As it had been threatening to do for the past twenty or so seconds, his heart exploded like dynamite in his chest, not killing him but paralyzing him and filling him with as much hammering pain as the increased horror he felt when he saw the shiny-scaled, locomotive-sized, winged creature sweeping over the castle and favoring him with one large, copper-colored eye, like a small, leering sun.

"Oh, no," he rasped. "Don't tell me there's dragons now, too!"

8

THE HOBGOBBIE TRAIL

The silhouettes of mesquite branches shone like witches' fingers on the rocky slope in the light of the full moon rising over the West Elk Mountains near Sapinero, just north of the San Juans in Colorado Territory.

It shone like a giant, sun-bleached skull—so clear and vivid in the lens-like desert air that Angel Coffin could have surveyed the lunar plains and mountains if she'd lifted her head. But the deputy United States marshal out of Denver had no time to marvel at the night sky.

She kept her head down, eyes forward, as she scrambled up the side of the rocky knoll in a shallow, cedar-rimmed canyon, hearing the drunken, jubilant singing of the Mexican hobgobbies down the other side of the rise. Several were singing badly while another strummed a mandolin. Other sounds rose on Angel's left—strange grunting noises.

Angel stopped suddenly and crouched down behind a boulder, holding her Winchester carbine straight up and down in hands clad in black gloves from which she'd cut out the fingers. She was clad nearly all in black leather excepting a sleeveless, low-cut doeskin tunic that was drawn tightly across her full breasts, her deep cleavage exposed behind rawhide drawstrings. She didn't wear the revealing attire out of vanity, but only because it was comfortable in most climes, and gave her nearly six-foot but willowy and graceful frame ample ease of movement.

Over the tunic she wore a Spanish-style deerskin charro jacket stitched in red. Tall, black, lace-up boots rose nearly to her knees. Her skintight leather breeches were shoved down into the tops of the low-heeled boots.

Doffing her black Stetson, shaking her rose-red hair out, and setting the hat down beside her, she peered over a jumble of black volcanic rocks humping up on her right, and narrowed her jade-green eyes. On her smooth, tapering cheek, beneath her right eye, lay the sickle-shaped scar she'd incurred several years ago from a wolf's decisive swipe a half second before she'd blown the beast to hell.

Angel studied the two human-shaped shadows moving among a few mesquites and desert willows.

About fifty yards away from Angel's position, she realized they had to be part of Rafael Ortiz's band, who'd been robbing banks and raiding ranches throughout Colorado Territory for months. The living demons, who could occasionally pass themselves off as humans despite their long noses and close-set eyes and the fact that they were no more human than a rattlesnake, which made them particularly hard to run down, had left clear signs south of Leadville. Some said the hobgobbies were the offspring of the Devil himself, and Angel, who'd had plenty of experience with the wretched vermin, had found no reason to contradict the theory.

There they'd robbed the second bank in their month-long raid, after enjoying a show at the opera house, oddly enough. Judging by their southward bearing, they were probably intending on returning to Mexico where the devils were welcome if they had pocket jingle, and if they limited their desecrations to the Apaches and relatively defenseless peons, both a bane to the current Mexican government. Also, the Mexicans were more tolerant of hobgobbies because they were natural enemies of the werebeasts that were as nettling south of the border as north of it, and they were more effective than Mexican bounty hunters at thinning the renegade packs.

Angel had tracked them along with her partner, Deputy Dwight Curry, who had been gunned down six days ago. Angel and Curry had been so intent on the hobgobbies' trail that they'd made the mistake of not keeping a close eye on their own backtrails, and several of the band had swung back and flanked them, killing Curry but not before he'd taken out one of the devils and wounded one other. Angel had dispatched the other two before burying Curry and getting back after the main band comprised of the remaining five riders, heading as due south as possible in this demon's playground of towering ridges, slanting mesas, and the maze-like, rocky, snake-infested slashes of canyons.

Angel Coffin had been a deputy U.S. marshal for six years and was as respected as any of the men in a profession that, since the War, did not discriminate against women because, due to the depredations of the ghouls, women outnumbered men on the frontier nearly two to one. There simply weren't enough men any longer to fill all the traditional male occupations, which gave women the opportunity to fill them. Angel had honed her skills and was confident, though not overly so, that she could handle the Ortiz bunch well enough solo.

Still, she didn't like that moon coming up. Not only was it too damn bright, but she should have known better than to night hunt during a full moon when anyone with any sense was holed up in a werewolf-proof cabin. She'd been so eager to run Ortiz's bunch down, however, that she'd lost track of the lunar calendar—an embarrassing, tinhorn mistake that was too damned dangerous to make twice.

Ortiz was out here, though. Maybe he knew something about the hunting habits of the wolf packs in this area. Maybe the werewolves were sticking close to their home country again and dining mostly on Indians, wild horses, and ranch cattle.

Just thinking about one of those spooks getting on her scent out here made Angel shudder—something she took pride in rarely doing. The deputy marshal was no hothouse flower, but even a man like the notorious Uriah Zane, her sometime lover and trail partner—a moody loner who hunted the devils for a living—shied from the thought of a pack of the howling hordes cutting his trail. Werewolves were hardly ever outrun or dissuaded. In fact, Angel had never heard of anyone surviving a werewolf attack unless they were somehow able to make it to a stout-walled shelter with a wolf-proof, iron-banded door.

The deputy marshal pressed her tongue to her lower lip as she peered over the rocks to her left, trying to get a fix on whoever was over there. Finally, wanting to keep track of all members of Ortiz's gang, so she could corral them all later, she pushed out from behind her covering boulder and made her way slowly, weaving among the rocks, toward where the two were grunting and groaning together and making belt buckles and spurs jingle. And then, when she found a nook in the rocks with a good view of the pair, she quirked her mouth corners knowingly.

The demons were fucking like back-alley curs. Not surprising. Male hobgobbies were even more randy than human men, but they were seldom outmatched by the females of their species.

One of the two shadows among the moon-silvered mesquites was bent forward over a flat-topped boulder while the other shadow rammed his pelvis against her round, naked bottom. The bell-bottomed charro slacks of Ortiz's hobgobbie sister, Leonora, were bunched around the young female's ankles while one of the males from the gang rammed her from behind so hard that he had to hold her hips taut in his gloved hands to keep her from sprawling to the ground.

Leonora cackled nastily, wildly.

"Damn fools," Angel muttered, staying low among the rocks and tufts of Spanish bayonet. "Liable to call the wolves down out of the hills, put us all in one helluva bind."

She began to pull her head behind the boulder, but couldn't quite get her eyes down behind the rock. Something about the pair hammering against each other, the male grunting savagely and the female cackling and hissing Spanish curses, gripping the sides of the rock in front of her, pulled at Angel's own loins.

She caught herself, rolling her eyes. Christ, she reckoned it had been too long since her own last tussle. A girl needed a roll in the hay from time to time, to keep her mind clear for more important things, like staying alive in known ghoul-haunted lands.

She studied the pair just finishing now in the mesquites not fifty feet away from her.

"*Mierda!*" Ortiz's sister said with an angry snarl. "I was nearly there, fool!"

The male—oddly tall, not so oddly humpbacked, and wearing a wagon wheel sombrero—backed away from her, awkwardly reaching down to pull up his pants, which had been bunched around his boots. "You take too long, Leonora," he whined in Spanish, in the bizarrely hoarse and high-pitched voice of his kind. The females spoke more like their human counterparts, slightly throatier.

"You don't take long enough, Rubio!"

"Shh! Keep your voice down, woman! You want to let every wolf in the territory know we're here?"

Leonora stumbled back, tripped over her slacks, and fell with an indignant yelp and rattle of spur chains. The small gold amulet that she wore around her neck glistened in the velvety moonlight.

"Leonora!" Rubio reached for her, but she pulled her arm away.

"Leave me, boy! Who is afraid of a fucking wolf, anyway? I'd like to roast one over the fire tonight. Go back to your friends!"

"But, *chiquita* . . ." he whined. He did not leave but stood back in the shadows a ways, his rounded shoulders set with chagrin while the woman dressed, the hump on his back adding to his air of grave defeat as it canted his head downward.

Finally, Leonora got her slacks pulled back up and her belt buckled, and wrapped her cartridge belt and pistols around her waist. Muttering angrily, she donned her black sombrero, adjusting it carefully on her black-haired head, then stomped through a crease in the hills, heading off toward Angel's right and out of sight.

Rubio followed, stumbling drunkenly, hanging his head in chagrin. They were heading in the direction of the singing and the strumming of the mandolin.

Angel waited. She wanted the entire gang together and in one place before she bore down on them, started planting beads with her Winchester '73, and commenced blowing their black hearts back to the particular hole in Hell they'd all slithered out of—though some said each hobgobbie was master of his or her own hell.

A wolf's howl rose and circled the night sky. It silenced the mandolin and the drunken voices from the direction of the hobgobbies' camp. Angel drew a sharp breath and hunkered low behind her covering boulder, feeling chicken flesh rise along her spine.

She waited, breathing shallowly, as though the beast could hear the breath rake in and out of her lungs. Relief loosened her shoulders when no other howls followed the first. There was only silence save for the faint crackling of the demons' fire and the beating of Angel's own heart.

Finally, the strings of the mandolin were strummed once more. They were not tentative strains but challenging ones. Angel ground her teeth. The males and lone female spoke loudly, as though intentionally drawing the werewolves in.

Angel looked down at her cartridge belt, saw the lead and silver bullets housed there in the leather loops for such nights as this. The Winchester was loaded with lead cartridges, ready to go. She had more than enough. No need yet for the precious silver, because hobgobbies could be taken down the same as men. Her silver-chased Colt Peacemaker was holstered low on her leather-clad right thigh, fully loaded as well, and her ancient but well-preserved, razor-edged, silver Spanish sword, a gift from her father when she'd followed in his footsteps and joined the ranks of the U.S. Marshals, was sheathed in a matching black scabbard on the outside of her right leg. Jutting from a boot was a ten-inch Mexican dagger she'd pulled off a swiller bathhouse owner in San Antonio.

In addition, she had three ninja-style shurikens with five points of thinly shaved silver tucked into two separate pouches inside her cartridge belt, over her belly. She'd trained herself to throw the discs nearly as well as a twelfth-century samurai.

She was well armed and well skilled, a formidable foe against even hobgobbies.

How many wolves could be out here, anyway? To avoid leaving a too-clear trail for hunters, they usually ran in fairly small packs.

Finally, when the music and voices dwindled and it seemed the hobgobbies were settling down, Angel rose from behind the boulder and began following the trail Leonora and Rubio had followed, moving quietly in her boots and keeping her eyes and ears skinned for a possible night guard. She doubted the demons would post a lookout—for all their savagery, they were a drunken, arrogant lot—but she hadn't climbed the ranks to deputy U.S. marshal by being careless. Moving as gracefully as a puma, she stole up and over a low rise, following the game path through the scattered trees and desert shrubs.

Ahead, the fire's pulsating glow shone—a circle of umber light in a slight clearing. The strummer had put away his mandolin and was at the far edge of the firelight, his back to Angel. By the set of his head and shoulders and position of his arms, he was relieving himself in the brush.

Leonora was arranging a bed for herself a few yards to the right of the mandolin player and casting jeering glances at Rubio. Her unsatisfactory lover was keeping his head down, scowling as he poured coffee from a black-speckled pot into a dented tin cup. The two other males in the group, one of whom was the leader, Rafael Ortiz, were resting back against their saddles, grinning mockingly at Rubio, their near-lipless mouths stretched wide beneath their long, pointed noses.

Angel heard the murmur of their voices, but she couldn't hear what they were saying. They seemed to be speaking to both Rubio and Leonora, who grunted her responses while keeping her dark-eyed, incriminating scowl on Rubio, who said nothing.

Good. They were all distracted.

Angel hurried forward, moving on the balls of her feet. She'd learned to tread quietly on the quietest of desert nights, always leaving her spurs in her saddlebags and wearing no ornamentation on her clothes. She gained a cottonwood about thirty feet from the clearing, crouched behind it, and drew the Winchester's hammer slowly back to full cock.

9

SOMETHING SNORTED

Angel had just started to take one final gander at the camp, hearing one of the men say, "You know, Leonora, back in Rio Juarez, the senoritas all marvel at my love skills," when Leonora's brother yawned suddenly, and said, "Forget it, Pedro. No one can satisfy my sister's goatish lust. No one. Not even I—her brother!"

He laughed and began to haul himself to his feet, casting his eyes toward the tree behind which Angel was hunkered. She drew her head back behind the cottonwood and gritted her teeth as Rafael continued to laugh his menacing, high, squeaking laugh, and said in slurred Spanish that it was time to drain his dragon.

Leonora said, "Thank God I was that drunk only once, Rafael!"

"As I remember, *mi hermana*, you came pretty close to enjoying yourself."

Spitting sounds of revulsion rose from the other side of Angel's tree. At the same time, she heard Rafael's laughter and saw a long shadow stretch across the ground to her left. The hatless silhouette continued to angle off through the trees in the direction from which Angel had come.

Rafael followed it, passing so close to the cottonwood

that Angel could smell the sour tequila sweat mixing with the typical death stench of the hobgobbie. The smell filled her nostrils and brought tears to her eyes, nearly making her choke.

Rafael stopped about ten feet beyond her, facing away. Angel held herself as still as possible. She could hear her heart pounding and hoped the demon neither sniffed nor heard her, as a hobgobbie's senses were nearly as keen as a wolf's. Rafael growled, hiccupped, and gave a grunt. His piss streamed down before him, steaming slightly on the cool ground.

Angel gritted her teeth resolutely, her heart racing, and raised her Winchester, flipping it end for end. So much for keeping the gang corralled. She stepped toward Rafael, and, closing her upper teeth over her lower lip, smashed the rifle's butt solidly against the back of his neck, just up from the hump on his back. She heard his neck crack, saw his head tilt at an odd angle just before he staggered forward, appearing even drunker than before, and wheezed.

"What the hell was that?" said Leonora. "*Mi hermano*, you all right over there?"

Rafael gave a long, last sigh and fell face forward on the ground with a thud and a fart.

Angel swung around with the Winchester, dropped to one knee, raised the rifle to her shoulder, and aimed into the clearing, drawing a bead on Rubio sitting on his saddle, knees spread, holding his steaming cup to his lips but scowling over it toward Angel.

She squeezed the Winchester's trigger. The rifle roared, punching a hole through Rubio's wool serape and causing his eyes to widen suddenly. He dropped his coffee cup. Angel quickly racked another shell into the Winchester's breech. There was no arresting ghouls, only dispatching them.

Before her, the others, including Leonora, had all

reached for weapons, but only the male nearest Angel, a fat, bearded Mexican ghoul with one milky eye, had wrapped his hand around the Schofield jutting from the holster beside the saddle he'd been reclining against. Angel calmly drilled a bullet through the dead center of his forehead and was ejecting the spent, smoking casing, when the fifth man bounded off his heels with the agility the hobgobbies were known for, and dove like a demon missile toward the marshal. Angel nimbly threw herself to one side, rolling up off her right shoulder and springing back to her feet, but not before the fat ghoul was on her again, bulling into her chest with his head and shoulders.

Angel dropped the rifle and hit the ground hard on her back. She groaned. The hobgobbie half snarled like a wolf and half hissed like a diamondback, his eyes glowing red as coals as he peeled his nearly nonexistent lips back to show his fangs that, when the ghouls were aroused, became even longer and more savage-looking than a swiller's.

The light in his eyes dulled, and his fangs retreated a little. Angel withdrew her ten-inch Mexican dagger from the ghoul's side, feeling his hot, piss-yellow blood wash over her hand. She stuck it into him again, angling upward toward his heart. He made a gurgling sound and, staring incredulously at Angel, shook his head and closed his eyes.

Leonora had frozen halfway to her feet and was staring at Angel with her lips bunched, a knife in one hand while she raised a Colt with the other. Her pointed-nosed face with close-set, dull brown eyes was twisted with near-hysterical rage, showing her curved yellow fangs, but she held fire.

In her right hand, Angel held her cocked, silver-chased Colt around the shoulder of the ghoul still sprawled and death-spasming on top of her. She narrowed an eye as she aimed down the barrel at Leonora, crouched as though ready to spring.

Leonora said throatily, just above a whisper while narrowing her devil's eyes, "What did you do to my brother, Scar Face?"

"He was resisting arrest."

"He was taking a piss!"

"Got me."

Leonora screamed and triggered her pistol with one hand, then threw the knife with the other. The male atop Angel jerked as the slug and the bowie ripped into his back. The Smithy in Angel's hand roared once, twice, three times. It barked once more, flames and smoke streaking across the camp.

Leonora was sent staggering backward with the first shot, and the following rounds kept her moving and screaming like a wounded hyena, hair flopping around her head.

Somehow still on her feet, she turned around and, holding her arm across her belly, staggered off toward the edge of the firelight, dragging her boot toes and howling. Several yards beyond the light, under a drooping willow, she dropped to both knees, screamed once more, and fell flat on her face.

Angel shoved the body off of her and gained her feet, breathing hard, chest rising and falling heavily behind her doeskin vest. She stooped to clean the dagger on the dead male before her.

A wolf howled.

Angel froze.

The high-pitched wail was louder than before, and Angel jerked her head up toward a ridge forming a saw-toothed, black velvet silhouette against the stars about a half mile away. Her heart shuddered. The hobgobbies' horses nickered and shifted uneasily off in the trees to Angel's right, about thirty yards away.

Something snorted.

There was a thud of something heavy hitting the

ground behind her. Dropping the dagger and the empty Colt, Angel wheeled, automatically plucking a five-starred shuriken from the pouch in her cartridge belt. Her eyes had just skimmed the shaggy, gray-black wolf standing crouched before her, hackles raised, before she threw the deadly silver disc with a flick of her right wrist.

The beast's shrill scream sounded like a train whistle as the shuriken cut into its chest, instantly stopping its heart. The beast itself lurched up on its back legs and twisted around before tumbling in a heap, quivering.

She couldn't be sure it was a werewolf, but the way the shuriken had stopped it was a pretty good sign. . . .

Angel picked up her Winchester. On one knee and looking around wildly for more beasts, she quickly loaded the Winchester with silver cartridges. Off in the darkness beyond the fire, the horses danced and nickered. Brush snapped, and faint snarls and mewls rose. They didn't seem too close yet.

Angel racked a live round in the Winchester's chamber, then set the rifle aside and loaded her .45, plucking the silver cartridges from her shell belt without looking but keeping her eyes on the darkness beyond the fire. Quickly, she decided to make a run for it. Probably, the wolves would linger over the bodies of the dead hobgobbies, devour them first before they came after her. If they did, and if there were only five or six in the pack, she'd be able to hold them at bay with her rifle.

Having made up her mind, she holstered the Peacemaker, fastened the keeper thong over the hammer, grabbed her Winchester, and ran. She'd run about fifty feet before the snarling rose from the hobgobbies' camp, and she could hear quick, padded feet moving toward her from both sides of the trail.

Shit.

She might have made the wrong decision.

She kept running as fast as she could on the treacherous terrain, holding the Winchester in her right hand, pumping her left arm. Her black Stetson blew off her head and flopped down her back by its horsehair chin thong.

A cold stone dropped in her chest when she heard the thuds of the running pack growing quickly louder, and she could hear the throaty, slathering snarls. She didn't look back, knowing it would break her stride, but kept running until, when she sensed at least one beast getting too close, she stopped, swung around, dropped to a knee, and raised the Winchester to her shoulder.

A big wolf nearly as black as the night but limned in silver moonlight was twenty feet away and closing by fluid leaps and bounds. His eyes glowed yellow red. Angel raked the Winchester's hammer back and fired.

The beast snarled and yipped, dropped, and rolled, piling up on itself four feet in front of Angel's knees. She cut a glance around, saw at least three more shadows bounding toward her from both sides of the trail, their strides now slowing in light of what had happened to the black.

"Come on, you bastards!" Angel shouted, angrily racking a fresh round into the chamber. "Come and get it!"

The shadows sort of hunkered low to the ground, making them hard to see even with the milky moonlight radiating from a big, round moon hovering about a quarter of the way from its zenith and casting the night in an eerie twilight.

One of the silhouettes moved. Angel snapped a shot at it, heard the precious silver round spang off a rock. She ejected the cartridge, heard it clang onto the gravel behind her.

"Shit!"

Levering a fresh round into the chamber, she rose slowly and began backing away, sliding the rifle from right to left and back again. She couldn't tell if the beasts were following her or not. When a werewolf had turned completely into a wolf and not some man-wolf amalgam, they were especially cunning and dangerous. These might be trying to get around her and cut her off.

That thought fired adrenaline into her veins. She twisted around, took the rifle in one hand once more, and broke into a full-ahead sprint. She'd seen a cave near the place where she'd tied her horse. If she could get in there, she could hold off the wolves till morning if she had to.

Liquid breaths rumbled in wolf lungs behind her. Padded feet thudded. Sage branches snapped and gravel crackled. She glanced over her shoulder, saw what must have been a whole dozen of the shadows lunging toward her, several pairs of eyes glowing fiercely in the moonlight.

She dug her heels into the ground, pushing harder, her heart racing now, blood flowing hot through her veins. She ran past the place where she'd stumbled onto Leonora and Rubio fucking, and followed a path down a steep incline. The wolves were on both sides of her now. One was lunging toward her so quickly he almost appeared to be slowing so he wouldn't overtake her. Another was coming hard on the other side, fangs showing pale between gaping jaws.

Angel wanted to stop and shoot but she couldn't. Something told her that if she did that, she'd be dead almost instantly. Even if she got one of the beasts, the others would be on her in seconds.

"Oh, Christ," she heard herself nearly sob aloud.

She should have stayed by the fire.

Ahead was the sand-bottomed draw she'd crossed on her way to the hobgobbies' lair. The wolves would get her down there. The deep sand would slow her. She glanced once more over her shoulder. One was so close to her now that she could smell the rancid stench of his breath, see the foam flecking from his jaws as he breathed.

Angel bolted into the draw. A strange resignedness

overtook her as she felt the deep sand grabbing at her boots, slowing her.

On the draw's opposite bank, she glimpsed something that she only vaguely registered as odd. A hatted figure silhouetted against the sky hunkered over something that appeared mounted high up off the ground and that flashed like gold sequins in the lunar light.

At the same time that she recognized the bullet-crowned hat, she heard a man's voice shout, "Down, Red!"

Angel probably would have gone down, anyway, as the sticky hands of the sand were grabbing at her heels. She hit the draw, rolled, and buried her face in the sand as a great cacophony shattered the night's bizarre silence.

Bam-bam-bam-bam-bam-bam-bam-bam-bam-bam!

Beneath the din, wolves yelped and yowled. A furry, rancid-smelling body hit the ground beside Angel and rolled beyond her until it piled up against the base of the draw's opposite bank. She heard the thuds of several others, and the wild thrashing of brush as a couple of the wounded tried to crawl away.

When the gun had hammered away for nearly twenty seconds, Angel lifted her head and glanced up to see the flash of the revolving maws and the quicksilver of its bullets streaking out over her head and off across her backtrail.

After another fifteen or so seconds, the din died suddenly, leaving only swirling echoes growing softer and softer, as though the moon were swallowing them piecemeal.

The gun blazed once more, causing Angel to jerk with a start and again mash her cheek against the sand, watching her backtrail with one eye. Several more streaks of silver flashed across the draw.

A final, agonized yip rose. A body thumped to the ground.

After a few more seconds the Gatling gun fell silent.

On the chill night air, Angel smelled the coppery stench of hot, flowing blood.

The silence was broken by a scratching sound. Angel gained her knees as she looked up the bank before her. The silhouetted figure crouched over the smoking Gatling gun mounted in its open casket, touched a match to a cigarette protruding straight out from between his lips.

Blowing gray smoke, Uriah Zane said, "Damn, that's a lot of 'em."

Angel drew a deep breath, the blood only just now beginning to slow in her veins. The terror was still there, but it was mixed with embarrassment and an automatic defiance. "I hope you're not thinking I needed your help, Uriah."

"Oh, no," Zane said, a ghostly silhouette smoking atop the casket. "They were just about to turn tail and run in the other direction."

10

"NOT YOU, TOO, URIAH!"

WHEN ANGEL SAID NOTHING, only stared up in anger and a sickening feeling of humiliation at the giant wolf-killer towering over her, Zane gave a disgusted grunt, leaped out of the casket, and strode down the slope to drop to one knee beside her, puffing his cigarette. "Where you hurt?"

"My pride."

"Fool woman."

She could smell the musky horse-and-sage scent of him as he bored his gaze into her, blowing smoke in her face. Only vaguely did she admit to herself that she was relieved to see him, that, in fact, she wanted to throw her arms around him and bury her face in his chest. It wouldn't do for him to know that, however. She'd never been a damsel in distress, and even though she'd come to within inches of being wolf bait, she wasn't about to start now. There was a bone-deep need in her to be respected . . . especially by Uriah Zane, for some damn stupid reason.

Not going easy on her, he said, "What in blue blazes are you doin' out here on a full moon?"

Tears of fury oozed from her eyes, and she felt a great convulsion in her throat. A wave of rage as well as frustration and befuddlement exploded within her, snuffing expressible words from her racing thoughts and emotions. How was it only Uriah Zane that could make her—*her*, a deputy federal marshal, and a damn good one!—feel like a silly, little, pigtailed schoolgirl hysterical over a harmless spider crawling across the floor?

"Fuck you, Zane!"

The ghoul hunter snorted. "Don't take nothin' for granted. Where ya hurt? And don't mince words. We ain't got all night. I'm out of silver bullets for the cannon yonder, and I don't doubt other spooks are on the way."

Angel heaved herself to her feet, wincing at the pain shooting up her leg from her right ankle, which she couldn't put much weight on. She glared at Zane, who straightened his big frame that stood about five inches over hers, the quirley dangling from a corner of his mouth. He was the only man she felt physically dominated by, and she hated that about him despite being so infernally attracted to him. "I made a mistake. Leave me alone, damn you."

He stared at her in filial disdain, and she found herself averting her gaze from his and giving in a little. "I twisted my ankle." She lifted her arms, saw that her elbows were bloody and sandy. "Scraped my elbows."

"That it?"

"Yes, that's it," she returned scornfully. "You asked, and I told you. Sorry my throat's not cut."

"The night's still young."

"What're you doing?"

"Gonna help you up."

He gave a grunt, and then suddenly she was in his arms, snaking her hands around his neck with a gasp. As though she weighed no more than a straw stock, he carried her up the side of the ravine and set her down on a rock beside the wheeled casket, the Gatling gun jutting up from it.

Zane's horse, General Lee, glanced at her over his shoulder and gave his tail a swish in greeting. Tendrils of white smoke were still unraveling from the machine gun's six nasty maws.

"It's not worth all that," she said, feeling the heat emanating from the Gatling gun beside her. At least, she thought the heat was coming from the gun. She had a soft feeling in her belly as she watched him standing before her, his broad-shouldered frame silhouetted against the moon. His long, coal-black hair hung down from his bullet-crowned sombrero to flow over the shoulders of his wolfskin vest. "I could have walked, saved you a backache. How'd you know I was out here?"

He crouched, picked up her right foot, wrapping his hands around the boot and pressing slightly against her ankle. "Lomax in Gunnison said you were looking for me."

The truth was he hadn't planned on searching for her till the next morning. But he hadn't been able to keep her off his mind, so after a few beers and whiskey shots with Junius Webb in the Ace of Diamonds in Gunnison, he'd paid the old prospector his share of the bounty gold, retrieved General Lee from the livery stable—the horse had enjoyed sufficient rest, water, and feed—and headed out well before sunset.

Angel winced as the pain shot up into her shin, and dug her fingers into the rock she was sitting on. "Figured you was on the grub line again and might need a job. I lost Curry two days ago."

Zane straightened and started walking away from her into the brush and low, rocky buttes. "I'll fetch your horse. You hear any more wolves, give a holler."

Angel barely heard that last, because he was just then disappearing through a notch between the buttes, moving as soundlessly as a jungle tiger in his high-topped fur moccasin boots from the tops of which bowie knives jutted.

"How did you find me *here*?" she called after him, receiving no reply. "I mean, this is big country, Uriah . . ."

She sat there, angry again and feeling frightened because he'd left her and hating the feeling, because she was a marshal, goddamnit, and she had no business fawning over the likes of some unheeled wolf killer.

Damn Lomax for letting Zane know she'd inquired about him. She must have been drunk. When he was around she sometimes lost her confidence, found herself feeling dependent on his admittedly superior hunting and tracking skills, and that graveled her no end.

"Seen your horse," Zane said later, when he'd retrieved Angel's paint mustang, and they were heading along a faint Indian trail to some cabin where the wolfer had said they'd find safety from the creatures of the full moon.

"What's that?" she said.

"Seen your horse."

"I got that much, Uriah. You saw my horse."

"That's how I knew you were out there. Tracked you up to that little box canyon you tied ole Cisco in."

She looked at him riding off her left stirrup. He rode easily in the saddle of the big golden stallion, trailing the wheeled casket.

"You didn't have to come."

He didn't look at her but stared straight and didn't say anything.

"One thing about shootin' wolves during a full moon," he offered after a time, "is they're sure to stay dead."

"Yes, I remember." Angel lifted her gaze to the full moon that had shrunk down to the size of a newly minted dime and was riding straight above her head. "If you kill them when they're men, their souls will haunt you, depending of course on the strengths of said souls. But if you kill them when they're in bad need of a shave, like the bunch back there, they *stay* dead."

"They go back to Hell where they come from."

She looked at him again in the darkness. "You really believe all that hillbilly lore?"

"I surely do, Red."

She couldn't keep the admiration from her voice as she said with a tender smile for him, "You're one of a kind, Uriah. I'll give you that." She hardened her eyes at a remembered slight. "You son of a bitch."

He widened his eyes innocently. "Now what I'd do?"

"Why didn't you wake me before you left last time? In Nebraska. Coulda said you were pulling out, said, oh, I don't know, maybe *good-bye*? You know how stupid and cheap that makes me feel? Goddamnit, Uriah—I got a reputation to look after the same as you, and you know how many folks in that relay station knew you left me sound asleep up there in the dark after you rode out, like I was your six-peso *puta*?"

Zane hiked a big shoulder. "Sorry, Red. I reckon I shoulda woke everybody up and told 'em I told you I was leaving and didn't pay you for your services." He arched a skeptical brow at her, emphasizing the irrationality in her thinking.

"And I—*I*, Uriah—led you to those three spooks! Because I knew you were riding the grub line and in need of a stake! And that's how you repaid me, by making me look *cheap*!"

"I ain't no grub-line rider, goddamnit!" He'd raised his deep voice with its rolling accent, and it caused Angel's paint to jerk its head up with a start.

Uriah's fury, and the way it made his eyes turn a dark shade of amber, always took her aback. She'd seen him furious—raving mad—and it had caused her to close her hands instinctively over her Colt's butt, in case his fury would turn toward her. It never had. But it always made her ill at ease. She'd always figured it was his brooding nature and violent temper that held him back from others, that kept him riding his own lonely trails.

"That's not the point, Uriah," she said finally, softly, turning her head forward in silent supplication. He'd saved her hide tonight, and she had no good cause to rile him. Besides, she knew that what she'd really wanted back in the Nebraska relay station was for him to have stayed with her another day or two. She hadn't wanted him to leave so soon. Waking and finding him gone—his side of the bed cold—had hurt her feelings, and that, in turn, had embarrassed her.

Since she was a girl, her embarrassment had always turned to anger. And her anger, like Zane's, held her aloof.

For another half hour, they followed the trail between steep sandstone ridges, the one on the right curling out over the canyon like a massive stone tongue, blocking out the moonlight and the feeble starlight.

"Good Lord! Where are you taking me? We'll be in Wyoming before long," she said as they climbed a low rise, having to ride single file now as the trail pinched down to only a few feet between piles of boulders that had fallen from both ridges, nearly blocking the canyon in places.

"Here." Zane stopped the big golden and stared under the overhanging ridge where a small cabin hunkered, seeming to glisten as though outfitted with jewels of some kind. "It ain't the Larimer House in Denver, but I reckon it'll do for a full-moon night."

Angel heeled her horse off the trail's right side and into the massive shadow of the canyon wall. Out of the moonlight, she gained a clearer view of the cabin—an incredibly stout hovel constructed of what appeared to be full pine timbers, with a slightly peaked roof also of pine. The door was two pine trees joined by a heavy Z-frame and bearing a stout iron latch. On either side of the door were steel brackets apparently for locking the cabin from the outside.

The shiny ornaments on the cabin's outside walls were not sequins but silver-chased horseshoes and deer and elk antlers. There was even a silver-chased bear skull mounted over the door, under the overhanging roof.

Angel turned to Zane, who'd ridden up beside her and swung heavily down from the stallion, shucking his Henry repeater from his saddle sheath and racking a shell into the chamber. "Wait here, Red."

The big man strode to the cabin and tipped an ear to the door. He pulled his head back, and called just loudly enough to be heard from inside, "Hello, the cabin. Anyone here?" His deep voice sounded bearlike in the heavy silence.

He waited a few seconds, tipped his head to the door once more, and then tripped the steel latch and drew the door open with his rifle barrel. The heavy door came open, its hinges squawking like red-winged blackbirds.

He stood in the black opening for a time, holding his rifle across his chest, then ducked under the low door-frame and disappeared inside. Angel remained aboard her paint, watching, looking around this cool, dark side of the sheltered canyon, the moonlight washing over the ridge above her to fill the canyon beyond with liquid pearl.

Inside the cabin there was the rattle of a lantern mantle. A match scraped, and a dull, gradually intensifying glow leeched out the open door. The mantle pinged again, and then Angel saw Uriah's big frame move just inside the door, where he laid his rifle across a table before ducking back outside.

"How'd you know about this place?" she asked him.

"Belongs to a friend of mine, Abel Lundquist. We're on his ranch. Leastways, it was his ranch."

She stared at the hovel's silver trimmings. "Abel's a spook, isn't he?"

"Yep." Zane stopped in front of the cabin door, hooked his thumbs behind his wide shell belt, and stared out over the canyon. "*Was* a spook. Got bit just after the War, when the Hell's Angels first come west."

After a long, brooding pause, Zane said, "Abel built this cabin for nights like this one here." He tipped his head to look at the moon kiting across the gray-blue sky. "He was worried he'd kill his family and the men who worked for him. One of those men, his *segundo*, put a silver slug in him last month when he refused to lock himself in the cabin before the moon filled out. Mary, his wife, gave the order. But only because Abel had told her to if he ever got too weak, too savage, to seclude himself here."

"I'm sorry, Uriah."

"Ah, hell, it's the same old story, ain't it? Hell's opened its doors, and there's no closin' 'em now."

"They've always been open. At least, as long as I can remember."

The big man gave a dry chuckle. "Keeps my larder filled, anyways, I reckon."

Angel stepped out of her saddle, forgetting the nasty twist in her right ankle, and sucked a sharp breath against the pain shooting up her leg.

"Ah, hell, I'm sorry, Red." Zane left his horse and strode quickly over to her, grabbing her arm. "Here I was wool-gatherin' during a full moon when I should have been getting you inside."

"I have to unsaddle—"

Again, she was in his powerful arms before she could finish protesting, and she wrapped her arms around his neck as he carried her toward the cabin. "Uriah, *please*!"

"Hush, now, damnit."

He carried her inside the sparsely furnished hovel, turned left, strode past an eating table on which the lantern flickered, and laid her down on a large, high bed covered with bobcat hides. He sat down beside her, shucked out of his gloves, and picked up her ankle, gently probing with his thick, brown fingers.

"Where's it hurt exactly?"

She looked down her legs at him, his soft eyes merely

hazel now and filled with concern as they stared at her. She looked at his broad shoulders and the hard expanse of his chest under the wolf vest and his tight buckskin shirt to his flat belly, then returned her gaze to his hands.

They were large and thick and brown from years of the frontier sun. Powerful. A killer's hands. But she could feel the warmth of them seeping into her twisted ankle, assuaging the pain. The heat oozed up her legs and into her belly, ensconcing her heart, which quickened.

She swallowed as she lay back on the pillow and stretched her arms toward him, flexing her fingers desperately. "Goddamnit, Uriah."

He removed his hands from her ankle, crouched over her, lowered his head, and closed his mouth over hers.

Her body turned warm as summer honey. She opened her mouth for him, welcomed his hot tongue with her own. She rose up a little, pressed her breasts against his chest, squirmed around, feeling her need for him growing in her loins, and groaned for him.

He pulled away from her, stared into her eyes, and pushed her back down onto the bed. "I'm gonna tend the horses. I'll be back."

He swung around and ducked out of the cabin. She lay there, feeling desolate, hearing him outside tending the horses, leading them away, likely to some hidden corral.

She squirmed around with the need for him, hating herself for feeling this way about one man when the frontier had plenty. Not that she hadn't sampled others, but it was this burly, hillbilly ghoul hunter from Carolina who stuck in her craw, who made her want him and need him when she wanted to need no one.

When he returned, he closed the door, shutting out the moonlight, and walked over to the bed and began shucking out of his clothes. Angel's breasts swelled under her tight vest as she watched him slip out of his wash-worn balbriggans that clung to his brawny, towering frame like a second skin. Naked, his big member flopping against his thighs beneath his hard, corded belly, he turned to open a window shutter, and stare out into the night.

"No one followed us, Uriah," she said, appreciating his white, muscular buttocks and the backs of his bulging thighs. "I'm sure of tha . . ."

She let her voice trail off as she stared at his broad back, the right shoulder blade protruding slightly as he crouched to peer out the window. Angel's lips parted as she gazed at him, awestruck. At the bottom of the wing-like blade was a mass of knotted flesh about the circumference of one of Zane's own hands.

It was jagged and ridged with scar tissue. The scars were teeth marks—two larger than the others.

Fang marks.

Angel gasped.

"Don't hurt to be careful," Zane said before straightening and closing the shutter. He turned to her, his black-bearded face twisted in a wry grin, eyes spoking at the corners, his member jutting with raw, masculine desire.

He frowned. "Figured you'd be out of them duds by now." He moved toward her. "Never knew you to be shy, Red."

She had risen up on her elbows. Her heart throbbed. Her voice was too dry for speech.

She stared at his eyes, in which she could detect little amber sparks, like the coals of a burned-down campfire, and her belly twisted with horror. As he sat down beside her, making the bed's wooden frame creak under his weight, part of her wanted to bound up off the bed and run away from him, to go screaming and crying into the night.

No, Uriah, not you, *too!*

But he had her out of every stitch of her clothes in a minute, his breath raking her naked, tingling skin as he breathed harder and harder with his passion. He buried his face between her full, ivory, pink-tipped breasts, raked his thumbs across her nipples, and drew a deep breath as though to capture the raw essence of her in his lungs.

And then he flung himself between her legs, which her own raging desire spread for him. He cupped her breasts in his big hands, mashed his mouth down on hers, sliding his hot tongue between her lips as her hands closed over the taut, hard slabs of his buttocks.

And then nothing in the world—not even that he might be one of those he himself hunted—seemed to matter anymore except their two bodies toiling and writhing together.

11

THE BURNING WAR PARTY

"SHY LAST NIGHT and quiet as a church mouse today," Zane said the next morning, as they followed a wagon road northwest, in the general direction of Denver. "Red, what's got into you?"

She turned toward him. Her eyes were troubled beneath curved, red brows. Her hair, tinged with orange in the midmorning light, blew around her tapered, fine-boned cheeks in the cool breeze. She turned away from him and brushed her knuckles across her scar, as she did from time to time, mostly when she was upset about something.

She didn't say anything but he could tell that her head was filled with unexpressed thoughts and emotions.

Zane reined General Lee up sharply. "What's got your neck in a hump? You haven't said one word since breakfast, and then you only said 'no' when I asked if you wanted more coffee. If I was a self-doubting man, I might think you didn't enjoy yourself last night, Red."

Angel doffed her black Stetson and ran her gloved finger around the sweatband inside the crown, not looking at him. "How is it you know so much about the wolves, Uriah?"

"What're you talkin' about? Haven't I been huntin' 'em since I came out here ten years ago?"

"How do you know you have to kill 'em while they're changed or they'll come back and haunt whoever killed 'em?"

Zane studied her beneath ridged brows shaded by his sombrero's broad brim. "Hell, that ain't no big secret. The Injuns have known that for a long time. I heard it from a Crow medicine man up in Montana, when I first came out here lookin' for the Angels."

She slanted a skeptical eye at him, holding her hat in her hands. "That's how you learned it? The only way you learned it?"

Zane sighed and poked his hat up his forehead. "How else would I . . . ?"

He let his voice trail off, and then a sourness settled in his gut, like a swig of bad milk.

"I saw your back." She set her hat on her head and looked away from him, staring off at a distant dust devil. "Why didn't you tell me, Uriah?"

"Ah, hell."

"Why?"

"I didn't see the point. You'd just see me as different and there'd be no convincing you otherwise." Zane gestured behind them as though to indicate the wolves they'd killed last night. "I'm not one of them, Angel. I'm still me. I have it in me, true enough. But I've learned to control it."

She shot a cold, incriminating look at him. "Like hell."

"I've told it straight, Red. I am one of them, but then again, I'm not. I talked to a Comanche shaman down in Texas. He taught me how to keep the devil on a leash." Zane paused, studied her as she studied him with that cold look of accusing. "But if you want to ride out, go ahead. I won't stop you."

She continued to study him but her expression had

gradually changed to one of utter befuddlement. "There was a full moon last night, and you . . ."

She remembered the frantic grabbing, clutching, caressing, sucking, grunting, the throbbing light in his wolfish red eyes as he'd brought her several times to heights of passion she'd not only never before experienced but never even realized were attainable. Even now, despite herself, a wave of near-savage desire washed over her just thinking about it. If he rode over to her now, grabbed her, thrust himself against her, she'd have a hard time stopping him, because she wouldn't want to.

But she had to. She'd never share his bed again.

He was one of *them*—one of the demons they hunted.

He was reading her mind. "I didn't tear your throat out, did I?"

"Why didn't you?"

"I told you. I can control it." He looked at her pointedly. "It's not like your father, Red."

She'd just opened her mouth to respond when a stone rattled down an escarpment behind her.

"Down, Red!" Zane clawed the Colt Navy revolver from the holster positioned for the cross draw on his left hip.

Angel threw herself sideways out of her saddle, hitting the ground on her left hip and shoulder as an arrow whistled through the air where she'd just been sitting to clatter among the rocks on the trail's other side.

Zane's pistol quickly roared three times. A shrill cry sounded from the escarpment, and Zane leaped off the palomino's back, hitting the ground running as the Apache rolled down from the niche in the scarp where he'd been drawing back a second arrow knocked to his painted ash bow.

As the Indian in deerskin leggings and calico shirt piled up against a boulder at the base of the scarp, the wolfer dropped to a knee and aimed his Colt up the slope, sliding the barrel from right to left and back again, ready for another flat brown face to appear among the rocks and crags.

Behind him, Angel rose to her butt, palmed her Peacemaker, and rocked the hammer back. She'd lost her hat, and her hair hung in a mess about her shoulders.

"Any more?" she asked.

Zane squinted one eye as he aimed up the slope. His heart thudded, but his hands wrapped around the gun were steady.

"Not yet."

He drew a deep breath. One advantage—maybe the only advantage aside from slightly keener vision—of having been bitten by the raggedy-heeled stage robber Alden Woodyard, north of Laramie, was having a heightened sense of smell. Like his magnified vision and hearing, he didn't always have it, but when he needed it most it came to him, and he could smell the wild musk and blood scent of the dead Indian lying nearby.

But in the slight breeze wafting over the top of the escarpment he could detect only sage and cedar, maybe the cucumber smell of a snake den up there among the boulders.

Lines cut across his broad, sun-leathered forehead.

No. There was more. And he could hear something else now, too—the clomp of unshod hooves.

"Wait here."

He straightened and, lowering the rifle, bounded up the slope, leaping from one boulder to another until he'd gained the crest of the ridge. Hunkering low and doffing his hat, he peered between two boulders and through a scattering of gnarled cedars, down the slope's other side and to his right.

Dust rose about a quarter mile away. Beneath the sun-burnished cloud was a string of galloping horses ridden by small, brown men in calico shirts and bandannas, long, black hair flying out behind them in the wind.

Some were armed with bows and arrows, spears lashed to the sides of their mustang ponies. A couple had what appeared to be repeating rifles—both Winchesters and Spencers, Zane could see now, squinting—jostling down their backs by rope lanyards. The Apaches—Lipans, judging by the design of the war paint on their cheeks and foreheads and on the withers and rears of their galloping horses—were cutting across a sage-stippled flat on an interception course with the trail that Zane and Angel had been following.

Through the roiling dust, Zane counted fourteen braves. The pack had heard the reports of the wolfer's pistol, and now they batted their moccasined heels against their ponies' flanks, heading toward the scarp.

Zane doffed his hat and ran back down the escarpment, leaping from one rock to another, moving easily, with a light-footed grace and agility that was a by-product of his new condition. "Mount up," he told Angel, who was holding the reins of both their horses. "War party behind us."

She tossed his reins to him and swung up into her saddle, wincing a little at the ache in her ankle. "Apaches?"

"Lipans."

"Wolves on the prowl last night must have stirred 'em up." The Indians held the white-eyes responsible for increasing the werewolf activity in their native lands, since they also blamed the whites for driving the beasts west in the first place.

"Yeah, a full moon will do that."

Zane hammered his heels into General Lee's loins, and the big palomino bounded up the trail, the casket clattering along behind. Zane glanced over his shoulder as Angel galloped up beside him. He could hear the thudding of the Apaches' unshod horses as they approached the scarp from the far side.

"How many?" Angel asked, pulling her hat low on her forehead.

"Too damn many, and they're well armed. If we can make it to Cimarron, a couple miles ahead, we should be in the clear." Zane holstered his coat and shucked his Henry from the saddle boot, cocking it one-handed.

"Cimarron's farther than that, Uriah. It's a good five miles from here."

The ghoul hunter shook his head as he held his reins in one hand, his rifle in the other, its barrel resting across his saddlebows. His crossbow jostled from where it hung from his saddle horn. "Don't think so."

"I think so!"

"You got no sense of direction, even less of distance."

Angel said something that Zane couldn't hear because just then a war whoop rose behind him, above the thudding of the hammering hooves and the cracks of rifle fire. A bullet spanged off a rock just left of the trail, and General Lee shied slightly.

The wolfer ground his heels against the Appy's flanks once more, urging more speed. Angel followed suit, reaching forward and sliding her Winchester from the sheath lashed to her saddle beneath her right thigh. "We're gonna have to make a stand, Uriah. They're comin' fast, and those mustangs are built for speed!"

Zane glanced behind. Angel was right.

He nodded in reluctant agreement as they followed the trail around another escarpment. When the Indians were out of sight on the scarp's other side, though their hooves continued thudding, their savage war whoops rising, Zane pointed over his horse's head toward where two mounds of volcanic rock humped on the left side of the trail. The dykes lay side by side with what appeared a twenty- or thirty-foot-wide crease between them.

"See them rocks?" he shouted. "Pull in there. They'll have to swing back, and that's when we'll take 'em!"

After three more strides, they checked their horses down suddenly. Both gave indignant whinnies as they spun on their back hooves and were sent storming into the gap between the two volcanic dykes pocked with solid bubbles and streaked with bird shit. Ahead along the crease, Zane saw a ragged fox leap across the path and disappear into a hollow at the base of the right-side lava mound.

He and Angel reined their horses down at the same time. They swung down from their saddles, Angel cursing when her right foot touched the ground. They'd both just raised their rifles and had started running back toward the trail, when a weird rumbling sounded and a windy whooping noise that was much louder than anything the Indians had voiced earlier issued from overhead.

A foul-smelling wind picked up dust and weed seeds, and there was a rumbling like that of a distant twister. The air warmed instantly.

Screams cut the air above the thudding of the loudening horse hooves, and then the war party was riding past the mouth of the gap in which both Zane and Angel crouched, rifles raised to their shoulders. Instead of aiming down the barrels, they were both looking around with incredulous, haunted looks on their faces.

The entire pack of Indians and horses galloped past the gap as a large ball of licking, crackling, smoking orange flames consumed them. Men and horses screamed shrilly, raising gooseflesh across the wolf hunter's broad back. The stench of charred flesh and horsehair filled Zane's nose as he heard Angel gasp beside him.

A half second later, a vast shadow passed over them, and they both looked up in time to see what appeared to be the striated belly of a giant fish fly over them from about twenty yards above the rounded tops of the two dykes. A snakelike tail of scaled, burnished bronze flicked and curled. The creature was so huge that it made a rushing sound, kicking up its own wind, lifting another small twister around the ghoul hunters.

"What the hell was that?" Angel asked, looking wide-eyed up at Zane and blinking against the windblown grit.

The ghoul hunter was startled out of words. He blinked as he stared out the mouth of the gap between the escarpments, where he'd just seen what he couldn't possibly have seen—the entire war party, men and horses, galloping inside a great ball of orange fire. He could still hear them screaming, smell them burning, though he could no longer see them behind the dyke.

Lowering his rifle, he ran forward, then stopped at the mouth of the gap and looked to his left, the direction in which the burning riders had been galloping.

Slowly, he moved out from the gap and into the trail, still blinking in disbelief at what he was seeing—all the Indians and horses now strewn in ragged black mounds along the trail and in the desert to both sides. A few of the horses thrashed as they continued to burn, but they and the braves were all down, scattered as though they'd fallen from the sky.

Most of the braves appeared dead. One was crawling into the desert off the trail's right side, shrieking while orange flames licked up around and over him. He was fried to black cinders. Finally, he stopped, rose to his knees, lifted his head, shrieking still louder and raising his arms as though in supplication before flopping to the ground and falling still.

Zane heard Angel's spurs ring as she walked up beside him and stared at the burning horses and fallen braves.

"Law," Zane muttered in his soft Southern drawl, running a hand down the black stubble on his face, his eyes glassy with shock. "Seen it once. Hoped I'd never see it a second time."

"In case you weren't paying attention," Angel said, her

voice rising as she raised an arm to point at the sky, "you're about to see it a third time."

Zane followed her finger. The dragon had banked, and, flapping its great jointed wings and flicking its long, kite-like tail, was headed back toward them, narrowing its snakelike eyes as it homed in on its prey, black smoke licking from its nostrils.

12

WOLVES AT HIGH NOON

THE FOUR WOLVES ran as one across the mesa, long, thick hair of varying shades of gray and brown ruffling at their necks and glistening in the high, dry Colorado sunshine. They ran side by side, none breaking stride until the willowy, square-headed beast on the far right was distracted by a jackrabbit and swerved away from the main group to give brief chase until the jackrabbit dove into a hole among some rocks and prickly pear and stared out, quivering.

The wolf gave a taunting howl, snapping its jaws, and raced after the others who were just now approaching the mesa's edge.

Tongues hanging, panting, mewling and yipping eagerly, the four wolves stopped and looked over the lip of the ridge. The stage trail angled around the base of the mesa, and just now a coach was fast approaching from the southeast, the team running full out under the driver's blacksnake, which cracked over their backs with the sounds of pistol shots. The sweat-lathered team appeared bathed in silver under the high-noon sun.

The driver cursed and yelled. The shotgun rider sitting beside him held on to his seat for dear life, his double-barreled shotgun wedged between his legs. The coach rattled and clattered. Dust roiled up to glisten like burnished copper.

"Got a timetable to keep, Lucy!" the driver shouted through the bandanna drawn up over his nose, jerking his arm up to crack the popper at the end of the whip once more, making one of the wolves give an instinctive start, leaping up off its front paws and groaning.

"Get up there, Jeremiah!" the driver bellowed. *"Lift some dust, Abilene!"*

One of the other wolves nipped another in its eagerness, then all backed a few feet away from the lip of the ridge, so they wouldn't be seen by the shotgunner or driver, and hung their heads low. Their eyes darkened in hungry anticipation. They snapped their jaws and licked their chops.

The thunder of the approaching coach grew louder and louder until the stage was nearly directly below the wolves. The largest of the beasts glanced at the others, giving the signal, then hurled itself over the side of the ridge, plummeting twenty feet in an arc of gray-brown fur and glowing red eyes, to land on its front paws squarely atop a long steamer trunk lashed to the top of the stage, behind the driver and shotgun messenger.

Two others landed on the roof, as well, while a third—the lightest colored of the four wolves—came to rest directly upon the shotgun rider and went immediately to work, snarling loudly and savagely as it tore the unsuspecting man's throat out.

The shotgunner screamed as he dropped his greener and reached for his bloody throat while the wolf shook him like a bone.

The driver's eyes nearly popped out of his skull as he watched the attack, his wide-open mouth pushing a circle out from behind his red bandanna.

Blood sprayed, covering the driver, who then

commenced screaming, kicking his feet as though to run, until one of the three wolves closed its jaws around the back of his neck from behind and, with the strength of six common wolves, jerked the man up and out of the driver's boot and onto the coach roof. The wolf promptly tore the driver's throat open, silencing the man's hysterical screams, then rolling him off the coach to hit the trail and tumble, limbs akimbo, blood flying.

A woman inside the coach screamed.

One of the other wolves atop the coach grinned at the wolf who'd killed the driver, then pivoted off its back legs. It grabbed the edge of the roof with one paw while throwing the rest of its body over the side.

When it had its back feet inside the coach window, it removed its paw from the edge of the roof, and the coach bounced as it landed inside the carriage. Screams rose in earnest below the other three wolves, who hunkered together on the roof, turning at nearly the same time back into One-Eye Langtry, Lucky Snodgrass, and their particularly savage leader—Charlie Hondo.

There they were—three of them fully outfitted in their Western trail garb complete with six-shooters and battered hats, as though they'd never been wolves at all. Charlie Hondo, born to Romanian nobility, was tall and thin, with bulging crazy eyes and long, sandy hair hanging down from the sides of his head, while his pate was as pink and bald as a baby's rump. Gold hoop rings dangled from his ears. In mockery of the Lutheran church, having been sent to an orphanage after his family had banished him for raping and chopping two serving girls up into tiny bits that he then dumped in the castle's well, he wore on each cheek two dull green tattooed crosses. They were in grisly contrast to his bulging, glittering, light brown eyes.

Due to a fairly common shape-shifting magic, the Angels' clothes worn while in their human forms had not materialized in their wolf forms but had come back through the second shifting of their shapes. Now wearing the blue Army uniform of Warden Mondrick of Hellsgarde Prison, complete with Cavalry sword, holstered Colt Army .44, and even the pocketknife, matches, and other paraphernalia the man had had in his pockets when Charlie had eaten out his heart and then beheaded him, the leader of the formidable wolf pack gave a tooth-gnashing rebel yell.

He leaped down into the driver's boot and took up the reins that the driver had dropped on the floor. He almost lost the warden's blue hat on the wind, but grabbed it and stuffed it under the seat.

The horses had heard the screams and smelled the blood and were still smelling it now as Curly Joe Panabaker was hard at work inside the carriage, raising shrieks and bone-splintering screams from the two drummers, one doctor, and two women riding in there, on what had been, only seconds before, a pleasantly eventless midday trek between Dead Horse Gap and Wild Rose, in the far-southwestern corner of Colorado.

The team was running wildly and trying to leap out of its hames and harnesses, but Charlie Hondo, hoop earrings thrashing and flashing, got them back on their leashes, holding them steady to the trail. One-Eye climbed onto the box beside Charlie, while Lucky Snodgrass remained on all fours, grinning delightedly over the side of the carriage roof as the savagery continued below.

Presently, one of the now-headless drummers flew out the coach's right-side door to hit the trail rolling, and Lucky whooped and clapped his hands maniacally. The doctor, also headless, was thrown out the opposite door, where his blood-geysering corpse bounced off a boulder beside the trail. Lucky glanced over his shoulder as the sawbones disappeared in the roiling dust cloud behind the carriage.

He whooped and hollered and pumped his fists in the

air. "Wolves at high noon! Can't beat *that*!"

The wolfish growls and snarls and angry yips intermittently drowned the women's screams until the throatless, disemboweled women were both rolling like rag dolls in the trail behind the coach, quickly lost in the distance.

A loud snarl rose, followed by a howl. And then the carriage jerked, and two hairy human hands appeared at the edge of the coach roof. Curly Joe lifted his head up above the roof, his funnel-brimmed hat snugged to his head by the rawhide thong secured taut to the underside of his chin. His red eyes turned blue, and the hair on his hands disappeared.

He grinned and gave another howl, this one belonging to a man, and hoisted himself up onto the roof where he sat with his legs raised, arms wrapped around his knees, grinning and looking around at the sunlit afternoon sliding past the carriage.

"I like this," he said, slowly shaking his head in awe-full appreciation of his new abilities. "I really do like this a lot, pards."

Charlie Hondo glanced over his shoulder at Curly Joe, looked away, then looked back again, widening his pale, lifeless eyes under the brim of his dusty blue cavalry kepi with the gold braid around the crown. "Curly Joe, you keep smilin' that hard, you're liable to break your face in two!" He loved being a "Westerner" as much as the others.

One-Eye had his Schofield out of its holster. He broke the piece open to check the loads. "Curly Joe's just enjoyin' his new abilities, Charlie. You should, too—since it's bein' able to turn whenever we want, day or night, full moon or not, that got you outta Hellsgarde."

"That and that dragon," added Curly Joe.

Hondo, the alpha wolf, shook his head and stretched his lips back from his rotten teeth in revulsion as he held the six-hitch team's reins deftly in his long-fingered hands, and stared ahead along the trail. "Glad to be out of that fuckin' perdition. Wish I coulda killed that warden one more time. Ripped his head off with my teeth just once more!"

The former Ludwig Jurgen Abelard Kiesler grinned at his compatriots. "Much obliged, boys. Oh, I woulda got outta there eventually, but you and that fire-breather sure made it a whole lot easier. I owe you a round of ale . . . if there's anything excepting coffin varnish to be found out here."

Dubiously, he studied the parched desert terrain sliding past the coach, and batted his lashes against the dust.

"Where'd the dragon come from, Charlie?" asked Curly Joe. "Don't recollect anyone mentionin' dragons."

"I reckon," said Charile, planting his cavalry boots on the dashboard and leaning back in the jehu's stiff wooden seat, "the dragon was a little something extra provided by our lovely, bewitching benefactor, Senorita Ravenna." He grinned in delight, remembering the beguiling, crotch-stirring image of Ravenna sprawling nude on a corn-shuck mattress in a Dodge City flophouse, the day after he'd met her in the Long Branch Saloon. "I suspect she'll be catching up with us soon."

"Ah," said One-Eye eagerly, snapping the Schofield closed, spinning the hogleg on his finger, and sliding it back into the holster thronged low on his denim-clad right thigh. "Miss Ravenna."

"Senorita Ravenna de Onis y Gonzalez-Vara," said Charlie, letting the long and regal Spanish name roll lovingly off his tongue. "A fitting name for that Mex piece of horny ass."

"You sure we can trust her?" Curly Joe said, trying feebly to roll a cigarette in his thick, brown fingers, despite the stage's violent jostling and the hot wind. "I never have known a Mex—male or female—I trusted any more than I could throw uphill against a Oklahoma cyclone."

"Oh, we can trust her," Charlie said with a self-satisfied air. "The girl's powers might be as strong as that cyclone"—he glanced over his shoulder at the others, winking assuredly—"because she needs us as much as we need her. Besides, she fancies my pecker!" He threw his head back and howled, snapping his jaws.

Curly Joe gave up on the cigarette and let the wind take the paper and tobacco, brushing his hands on his patched, checked wool trousers. "And once we get to Mexico?"

"She'll be sharin' in our newly acquired fortune, Curly. Once we find it, that is. You don't think she and her spells helped you spring me from Hellsgarde just for my pecker, do you?"

"I reckon not," said Lucky Snodgrass, who sat back with his hat tipped over his eyes, trying to catch a few winks. "But you never know about a witch. Ever'one I ever known has made me nervous. They're a selfish lot, I tell you. And their powers make 'em dangerous. I hope she ain't just toyin' with us."

Charlie slapped Lucky's knee, fairly teeming with confidence. "You let me worry about Senorita Ravenna," he said, shaking the ribbons over the team, urging more speed as they started up a long, easy grade. "Ravenna needs us as much as we need her. She followed me to Dodge City for some reason. If I hadn't gotten drunk and careless in Denver and thrown in Hellsgarde, I might have found out." He paused, sucked at a gap in his upper teeth. "Oh, she's got somethin' wicked on her pretty little mind, all right. But I think it's to our benefit." He grinned at the others. "Besides, I got her eatin' outta my pants!"

Again, Charlie howled.

The others glanced at one another uneasily as the stage shot up and over the hill, then moved even faster down the other side. Ahead, at the bottom of the grade and in a broad horseshoe amid a jumble of high boulders piled on the trail's right side, the Sandy Wash relay station appeared—a low-slung, L-shaped cabin with a broad-roofed gallery angling off its front, a barn and two corrals, and a windmill spinning lazily in the warm fall breeze.

One-Eye sniffed the air in the direction of the cabin. "I do believe I smell beer, Charlie!"

Hondo worked his nose, then shook his head. "You've been too long in America, One-Eye. That's not beer. That's a flooded hog wallow tainted with alkali and stinkweed. But just what the doctor ordered!"

Charlie pulled the stage up between the barn and the cabin, and the horses had barely settled back in their collars before the cabin's timber door squawked open, and a short, potbellied old man in ragged pants and suspenders came out, blinking his eyes sleepily and tucking his shirttails into his slacks.

Two other, younger men came out behind him, and as the old man stepped off the wide gallery shaded by a brush roof, the younger men angled off away from him toward the team and began unbuckling straps while casting wary eyes at the men atop the stage. The old man ambled, limping slightly on his right leg, toward the coach. As he did, he glanced at the driver's boot and slowed his pace, frowning.

"What the hell . . . You ain't Mike 'n' Rascal. . . ."

He stopped, staring up at the four men riding the coach's roof, blinking as though to clear his bleary blue eyes. The tip of his red nose was nearly as large as an apricot, and badly pocked and pitted.

"You're an observant son of a bitch," said Charlie Hondo, throwing the brake and wrapping the ribbons around it. The other three Angels glanced around at one another, grinning and chuckling. The two young hostlers, working quickly and automatically, well versed in their profession, continued unharnessing the team, casting wary glances from the newcomers to each other and back again.

The fresh horses in the holding corral off the barn ran around with their tails humped.

"Hey, old-timer," said One-Eye, waving his hat at the dust just now catching up with the coach, "you got any beer in there worth drinkin'?"

"I . . . I don't see no passengers," the old man said, tentatively, as he took a few more steps toward the coach, lifting his chin to peer in a window.

"And you won't, neither," said Lucky, as he stepped down to the left front wheel, then dropped to the ground. "'Cause they're all wolf bait litterin' the trail back yonder."

The old man made a face as he turned away from the blood-coated interior of the stagecoach. "Oh, Jesus!"

"Jesus won't help you now!" Lucky said, suddenly back in his sleek wolf form.

Lucky the wolf leaped atop the old man and had him flat on his back and dying in seconds, while Charlie and One-Eye, also in wolf form, leaped down from the front of the driver's boot and onto the backs of the two horses nearest the stage. In seconds, they ran up across the backs of the other horses that had only seconds ago been released from the hitch, and leaped on the two young hostlers who could only stand there, lower jaws hanging, as the two wolves pounced on them under a high, copper sun.

Just as the old man's had been, their screams were short-lived.

The terrified horses, still strapped to each other but free of the wagon tongue, ran off across the yard, dragging the double tree and kicking their back legs in horror.

Charlie Hondo changed back into his cavalry-suited man form. Then both Lucky and One-Eye changed into their more soiled but well-armed frontier visages. They stared down at Curly Joe, who lay facedown in the dirt beside the recent wheel ruts made by the stage.

Lucky ran to him, placed a hand on his arm. "What the hell happened, Curly? The stage run you over?"

Curly grunted and pushed up onto his knees, snatching his hat off the ground beside him. He looked at Charlie. "I didn't change!"

Charlie scowled back at him, confused. "Say *what*?"

"I didn't change, Charlie. I was just about to—I could feel the hairs pushing out and my hands and feet growin' big, and just as I was about to jump off the coach, I went back to myself so quick I couldn't catch myself. I was expectin' to land on all fours, and . . ." He winced as he hauled himself heavily, painfully, to his feet.

"Same damn thing almost happened to me, Charlie." One-Eye adjusted his black eye patch and rubbed the slight paunch pushing out his blue wool shirt, the V-neck of which was held together with strips of braided rawhide. "I felt a little hesitation, sort of a weakness. And now . . ." He made a face and continued to rub his belly. "I don't feel so good. This never happens during a full moon. Of course, I don't change so quick then. . . ."

Charlie snapped his head at Snodgrass. "What about you?"

Lucky shrugged. "I didn't have no problem. What about yourself, boss?"

Charlie had just opened his mouth to speak when the cabin door, which had been standing open, closed with a *bang!* A girl's voice shouted from inside, "You mangy wolves pack up and fog the dusty trail. I got a shotgun loaded with silver dimes, and I'm just itchin' to use it!" Her voice grew shrill. "Wolves at high noon—I never seen the like."

The four killers looked around at one another. Their moods lightened. Charlie smoothed his long, shaggy mustache with the index finger and thumb of his left hand.

Smiling wolfishly, he began striding toward the cabin. "Fellas, I smell purty young female flesh."

13

RAVENNA AND THE DRAGON

"SHE SOUNDS like she's got some spunk," said Lucky as he and the others followed Charlie to the cabin. "I like my wenches spunky."

They stopped just off the edge of the ten-foot-wide gallery as Charlie mounted it, stepped to one side of the door, and hammered it three times with his fist, causing dust to leap from the cracks.

"You, in there," the alpha wolf called. "You'd best open this door and toss the gut-shredder out. You got me mad already, callin' us names who you've never met. And you had the nerve to threaten werewolves with silver? Come on, you little bitch, what's got into you? I'm so mad now, I'm liable to suck your throat out your asshole and spit it back in your face!"

"Might just do that, anyway," said Curly Joe, bending his knees slightly and adjusting his crotch. "After I drill her, I mean. I ain't had me a mattress dance in a month of Sundays." He grabbed his crotch and lurched hungrily up and down, bending his knees. A thoughtful cast entered his gaze. "I wonder if I can do it changed. . . ."

"You mean as a wolf?" Charlie asked.

"Why not?"

Charlie shrugged as though the idea hadn't occurred to him but it was worth considering.

"Best proceed with caution," advised Lucky, sliding his long-barreled Remington and rolling the cylinders across his forearm. "You heard—silver."

"Where in the hell'd she get silver out here?" One-Eye wanted to know. "Silver dimes, no less!"

There was no mineral, not even gold, more precious than silver. The only thing more sought-after on the entire frontier was blood-swilling girls with Indian blood—especially blood from the most savage tribes like the Crow up in Montana, the Utes in Colorado, and the Comanche, Apache, and Yaqui in the Southwest and Mexico. They were ferocious as well as rare, and it was said that if a man survived a night with one, no other woman could ever satisfy him again.

"Mr. Jipson done stored 'em up," the girl obliged One-Eye's inquiry. "And I got two loads snugged down in both these ten-gauge barrels, so you take your hairy, foul-smelling asses and vamoose!"

Her shrill voice broke on that last.

" 'Hairy, foul-smelling asses'?" Charlie said, gritting his rotten teeth and glaring at the door, blood vessels bulging in his forehead. "Listen, you fuckin' little bitch, you open this door or I'll break it down. If I have to do that, I'm gonna be even madder than I am now!"

On the other side of the door, the girl sobbed.

Charlie grinned.

He licked his lips, absently massaged the cross tattooed on his right cheek, and gentled his tone. "Honey, look. Werewolves, we are, indeed. You got us pegged. But, while we are werewolves and we did kill your employers merely for the enjoyment of a bloody kill, we're tired now. We'd just like food, beer, and rest. We got money. We'll pay you."

He paused, taking a deep breath as though speaking so gently, suppressing his rage, was sapping his energy. "Best yet, we'll let you live. Now, won't you please open the door?"

The girl's strong, defiant voice was gone. Weakly, befuddledly, she asked, "How in the hell'd you fellas change into wolves right here in broad daylight? The full moon was *last* night!"

"Let us in, honey, and we'll tell you all about it," said Curly Joe, voice pitched with lust.

"You'll turn again," the girl said, "and you'll do me like you did Mr. Jipson and Eb and Leonard."

"No, no, no," said Charlie. "But I'll tell you what we will do if you don't open this door." He calmly removed his hat, inspected the gold braid, flicking bits of dust and weeds off it with his fingers before lowering the hat to his side and, face swelling up and turning as red as an Arizona sunset, shouted, *"We'll burn this bloody place right down to the ground, and you along with it, you defiant little whore!"*

Silence.

Curly Joe snickered as he and One-Eye and Lucky stood just off the gallery, thumbs hooked behind their cartridge belts, Lucky holding his Remy pointed at the door, in case the girl should storm out firing.

From inside, the girl's frightened voice: "You promise you won't kill me."

Charlie swallowed. "I promise," he said as gently as he could, his voice quavering.

Another stretched silence. Then there rose the scraping of a locking bar being removed from over the door. The steel and leather latch clicked, and the door squawked as it drew inward a few inches to reveal a young girl's pretty, freckled face staring through the crack. Deep furrows cut across her freckled forehead, and her eyes were suspicious, fearful. "Remember, you promised."

She screamed as Charlie rammed his shoulder against the door. As the girl fell back into the stage station's thick shadows rife with the smell of grease, tobacco, and woodsmoke, Charlie bounded inside and grabbed the shotgun out of her hands. The girl hit the floor on her butt with a yelp, and Charlie stood just inside, his long shadow falling across her body clad in a low-cut flour-sack dress.

She was barefoot, and her pale blues eyes sparked with fear between wings of her long, straight, tawny hair.

The other men sauntered into the station behind Charlie.

"She's purty, all right," said Lucky, swallowing hard and glowering down at the girl.

"Right well set up, too." Curly Joe doffed his hat and started forward, tossing his hat onto the table. He glanced over his shoulder at Charlie. "You want her first, boss?"

Charlie scowled, his fists still balled in fury at his sides. "Nah. You boys deserve first turns with her. I reckon I owe you that. Besides, I think she stinks worse than we do."

Curly Joe turned back to the girl and began unbuckling his cartridge belt. "You an' me, girl, we gonna have us some fun."

"No!" The girl jerked her arm away from him and heaved herself to her feet. "You promised!"

"Promised we wouldn't kill ya," said Lucky as he and One-Eye followed Curly Joe after the girl, who scrambled, stumbling and falling and trying to run barefoot on the scarred wooden floor. He gave a whoop. "You ever tumble with a werewolf before?"

As Curly Joe, One-Eye, and Lucky went after the girl, Charlie walked back out onto the veranda, at the edge of which he stood and, tipping his face to the softening sunlight and a slight breeze wafting down from the high country in the northwest, dug a long, black cheroot from the breast pocket of the warden's rough wool shirt. From behind him came the girl's curses and sobs as the men apparently cornered her in the cabin's north corner.

Charlie scratched a match to life on the warden's black cartridge belt and touched the flame to the end of his cigar.

A whirling sounded in the far distance.

Charlie passed the sound off as merely a gust in the freshening breeze, but as he blew his match out with a puff of cigar smoke, he curled a dubious brow as he stared into the rolling, rock-, sage- and cedar-stippled desert beyond the station.

The whirling grew louder and louder, and for a moment Charlie wondered if the station wasn't about to be hit with one of those infernal cyclones that plagued the flat, less arid country a little to the east, when a large, dark cloud slid into view, its fishy white belly raking the top of a high, northern ridge. Charlie scrutinized the shadow as he blew more cigar smoke out his broad nostrils, and felt his lips part as his lower jaw sagged slightly.

The cloud had enormous, flapping wings and, all alone in the cobalt sky gaining a darker cast as the afternoon waned, was fast approaching the stage station. It wasn't a funnel cloud. It wasn't a cloud of any kind, Charlie saw now as the sunlight winked off the lime-green and golden scales, and the dragon's wagon-sized head, like the head of a deadly, giant diamondback rattlesnake, turn toward him, eyes like burning green and red coals.

Flames shot out of the dragon's nostrils—two slender jets of orange fire flicking out like twin tongues merely testing the air before receding again into the bizarre beast's antenna-adorned head. The flames' black smoke was torn away on the wind.

"Yeeeee-HAWWWWWWWWW," came a cry beneath the whirling sound of the dragon.

Charlie looked away from the fast-approaching winged beast then, realizing that the sound had to be coming from the dragon itself, turned back to it as its great, bat-like wings rose and fell while its finned tail curled out behind it, propelling it along from behind.

The cry came again, and as the dragon approached the station from a mile out now, dropping and coming on fast,

Charlie made out a slender figure astride the dragon's back, throwing one arm out and whooping as though the fool were riding a bucking bronco in a Fourth of July rodeo in Abilene.

Charlie squinted his eyes incredulously.

A *female* fool. Long, black hair flew out behind the woman's head in the wind. Her willowy, curvaceous body was clad all in black and brown, with a red sash and matching red boots angling back against the dragon's broad body. In contrast to the dragon's girth—the beast was the size of a small barn—the girl appeared little larger than a cat as, yipping and yowling and throwing up her arm, she held in her other hand the leather ribbons of a braided gold harness of sorts that curved around the beast's stout neck. Beneath the woman was a red velvet blanket trimmed in gold, with gold tassels fluttering in the wind as the beast now made its final approach, the sage and cedars shivering in the wind of its sinewy wings.

Charlie tipped his brim low against the ground fog of dust, straw, and horse shit. He couldn't help chuckling then, as he recognized the woman astride the dragon, and stepped down off the veranda and walked across the yard as the dragon set down between the crazily spinning windmill and the cabin.

"What the hell's that?" shouted one of the men from inside.

The girl's cries had died to mere whimpers and occasional snapped curses.

Boots thumped on the worn puncheons behind Charlie, as the pack leader strode several yards out from the veranda and stopped, grinning around the cheroot smoldering between his teeth, crossing his arms on his chest, and rocking back on the heels of his polished cavalry stovepipes. Sitting atop the now-idle dragon, who blinked its copper eyes slowly at Charlie, shorts bits of fire curling from its nostrils and its wings flexing slightly as they settled against its sides, Ravenna de Onis y Gonzalez-Vara pinched her black hat brim in salute.

The pretty Mexican *bruja*, or sorceress, swung her right leg up in front of her, where a saddle horn would have been had she been using a saddle, and dropped spryly down to the dragon's left wing. From there, spreading her arms out for balance, the red sash and the tails of her long, black leather duster fluttering out around her, she dropped straight down to the ground.

Striding toward Charlie, the witch glanced over her shoulder at the idling dragon, and said, *"Siente y comportese, Chico!" Sit down and behave yourself.*

"You are even a better witch than I imagined," Charlie said, letting his flat brown eyes roam lustily across the woman's exquisite, black-and-brown-clad, well-armed figure.

"How's that, *mi amigo*?" Ravenna asked as she stopped before him, smiling and showing all those perfect white teeth though his eyes were lingering on the black vest, which was all she wore beneath the duster and which revealed more of her full, enticing, olive-hued breasts than they hid. The top of each one was tattooed in black with a weirdly shaped symbol—a totem of some kind.

"I was just thinking of you before I saw . . ." Charlie glanced past her at the dragon, whose sides expanded and contracted slowly, heavily, as he breathed, his scales sparkling as the light dashed across them with each expansion and contraction. "Your crazy bird there . . ."

"Be careful, Senor Charlie," Ravenna said, lifting her chin to smile up at him while waving a finger in good-natured admonishment. "Chico does not like to be called a bird." She glanced over her shoulder at the dragon. "What the hell, Chico. *Va la causa un cierto apuro, huh!" Go wreak some havoc!*

Eagerly, Chico flapped his great wings, rising up on his giant, birdlike legs, and heaved himself into the sky. The wind of his wings lifted dust and grit against which Charlie and Ravenna closed their eyes and held their hats down tight to their heads.

"What are dragons, anyway?" Charlie asked when the bird was winging off to the west and banking north, as if suddenly sensing prey in that direction.

"They are dragons, fool." Ravenna rose up on the toes of her fancily stitched, red, black-topped boots to plant a kiss very lightly on his lips. "You were thinking of *me*, *Major Charlie*?" she said, running her fingers over the shoulder straps on his greatcoat, obviously surprised and flattered.

"Encountered a little problem we need to disc—"

He stopped when one of the men inside the cabin cursed loudly. Running footsteps sounded, emanating out the open door until the girl, looking frantic, a torn strap of her dress hanging down to reveal a wash-worn camisole behind which her right breast jiggled, dashed across the veranda and bolted past Charlie and Ravenna. As the girl headed for the barn, leaping the stage driver's bloody carcass, One-Eye came running out of the station house, flanked by Lucky and Curly Joe, whose lower lip was bleeding.

"Bitch bit me!" he raged.

The three stopped when they saw Ravenna with Charlie. "What the hell is that?" said Curly, slowing as he came down the steps and pointing at the dragon now winging back over the stage station. The other two were casting incredulous looks between the dragon and the beautiful senorita in the black duster and revealing fawn vest from behind which her ample breasts swelled invitingly.

"My horse!" said Ravenna delightedly. "I've put him out to pasture for the time being." Looking at Charlie, she said, canting her head toward the barn, "Who's the whore? You haven't been cheating on me, have you, Charlie?"

She nudged one of her round hips against Hondo's crotch, stuck a finger through one of his gold earrings, and gave it a gentle, chiding tug. "I've been saving myself for you ever since Dodge City!"

Charlie tittered. "The hell you say!"

"Be careful or I'll send you there," she chided with just enough of an edge to rock Charlie back on his heels. "You know I have the magic for it."

Glancing again at the dragon just now fading from sight but obviously more compelled by the prospect of toiling between the station girl's legs, Lucky bolted away from Charlie and Ravenna, heading for the barn.

"Hey, slow your horses!" shouted One-Eye, sprinting for the barn.

Curly Joe wiped blood off his lip and took off after the others. "I git her first, goddamnit! She drew my blood!"

Charlie watched the three, hearing their spurs chinging, shaking his head and chuckling.

"Were they so depraved in the Old Country?"

"Oh, I reckon." Charlie looked at the witch and necromancer and gave her low-cut vest a commanding tug. "We best talk business, *chiquita*. We got problems. "

"Business?" Ravenna stuck her two index fingers behind the waistband of Hondo's pants and returned the tug. "But I just got here, and I smell like Chico. I must have a bath. *Vamos!*" She grabbed his hand and jerked him along behind her as she mounted the veranda. "We'll take one together, Charlie! It'll be fun. *You'll see!*"

She laughed and dashed into the cabin. Unable to resist such a delectable creature, and forgetting for the moment that she could send him to the devil's own Hell in pieces, he ran in after her and closed and locked the door behind them.

One-Eye and the others could sleep in the barn.

14

HATHAWAY

As the dragon careened toward him and Angel, Uriah Zane raised his Henry repeater to his shoulder, took hasty aim, and fired.

He didn't wait to see if his paltry round had any effect on the beast, but swung around and followed Angel back into the crease between the rounded mounds of ancient lava. He'd only just pulled his left foot behind the cover, when a great rumbling and *whoosh* sounded and orange flames licked over the top of the dyke, curling down its sides to within a few feet of Zane and Angel.

The heat was like that of blacksmith's fully stoked bellows, and it smelled like brimstone.

"Uriah!" Angel shouted, ducking into a two-foot-high notch cave at the very base of the dyke.

Zane threw his big body down and rolled into the notch behind the redhead just as another stout, roiling lance of fire hammered into the ground behind him. He rolled away from the flames that curled a few inches into the gap. He half rolled on top of Angel, shielding her body with his own. There was a great rushing of wings, and as the smell of scorched earth permeated the cave, what sounded like the squeals of an enraged pig rattled Zane's eardrums.

He gritted his teeth against it. Her face turned toward his, Angel did the same.

The squeals dwindled into the distance, as did the rushing of the wings.

"Christ!" Angel said.

"Not even close."

Zane started to roll away from her. She grabbed his arm. "Wait. It might be circling."

"I'll see."

Her face reddened in anger, making the hooked scar beneath her eye turn pale. "Give it another minute, goddamnit, Uriah! We know nothing about those . . ."

She let her voice trail off. Zane, ignoring her as he usually did, had rolled out of the notch cave and, on one knee, holding his Henry in his hands, surveyed the skies. All clear. The ground around him—the sand, gravel, sparse tufts of sage and Spanish bayonet—were black and smoking.

"It's clear."

Angel rolled out and climbed to her knees, looking around. Zane remained there, too, scowling up at the blue sky, wondering if he'd really seen what he thought he had.

He'd heard the legends, of course. What kid hadn't? A few people claimed to have seen such winged dinosaurs, but none of the stories had even been corroborated. But then, when he'd been a kid growing up on his father's plantation north of Atlanta, blood-swillers and shapeshifters had been legends, too. They'd been thought to exist only in Europe and isolated pockets here and there about the West, but few white men had yet seen them.

For him, tales of the shape shifters from far away lands had dissolved in a cold rush of bloody reality that night in the hollows of the hills near Gettysburg, when Grant and

Buford had turned loose their recruited horde of werewolves.

Zane gave a shudder, remembering that awful night, seeing the man-beasts—wolves twice the normal size and with vaguely man-shaped heads but wolflike fangs and claws—running upright and storming into the Confederate bivouacs even as the pickets screamed and fired on them with their crude trapdoor Springfields, and soldiers poured out of their tents in terrified confusion, thinking it was the blue bellies attacking at night.

In just a few hours, every Confederate soldier save a lucky few, like Zane himself, wounded earlier that day by a Union minié ball to the neck, had been ripped to bleeding piles of viscera steaming in the full moon's pearl light. Zane's own brother, Zachary, had been one of those piles. . . .

"Where are the horses?" Angel said after a time, breaking the pregnant, eerie silence.

Zane heard her as though she were a half mile away. He was still staring at the sky, hearing the howls, snarls, and squeals of his doomed Southern brethren.

Angel placed her hand on his forearm. "Uriah."

He turned to her sharply, startled. "What?"

"Did you see the horses?"

Zane looked around. He'd forgotten about them. He didn't think they'd been in the crease between the dykes before he and Angel had fled from the fire-breathing demon. "Must have run off. Good thing." He ran a big hand down his bearded face, pressing away the horrible memories aroused by the beast who'd nearly burned him and Angel to cinders. "I'd hate to be stranded out here afoot with that winged devil flying around."

She closed her fingers a little tighter about his arm. "You okay?"

The question annoyed him. In his line of work, a man didn't have time for the distractions of memory. Furling his brows angrily, he pulled his arm away and said, "Yeah."

He heaved himself to his feet, walked out the opposite end of the notch, and looked around. General Lee and Angel's paint, Cisco, stood a good half mile off, reins dangling as they nervously looked around, twitching their tails, as terrorized by the winged beast as Zane and Angel were. The wheeled casket was still in the Appy's tow, looking none the worse for wear.

"What's going on, Uriah?" Angel came up to stand beside him. "You've been hunting spooks longer than I have. You ever see anything like that before?"

"Not since yesterday. Caught a brief glimpse of one, maybe the same one, on the way into Gunnison."

Zane was still squinting up at the sky. A winged giant that spat fire would be one hell of a formidable foe. He doubted even the Gatling gun would be of use against it, unless he could get it in close. But then you had the fire to worry about.

"Till then, I never seen one. Heard somethin', though. . . ."

He tried to remember the story he'd heard a couple of years ago in Mexico.

"Somethin' about a young girl from a wealthy hacienda down Sonora way . . ." Again, he let his voice trail off and jerked his head to the north, in the direction he and Angel had been traveling. Beyond a low jog of brown hills sounded the muffled snaps of gunfire. In the sky careened a winged figure, a column of orange light angling groundward.

Angel said tonelessly, "It's after somebody else."

Distant screams sounded amid the shrill whinnies of terrified horses.

"Let's go," Zane said, jogging in the direction of his and Angel's horses, resting his rifle on his right shoulder.

He moved fleetly for a big man, and it was all Angel

could do to match his long strides. When they gained the horses, they quickly went over the tack, tightening latigo cinches and pack straps that might have come loose when the mounts had fled the dragon. When he was sure that the wheeled coffin was still harnessed properly to General Lee, Zane swung up into his saddle and slid his Henry repeater into its sheath, which was angling forward across his right stirrup, and touched spurs to the Appy's flanks.

General Lee had great power in his legs. The stallion bounded off its rear hooves with a shrill whinny, it and the trailing coffin angling northward. Zane stayed wide of the burned Indians and their dead horses, knowing his own horse would be repelled by the stench.

He glanced over his shoulder to see Angel galloping about twenty yards behind him. The woman was a wonder to him. She could be as much female in bed as a man could ever need or want, yet she had the sand of a seasoned frontiersman to boot. He knew she was afraid, because she wasn't crazy—hell, his own guts were pulled in a hard knot—but as she crouched over her paint's neck, her hat brim pulled low against her jade eyes, red hair flying out behind her, she looked more determined than anything else.

But what did Zane expect from the daughter of the famed lawman? She wore his boots well. At least, the boots he'd once worn.

Ahead, as Zane and Angel headed for a notch in the brown, boulder-strewn hills, the shots grew louder but then dwindled as Zane saw the dragon pull off to the northeast. The flapping wings and body merged into a single dot, and then the dot was swallowed up by the sky, leaving Zane to clench his belly tight as he wondered what devastation it had left in its wake.

Rising smoke told him where to head, and, following a crease between the rocky hills, he came to a broad bowl cut into the side of a high bluff. Here, horses and men lay scorched and sizzling, strewn about the rocks and brush of the bowl as though, like the Indians, they'd been dropped from the sky. Zane rode ahead, and Angel followed suit, widening the gap between them as they both surveyed the carnage.

Most of the horses and bodies were charred beyond recognition, but Zane saw a sleeve on one of the cadavers that was burned down to the charred bone, smoke slithering out its eye sockets. The sleeve was blue wool and had a cavalry sergeant's three bars worn point down on it. Elsewhere, Zane saw a blue cavalry kepi and a mule-eared, low-heeled, stovepipe cavalry boot with a smoking black leg bone sticking up out of it. On a horse's wither he saw the customary U.S. brand.

Zane had ridden only halfway through the carnage before his eyes were aching from the stench of burned flesh, leather, and horsehide combined with the dragon smell of brimstone he'd noted before.

"There must be twenty soldiers here, Uriah." Angel's voice was muffled by the red neckerchief she held to her mouth and nose. She stopped her paint beside a boulder near which another horse, its burned rider's right leg poking from beneath it, smoked and sizzled, the belly expanding and contracting from the gases inside. "They must be out of Fort Saber near Socorro."

"This is Abner Dean's command."

"Who?"

"Buddy of mine. Captain of the first cavalry who rides patrol around here." Zane looked at a horse and a charred black skeleton several yards to his left. "A good man, for a blue belly. Poor bastard didn't know what hit him."

"Hold it right there!"

Zane snapped his head around, trying pinpoint the owner of the burly voice. His eyes stopped on a short, portly black gent in buckskins and blue Cavalry hat standing in a deep notch in an escarpment against the base of the bluff. He was round-faced, and his woolly black beard was liberally sprinkled with gray. He held a Sharps carbine to his shoulder and was squinting as he aimed down the barrel.

"One wrong move out of either one of you, I'll drill ya good, kick ya out with a cold shovel!"

Zane studied the black man. "Who the hell are you?"

"Scout. Ride over here, both of ya." He added with menace, "*Slow*. And keep them hands where I can see 'em."

Zane and Angel shared a glance, then moved their horses forward across the hollow. They halted near the mouth of the ravine where the short, stocky black man stood, aiming his cocked carbine, coffee-brown cheeks bunched as he squinted against the sun.

Angel glanced in revulsion at the carnage around them. "Put the gun down, mister. You overestimate us if you think we did this."

Zane, within twelve feet of the man with the rifle, could see that despite the rough features and smoke-stained buckskins bespeaking a man of a long career on the Western frontier, the officer was as stunned by the bizarre happening here as Zane and Angel were. His chocolate eyes were rheumy and uncertain—an uncustomary look for the man, obviously. Like the wolfer and the marshal, he was as frightened as a kid just run out of a haunted house by an ax-wielding blood-swiller.

"I seen it." The black man mashed his lips together inside his thick, curly beard. He seemed a little incredulous about the rifle, but he was too stunned to lower it.

Vaguely, he wanted to put human or known ghoul form to the killings. Humans, swillers, and the like were more easily understood, more easily held responsible for their actions than that winged, fire-breathing, man-incinerating creature known only in fairy tales.

He said in his deep, quavering voice, "Don't know if I

believe what I saw. I take it you seen it, too?" The skin above the bridge of his freckled, wedge-shaped nose wrinkled.

"We saw it," Zane said. "Saw it a while ago, too. It took out a passel of Apaches on our trail. Torched 'em just like Abner Dean's boys."

The black man lowered his rifle to hip level, keeping it aimed in the general direction of Zane and Angel, canting his head to one side. His buckskin shirt was sleeveless, and his black upper arms hung like slabs of charred beef at his sides. "You knew Dean?"

"That's right. When he was stationed at Fort Bowie, I rode scout for him against a pack of Injun swillers in the Chiricahuas. I'm Uriah Zane. This here's Angel Coffin, deputy U.S. marshal out of Denver."

"I'm done having that carbine aimed at me, mister," Angel said tightly.

He depressed the Sharps's hammer and raised the barrel, pressing the stock against his double cartridge belts from which several knives and pistols jutted. A thin smile parted his cracked, pink lips, and his weary eyes flashed in recognition. "You got your father's disposition, Marshal Coffin."

Angel frowned.

"You don't remember. I don't blame you. I was your father's deputy when he was sheriff o' Julesburg." He patted his hard, black belly angling roundly out from behind his worn buckskin shirt trimmed with Indian designs that Zane recognized as Coyotero. "And I was, oh, about fifty pounds lighter."

"Alpheus Hathaway!" Angel's face lit up, white teeth flashing, as she swung down from her saddle and ran into the broad arms of the burly Army scout.

He laughed and held her tightly, patting her back. His face sobered quickly, and he glanced from Zane to the burning shrubs and charred bodies around them, the stench not so bad here as the breeze was out of the north. "Sorry place for a reunion, huh, girl?"

Angel pulled away from him, following his gaze, her own smile fading quickly, as well. "At least twenty men, Al."

"Twenty-three. I rode with 'em as chief packer and scout. I was ridin' ahead, as the Lipans been on the prod of late, though it wasn't the 'Paches we was after. We was headed for Hellsgarde Penitentiary over in Devil's Canyon." He canted his head to indicate southwest, talking to Zane now, too. "I was up there on the saddle, headin' back this way, when I seen the bird."

He shook his head and looked truly befuddled, almost out of his mind in confusion and bereavement. "A fire-breathin' bird."

"A dragon," Angel said softly, as though to herself, as she looked around.

"Yessir. As real now as the blood-swillers and shape-shiftin' wolves from across the ocean. What's the frontier comin' to?" Hathaway looked at Zane, furling his brows. "It's almost like Hell's doors done opened again, just like they did back in 'sixty-three, lettin' ghouls from our worst nightmares out."

He paused, grimaced sadly. "I'd like to bury these boys. But there's no time. We was headed for Hellsgarde. Been a break there."

"Nah," Zane said. "Not possible. Hellsgarde's an impregnable castle. Hell, Devil's Canyon itself allows no way in or out except through a stout steel-mesh door."

"That's what I said when Major Dean told me about it, and signed me up to scout the expedition." Hathaway studied Zane. "You're Uriah Zane."

"That's right."

"I'd recognize you anywhere, Mr. Zane." Hathaway walked over and extended his hand, and Zane shook it. "Pleased to make your acquaintance. You'll be interested to know that the four survivin' Hell's Angels broke out of Hellsgarde. Three broke in, broke Charlie Hondo out."

Zane straightened in his saddle, stared at the man as though he'd spoken in a foreign tongue. Rage bit him like an Apache arrow. Rage and fear. That the man who had led the wolf pack that had wiped out several Confederate companies including his brother and several cousins and an uncle was beyond belief.

He hardened his jaws and shook his head. Suddenly, he neck-reined General Lee around, ground his heels into the horse's flanks, and bounded off at a dead gallop toward the blue, serrated ridges of the San Juan Mountains rising in the west.

15

A BREED OF FLYIN' CRITTER

ZANE CHECKED General Lee down after a quarter-mile sprint, realizing that killing his prized horse wouldn't get him to Hellsgarde. Gradually, Angel and Hathaway, who rode a tall and surprisingly quiet gunmetal-gray mule, caught up to him and kept pace to either side of him.

"How'd it happen, Hathaway?" Zane asked the cavalry scout.

"Don't know the answer to that question, Mr. Zane. All I know is most of the guards was killed, but they sent a telegraph message to the fort yesterday, asking for help to track the killers down and manpower to keep the rest of the ghouls in their cages."

"Any others get away?"

"Don't believe so. Three Angels were hauled through the gates in a jail wagon, though no one knew they was Angels. Didn't even know they was ghouls. Killed some federal badge toters to get themselves hauled to Hellsgarde, then shapeshifted soon as they got inside the main door, sprang Charlie Hondo, killed the warden and a passel of guards."

"They changed in broad daylight?" Angel was dubious. No ghouls were ever hauled by night. Not on any night.

"That how I understood it, Miss Angel."

Zane said, "How'd they get out the tunnel? You couldn't drive a Baldwin locomotive under full steam through those bars. And not even a ghoul could climb those canyon walls."

"Don't know the answer to that, Mr. Zane. The message that come in didn't tell us much, just to fog the trail out to Hellsgarde as fast as we could."

"You can call me Uriah."

"All right. An' I'm Al. What do you suppose ole Charlie's intentions are now that he's free?"

"No tellin'," Angel said, riding on the other side of Zane. "But I'd bet the seed bull he's not aimin' to start a church."

They pushed their horses hard toward the steep ridge wall behind which the appropriately named Devil's Canyon and Hellsgarde prison lay.

The ridge stood tall and dark and fittingly ominous, owning the shape of a black-scorched sawtooth blade. While they'd spotted the ridge not far from where they'd met Hathaway, the formation rose before them slowly across the cedar-stippled flat scored with sudden arroyos and pocked with low bluffs. Slowly, the pits and troughs and fissures in the ridge's sheer wall gained shape and dimension.

The October sun hammered down, and the day grew hot. The air smelled of greasewood and sage, and there were occasional tinges of blossoming autumn wildflowers. The sky, to the group's relief, remained free of dragons.

When the trio had slowed their mounts after a long lope, giving them a rest, Angel swung her paint up beside Hathaway's mule, which the black scout called Annabelle and which he'd been riding for nearly six years, preferring the mule's bottom and sure-footedness over what he called the clumsiness and unreliability of horses.

"Sure is nice to see you again, Al," Angel said. "Though I wish it were under better circumstances."

"Them boys didn't deserve to die like that. Personally, I'd like to give that bird about twelve rounds of twelve-gauge buck, if I ever see him again." Hathaway patted the long, double-barreled shotgun that rode in a saddle sheath on the opposite side from his rifle. Like most frontiersmen, he also had a crossbow lashed to his saddle, draped across one of his saddlebag pouches, the flap of which was stamped U.S. He frowned apprehensively. "Why is it I have a feeling I will?"

"Why is it I have a feeling that twelve rounds of twelve-gauge buck won't bring it down?"

Hathaway glowered, then, as he studied the young woman he'd known long ago, gave a low whistle. "Look at you. The last time I seen you, you was in pigtails and tendin' chickens behind you and your pa's house when you weren't out trying to bring down sage hens with your sling-shot. Now . . . why, you're a full-grown woman."

He grinned brashly, showing a nearly full set of large, white teeth. "With all the curves to prove it!"

Angel colored with embarrassment.

Hathaway glanced over at Zane. "Ain't she a fine-lookin' woman?"

Zane glanced over at Angel, who did not look at him. "About the finest I've seen."

"I know it ain't none of my business, but are you two . . . ?"

"Hell, no," Angel said too quickly. Then, to soften it: "You best get yourself under rein, Mr. Hathaway. I'm also a federal marshal and I do not cotton to bein' harassed by an old saddle tramp."

Hathaway shifted his questioning gaze between Zane and Angel, then chuckled uneasily.

After a time, as they rode straight toward the ridge, following the wagon trail they'd picked up several miles back, he said without looking at Angel, "Again, this ain't none of my business, but any word about your pa?"

"No."

Zane hadn't expected her to elaborate, as she rarely spoke of her father since the respected lawman James Coffin had been turned into a swiller by a pack haunting the Missouri River breaks up in Dakota. They had attacked him and two other federal marshals when they were investigating illegal shipments of whiskey to the Sioux reservation near Bismarck. So he was surprised now to hear her say, "Last I heard he was spotted in Montana. That was two years ago. He sent me a letter once, but I didn't open it."

"Why not?"

"He's a killer, Al. There's a high bounty on his head. Like most, he just can't resist human blood. Even if he could, once they've changed, they're no longer the people they were." She turned her head slightly to give Zane a quick, sidelong glance.

He was glad when they saw the tunnel mouth at the bottom of the ridge, and the six or seven soldiers milling around a Gatling gun on a tripod aimed straight into the hand-hewn and dynamite-blasted cavern. Two others were hunkered in rocks on both sides of the trail, sitting smoking against the rocks until one swung his head toward Zane's group and whistled at the guard on the other side of the trail from him. Both soldiers jerked to life and grabbed their carbines.

"Who goes there?" shouted the young soldier on one knee atop a boulder on the trail's right side. They were skittish as hell.

Angel called, "I'm a deputy United States marshal. We got word of the attack on the prison and are here to investigate. Who's in charge?"

The rifle-wielding guards glanced at each other. Another swung the Gatling gun around on its wooden tripod, and aimed the six-barreled weapon at the group.

"You're not gonna need that, fellas," Angel said. "I have stamped papers in my saddlebags. With me are Uriah Zane and Alpheus Hathaway, and I'll vouch for both."

The guards lowered their rifles only slightly, glancing at one another nervously, and came skipping down the rock piles, leaping onto the trail. One was tall and skinny, a quirley smoldering between his lips. The other was medium tall, paunchy, with curly orange hair puffing out from beneath his tan kepi.

He waved the group over, and Angel took the lead as she, Zane, and Hathaway rode up to the young guards. Angel slowly reached back to dig around in a saddlebag pouch, and showed the guard her papers encased in a small leather portfolio.

When the guard seemed satisfied with the documents, he gestured to the others to stand down. Zane rode up to the cave mouth, where the other soldiers were slowly, almost reluctantly lowering their rifles. They were all young and bright-eyed, and their muscles seemed to jerk under their ill-fitting uniforms.

Zane turned to the soldier manning the Gatling gun. "How in the hell did those ghouls bust through the tunnel?"

"Didn't bust through it," said the guard in a faintly sulking tone, turning toward the tunnel mouth. "That flyin' devil melted the door."

Zane swung down from General Lee's back and, ground-reining the palomino, walked over to the tunnel mouth, gazing at the ground. His heart skipped a beat.

When he'd first seen it, he'd thought that the material littering the cave mouth was a large mud puddle from a nearby spring. But now he saw that the hardened, twisted sheets of melted steel were all that remained of the door that the government had promised was absolutely indestructible to any and all forces, be they men or beasts. It had been built of the stoutest grade of steel found anywhere in the world. Stronger even than its own density in stone.

Hathaway and Angel rode up behind Zane and looked down at the mass of melted minerals.

"Holy hob," said Hathaway, removing his floppy-brimmed black hat and scratching his head slowly. "I guess we know what kind o' flyin' critters done that—don't we, pards?"

"I reckon we do," Angel said, casting an anxious glance at the sky.

16

THE COVEN

Lieutenant Andrew Jackson McAlpine, assistant warden of Hellsgarde Penitentiary, scratched a match to life on the surface of the late Warden Mondrick's broad desk, and, with fingers shaking as badly as if he were aboard a train traversing a stretch of bad track, touched the fire to his long, black cigar.

Leaning forward in the late warden's leather-upholstered swivel chair, he planted his elbows on the desk and blew smoke out his nostrils as he tossed the stove match into an ashtray carved in the form of a bear's open paw, and thumbed his spectacles up his long, slender nose.

"You have any idea what it's like here now?" he said, his voice quaking as badly as his hands. "I have just barely enough men to run this place, let alone keep the two hundred and fifty ghouls housed here under lock and key."

"I'm sure you're under a lot of stress," said Angel.

"Stress?" Warden McAlpine chuckled without mirth and lifted a brandy snifter to his lips. He swallowed, making a pained expression. "No, it's far from stressful wondering when one of the bastards is going to get loose and suck your blood and turn you into one of them. 'Horrifying' is a better word. I just hope, when it happens, and it will surely happen if I don't get some *fucking support out here, goddamnit*!"—he punched the top of warden's desk so hard his spectacles slid down his nose and the Tiffany lamp rattled—"that they just tear my throat out and let me die!"

"Easy, partner," Uriah said from where he stood at a casement window, one elbow propped atop the coping as he smoked a tightly rolled quirley of strong Mexican tobacco and sipped the late warden's whiskey from a water glass. "Givin' yourself a heart stroke ain't gonna make the situation any easier."

"Sorry the soldiers didn't make it, Lieutenant," said Hathaway. "Sounds like we ran into the same winged devils that attacked the castle." The black scout sat in an overstuffed leather couch near the oak door at the back of the large room outfitted with game trophies, maps, and heavy, exotic wooden furniture acquired during Warden Mondrick's hunting adventures throughout the world. He'd been a prominent member of Lincoln's and then Sherman's cabinets, and, since he had no wife or family and didn't mind living beyond society's fringe, had volunteered for the warden position at Hellsgarde.

Zane doubted that that was the case with McAlpine. The young assistant warden looked ready to resign and gallop back East just as soon as he could.

A fire danced and crackled in a fieldstone hearth. Mondrick had tried to make the office as homey and familiar as he could in attempt, most likely, to assuage the fact that he was surrounded by screaming devils, any one of whom who would send him to Hell if they ever got their talons or claws into him.

And one eventually had. . . . Hondo had even taken the man's clothes.

"If the courier gets through," Angel said, sitting in the visitor's chair angled in front of the desk and turning her own brandy snifter in her fingers, "Major Dean will send more men. I'm sure more will be coming from Fort Reynolds, as well. We'll find a way to handle those dragons, just like we've found ways to handle everything else."

"Yes, everything else." McAlpine curled his upper lip and, drawing a deep, calming breath, sagged back in his chair. "I know this isn't the ascribed view, but why the hell not kill them all? Kill them all now before they all get away!" He threw back the last of his brandy and, fumbling with the cut-glass decanter on his desk, refilled it.

"Don't want to make the situation any worse than it already is," Hathaway reminded the man. He sucked on a fat stogie from the warden's humidor, blowing a large smoke ring. "Part of me wants to agree with you, though, Lieutenant. Especially after what happened to my detail. Sooner or later, somethin' real bad's gonna happen because we got so damn many o' 'em all over the West. And now we got some we didn't even know we had."

His heavy, rounded shoulders jerked as he chuckled fatefully, shaking his head. He was thinking, of course, about the dragon.

"Look, we can discuss politics all we want," Zane said, blowing a lungful of cigarette smoke out the open casement window, looking out over the scorched yard that had only recently been cleared of charred, dead soldiers, "but what we really need is to haul ass out of here and try to cut Charlie's sign."

"It's too late in the day, Uriah," Angel said wearily, showing her own frustration. "We're gonna have to hole up here for the night whether we like it or not. The sun'll be down soon."

Zane blew a smoke plume out the window over the darkening yard. Angel was right. It was too late in the day to start out. They and their horses needed food and a good night's sleep.

But he had a bad feeling, whether due to his recently acquired and troubling condition or not, that something bad was going to happen, and the chance of that occurring grew by leaps and bounds with every minute Charlie Hondo and his men were running off their leashes. If he had hackles at that moment, they'd be raised.

"You have somewhere we can bunk?" Angel asked the lieutenant.

"Sure, sure. We have an entire wing for visitors, if you'll pardon the ghouls' screams, which tend to pick up after midnight, though begin to fade slightly after three." McAlpine blinked slowly. "I'll send someone to make sure the beds are made. You can dine with me, if you like, in the warden's quarters. Thank heavens none of the cooks were burned to ashes. Little good they'd do if we were under siege again—most being women."

"You'd be surprised what a woman can do with the right weapons, Lieutenant," Angel said crisply, throwing back her brandy.

McAlpine, a pale, light-skinned man with large ears and pomaded hair, looked chagrined.

Zane took another puff of the pungent Mexican tobacco he liked so well for the peppery tang it left in his throat, and blew the smoke into the room as he said, "Does the name Elaina Baranova ring a bell with you, Lieutenant?"

McAlpine looked at him, the lines of weariness in his forehead cutting deeper. "Of course. Our resident black sorceress, one of three we have imprisoned here. We call her 'the queen' because she acts like one and seems to carry the respect of nobility among the other ghouls. Oh, God, why bring her up now?"

"I'd like to speak with her privately."

Angel threw back the last of her brandy. "Why? Who is she?"

"Oh, that won't be possible, I'm afraid, Mr. Zane. No one speaks privately with any of the prisoners here. All conversations must be overheard by second and third non-ghoul parties out of fear, of course, of spells being exchanged or imparted." He spoke that last as though reading the words out of a regulation manual.

"All right, you can join us. But I would like to speak to her."

"Uriah . . ." Angel said.

"I'll tell you later."

"If you're to speak with 'the queen,' Mr. Zane, we'll need a third party in addition to a couple official jailers. I'll summon them in the morning."

Zane flicked his cigarette butt out the window. "We're pullin' out first thing in the morning. I'd like to speak to her now."

Angel hiked a shoulder. "I'll be that third party, Lieutenant. If Zane thinks it's important to talk to the witch, I'd like to hear what she has to say."

"You don't want to go in there," Zane said.

"Why wouldn't I?"

"Look, look," said McAlpine, looking pained. "I would rather do this tomorrow, Mr. Zane. My nerves are all leaping up and down my spine, and . . ."

"I need to talk to her tonight, Lieutenant."

"Good God, man, *why?*"

"She could save us a whole lot of time and make a big difference whether we catch up with old Charlie Hondo or not."

They all stared at him.

Hathaway broke the silence after blowing another smoke ring. "Well, hell." He stubbed his stogie out in an ashtray on the sofa beside him. "I reckon I'll trail along, too. Me, I'm partial to witches myself. Had one put a hex on all three of my ex-wives."

Half-drunk, he grinned.

McAlpine summoned a couple of jailers armed with carbines and stone talismans draped around their necks, which some believed would ward off spells and incantations of doom founded in the darker forms of known magic.

They were a burly pair, tough-nut soldiers who'd survived the War and who obviously prided themselves on having the courage it took to guard the ghouls at Hellsgarde. They wore sweat-stained sombreros with the brims turned up in front and fastened to the crows, cavalry-fashion. Each carried a Model '67 Winchester carbine, and in addition to the talismans, they wore bandoliers of both brass and silver, though there were no werebeasts of any stripe in the Witches' Wing of Hellsgarde.

Crossbows dangled from their hips. Several knives of different shapes and sizes bristled about their uniforms.

The wing was on the opposite side of the castle, and the two gravely silent guards, holding flaming torches aloft, led Lieutenant McAlpine, Zane, Angel, and Hathaway down endless stone cavern-like corridors lit with flickering torches. Their boots clacked and chinged on the cracked, heaving stones. The warden shamelessly cradled the cut-glass brandy decanter to his chest, as though it were a suckling baby, and took occasional pulls directly from the bottle.

No cells opened onto this main, circuitous artery through the bowels of the castle, but eerie sounds of all pitches emanated from the thick stone walls, almost as though the walls themselves were making them. Occasionally, Zane could feel a vibration in the floor beneath his boots.

Once, he put his hand on the wall and felt the shudder there, as well. He remembered the cave in which he and Junius Webb had found the high-brow swillers, and the hair on the back of his neck pricked. He almost wished he'd fortified himself with one more shot of whiskey. Odd, he vaguely thought, that as a ghoul himself he'd be so squeamish.

He gently closed his fist, shutting away the thought as

he believed he'd closed off that dark side of himself, forever able to keep it from reaching the light of a full moon as it had but only once in the year since he'd been bitten.

When they came to intersecting corridors, they stopped in front of two broad, timbered, iron-banded doors. Overhead lay a wood sign on which WITCHES COVEN had been burned. While one of the guards fumbled with a key ring, Zane glanced to his left and saw several barred doors opening off both sides of the corridor. Cells, most likely.

What else could they be? He looked down the right corridor and saw the same thing—more doors.

Ghouls of some sort must lurk inside, though there were no sounds here but the murmurings in the rock walls and the clatter of the keys on the heavy iron ring. There was also the gurgle of liquid as Lieutenant McAlpine threw back another slug of the brandy. Chairs on either side of the door the guard was unlocking said that guards were customarily posted here, but due to the sudden lack of manpower at Hellsgarde, they were probably all out guarding the canyon to make sure no spooks got out.

Or in again.

The locking bolt clicked. The guard opened the heavy door that rocked back slowly, like the door of a vault, on stout hinges. Unexpectedly, a pleasing odor, a homey odor, wafted into the dank hall from beyond the door, and as one of the guards led the company into the room beyond while the other closed and locked the door behind them, Zane was surprised to find himself in a large room outfitted much like the first floor of a cozy albeit modest house in your typical frontier town.

One in which supper was being cooked. The smell of fried liver lay thick in the pent-up air.

There were two rooms partitioned off from each other by a crude-hewn set of stacked cupboards, a sitting area with comfortable chairs and a fainting couch to the left, and a kitchen with a cloth-covered table and a black range to the right. Two lumpy old women in shapeless dresses, heavy shoes, and aprons were cooking in the kitchen while —Zane blinked and felt his hand edge toward the butt of the Colt Navy slanting across his belly—a sleek black puma lounged on a braided rope rug before a snapping fire in a fieldstone hearth.

In front of him and the warden, the burly guard stepped back, pivoted on his hips to face the cat, and cocked his Winchester loudly.

The deputy warden made a gurgling sound in his throat and pointed at the beast sitting there as though on a sunny slope, slowly flicking its tail, yellow eyes shiny with reflected fire and lamplight. "She . . . G-goddamnit! She's not supposed to do that!"

The old woman forking beef liver around in a sputtering pan turned to see the cat, and said in a scolding tone, *"Elain-ahh!"*

Throaty laughter sounded a half second before the cat on the rug sort of melted, waxlike, shifting its shape to become a beautiful, blue-eyed brunette with gold hoop earrings and a high-busted, full-hipped figure in a green velvet dress trimmed in wolf fur. Lounging on the rug before the fire, her long legs curled beneath her, Elaina Baranova threw her head back and laughed her hoarse, husky laugh, showing all her white teeth glistening like porcelain between full, red-painted lips. Her blue eyes, which owned a Slavic slant in a heart-shaped face, shone like polished marble.

"Miss Baronova, you've been warned countless times against shape-shifting, and if this . . ."

"I do apologize, Lieutenant McAlpine," Elaina said, though her exotic eyes were riveted on Zane with the zeal of a stalking huntress, "but a girl gets bored, you know. I don't shift my shape regularly but just to get the guards' goat."

Her lips stretched pleasingly. "Zane." She almost whispered it, scrutinizing him as though he, too, were a figure that might shift and be suddenly gone or merely a figment of her imagination.

"Hello, Elaina," Zane said. "Been a while."

Her bosom heaved behind the dress, the cleavage-baring neckline of which was fringed with wolf fur as black as the puma she'd just been. She slid her eyes from Zane to the others, her gaze lingering on Angel.

"Well, you certainly bring a crowd, don't you?"

"Yes," Angel said coolly, her own eyes appraising the strangely beautiful woman before her. "He does."

17

ELAINA BARONOVA

ELAINA'S LONG, slanted eyes narrowed with a feline-like knowingness as she said, sliding her gaze from Angel back to Zane, "She's jealous."

Angel snorted. "Like hell. Uriah and I are after Charlie Hondo and the ghouls who broke him out of here. We'd just like to ask you a few questions, if—"

"Red." Zane looked at her sharply. "Let me handle this."

"Handle what? I certainly never expected to see you again, not after I ended up here on a handful of rumors and innuendo that spread like a wildfire around New Orleans." Tears shone in Elaina's eyes, and her lip trembled a little as she said, "Crowd or not, it is good to see you again, Uriah."

McAlpine turned to Zane. "How well do you two know each other, anyway?"

"Lieutenant, let us have a minute, will you?" McAlpine began to object but Zane interrupted him with, "I know it's against regulations. But I believe Miss Baronova has some information about the folks who busted Hondo out of here, and if we want him back in his cage, I need a moment alone with Elaina. It could be the difference."

McAlpine slid his eyes between the pair, then drew a sharp, resigned breath. "All right, all right. It's against regulations but I don't hope to be here much longer, anyway. And I reckon things couldn't really get much worse than they already are."

He canted his head toward a curtained doorway in the middle of the back wall. "You have five minutes. No weird stuff. If she were to loose some spell she's privy to, it wouldn't do much good for us to have her locked up in the first place, would it?"

"Elaina?" Zane said.

"Anything you want, Uriah. Just wish we had more time." She quirked her lips devilishly as she glanced at Angel, who regarded the witch blandly.

Elaina walked to the curtained doorway, her long, green crinoline skirts rustling softly across the floor carpeted in a deep, plush, wine-red rug without any design whatsoever, due, most likely, to the government's fear that Elaina and the other two sorceresses might turn one into a talisman of sorts.

Zane followed the Russian witch through the curtain and found himself in a room not nearly as well outfitted as the two he'd just left. In fact, it was a jail cage with two large cots in it, all appointed with heavy skins and furs. There were only two windows, hardly larger than rifle slots, high up in the walls.

The curtain had just barely fallen back into place before Elaina spun around, hair and skirts flying, and flung her arms around Zane's neck, pressing her soft lips to his. At first, he resisted. But even with Angel in the next room, he couldn't resist an embrace from his old lover Elaina Baronova, witch that she turned out to be. A deadly witch, he well knew. But one who he hoped was still in love with him.

They'd met when Zane had taken a riverboat to New

Orleans hunting Cajun ghouls and ended up spending the long, rainy winter there.

As he mashed his own lips against hers, feeling her suck at him gently, her saliva warm and tasting as he remembered it had when they were about five years younger and holing up in one of the brothels owned by Elaina's father, who himself was a medium who had built a nice stake before the War operating a circus and traveling carnival show throughout Louisiana and Texas that specialized in fortune-telling.

She pulled her head back slightly, then rubbed her nose against his. "Did you come to spring your witch, Uriah Zane?"

"I came to ask for your help."

Vaguely, he was wondering if she'd noted the change in him, but nothing registered in her eyes, and he thought that a good thing. Maybe he'd suppressed it so far that not even a witch of Elaina's caliber could detect it.

"Anything for you, Uriah." She leaned into him, pressing her breasts lightly against his chest and resting her wrists on his shoulders. "You know that. You tried to save me once, made a genuine effort to make an honest witch out of me, and I was too pigheaded to listen. Thus, I am fated to remain here with those two old crones whose powers can't hold a candle to mine, for the rest of my life."

She brushed her lips once more across his. "Or until you rescue me."

Zane placed his hands on her wrists, gave them an affectionate squeeze. She was as wicked as they came. She'd wielded her powers with aplomb in New Orleans, gaining power over her father's competitors and even casting a spell to turn one into a spider, which she then crushed beneath her shoe. So she'd been incarcerated here in Hellsgarde, a prison reserved for only those most diabolical of witches who, unable to resist their own powers, had proved beyond rehabilitation. She'd have been hanged if there'd been a judge brave enough to pass sentence on her.

Still, Zane felt a pull toward her. Before he'd known what she was, they'd had a wonderful couple of rainy months in each other's arms.

Knowing he didn't have much time, he leaped to the point of his visit. "Who helped those three wolves rescue Charlie Hondo, Elaina? Who's the dragon-speaker?"

"Something tells me you already know the answer to that question, Uriah."

"Ravenna?"

"That's right." Admiration shone like guttering candles in Elaina's long eyes. "The god Elyhann has taught her very well. Makes me jealous."

"Oh, you didn't do too bad."

She stepped back and crossed her arms on her breasts. "Dragon conjuring. Even I have to admire such gall. Elyhann never cast such spells my way, and that truly does gravel me, Uriah. Oh, the fun I could have had!"

"Maybe you didn't ask."

"I shouldn't have had to ask. Ravenna . . . I have to admit that her harsh upbringing in Mexico, where witches are tolerated even less than here, made her riper pickings for Elyhann. Whatever the reason, if you're going after Charlie Hondo, Uriah, tread carefully. Ravenna has used the black powers of the meanest demon in Hell to her best advantage. There will be more tricks up her sleeve besides dragons."

"Why? Why would Ravenna help the Hell's Angels?"

"Charlie Hondo, you know, is a rakish ole devil. There's just something about a man who gets a nasty need for a shave every full moon. But Ravenna is a girl of opportunity, if she's anything, so I doubt it's merely sex or love. I really couldn't tell you, Uriah. But if he threw in with Ravenna to get him out of Hellsgarde, I'd bet my papa's last whorehouse that their partnership goes beyond the prison break.

They've partnered up for a good, dark reason. She needs Charlie, and he needs her."

She dug her fingers into her arms. "It give me the shivers just thinking about it. So much power in a vessel even less restrained than myself."

"You know that Charlie and his pards turned several hours before the full moon rose, don't you?"

Elaina winked. "Like I said, Ravenna has some mighty powers, Uriah. Takes quite a woman to haze a dragon around the skies and to allow shape shifters to shift at will. I'm betting that her powers are a little sapped, however. If you're going to catch up to them, it had better be soon, before she has time to replenish herself. No witch in human form, not even Ravenna, can stay strong forever."

"You have no idea where they're headed or why?"

Elaina's eyes became oddly uncertain as they dropped to Uriah's chest. The skin above the bridge of her nose wrinkled. "I tried to tap into that, but without my cards and amulets it's very difficult. The guards even scour this place for spiders! I did get a feeling, though, Uriah." She looked up at him, her eyes still apprehensive.

He waited.

"I felt that she's been sent by Elyhann herself. That Elyhann wants something . . ."

"What?"

"I don't know—maybe his favorite, dead son, Eurico—"

"Eurico?"

"Yes," Elaina said. "The Lord of Darkness. The long-dead werewolf god, slain by a demon even greater than himself. His death is what caused the werewolves on earth to lose their power—long, long ago—and for the humans to get the upper hand and run them into the proverbial hills."

Zane stared at her, wondering if she were mad as well as demonic.

She gazed back at him, her eyes owning an uncustomary graveness. "If they find what they're looking for . . . and if what they're looking for is the final resting place of Eurico . . ." The tip of her tongue flicked across her lower lip, and her eyes became so fearful that Zane felt a cold, heavy stone drop in his loins. ". . . And if it's true, as legend has it, that Eurico, with the right spell, could be reborn into another vessel, a werewolf vessel . . . it might not mean the end of the world, Uriah, but the start of so much darkness and chaos that we, all of us—humans, magicians, and even some ghouls—will be wishing it were."

Zane pondered this. "You think Hondo and Ravenna are out to resurrect the Lord of Darkness?"

"I don't know." Elaina pursed her lips. "Like I said, my resources are limited here. But if they do resurrect Eurico, it'll mean a return to the old days when the werewolves ruled the earth—night *and* day—and humans—even witches without the power to defy the snarling hordes—will be back cowering in caves."

Zane tugged at his beard. "Personally, I don't much care for cave life. Why, just the other day I found a whole cave full o' . . ." He broke off his own uncustomary nervous chatter. "Oh, well. 'Nough o' that." He kissed the witch's cheek. "Thanks, Elaina."

He began to turn away, but she placed her hands on his face and looked sadly into his eyes. "I'm so sorry, Uriah."

Zane frowned. Then he saw it in her gaze.

He hadn't buried the wolf in himself as deeply as he'd thought he had.

"But it's really not as bad as you think," she added.

A little later that same night but forty-five miles to the southwest, on a cot in the bowels of the Saber Creek Station, Charlie Hondo said as he closed his hands over the breasts of the witch bouncing up and down atop him, "Ravenna, dear, it's kinda hard to give you the full attention you deserve with your dragon staring in the window at me like he's fixin' to turn me into a pile of smoking ashes."

Ravenna stopped bouncing up and down on her knees and shook a thick tangle of hair from her eyes as she turned to the window. Two smoldering eyes shone a few feet beyond the open shutter, the beast's devil-like head silhouetted behind it.

She rapped her hand against the shutter and scolded, "Chico, you randy rascal. Get away! Go on! This is private business! Go find a hollow to curl up in, and I'll see you in the morning!"

The eyes blazed, then dulled, as the head lowered and slowly withdrew against the hulking body behind it. Charlie could hear the crunch of gravel and brush beneath the beast's taloned feet, smell the hot, stony breath and the general, indescribable sweetness and musk of the creature's ungainly body. Oddly, it sort of smelled like burnt squash.

There was a deep-throated groaning sound, and then the beast gained flight and rose up over the desert. The voices of the other three men could be heard in the near distance as they sat around a fire out there. They had finished long ago with the girl, though her screams had taken a long time dying and had added to Charlie's efforts at staying attentive to the rapacious Ravenna.

"Right protective, ain't he?"

"Shh!" Ravenna dropped her rump to his thighs and waggled around on him, sandwiching his face in her beringed hands, pressing her fingers hard against his temples. "Finish me!"

Charlie groaned and squeezed her breasts as she began pummeling him wildly once more.

After he'd brought her to the heights of passion during which she mewled like a bobcat and fairly shredded his chest to ribbons with her fingernails, she kissed his nose and rolled onto her back beside him. "There is nothing like riding a wolf!" she said huskily, regaining her wind. "I love the savage in you, Charlie."

"I was about to return the compliment, Ravenna."

She chuckled and patted his thigh as she reached over to a crude wooden table beside the bed for two long, thin cigars, one of which she gave to Charlie. He rose up on his butt, adjusted the water-stained, corn-shuck pillow covered in blue-striped ticking, and stuck the cigar between his lips.

Ravenna fired a stove match to life on the table and slid the flame toward Charlie. It danced in her brown eyes. "You like your new powers? To be able to change at will—even during the day? Someday, you will change even when there is no moon to be found!"

As Charlie puffed his cheroot to life, Ravenna lit her own cigar, which was sticking out from between her perfect white teeth.

"Yeah, well, you see, that's what I been meaning to talk to you about, Ravenna." He inspected the cigar's glowing coal and blew smoke out his nostrils. "Ya see, a coupla the boys had a hard time changing a little earlier. Curly Joe made a complete fool o' himself jumpin' off the stage thinkin' he'd be landin' on four feet instead of two. The kid coulda hurt hisself."

Ravenna laughed.

Raw fury boiled up in Charlie. His face darkened, and his eyelids drooped. His jaw hinges dimpled, and he reached over the side of the bed and brought up a big skinning knife he'd found in the station, the blade flashing umber in the light from the little sheet-iron stove burning piñon pine in the corner.

Tossing his cigar on the floor, he rolled toward Ravenna, grabbed a fistful of her hair with one hand, using it to pull her head back hard against her pillow, and slid the knife up tight against her throat.

"Listen, you crazy little *puta* bitch, you make a fool o' Charlie Hondo and I'll be the last wolf you ever ride into ecstasy. You got that?"

Her two brown eyes stared up at him fearlessly.

The fury burned brighter behind Charlie's heart. He was accustomed to his threats evoking fear and trembling in women.

"Back in Dodge, you told me you knew where the Lord of Darkness is buried. You told me you'd not only get me there but see that his powers become mine." Charlie spat through gritted teeth. "Are you just bullshittin' me, Ravenna? Is this all just fun and games to you 'cause you're bored and lookin' to tumble with a werewolf?"

His brows bunched suddenly. A sharp fear shone in Charlie's eyes. He gulped and slowly relaxed his grip on the witch's hair. His palm gripping the horn handle of the skinning knife turned soft and spongy.

Beneath the covers and way down past his belly, there was a sharp pressure against his balls. He couldn't see what was causing such a minor but menacing pain, but he could picture the slender stiletto, no doubt as sharp as Charlie's own knife, snugged up taut against his scrotum.

One twitch of the witch's hand, and he'd be howling in the pitch of a she-bitch forever.

18

THE POWER OF EURICO

RAVENNA KEPT her placid eyes on him and applied just a little more pressure to his balls.

"You've made a mistake, Charlie." She blinked, quirked her mouth corners menacingly. "Don't let it be your last."

Charlie's heart skipped a beat. He, of course, had been bluffing. He'd just wanted to put some fear into the girl. She, of course, was not bluffing, and appeared to be yearning to stick that pig poker clear through his pelvis till it was showing through his asshole.

What they had here was akin to a Mexican standoff.

"Now, now, *chiquita*," he cautioned, pulling the knife away and releasing her hair, "can't you take a little funnin'?"

"Sometimes my sense of humor is sorely lacking, Charlie." She grinned delightedly and kept the stiletto pressed tight against his balls for several more seconds, but what felt to Charlie like hours, before withdrawing it, throwing her covers back, and dropping her feet to the floor.

Naked, full breasts jostling, her skin resembling varnished oak in the fire's umber light, she set the stiletto on the table and walked over to the stove. "I hope I haven't made a mistake about you, Charlie." She stooped to grab a piñon log off the floor beside the stove. "I chose you for this excursion as much as you chose me. In fact, I've been looking for you . . . or a beast like you . . . for years, ever since I learned about Eurico myself. I never wanted you for *you*, Charlie. You fool! I thought you were aware of that." She glanced at him in disbelief. "I wanted you for the *wolf* in you!"

Gruffly, she tossed the wood into the stove, then swung around so that her dark, magnificent body, all its womanly curves silhouetted against the crackling fire behind her, faced him. Gold hoop rings similar to Charlie's own dangled from her ears.

"If you knew the real secrets of Eurico, you would realize that. If you knew the kind of powers Eurico will unleash once we've found his last resting place and I use my powers given to me by Elyhann to awaken him, you would know I would not trifle with you, Charlie."

Charlie studied her, incredulous. He'd known about Eurico since he'd first been turned into a werewolf, when he was six years old while hunting in the forest with his father and brothers and was bitten by one who lived near their Romanian estate. Most who changed gradually grew aware of Eurico. He was like a soft whisper in your ear, a dream you could never get ahold of.

The desire to learn more could become almost as strong as erotic passion, consuming, filled with the promise that if you could know Eurico—the Lord of Darkness, the *first* beast, the *ruler* of all beasts—the power of all the dark magic in the universe would be yours. That was all Charlie knew.

And now that he knew that the Lord of Darkness was real and could be found somewhere in the known world, he had to find him. This bewitching sorceress, whom he'd met in a smoky saloon in Dodge City during a drunken debauch just days before he'd been run aground by a passel of bounty hunters who recognized his face from wanted circulars, was going to take him to this formidable ruler of all.

He wasn't sure what would happen, but he felt he knew that at least part of Eurico's ancient, formidable power would be within his grasp, and he and his kith would no longer be at the mercy of mortals. Nor the cycle of the moon . . .

"Well, hell," Charlie said, abashed. "Why's our powers growing weaker?"

"Because *I'm* growing weaker." Bewitchingly cupping one of her pointed, upthrust breasts in one hand, she extended a finger at the window near Charlie. "*Cristo!* I conjured Chico up from twelve eons. That takes a lot out of a girl! I am sorry if the powers I provided you and your compadres is weakening, but I am in human form now, and the powers I derive from Elyhann must ooze through my human vessel—splendid as it is."

She walked toward the bed, rolling her hips, breasts and hair jostling as she moved, and sat on the edge of it, bringing one long, dusky leg up beneath her. She leaned toward Charlie, hair spilling over one breast, and smiled brightly in the dimness.

"But when we conjure Eurico, all the black magic in this world and many others will be yours, and you and your kind, Charlie, will not only shapeshift at will but will have the humans cowering beneath their beds for all ages to come. Your kind ruled once and lived in great cities together, before Eurico was defeated by a spirit even darker and more powerful than himself. But that spirit is long dead on a dead world turned to dust so long ago that even the oldest witches no longer remember its spells and hexes. Your kind will rule again. And if all goes as I've planned, you will rule supreme!"

Charlie grinned slowly and placed the cigar between his teeth, leaning back against the wooden headboard. "I like the sound of that." He frowned. "But . . . what do you hope to get from all this, *chiquita*?"

"A witch who can tap into the black magic of Eurico, Charlie, will be the most powerful witch in the world. Wolves and witches, Charlie, will rule the universe." She reached out and placed her hand on his crotch. "Won't we be stomping with our tails up then, amigo?"

Charlie started to reach for her but stopped when the rataplan of distant hooves sounded outside. Several horses, moving at a gallop, were hammering along the trail from the west.

Charlie sat up slowly, listening, hearing the voices of his own men grow as the hoof thuds continued getting louder. He looked out the window over the wood stove but could see only the glow of the other men's fire in the front yard and the stars showing faintly in the desert sky beyond.

The hoof thuds stopped, and now unfamiliar voices sounded.

Charlie smiled wolfishly as he leaned back against the headboard once more, crooking an arm behind him. "I reckon the fellas at the next relay station must've gotten around to missin' the stage. Not to worry. Curly Joe, One-Eye, and Lucky'll take care of 'em."

"*Sí*, but I hope they are not expecting to change. My powers are plumb sapped out, Charlie. The spell is weak and grows weaker. Even Chico might be heading back to where he came from soon."

"Shit!"

Charlie sighed as he swung his legs to the floor, pulled on his long underwear suit, and wrapped his shell belt around his waist, quickly securing the holster thong to his thigh. Ravenna lay back on the bed, drawing the covers up and pensively puffing her cigar as Charlie stomped into his boots. Hearing the voices in the yard growing louder, he pushed through the little sleeping quarters' curtained doorway and tramped into the main part of the cabin. He pulled the front door open and stepped out into the chill night air, stopping on the station house's rickety front stoop.

About twenty feet straight out lay his partners' fire, around which the boys' gear was piled and eating utensils were strewn. A coffeepot smoked as it sat on a hot rock near the dancing flames.

To the right of the fire, Curly Joe, One-Eye, and Lucky stood facing the three burly men sitting three snorting, nickering horses and pulling back on the mounts' reins to keep them in check. The butts of holstered pistols jutted from behind the newcomers' jacket flaps. Rifles were snugged down in their saddle boots. None of Charlie's own three men was wearing his pistol belt or even held so much as a pigsticker in his hand.

They were relying on their newfound and irresistible abilities to change at will.

The middle man in the group of newcomers was saying, ". . . All I can tell you fellas is we been waitin' on the stage, and there she sits, and we're just naturally wonderin' why in thunder it's still *here*."

The man on the far right neck-reined his horse away from the group and galloped off across the trail and into the desert beyond, where coyotes were howling and snarling. He'd likely soon come across the dead station men and the girl.

"All right, all right, there, fellas," Charlie said, stepping down off the stoop and making his spurs ring as he walked toward the newcomers. "I think I can straighten this all out, make it all real simple and clear."

"Is that right?" said the chunky man who appeared to be the leader, whose unshaven face shone red-brown in the firelight. He wore no glove on his right hand, and that hand was splayed across his wool-clad right thigh, near the handle of the big Smith & Wesson jutting up from the holster nearly concealed by his buckskin coat. "And how is it you're gonna be able to do that when these three can't?"

"Hey, Burt." The voice came from the desert, crisp and clear and sullen on the night air. "Think I found 'em."

Charlie looked at the man called Burt and grinned. Burt's eyes widened and shone like gold coins in the firelight as his right hand jerked toward the walnut butt of the big Smithy.

Charlie gave a howl as he snared his own Colt in his hands, clicking the hammer back and going to work, the blasts rising like cannon fire in the otherwise quiet night. Smoke puffed and flames spewed. In little more time than it took to blink, both Burt and the other man beside him were grunting as Hondo's lead punched them back in their saddles. They bounced off their horses' rumps and tumbled on down to the yard, the horses pitching and screaming and lurching away to gallop off in the night.

The boys looked at Charlie. One-Eye threw up an arm in exasperation. "We coulda handled it, Charlie. No need for all that commotion."

Hooves thudded. Beyond the boys, the third rider was a shadow galloping off to the west, his silhouette bobbing against the stars. Charlie took long strides as he crossed the yard and stepped into the trail, raising one of his pistols once more, narrowing one eye as he aimed.

The Colt leaped and roared.

Charlie listened. The hooves continued thudding. Then there was the gravelly thump of a body hitting the ground.

Charlie lowered the warden's Colt, turned, and headed back toward the fire where the other three were still regarding him doubtfully. "You boys ain't gonna be changing' for a while," he said as he continued toward the cabin and the lovely, insatiable witch awaiting him there. "So keep your nasty ole selves on a short rein, hear?"

19

WOLF HUNT

TRACKING the wolves out of Hellsgarde gave even experienced trackers like Zane and Hathaway fits the next morning.

Inside the canyon, the prints were sometimes men's boots and then wolf paws and then back to boots again—as though the four were still trying to get steady on their wolf legs. The four had run down the tunnel as wolves, then sprinted along the Hog Wollop Trail for about a hundred yards before swerving off the wagon road and heading dead south across a high-desert bowl. The four were running all-out, obviously enjoying their new freedom.

They slowed their pace about halfway across the five-mile-wide bowl, milled around a long-dead deer carcass surrounded by coyote and bobcat tracks in a shallow dry wash, then followed another wash up through low hills stippled with Spanish bayonet, post oaks, and cedar. Here, the rough terrain made for slow going for Zane's and Angel's horses and even for Hathaway's mule. The wolf tracks were harder to follow, as the four spread out here across the hillocks and rocky knobs, but Hathaway found where they converged once more on a freshly killed elk.

They'd gutted the beast, ripping out most of the good meat and organs, including the liver and heart, and had a leisurely meal before drawing water from a nearby spring. Their prints were clearly etched in the mud rimming the moss-edged bowl in the rocks.

Refreshed, they'd continued southwest over a low jog of sandy hills.

The trackers had an easier time following the pack here but a harder time later on when they'd followed a rocky draw that rose up the side of a steeply shelving mesa. It was late in the day when they came to the mesa's lip, where all four prints simply disappeared.

Zane stepped down from General Lee's back, dropped to a knee beside the tracks, and looked over the edge of the cliff. A trail furrowed with narrow wheels tracks curved about fifty feet below, coming up an incline on the left and twisting and turning on down the grade to the right before straightening out and heading across a rocky flat. The sun was low, drawing shadows out from the sage and grease-wood clumps, brushing the cedars with soft copper light.

"That's the Drier-Phelps Stage Company Road. Follows an old fur traders' route from Taos all the way to Tucson."

Zane looked at the trail, unable to see any wolf tracks in the finely churned, pale brown powder. He looked at Hathaway crouched beside him. "You reckon they hopped the stage?"

"I reckon I wouldn't put anything past 'em."

"That must be what they did," Angel said.

The marshal was holding a pair of field glasses to her eyes and looking south along the stage road. "Buzzards ahead. Feasting on something along the trail." She glanced at Zane and Hathaway as she dropped the glasses back into one of her saddlebag pouches. Then she reined Cisco around and trotted along the edge of the mesa, scouring the ridge face for a way down to the trail.

She found it a few minutes later, and Hathaway and

Zane followed her down the perilous path twisting among red rocks and boulders. Zane brought up the rear, moving more slowly with the casket behind him, not wanting to crack a wheel or an axle. When they reached the trail, they scoured the area for more wolf prints.

Finding none, they decided to head south, the direction in which the stage's tracks said it was heading, and soon drew rein. Just ahead, buzzards were milling around a bloody woman's body dressed in a shredded dark red traveling suit. She lay parallel to the trail, hugging the right shoulder, one buzzard on her head, another on her belly.

The baldheaded, beady-eyed carrion eaters eyed the interlopers angrily, squawking their disdain and flexing their wings. Several more were hunkered down on both sides of the trail where they were dining on spilled entrails. A few more milled farther up the road, where Zane could see another body lying father off the trail about ten yards.

Zane stared down at the woman, whom he judged to be in her late forties, early fifties. A cameo pin was still stuck to her red jacket, which was spotted with the darker red of blood. Her limbs were stretched out to both sides of her, and she stared up at the sky through empty sockets.

Zane felt a keen revulsion. Murder for the sake of murder—that was the wolf's way. He thought of that vile predator lurking around inside him, and it made him want to throw his guts up.

"Take time to bury her?" Hathaway asked.

Zane shook his head. "Best not. Best to get on up the trail. She's dead. More'll soon be dead if we don't catch up to Charlie Hondo."

Angel gigged her paint on up the trail. Zane and Hathaway followed, stopping beside her near the other body, another woman, lying in the brush off the trail's left side. The shaggy black buzzards mewled and squawked in a half circle around her, one feeding on the navel exposed by the torn, spruce-green traveling suit.

Probably a sister of the other. Maybe a mother and daughter traveling together. Hard to say, with all the blood. Zane resisted the urge to shoot the buzzard off the woman's belly. Like the other woman, she was dead. And buzzards needed to eat, too. Even if he and the others buried these women, coyotes or wildcats would likely dig them up again.

"Let's ride." Zane mashed heels to General's Lee's flanks, and galloped on up the trail, Angel and Hathaway falling in behind him.

He didn't slow when he spied several more bodies lying off in the sagebrush. He saw a blood-splattered coach gun, too, leaning against a sage-shrouded boulder as though it had been purposely set there. Most likely, that was where it had tumbled after the shotgun messenger had dropped it.

They rode hard for thirty minutes before rounding the base of a broad escarpment. At the bottom of the gentle grade before them lay a relay station—the Saber Creek Station, Zane knew from having crisscrossed this country several times in the past, hunting spooks. The stage sat in the middle of the yard, between the stock tank and windmill. In the holding corral off the barn, several horses stood like statues, heads hanging, a couple lazily switching their tails.

The group continued down into the yard, looking around cautiously, all shucking their rifles from their saddle sheaths and racking rounds into the chambers. They paused at the edge of the yard. Zane detected a sickly sweet stench in the desert off to his left and recognized it instantly. Putrefying human flesh.

They continued on into the yard, Zane edging away from the others and moving toward the stage whose wagon tongue drooped to the ground. Before he was twenty yards away from it, he heard the flies, and now as he approached he saw the clouds of them swarming around the carriage.

He rode up and glanced in the window. It was as

though someone had taken a bucket of blood and sloshed it over both cowhide seats and walls and even the ceiling. There was more red than any other color in there. More blood lay thick in the dust beside the carriage, and as Zane gigged General Lee forward, he spied even more just ahead of the tongue. Men had been killed there, too.

He swung General Lee around and galloped across the yard and into the desert to the southwest, reining up when he saw the four bodies lying in the sage—dragged there and dumped unceremoniously. One older gent, two young men, and a young woman who wasn't wearing a stitch and whose pale, freckled body looked obscene in the harsh western light.

They'd been worked over by the carrion eaters, as well, until there were few distinguishing characteristics. Tonight, the coyotes and bobcats would return to fight over what was left.

Zane touched his moccasin heels to the palomino's flanks, and rode back into the yard, circling the holding corral twice and leaning out away from his saddle to inspect the ground etched with multiple sets of shod hooves. Angel and Hathaway were filing out of the cabin, holding their rifles and casting cautious glances around the yard.

As Hathaway dropped to one knee about thirty feet in front of the cabin, near the stock tank, Zane pulled General Lee back over toward the cabin, where Angel's horse and Hathaway's mule stood ground-tied.

"Nothin' in there," Angel said, grabbing Cisco's reins.

"No, they left early yesterday morning. They're long gone. Rode out on five horses."

Angel slid her rifle into her saddle boot. "Five?"

"Maybe one's a packhorse. Maybe they met up with someone else here. Ravenna Gonzalez-Vara."

"Got somethin' over here."

Hathaway was still down on one knee and staring at

the ground before him. Zane swung out of the leather and set his rifle on his shoulder as he and Angel walked past a fire ring heaped with gray ashes, and over to the scout, slanting their long shadows across Hathaway and the track he was inspecting. It looked like the print of a large bird. Zane had seen such prints embedded in ancient lava in Utah and Arizona, and had figured them to be the marks of a winged dinosaur from eons past. Not only strange to see one similar in the finely churned dust and horse shit of the station yard, but also chilling.

Walking around, he saw several more prints just like it. As though one of those winged dinosaurs had been walking around out here recently. Or something akin to it.

A dragon, say.

Hathaway walked a few feet away from the first print and stooped to run his gloved hand over a sage shrub, crunching the blackened branches in his hand. "Burned."

"I have a feeling your friend Ravenna was here," Angel told Zane, lightly jeering.

"One good thing." Zane raked a thumb down his bearded jaw and stared at the corral. "They not runnin' as wolves. They're in the saddle. Ravenna must be tapped out, saving her strength."

"For what?" Angel asked, moving up beside him. "Where are they headed and why? Elaina have any idea at all . . . during your private conversation?"

Zane shook his head slowly.

Behind him, Hathaway gave a fateful sigh. "Hell, they're Hell's Angels. They're probably gonna run and kill awhile for fun, then try to slip in among the usual crowd again, just like they done before ole Charlie was caught in Denver."

"I don't think so."

Zane stared down the trail colored gray brown with the sun tumbling behind the western ridges, remembering the fear in Elaina's eyes that had pricked the base of his spine with the point of a cold, sharp nail. The memory of it did the same again now, and he felt the urge to hurry.

"Nah, I don't think so. Let's mount up."

"Dark soon," Angel said.

"We have another hour of light left." Zane slid his rifle into its saddle boot, and stepped into the leather. "Let's make use of it."

He touched moccasin heels to General Lee's flanks.

They made camp that night in a box canyon south of Alamosa, and ate a meager supper of jerky, hardtack, and coffee. Wolves howled from the surrounding ridges and canyons. They took turns keeping watch from a scarp high over the camp.

During Zane's time on the scarp, he could hear the slightest rustle of burrowing creatures in the brush up and down the canyon they were in. He could hear the howl of a distant coyote, smell the blood of a rabbit killed by a hawk that the night breeze brought to him from the north, possibly far, far away.

Turning his attention to the camp below in which the fire guttered weakly, flames fingering up from a bed of umber coals, he could hear Angel's slow breathing as she lay curled in her blankets. From time to time, she gave a soft moan, and he wondered what she was dreaming about.

Him?

Her father, who had also broken her heart when he, too, had become a ghoul? James Coffin was a renegade now, running wild in the Montana mountains.

All Zane's senses were almost frighteningly keen and alive. The feeling made his limbs tingle thrillingly. At times, despite his trail fatigue, he felt a surge of raw power that made him want to run and climb and jump and . . . what?

Kill?

He tightened a fist against it.

No, he told himself, staring out at the star-capped night in which the waning moon climbed, relieved it was not full and feeling the fearful anticipation, as he always did, of the next time it would be full and high.

Would he once more be able to hold the wolf inside him at bay?

He and the others got started at first light. By midmorning they slipped across the Colorado border and into Arizona. Pushing the horses as hard as they dared, in the midmorning they followed the tracks of the Angels' five shod mounts into a small ranch headquarters.

There was a hay barn, two corrals including a breaking corral outfitted with a snubbing post, and a run-down, brush-roofed cabin.

They reined up near the windmill and stock tank, and Zane caressed the trigger of his Henry as he and the others got the lay of the place.

There wasn't much movement except four horses in the main corral off the barn, the lazily spinning windmill's rusty blades, and a tumbleweed bouncing off across the yard flanking the cabin from which emanated the squawls of a young child.

By the scuffed, windblown tracks in the yard—though with no sign of the dragon—the gang they were after had obviously ridden through here some time ago. Likely they'd moved on. But boot hills across the frontier were rife with men who'd banked too heavily on assumptions.

A child's face appeared in the window right of the cabin, two little hands closing over the window's bottom casing. A man's long face appeared over that of the boy, then just as quickly disappeared.

The cabin's front door opened. The man poked his head out, squinting his eyes, then drew the door wider and stepped out holding a .45/70 Springfield army carbine down low across his thighs. He was a gaunt, thin man with muttonchops and ragged pin-striped coveralls and a grimy undershirt. He wore stockmen's undershot boots, but both toes were nearly torn away from the soles. His shoulders were thick, his sun-browned hands on the Springfield large.

A wild horse hunter and breaker. Zane knew the breed. He eased his finger away from the Henry's trigger.

"We're friendly," he said.

The man had drawn the door closed behind him and haltingly stepped down off the cabin's dilapidated stoop and walked slowly toward the newcomers, squinting, a lock of gray-flecked hair hanging over one eye.

"Name's Zane," the bounty hunter said when the mustanger had stopped about twenty feet away. "The lady with the badge there is Deputy U.S. Marshal Angel Coffin, and on the other side of her is Al Hathaway, Cavalry scout. We're after the gang that pulled into your yard sometime back—I'm guessing the day before yesterday."

The mustanger looked uncertain as he dropped his eyes to the ground as though looking for the tracks these newcomers had followed to his ranch. He looked back up at Zane, flicking his eyes across Angel and Hathaway, then said, "What'd they do?"

"Broke out of Hellsgarde," Angel said. "Leastways, the men did. The woman gave 'em a hand."

"When did they pull in and when did they leave?" Zane inquired.

"You had it right," said the mustanger. "Midafternoon day before yesterday. Pulled out the next mornin'. Hellsgarde, you say?" His facial muscles stiffened, and the lids drooped halfway over his eyes. "Why on earth . . . ?"

"Spooks," Hathaway said with a grunt, leaning forward to run a gloved hand down his mule's neck. "Shapeshifters. Wolves. They show you that?"

"There wasn't no such nonsense as that. I invited 'em to go ahead and camp behind the cabin, and Angeline cooked for 'em, and before they left they bought two beef haunches from me and gave me five dollars for 'em, though it weren't nothin' but a scrub cow."

Angel cast a wary eye to the sky. "The girl didn't come packin' a dragon, did she?"

The man's face colored up slightly, and his eyes gained an indignant cast. He thought he was being toyed with.

"I ain't seen no such nonsense as dragons," he said finally. "Good Lord. I have enough trouble keepin' a pack o' hobgobbies away from my cattle. Whole ranch of 'em in the next watershed to the north. They love beef—any beef that ain't their own, that is. Sometimes they even come after my hosses."

The mustanger shook his head as he stared in silent beseeching at Angel.

"When we've done run our current quarry to ground," she told the mustanger, "I'll look into it."

"I'd be obliged."

"In the meantime," Zane said, "mind if we water our horses?"

"The water's good. You can stay for supper, if you like."

"Thanks," said Hathaway. "We best keep movin', sir."

The mustanger nodded. "I gotta go back inside. Little one's sick, and the missus needs help with the others." His eyes acquired a sad look. "Too bad about Charlie and his pards and that girl. They was right friendly." He grinned bashfully. "That girl—she was an eyeful."

"I bet she was," Angel said.

The man turned and went back inside the cabin. Zane, Angel, and Hathaway watered their horses at the stock trough, loosening the latigos and slipping the bits from the horses' mouths. They fed them a couple of handfuls of grain, letting them eat it slow.

Resting in the windmill's shade, Zane and Hathaway each rolled a quirley. Angel smoked one of her long, black cheroots she bought for a nickel each in Denver and which, at one time, had been her father's favorite brand.

Zane smoked only half of his cigarette. For some reason, the tobacco didn't taste as good as it once did. As the sun angled westward toward the White Mountains rolling up like severe clouds above the sage-stippled plain, they mounted up and headed along the trail once more.

After another hour's ride, they came to a right fork in the trail, the fork meandering up and over a distant rise among low buttes and mesas.

Zane halted General Lee and studied the trail with a speculative air.

"What is it?" Hathaway said.

"Gonna head up that canyon, see a man about a horse."

"What'd we need with another hoss?" asked Hathaway.

"I don't think he means a horse," Angel said. "Think he means silver."

Hathaway stretched a knowing smile. "Untaxed, I suppose?"

Zane shrugged.

Officiously, Angel said, "That's contraband, Mr. Zane."

"Nah, that's just affordable silver. Ain't much of it these days, with the increased demand since the War an' all."

Zane dismounted and quickly unharnessed the casket from General Lee. "I'm gonna make a quick run, leave this here. Don't need a busted wheel."

Grunting, he pushed the casket off into the dense brush and rocks along the trail.

"You sure you don't want us to go with you?" Angel asked.

Zane shook his head. "You two push on, find a spot to camp. If all goes well, I'll find you before sundown."

Zane remounted General Lee and galloped onto the forking trail, over the rise, and into a canyon between steep-walled tabletop mesas.

20

A VISIT TO THE SILVER-BULLET PADRE

ZANE LAY ATOP A RISE, focusing his field glasses on the lower canyon before him. The cut was abutted in the north and the south by steep cliffs leaning inward.

Up a brushy slope on the canyon's north side sat an old Spanish church flanked by a cemetery of tilting wooden crosses and engraved tombstones. A little ways down the hill from the church, and nearer Zane, lay a small mud-brick, brush-roofed shack from which a curl of smoke lifted. The sun's dying rays burnished the sandstone church above the shack so that it glowed like a new penny.

A thin stream flashed at the bottom of the canyon. On both sides of the stream were wood-frame shacks, seven in all. Sun-silvered and dilapidated, with brush growing up through the boardwalks fronting them, they were all that remained of a town built here by gold prospectors before the War and abandoned soon after. The stone ruins of an old Spanish pueblo could be seen around the newer buildings, only a few of them still sporting roofs.

There wasn't much gold in the stream, but the padre had found a healthy silver vein in a hidden canyon cut into the northern ridge behind the church. The Franciscan priests from Spain had been the first to exploit the vein, and they'd even processed the ore, a tradition that Padre Alejandro had been continuing for nearly thirty years with the help of his half-breed assistant, Tico Palomar. Few besides Zane knew of the silver cache, and he'd stumbled on it years ago when he'd holed up here to recover from an arrow drilled into his leg by a Coyotero Apache.

Despite Zane's lack of a spiritual bent, he and the padre had become fast friends. It was then that the padre had begun selling silver bullets to the ghoul hunter, as he did for a select few fighting the hard war against El Diablo, who would surely take over the world if not for the brave men who stood against him.

Spying no sign of danger below—he'd learned long ago to never ride into a place without scoping it out carefully beforehand—Zane returned his field glasses to his saddlebags, mounted General Lee, and galloped on down the hill and into the canyon. He cut away from the stream, mounted the northern slope, and drew rein before the humble shack.

"Padre?"

No answer but the breeze rustling the dead brush roofing the shack. An *ojo* hanging from the ceiling of the narrow front gallery twisted slightly in the breeze, its rope creaking faintly. The striped Indian blankets hanging over the windows from the inside fluttered.

"Padre Alejandro?" Zane called, louder. "It's Uriah Zane."

Still no reply from the shack. The door was closed. The padre was not in his garden to the shack's right, which the old Catholic watered each day from the stream, chanting and praying, as was his practice.

Zane gigged General Lee around the shack and up the well-worn trail to the church that stood like a hulking sandstone barrack. A cracked and tarnished bell crouched in an eroded belfry mounted high above the arched, wooden front door. Pigeons gurgled and fluttered. As Zane swung down from the saddle, they swooped into flight.

Zane dropped the palomino's reins, tripped the heavy oak door's latch, and shoved the door wide. His big frame filled the doorway as the door tapped the wall to the left, and he stared into the church's bowels that smelled of stone, wood, and candles.

"Padre?" His deep voice echoed.

The benches inside the place had long since rotted and crumbled and been hauled away. Now if any worshippers appeared—and there were damn few left in these hills—they simply knelt on the cracked flagstone floor. Beyond a dilapidated wooden rail and a rack of unlit candles lay the altar and a wooden cross.

Zane walked into the church, leaving the door open wide behind him, and followed his long shadow down the center of the church and around the altar to a small back door. He pushed the door open and peered into the cemetery.

Again, he called for the padre. Except for the breeze ruffling the brown, wiry weeds that had nearly overgrown the boneyard and the gurgling of the pigeons perched on the red-slate roof above him, there was no response. He raked his eyes across the cemetery. They caught on the large oak cross standing at the rear of the yard, and held there, his heart skipping beats.

Zane lunged into a run, leaping stones and small crosses until he stood in front of the large cross at the rear of the cemetery and stared up in horror at Padre Alejandro, who lay naked and spread-eagled and bloody, nailed to the cross just like his beloved Jesus.

Zane reached out and touched the man's thin, pale, blue-veined right ankle. Cold as stone. He looked at the gaunt face framed by long, grizzled, silver hair. The skin sagging against the concave cheeks was as dry as parchment. The man's brown eyes were half-open and staring almost tenderly down at Zane, his head canted to one side. The blood that had oozed down from the spikes driven through his hands and feet was dry. He'd been dead a day or two, his flat belly starting to pooch out away from his ribs from the putrefaction within.

Oddly, it appeared no buzzards had yet found him.

Zane backed away from his dead friend, the horror in his eyes hardening now to a keen rage as he lowered his right hand to the cross-draw holster on his left hip, and slipped the Colt Navy from its holster. He remembered the smoke lifting from the stovepipe jutting from the roof of Alejandro's shack.

Maybe whoever had done this was still here. Or was that too much to hope for?

He walked back through the church and out the front, swung up onto General Lee's back, and booted the horse down the hill. When he was fifty feet from the padre's shack, he slid down from the saddle while the palomino was still moving. He hit the ground jogging, and pressed his back against the shack's rear wall, near the closed back door.

He reached over and tried the metal latch lever. It clicked, and the door whined open a few inches. Zane gave a shove and stepped into the cabin. He was in the padre's kitchen, simply furnished with a small cookstove, eating table, and several plank shelves crowded with airtight tins and burlap food pouches.

Beyond lay the sleeping area with one rocking chair built of elk horns and hide and over which an afghan was draped that Alejandro used to wrap around his shoulders of a chilly night at this altitude and sip his home-brewed ale and stare into the hot fire provided by the small, mud-brick hearth in the left wall. The windows were covered by Indian blankets through which a dingy, washed-out light emanated, casting the cabin in misty gray shadows.

The padre's cot lay before the hearth, in which a small

fire smoldered. On the cot lay a man in threadbare long handles. He had long, obsidian-black hair and a long, sharp, upturned nose. The way he lay bespoke a hump on his back, neck bent at an angle. An empty whiskey bottle and a shot glass sat on the hearth on the far side of the sleeping beast. A cigarette stub lay on the floor a few inches below his sagging, knobby hand with fingernails shaped like arrow points.

On the room's other side, two more figures lay on a straw pallet—a naked male and a naked female only partly covered by a green wool Army blanket. Lice flecked the hair of each. Two whiskey bottles, one empty, one half-full, and several of the padre's beer bottles lay or stood around them. The male was spooned against the female, cupping one of her small, pert breasts in his pale, gnarled hand. His face was buried between her shoulder and her neck, and he was snoring loudly.

The female opened her eyes and stared at Zane through sleep fog. She blinked, recognition flashing in her pale blue eyes as she realized that she was not dreaming the big man in the room. She lifted her head with a start, stretching her lips back from yellow fangs.

A snakelike hiss rose from deep in her throat, and her eyes slanted devilishly. Zane's Colt roared, spitting smoke and flames into the dimness. The female tipped her head back and clutched her throat with both hands, making strangling sounds and staring wide-eyed at the herring-bone pattern on the ceiling, quivering.

The male behind her lifted his head up, coming awake instantly, snarling, and reaching under the pillow they both shared. Zane's Colt roared twice more, blowing the male back off the cot, both slugs exiting his back with a spray of snot-colored blood and viscera, and painting the whitewashed wall behind him.

The female had fallen onto her back atop the cot, and was flopping around like a landed fish. Zane shot her again, through the heart, then turned toward the other side of the room where the other ghoul was reaching under his own cot for a sawed-off, double-barreled ten-gauge.

As the ghoul brought up the coach gun, Zane drilled him through his left shoulder. The man loosed a shrill falsetto squeal that felt like a slap to the ghoul hunter's ears, rattling his eardrums painfully. The black-haired hobgobbie dove forward off the bed, turning a complete somersault as he hit the floor, rolling toward the door. As he came to a standing position in his threadbare, filthy white balbriggans, he tried to bring the shotgun up once more, shouting in his bizarre old woman's voice, *"Fuck you, you red-blooded coyote!"*

Zane's Colt belched twice more, punching one slug through the top of the man's center chest, another through his other shoulder. The man squealed louder, and Zane threw himself hard to his left as the double-barreled barn blaster roared like a cannon in the close confines, spraying a pumpkin-sized load of buckshot across the kitchen and into the table and wall and through the open back door.

Zane rolled off his left shoulder and hip, dropping his empty pistol and shucking the one holstered on his right side, thumbing the hammer back, narrowing an eye as he planted the bead at the end of the barrel into the V over the cylinder, and fired.

The slug hammered through the ghoul's forehead, just below his hairline. As he flew back against the door with a high wail, he triggered his gut shredder's second barrel into the ceiling. He lolled against the door, which wobbled in its frame on weak hinges until it gave way with a crunching splintering sound, and both the door and the ghoul went sailing into the padre's front yard.

The ghoul piled up atop the door. He sighed heavily and lay still. Greenish yellow blood oozed from the silver-dollar-sized hole in his forehead.

Zane looked around the room, in which powder smoke

billowed in blue webs, smelling like rotten eggs. The other two were down and still, oozing their putrid fluids onto the padre's hard-packed earthen floor.

"Sons o' bitches," Zane bit out, wincing at the pain his impact with the floor had caused in his left shoulder.

Slowly, breathing heavily, he gained his knees. He retrieved his empty Colt, then heaved himself to his feet, holstering the right-side gun, flipping open the loading gate on the left-side gun, spinning the wheel and letting the empty casings tumble onto the floor around his moccasins.

As he plucked fresh shells from his cartridge belt and punched them into the Colt's cylinder, turning it slowly, hearing each click, he walked through the open door and stepped over the dead ghoul. He looked around, expecting more ghouls from any quarter. They usually ran in packs, and it was odd to find only a few at a time.

He glanced up at the church, then toward a knob of rock looming on his left, then at the garden and clumps of brush and cedars all around the place. He heard a murmur of voices from the direction of the canyon, and stepped farther out away from the padre's shack to peer the hundred yards down the gradual slope into the deep arroyo.

Three figures were just now crossing the ghost town's single street and angling toward the base of the slope, looking up at Zane from beneath the brims of their battered hats. They were three ragged-looking hombres in worn trail garb. One wore a duster. He also walked with a limp and had a prominent hump on his back, giving him a twisted look. Zane inspected the other two more closely, saw that they, too, had humps lifting the backs of their shirts.

The one who wore a funnel-brimmed hat, red-and-black-checked shirt, and green neckerchief dropped suddenly to one knee and raised a pistol, aiming up the slope at Zane. The ghoul hunter wasn't worried about the hogleg. He was pretty much out of range of the short gun, unless the shooter was the best shot Zane had ever known. But ghouls were notoriously lazy and undisciplined, and it was hard to find a good shooter among them.

What had gained the brunt of his attention were the clumps of other ghouls just now spilling out of two of the other rickety, false-fronted buildings on the far side of the ghost town's narrow main street. They were all slouched and still pulling on shirts or denim jackets and checking pistols as they came on toward the slope. More movement caught Zane's eye, and he saw three more men filing out of the old Palace Hotel, and then three more men stepped out behind them.

And four more . . .

A pistol popped. Zane looked straight down below his position and saw smoke puffing in front of the hobgobbie in the checked shirt. The other two men were running up the slope now, taking long strides and casting savage looks up at Zane.

"Well, I'll be damned," the ghoul hunter muttered, swinging around and running over to where General Lee stood about fifty feet in front of the padre's shack, swinging his brown tail back and forth sideways and twitching his ears as he stared down the slope at the crowd headed toward him and his master.

"Easy, fella," Zane said, quickly shucking his Henry repeater from the saddle sheath.

He ran back to the brow of the hill and quickly, resolutely, dispatched the two ghouls running up toward him and laying out the pistol-wielding ghoul in the checked shirt. That didn't waylay the others a bit. In fact, it seemed to lure them on.

All twenty or so loosed a low roar and surged forward, filtering out between the dilapidated buildings and running up the slope. For all their sloth and the cumbersome humps on their backs, hobgobbies could run. It was almost as though they had springs in their ankles.

The group was coming on fast, triggering lead.

Zane lowered the Henry and ran back to General Lee.

"Hate to tell ya this, General," he said, catching up the reins and swinging into the saddle. "But I do believe we've done wore out welcome here in old Dry Wash."

General Lee replied with a shrill whinny and lunged into a gallop, kicking up great gouts of clay-colored dust behind him.

21

A SNARLING HORDE

As Zane, atop General Lee, angled down the slope toward the creek threading the canyon's bottom, he looked to his right. Now the horde of hobgobbies in the grimy garb of thirty-a-month-and-found cowpunchers was running along the road paralleling the creek, on an interception course with Zane.

Holding the General's reins in his teeth and giving the horse his head, Zane shouldered the Henry repeater and snapped off three quick shots. The slugs puffed dust along the road and the slope and skipped away, screaming. That didn't stop or even slow the hobgobbie horde, as the ghoul hunter knew it probably wouldn't.

Once a hobgobbie had you in his sights, there was little stopping him except a slug or an arrow. They could be snivelingly nonaggressive when they weren't excited, but whipped up by the bloodlust, they'd chase you barefoot across a smoking lava field and gut you with the short, razor-edged knives they favored, or shoot you with a pistol or hogleg. They lacked coordination, and their eyes were bad, but they could shoot within ten feet as well as your average greenhorn who'd been practicing only a week or two.

The really bad thing about them was how fast on their feet they were. Zane had less ground to cover to the canyon bottom than they did running out of the ghost town, but as fast as they were all moving, as one yipping, snarling, cursing horde along the trail, he judged they were running nearly as fast as General Lee, and the palomino had been cut and gentled out of a bronco mustang herd in the rough country around Arizona's Chiricahua Mountains.

As he approached the canyon-bottom trail, Zane cursed and snapped off two more shots. One hobgobbie, within fifty yards and coming hard, running abreast of three others, yelped, grabbed his knee, hit the ground, and rolled, nearly tripping one of the others.

They all kept coming.

The front of the snarling, long-striding pack was only thirty feet from the intersection of the two trails when Zane hit the canyon bottom. General Lee gave an indignant whinny at the closing horde, and swung hard left, faltering slightly before grinding his rear hooves into the turf and lunging forward until he was in full gallop once more.

Behind Zane, pistols and rifles popped above the hum and buzz of the frenzied ghoul pack. He heard the fast patter of running feet and glanced over his right shoulder just as the lead ghoul pistoned off his heels and made a mad dive forward, scissoring his arms as though to grab one of General Lee's hammering rear legs.

The ghoul missed by inches. He hit the ground with a shrill, enraged cry, and rolled off to the side of the trail, the one behind him wildly leaping at him, the others hammering on past him and after Zane.

Two of the front-runners were sporadically triggering shots, and several times the ghoul hunter felt the air beside his head curl warmly, saw the bullets plunk into the dust ahead of him. As he approached the rise atop which he'd glassed the canyon an hour ago, one bullet tore through his flapping wolf vest to kiss his right side, about a foot below his armpit. He felt little except the slight dampness of trickling blood.

He glanced behind once more. A few hobgobbies were slowing for the grade, but General Lee was, too, so the horde was continuing to gain on Zane in small increments. He could probably outrun them in time, because General Lee had more staying power than the hobgobbies, who could run like grizzlies for only short stretches, but this group was especially determined. He was beginning to feel the stony chill of the doomed in his bowels when, as he closed the gap between him and the crest of the hill, a familiar sight appeared between a boulder and a gnarled cedar right of the trail.

The Gatling gun's brass canister flashed as bright as a miniature sun, blinding Zane for an instant. As he snapped his eyes away, he heard the sudden ratcheting of the six-bored gun. Squeals and agonized cries rose behind him as the .45-caliber slugs tore and crunched through flesh, snapping bones. Zane rode on up and over the rise, leaped out of the saddle, and ran back up to the crest of the hill.

He dropped to one knee and raised the Henry to his shoulder.

Now he could see Angel kneeling behind the Gatling gun and working the crank for all she was worth, wine-red red hair spilling about her shoulders. On the opposite side of the trail, the bulky dark figure of Al Hathaway in his smoke-stained buckskins and blue cavalry hat knelt on a flat-topped boulder, levering rounds from his '67 Winchester, the empty casings flashing in the sun as they arced back over his right shoulder.

Straight down the trail, a good half of the hobgobbies were down and bloody, a few of the wounded trying to crawl away. Those still on their feet continued to come, showing their teeth between their thin lips as they snarled and raged, so infuriated by the human interlopers, and wanting blood so badly, that they continued heading fiercely, stupidly, straight into the bullet storm.

A few dropped down behind rocks on either side of the trail and tried to return fire, but the Gatling gun had them mostly cowering, unable to lift their heads.

Bam-bam-bam-bam-bam-bam-bam!

The hiccupping gun continued to tear through flesh, blow up dust, throw up sage branches, and hammer shards from rocks. Two well-placed bullets blew one of the ghouls' heads off its neck, which went tumbling in a geyser of snot-colored blood across the gravel, the body it had left kneeling as though in prayer, slowly lowering the Remington .44 in its quivering hand.

Zane added his Henry and LeMat to the fusillade, and when both guns pinged on vacant chambers, he emptied one of his Colts. Before he'd fired his last pistol bullet, the Gatling clicked empty. Hathaway had emptied his own rifle and two pistols and had leaped down off the boulder to reload behind it.

Through the sunlit smoke haze, Zane saw a hobgobbie poke its hatted head with its long, stringy hair out from behind a boulder. The hobgobbie gritted its tobacco-crusted teeth as it snapped off a shot. Before the one remaining ghoul could thumb his pistol's hammer back, Zane trigger his second Colt.

The ghoul's head snapped back as though he'd been hit in the face with a hammer. He dropped onto his back, flopped around, and gradually fell as still as all the others slouched beneath the wafting smoke, their pooling blood glistening like the skin of rotten lemons.

Angel rose from behind the hot Gatling, grabbing her rifle.

Hathaway looked down the slope from behind his boulder for a time, turning his head this way and that as he surveyed the carnage. Finally, he turned his broad, sweating, coffee-colored face with its black beard and wide brown eyes toward Zane and grinned.

"Looks like you got crossways with a hobgobbie camp."

"Somethin' like that." Zane started reloading and looked at Angel. "I thought you'd rode on."

Angel turned to him as she plucked shells from her cartridge belt and thumbed them through her Winchester's loading gate. "Ran into three other o' them demons along the trail. Drunk as lords, and when they saw me an' Al, they went into a frenzy and came at us shooting. They were heading this direction, so . . ."

She shrugged, jerked her charro jacket down at her waist and stared down the slope before her, one fist on her hip.

Zane rose slowly. He, too, was reloading his weapons but his mind was elsewhere. "Bastards killed Alejandro," he said tightly, almost under his breath, wanting to kill every hobgobbie he could plant his sights on. "Just an old padre, wasn't botherin' no one."

"Yeah, they do that," Hathaway said with a fateful sigh. "Ghouls hate men o' the cloth in partic'lar."

The stocky scout wagged his bearded face sadly as he started down the slope to kick around among the bodies and to shoot any that had a glimmer of life left in them.

While Angel and Hathaway headed off to find a secure night camp, for the sun had dropped behind the western ridges, Zane returned to Padre Alejandro. He used his considerable strength to lift and twist the cross out of the ground. Then he pulled the spikes out of the priest's lifeless limbs, and wrapped the man in the altar cloth he'd found in the church.

It was nearly dark by the time the ghoul hunter, working bare-chested, sweating in spite of the cooling air, had dug the grave, gentled the blanket-wrapped priest into the dark hole, and covered him. He took extra time to erect a crude cross of pine branches and rawhide.

When he'd finished the chore of running down Charlie Hondo's bunch, he'd return and erect a chiseled stone. Doubtless the priest would scoff at such ostentation. Zane had never known anyone simpler or more self-effacing, but the padre would have to indulge the ghoul hunter. He could think of no words to say over the mounded dirt and the rocks he'd gathered to ward off predators. The stone would be his attempt at compensating the priest for the lack. Whether the old man wanted it or not, Padre Alejandro deserved something to mark his passing and the sanctified ground in which he would lie forever.

In a cellar in the padre's shack, Zane found the padre's cache of silver bullets. There were several hundred freshly milled slugs laid out in a bed of dried moss. Zane knew the padre had molded them for him, so he took the entire peach crate filled with the precious cartridges that likely would have cost him upward of a thousand dollars on the open market, if he'd been able to find any, as silver was always in short supply.

Nearly an hour later, he found Angel and Hathaway's camp in a dry arroyo sheathed in stone escarpments and cedars, a good half mile off Hondo's trail. The camp was relatively secure, if there was such a thing, from hobgobbies or the wandering bands of Indian swillers this country was known for, as many Arizona Apaches sought out the swillers' curse for the gift of everlasting life and the unearthly powers over the white man.

Angel killed a couple of jackrabbits with her shurikens and chopped them up with her silver Spanish dagger. Hathaway, an ex-camp cook, took over from there, throwing together a surprisingly flavorful stew from the rabbits and several handfuls of wild herbs and roots he gathered from the banks of the arroyo. They dined hungrily, washing the food down with whiskey-laced coffee.

When they'd cleaned their plates and brewed another

pot of coffee, Angel offered to sew up Zane's bullet-burned right side.

The ghoul hunter reluctantly agreed. It wasn't a serious wound, but he could feel the sporadic discomfort of the oozing blood under his clothes.

"I'll be damned," Angel said, kneeling beside him and dabbing at the cut with a cloth she'd soaked from her canteen. "Looks like it's already started to heal."

"Wasn't much in the first place."

"I beg to differ. Looks like the slug ricocheted off a rib." She touched her finger to the bloody furrow. Zane felt only a slight numbness there, no pain. He shrugged but did not look at Angel, feeling the heat of her incredulous gaze on his face.

Hathaway refilled his coffee cup from the pot in the fire, and glanced at Zane's side. "I'll be damned. It does look to be healin'." The scout chuckled deep in his chest and lifted his cup, taking a sip. "You must be part werewolf. Imagine that—a werewolf huntin' werewolves."

He chuckled again, pulled a blanket coat on over his bear arms. "I'll take the first watch from atop one o' them scarps over yonder. Who wants me to wake 'em in a few hours for the next hitch?"

Zane stared into the darkness beyond the throbbing firelight. "I'll take it."

"All right, then." Coffee in one hand, rifle in the other, Hathaway strode off in his drag-heeled, bull-legged fashion.

When he was gone, neither Zane nor Angel said anything while she finished cleaning the wound. She said when she'd threaded her needle, "Probably doesn't need this—looks like it'll be all healed up by morning, but I reckon I might as well finish what I started."

Then she pinched the skin along the furrow together, and began sewing the wound closed.

Zane stared into the darkness across the fire and

sipped his whiskey-laced coffee, feeling nothing except for a gentle tug beneath his arm as she poked the needle through. When she finished, she lowered her head to cut the catgut with her teeth, then pressed her forehead against the ghoul hunter's shoulders.

She held her head there for a time. He felt the warmth of her skin against his. She wrapped her arms around his bare waist and pressed her forehead more firmly against his shoulder. She laced her fingers together, and squeezed him hard against her.

"Goddamn you, Uriah."

He felt a tug low in his belly. His blood surged. He turned to her, wrapped an arm around her, and lifted her chin. She stared back at him obliquely, lines cutting across her forehead, but she did not resist him when he pressed his lips to hers.

She rose a little on her haunches, pressing her lips firmly against his, opening them, lifting her arms from his waist to wrap them around his neck and squirm against him, mashing her chest against his. He felt the swell of her breasts behind the soft calfskin vest, and his heart beat faster. He was a little surprised when, driven by a hard desire, he drew her onto his lap and kissed her more passionately, and closed a hand over her right breast, kneading it gently through the vest, and still she did not resist him.

She groaned and placed her own hand over his.

Finally, she heaved herself to her knees and, staring at him with dewy eyes, quickly began untying the vest's rawhide drawstrings. Zane kicked out of his boots, waggled out of his buckskin breeches, and removed his own sweaty tunic and long handles.

He watched her stand and undress heatedly before him. Neither one said anything. Angel slowly revealed her delightfully rounded, full-breasted body to him, succulent hips swelling out from a belly nearly as taut as Zane's own.

When she stood before him naked, she swept her hat off brusquely, and her hair fell in a sexy, dark red mess across her shoulders, red strands curling up from beneath her arms to lick at her swollen, pink-tipped orbs.

She slid her hair back from her cheeks and dropped to her knees before him, one hand pulling at his hard, jutting shaft, the other sliding through the thick, black, sweat-damp mop of his hair. She pushed him back against the ground, and straddled him hungrily, grunting, whispering, "Goddamn you, Uriah. . . ."

22

"HOW'D IT HAPPEN?"

ANGEL ROSE UP and down on her knees for a time, straddling Zane, groaning and kneading the hard, bulging slabs of his pectorals. The firelight illuminated faint copper streaks in her hair. Her narrowed jade eyes smoldered at him as the firelight shunted across her naked body, her jostling breasts casting shadows across her belly and ribs.

Her held her hips in his strong hands, moving as she moved, up and down, until she leaned down, pressed her breasts against his chest, and kissed him, moving her head and stabbing her tongue deep into his mouth. He gave a groan and rolled her over, then propped himself on his outstretched arms, and hammered against her—hard, even thrusts.

He lifted his head, fought back the impulse to loose a howl. The blood ran hot in him.

She rolled her head from side to side, pulled at his hair, tugged at his ears, his beard. She dug her heels into the backs of his legs, her knees flopping like wings, and closed her eyes and turned her head to one side. She arched her back, bucking up hard to meet his wild thrusts, closing her upper teeth over her lower lip, sobbing and groaning.

"Oh . . . Jesus . . . *God* . . . !"

They'd lain together enough times to know when the other was ready. She opened her eyes and stared up at him meaningfully as she wrapped her hands around his corded forearms from which the veins stood out in sharp relief against his sweat-damp skin bronzed by the firelight. She frowned up at him, puzzled.

"Stop, Uriah," she whispered, caressing his arms with her hands.

He hadn't heard her above the thunder of the blood in his ears.

"Uriah!" she said, looking frightened now, lifting her head.

Zane forced himself to stop hammering against her. He ground his teeth and lowered his chin hard, clutching at the ground on either side of her, and withdrawing his pelvis from hers. It was like trying to stop a Baldwin locomotive on a steep downgrade under full steam.

She scuttled down until her head was below his belly, and he closed his eyes tightly, grinding his teeth, as she finished him with her mouth.

It took a long time. She writhed beneath his belly, making choking sounds.

He rolled over onto his back and she rested her head upon his chest.

"Jesus," she said raggedly, running her arm across her mouth and trying to catch her breath.

They lay there for a long time, entangled, Zane running his fingers through the silky strands of her hair, until he felt a wetness on his chest. He glanced down at her, saw tears dribbling out of her squeezed-shut eyes. One rolled down across the hooked scar on her cheek and into the hollow of his breastbone, showing gold in the firelight.

After a long time, she pushed off of him, slowly gained her feet, and gathered her clothes and myriad weapons including the silver Spanish sword. When she had them all in her arms, she set them down beside the fire, and, facing the flames, her back to Zane, she slowly dressed. When she had everything on except her boots and her hat, she tossed a piñon log on the fire, walked over to the other side of the blaze, and lay down in her blanket roll, resting her head back against her saddle.

Zane stood up and also dressed before walking off in the brush beyond the fire to evacuate his bladder. He came back, refilled his coffee cup, splashed some whiskey into the hot brew, kicked out of his boots, and got out his hide makings sack. He lay back against his saddle with a weary sigh. Troughing a wheat paper between the first two fingers of his right hand, he dribbled chopped tobacco into it.

Angel's voice came quietly from the other side of the fire. "How did it happen?"

Zane didn't speak for a time as he slowly built the quirley. "You know that old stage robber Alden Woodyard?"

She nodded, staring up at the sky, not looking at him.

"After tracking him for five days north of Laramie, I ran him down in a box canyon in the Big Horns. Moved into his camp one night. There was a full moon. I shouldn't have been out there, but I wanted to run him to ground before he met up with the rest of his gang. He lured me in, leaped on me from a rock, and tore that hunk out of my back before I drilled a silver slug through his heart."

She didn't say anything for a long time. She just stared up at the night sky. The firelight played across her hair. The fire cracked and sputtered.

Zane sipped his coffee and whiskey, set the cup down, licked the edge of the wheat paper, and rolled it closed. He stuck the cylinder in his mouth, sealing it with his tongue.

"After this job, Uriah," she said in the same even tone as before, "I reckon we'll be forking trails for good."

She turned away from him and drew her blankets up across her shoulders.

"If that's what you want, Red."

Zane stared at the newly built quirley. Finally, he tossed it into the fire. The flames licked at it, causing white smoke to curl up from the cylinder. The fire consumed it, leaving only a line of gray ash beside the coffeepot.

Zane leaned back against his saddle once more and took another sip of his coffee. It tasted sour. He flipped the cup back over his shoulder, sending the coffee and whiskey splashing into the brush.

He lay back against his saddle and drew his hat down over his eyes.

Wet and naked, the bewitching Ravenna Gonzalez-Vara sat Indian-style on a flat stone slab above a steaming hot springs pool. She sat with her chin up, shoulders back, black hair behind her shoulders, eyes closed. Her invitingly fleshy, copper-colored belly moved in and out as she breathed.

A gold amulet in the shape of a hexagon and the size of a saucer hung from a rawhide cord around her neck. It lay with one edge tipped into her cleavage. Her full, dark breasts angled out slightly from each other, one a little larger than the other. The larger one had a faint brown birthmark along its bottom curve.

Charlie Hondo's loins sputtered and tingled as he watched from a niche in the rocks of this hidden canyon. He grinned, brushed a hand across his nose.

Steam bathed the Mexican witch, lifting all around her and causing her skin to glisten. There was a thin, warm trickle of water tumbling above her and onto the ancient stone trough behind her. The water slid darkly, steaming down to caress her buttocks and split and flow in two separate streams around her bent legs before continuing into the warm pool below the slab of rock she was perched on.

The water rattled like delicate wind chimes. It smelled of sulfur and moss.

Charlie thought he could smell the wild musk of the woman as well. His heart heaved. Warm fingers tickled his groin.

Moving stealthily on the balls of his boots, he stepped back into the niche and walked along the corridor of sandstone by which he'd stolen in here from the camp that he and the boys and Ravenna had set up late last night in this remote, unnamed sierra in north-central Arizona Territory. He came to a cut in the rock to his left and followed its circuitous route until it opened again just up the waterfall's bed from the meditating witch.

Warm, salty-smelling water tumbled onto the black volcanic rock to Charlie's left. He stepped out around it and into the trough of the falls, the water feeling hot as it closed over his boots. Ravenna sat about ten feet ahead of him, her back to him, her wet hair tumbling down her shoulders to nearly cover her plump, glistening buttocks.

Charlie stretched his lips back in devious delight as he stepped softly toward the woman, biting his lip with the effort of silence, lifting one foot at a time in the four-inch-deep black water. Humor rippled through him, and he had to pause a moment to choke it back down into his chest.

He continued forward. Ravenna was within four feet of him. He could see the pores in her skin, the droplets beading on her hair ends, tracing jagged routes across her shoulders and the backs of her arms.

Charlie held his arms out to both sides, crouching, cupping his hands, getting in position to grab the young, ravishing sorceress from behind, to grab her big breasts, scaring the holy hell out of her, and steal a wild kiss.

Ravenna was smiling, only Charlie couldn't see her face. She glanced behind her to see the javelina she'd conjured blinking up at her through Charlie Hondo's bright, horrified eyes.

It was a typical desert javelina, brown and gray, with a ridiculous-looking face that resembled that of a bear cub but with a long nose and flaring pink nostrils. The nostrils were really flaring now, the sides of the javelina that was now Charlie heaving as he breathed frantically, snorting his dismay at the sudden transformation.

Ravenna poked a finger to a corner of her mouth and tittered delightfully. "That'll teach you to sneak up on a girl saying her prayers to Elyhann!"

Charlie lowered his head and shook it wildly, as though to rid himself of this ugly, wild pig's body. His sides heaving faster and faster, he ran off squealing down the stone trough around the steaming pool, his little black, cloven hooves slipping and sliding on the slick rock.

He bulled forward into some manzanita grass and willows growing just beyond the spring and along the cut the runoff made through the middle of this canyon that slanted gradually down to the Salt River and then out of the mountains to the open Arizona desert beyond. He came back through the brush, splashed across the runoff creek, squealing and oinking madly, his eyes still the brown eyes of Charlie Hondo but now owning a horror that Ravenna doubted they'd ever shown before. Gold javelins of stark-raving terror shot from them as Charlie dashed up the ravine and into more brush on the stream's opposite side.

Ravenna threw her head back and laughed huskily with unabashed mirth, cupping her big breasts in her hands, as she watched the brush thrash and jostle, catching occasional glimpses of Charlie's pig head and curled tail above the weeds, willows, and black volcanic rocks.

Charlie arced away from Ravenna, then dashed back into the narrow ravine, splashed across the stream, and mounted the left-side bank, heading back in Ravenna's direction. When he reached the misty pool below her perch on the slab of rock, she touched the amulet with both her hands, muttered a phrase or two, and watched as the pig's front legs buckled. The javelina was suddenly Charlie again, lying belly down in the mud and moss and manzanita grass beside the pool.

Charlie's back rose and fell as he breathed. He pressed his cheek against the ground, grinding one of his hoop earrings into the mud, and blinked his wild eyes as though trying to reassure himself that he'd regained his human form. The cross tattoo on his right cheek shone spruce green against his terror-bleached skin.

Ravenna cradled her knees in her arms and loosed another volley of wicked, elated laughter.

"I'll put good money on the barrelhead that you'll never try that again!"

Charlie winced, pressed his hands to the ground on either side of him, and pushed himself up. He looked at Ravenna, his eyes hard with fury, teeth gritted, pale cheeks mottled red. Ravenna pointed at him and laughed all the harder, rocking back and forth on her naked bottom.

"You fuckin' bitch," Charlie bit out angrily, though instinctively knowing he had to restrain himself. If she could turn him into a javelina, she could turn him into a spider that she could crush under the heel of her hand.

And he had a feeling that if he pushed her at all, she'd be thrilled to do just that.

He got his knees beneath him and, drawing deep breaths of calming air, sat back on his heels. He ran a sleeve across his sweat-slick forehead. "Whew! You really had me going there."

"Sí," Ravenna said, her laughter slowly dying. "I had you running everywhere, Charlie." Suddenly, the laughter died and she looked at him coolly, narrowing one chocolate-brown eye. "I can do it again. Anytime."

"I thought you was tapped out."

"Too tapped out to conjure dragons, maybe. Too

fatigued to let you boys turn into wolves just any old time. But any witch worth her salt can cast a spell like that in her sleep."

"Thanks for the warnin'."

Charlie heaved himself to his feet, grabbed his hat off a willow branch, pulled it down tight on his head, and strode off sulkily toward a wide crack in the canyon wall.

"Oh, come on, don't go sour on me, Charlie. I was only fooling around, just as you were, *mi amor!*"

"I didn't turn you into no pig," Charlie snapped, wheeling at the entrance of the defile that led back to the camp. "Hell, Ravenna, don't you know that during full moons, I *eat* pigs!"

"I apologize, *mi amor.*" Ravenna raised her eyebrows beseechingly. "Forgive me?" She drew her arms away from her breasts, lifted her chin, and threw her shoulders back. Alluringly, she said, "If you forgive me, you can have me. . . ."

Charlie would have none of it. He'd been scared shitless, and he wasn't used to the feeling. Didn't like it a bit. "Where we goin', anyways? You say we're getting close. Don't you think it's time you let me an' the boys know?"

"You'll know by the next full moon, Charlie."

"Goddamnit, Ravenna. Why's it such a big secret?"

"It is the biggest secret in all the world, Charlie. And not to be taken lightly. No offense, but if I tell you, you might blab it to the others. I know how you boys like to drink and carry on. We'll be laying in supplies in Tucson, and I don't want anyone there having any inkling about where we're headed."

"Me an' the boys don't like bein' kept in the dark by no . . ." Charlie let his voice trail off, frowning in frustration, averting his eyes.

"By whom?" Ravenna arched a severe brow. "By a girl? By a Mexican witch . . . ?"

She wagged an admonishing finger and clucked her tongue. “Never forget what I’m capable of, Charlie.”

“Ah, hell.” Charlie snorted, miffed, and stomped off down the rocky defile.

Ravenna laughed, funneled her hands around her mouth, and called, “I’ll make it up to you soon, *mi amor!*”

23

CUTTING THE TRAIL DUST IN TUCSON

Two weeks later, the dust-laden wooden sign leaning along one side of the stage and freight road and in the shadow of a tall, one-armed saguaro warned:

BY ORDER OF THE TUCSON
CITY COUNCIL ALL GOOLS
WILL BE SHOT ON SITE!

Someone had scrawled in faded green paint below the main admonishment: *"Specially hobgobs!"*

"Now, that ain't no way to treat us ghouls that got jingle in our pockets," said Curly Joe Panabaker, riding directly behind Charlie and Ravenna, who headed up their small pack.

"Yeah," said Lucky Snodgrass indignantly. "Here we was, aimin' on payin' for our trail supplies. Maybe we ought not be so damn nice, if'n they're gonna treat us like third-rate citizens!"

Ravenna chuckled. "I don't think they'd call us any kind of citizens, amigo."

"What I'd like to know is how they think they can pick a werewolf out of a townful of humans. They know and we know they can't, less'n there's a full moon, o' course."

Ravenna said, "Don't get cocky, Charlie. Word is probably out about your break from the pen, no? Telegrams have probably been flying all over the frontier—with your descriptions on them."

"Hell, you know there ain't no telegraph wire up longer than two days anywhere in the West without a ghoul of some sort rippin' it down." Charlie looked around with interest as he and the others rounded the trail and entered the outskirts of Tucson with its smelly stock pens and ancient adobe hovels from which the smell of spicy Mexican meat rose from brick chimneys. "Word of our escape from hell won't get out here for another month yet."

"Ah . . . Tucson." One-Eye sat up straight in the saddle, his lone dull brown eye sparkling beneath the brim of his shabby brown bowler hat. "Been a while since we been to a town, amigos. I say it's time to do a little stompin'." He glanced at a narrow, three-story building with FOUR ACRES painted in arcing red letters over the high false façade. "And ruttin'," he added with a wolfish growl.

"Three days here at the most, boys." Ravenna looked around uneasily at the heavily armed men in skins and furs walking the boardwalks or slouching out front of quiet, dark Mexican cantinas or the more rollicking saloons. Bounty hunters, most likely. "And we keep our heads down and stay out of trouble. A few drinks, a few girls, a little harmless fun."

She narrowed her eyes as she swept her admonishing gaze around the group. "But no trouble. Not even if it comes stalking. We avoid it at all costs. We are choir boys —remember that. We are the humble and meek and we give trouble of every color a wide berth. We have, as the gringos love to say, bigger fish to shoot."

"I think that's 'fry,' *chiquita*," Charlie corrected her, giving a snort as he ran his glance across a long, low-slung building on the south side of the pueblo's main street, which a board over the shake-shingled roof identified as a U.S. Bounty Office.

"Whatever," Ravenna said, as Charlie led them toward the Rincon Mountain Dance Hall and Beer Parlor on the street's right side, across a side street from a whitewashed Catholic church with a half-ruined wall around it. Several Mexicans in striped serapes and straw wagon-wheel sombreros lay atop the wall, hats tipped over their eyes. One had his arm hanging down the side of the wall, his brown hand still wrapped around the neck of a half-full tequila bottle. Another Mex lay slumped at his side against the wall's base, a brown cur sniffing around the pockets of his white cotton slacks.

Ravenna held back, looking up and down the street as the others drew rein at the hitchrack before which ten or twelve horses were lined up, the autumn-cool, late-afternoon sun shining on their backs.

"Come, *chiquita*," Charlie called to the witch as he swung down from the leather. "I'll let you buy the first round." He grinned, hitched up his blue wool cavalry trousers that showed the wear, tear, and campfire smoke of their long trek from Colorado, and adjusted the black holster containing Warden Mondrick's .44.

"Me . . ." Ravenna said, narrowing her eyes at a building farther up the crooked main street. "I'm gonna have a long, hot bath. Scrub some o' the trail dust off my lovely body. I'll find you scalawags later."

"Ah, come on." Charlie beckoned to the black-haired sorceress. "One drink, and I'll join you!"

He grinned again.

Ravenna turned to him, one eye narrowed speculatively. She looked at the big, gaudily decorated building before her and from which came manic piano patter and the low rumble of male conversation. "I guess it couldn't hurt to see that you boys get our little sojourn here off on the right, quiet foot." Ravenna put her horse up to the hitchrack, swung down from the saddle, and tossed her reins over the tie rail. "And I sure could use some tequila and carne asada!"

"Now you're talkin'!" Charlie wrapped a long arm around the young woman's neck, leaning into her and glancing down her open vest as they followed the others up the porch steps and through the batwings. He'd forgiven the mercurial witch for changing him into a javelina under the waterfall. Or, at least, with the prospect of the treasure she was leading them to, he'd filed the transgression in the back of his mind for later.

"Welcome, gents . . . and, uh . . . senorita!" rumbled a jovial voice from the bar. The barman, a big, mustached, square-headed gent in a white silk shirt, string tie, and paisley vest, was filling a schooner from a beer spigot. "Sit an' light a spell. Less'n you're spooks, that is. Don't allow 'em on the premises even if their pockets are loaded with silver!"

He tipped his head back and laughed as he swiped a flat stick across the frothy head of the beer schooner, sending a white spray of creamy foam shooting onto the floor behind the bar. He glanced at the plank sign nailed to a two-by-two ceiling beam about ten feet in front of the batwings. On it was crudely painted in a firm hand:

NO GOOLS ALLOWED.
IF YOUR A GOOL
THIS MEANS YOU!

Ravenna glanced at Charlie, who was still moving his lips and sounding out all the words, as he'd never learned to read above the third-grade level in his native tongue and was almost illiterate in English, as well.

"Like I said," announced the bartender, beckoning with a large, freckled arm revealed by a rolled-up shirtsleeve, "come on in an' sit a spell. I'll bring your drinks out in a minute!"

As the barman set the freshly poured beer on a tray and then carried the tray out from behind the bar, heading for one of the dozen or so tables, a good three-quarters of which were occupied by swarthy, bearded, sunburned frontiersmen of every stripe—mostly Americans—Charlie cut his perplexed gaze away from the sign, glanced at the other three men, and began tracing a zigzagging route toward an empty table toward the room's rear.

Ravenna remained in front of the batwings and jammed her thumbs behind her cartridge belt, a little apprehensive about the setup of the place. There seemed to be a lot of ghoul hunters in town, and that worried her. Not so much for herself—although she did have a sizable bounty on her own head in Arizona as well as New Mexico Territory and even western Texas. She was mainly worried about Charlie, One-Eye, Lucky, and Curly Joe. She didn't have the power to allow them to turn at will, so they couldn't turn until the next full moon, a week away. That meant they were relatively easy pickings for ghoul hunters.

But only if said ghoul hunters knew they were ghouls, that was. And Charlie himself had said it best—there were few ways to tell if one was a werewolf at any other time but the night of a full moon.

That thought relieved her apprehension somewhat.

Another one took its place, tying a little hitch in her belly. Werewolves and ghoul hunters were natural enemies. Could Ravenna's boys keep their heads when surrounded by the breed? Even after they'd had a few drinks and were hearing their wolves' howl?

Well, she'd never be able to get them out of here now. She doubted the crazy beasts realized how important it was they stay out of trouble, and what was at stake, all the power that was theirs for the taking once they got out of

Tucson in one piece, with plenty of trail supplies, and reached the Lobo Negro Mountains three days southeast.

Deciding that she, a witch of her formidable powers, couldn't control three male wolves even in their human forms, she sauntered over to the bar, raking her spurred heels across the floorboards. She glanced at Charlie and the others just now doffing their hats and sagging into kicked-back chairs. Charlie eyed Ravenna with one brow arched questioningly.

She indicated with a toss of her head that she wanted to stand at the bar, then clutched her rump and grinned to signify she was sore from the long ride. She continued striding along the varnished mahogany counter with its brass footrail, past the half dozen men standing there chinning and drinking and casting lusty glances Ravenna's way.

Ignoring the leers she was so accustomed to, she drew up to the gap about two-thirds of the way down and was met there by a second bartender, a stocky, black-eyed gent with a nasty scar on his lower lip that was in contrast to his slicked-back and pomaded black hair. A citified half-breed, Ravenna reflected. Probably Pima or Apache.

Vaguely, she felt a little sorry for the man. She knew how it was to be an outcast, growing up as she had—a witch in the sprawling hacienda of a wealthy Mexican landowner who'd cast her out at an early age. Secretly coached by a half-breed peon witch whose family raised chickens and hay on her family's sprawling hacienda in southern Chihuahua, she'd finally been unable to suppress her powers. In a fit of pent-up rage, she'd turned her taunting older brother into a lobo who'd run away into the hills howling and yipping like a moon-crazed hyena, never to be seen again.

The half-breed gave Ravenna a dully inquisitive stare.

"Tequila," she said. "Put it up there with a beer, amigo."

While the Indian set about filling the witch's order, the jovial barman took the orders of Charlie and the boys.

Ravenna threw back her first tequila, picked up her beer schooner, and turned to face the room, hooking a boot heel over the brass rail at the base of the bar behind her.

The jovial bartender hauled the tray of beer schooners and a whiskey bottle out to Charlie and the boys. He was the chatty sort, and as he passed around the beers and shot glasses and set the bottle on the table, he said, "You fellas don't have to worry about no ghouls in Tucson. No, sir!"

He turned to cant his head toward the rough-hewn men playing cards at the tables between Charlie's group and the door. "We got some o' the best ghoul hunters anywhere in the West right here in my very own saloon, and I'm proud to welcome Mr. Jesse James, his brother Frank, and their cousin Cole Younger to our fair territory."

He said this loudly enough to be heard above the patter of the scrawny little piano player in armbands and green eyeshade, smoking a loosely rolled quirley and hammering away at "Little Brown Jug."

A small-boned man with frosty blue eyes and a sparse blond mustache glanced toward Charlie and the boys and gave his chin a cordial dip. The man with the black beard beside him, a little bigger than Jesse James but with the same blue eyes, reached up with a sun-browned hand to pinch the brim of his battered felt sombrero. Cole Younger wore a tattered serape crisscrossed with bandoliers holding a good number of silver cartridges among the brass. There were six men with James and Younger, and the bartender proudly pointed them out, as well.

There were James Younger, Frank James, Bob Younger, Bill Chadwell, Clell Miller, and Charlie Pitts. These others barely acknowledged the introduction. They were a trail-seasoned, sour-faced lot, their hair and beards dusty and sweat-matted, and they were more interested in the stud poker they were playing than their ghoul-hunting fame.

"The only one who can compete with these boys for takin' swiller heads and wolf teeth and fer puttin' the fear o' god in the western hobgobbies is Uriah Zane his ownself." The barman said this to only Charlie's bunch, keeping his voice down. "But everyone knows Zane rides alone. Always has, likely always will. He was in here once, wasn't all that sociable, but I reckon I never knew an overly sociable ghoul hunter. Odd breed."

The apron jerked his head covertly, meaningfully, toward the James and Younger bunch behind him.

"Hell," Lucky Snodgrass said, sneering over the beer he was lifting to his yellow-mustached lips, "everyone knows the Jameses and Youngers ain't nothin' but back-shootin', no-account robbers of small-town banks and slow-movin' trains. Hell, they'd shoot a hunk o' rock candy out of a child's fist."

Lucky snickered as he dipped his upper lip into his creamy beer foam.

The jovial barman looked suddenly stricken.

Someone cleared his throat loudly behind him. "What'd that sack o' burnin' ghoul shit say about me an' my boys?" Jesse James inquired, his blue eyes flat and mean.

24

THE DEMISE OF THE JAMES GANG

THE VOICE of steely eyed Jesse James, while not lifted inordinately high, cut through the din of the Rincon Mountain Dance Hall and Beer Parlor like a razor-edged stiletto through hog tallow.

The low roar of conversation died suddenly. The little man playing the piano turned his head toward the James-Younger table, frowning through the smoke curling up from the quirley in his false teeth, and lifted his pale hands from the ivory keys. It was so quiet that Ravenna, still standing with her back to the bar, her belly tied in a half-hitch knot, could hear the piano keys' dwindling reverberations inside their drink-stained, bullet-scarred box.

The jovial barman standing between Charlie Hondo's table and the James-Younger table twisted around on his hips to stare, aghast, at Jesse, who sat slumped back in his chair. The Missourian held his pasteboards in his left hand, resting on the edge of his table, his battered gray Stetson tipped back off his domed, sunburned forehead. The flap of his threadbare wool coat was pulled back behind the carved ivory grips of the .45 Peacemaker angled across his belly from the soft, brown leather holster on his left hip.

His pale blue eyes were menacingly dull as they stared across the fifteen feet toward Lucky Snodgrass, who sat slouched over his beer, both hands resting on the edge of his table, his eyes hard and cold, nostrils flaring. His long, dusty yellow ponytail curved down over his shoulder to disappear in his lap.

Charlie and the others wore similar expressions.

It was so quiet that Ravenna thought she could hear the jovial barman dribbling down his leg.

She broke the tense silence with, "Amigos! No, no, no, I think you misunderstand my friend Lucky over there. Lucky was only talking about that strange loner, big as a grizzly bear and twice as ornery—Uriah Zane!" She cast a cold smile at Lucky. "Wasn't that who you were talking about, Joe?"

She put just enough steel in her voice to get Lucky's attention, to communicate to the cork-headed fool the gravity of their situation and her previous admonishment to the boys to keep their noses clean here in Tucson.

"Yeah, that's what Joe said," Charlie said, all wide-eyed innocence in sharp contrast to the weirdly menacing tattoos on his cheeks. "He was talkin' about that loco Uriah Zane. Not you, Jesse, for Pete's sake." He chuffed ironically and lifted his beer to his lips.

"Yeah," Lucky said, fidgeting around with his own beer. "I meant that old coyote Zane." Softer now, really biting hard on his tongue, he added, "Didn't mean no offense to no one else . . . I reckon. . . ."

He threw back an entire whiskey shot and chased it with a long pull of his beer.

"There. See?" Ravenna said, swinging her hips as she sauntered over to where Jesse James still sat slouched down in his chair, his dangerous eyes still riveted on Lucky Snodgrass. "I tell you what—just so we can all get our friendly moods back, I will buy the next round for the James-Younger gang!" She pivoted, snapping a thumb above her head. "Apron, another round over here. Pronto! Anything they want! Add it to my tab. *Vamonos!*"

"Yes, ma'am! Yes, ma'am!" The jovial bartender, his face flushed deep russet, sweat glistening on his forehead, hurried around behind the counter and motioned for the half-breed apron to begin pouring and drawing fresh drinks. "Yes, ma'am, you got it! Whiskey and tequila all around for the James-Younger bunch! Really makes me proud to see them blessin' my humble establishment with their Yankee-killing, ghoul-huntin' presence. Yes, sir! Hurry up, there, Alfred. Pour them beers! No one gets thirsty in the Rincon, by God!"

When the James-Younger gang was all set up, the conversational din built up gradually again, the tone pitched with relief. The last thing anybody in the place wanted, least of all the jovial bartender, was a lead swap in such close, crowded confines.

The old man at the piano began hammering away at the ivories again, Charlie and the boys became distracted by their own conversation, and Ravenna herself breathed a sigh of relief as she turned to slouch over her beer and second tequila shot atop the bar. Soon, very soon, she would go over and lasso Charlie and the boys and haul them on out of the saloon and over to some quiet, side-street hotel.

"*Muchas gracias* for the drinks, senorita," a man's slightly slurred voice said behind Ravenna. She smelled horse sweat and whiskey. A finger poked her shoulder. "How 'bout you haul your pretty Mex self over to our table and join us?"

Ravenna cast a weary glance over her shoulder to see a ferret-faced young man in a bowler hat and a long, cream duster staring at her brightly. His eyes were spaced too far apart, and his nose sat oddly low between them, giving him the look of a moron. "Jesse's taken a shine to you, said he'd like an introduction."

The young man standing next to this one, a little shorter than the first and with a small knife scar on his knobby chin, chuckled, spraying spittle on his lower lip. "My brother Cole thinks you're just about the best-lookin' Mex piece o' ass he's seen in a month of Sundays!"

He rocked back on his undershot boot heels and nervously flicked one of his suspenders over and over again.

Ravenna couldn't help scowling at the pair. She recognized both from the James-Younger table, and she knew who they were. The first was Bill Chadwell. The other was Cole Younger's younger brother, James. She glanced behind them to see Jesse James, slouched casually as before, but staring between several standing men, casting his dully menacing, slightly jeering blue gaze at Ravenna. Cole Younger sat beside him, one stovepipe boot hiked up on a knee, his lips stretched drunkenly inside his shaggy black, tobacco-crusted beard.

"Tell senors James and Younger I am deeply flattered," Ravenna said huskily, unable to conceal her disdain for the arrogant Confederate ghoul hunters, "but I prefer to drink alone. Besides, I am leaving soon, on to better and bigger things—*comprende*?"

She blinked slowly and tossed her hair back from her face as she slumped forward over the bar once more. In the back bar mirror, behind pyramids of sparkling mugs and shot glasses, she saw Bill Chadwell's face flush. James Younger furrowed his dark brows and reached forward, grabbed the tail of her red sash, and jerked her around sharply.

"Don't turn your back on us, greaser bitch!"

"Yeah," said Chadwell, hardening his jaws, "we was talkin' to you on behalf of Mr. Jesse James his ownself!"

Ravenna's own face flushed. Miniature silver javelins of raw fury shot from between her narrowed eyelids.

Rage swept through her like a tidal wave, and before

she knew it she'd muttered three words of a spell the peon witch had taught her long ago in Mexico. Bill Chadwell was suddenly gone, disappeared into thin air. Where his boots had been on the floor was now a yellow and green scorpion curling its striated tail with the venomous stinger at the end, and opening and closing its raised pincers.

James Younger looked around wildly. He dropped his eyes to the floor and stumbled back, lower jaw falling nearly to his chest. He made a choking sound, and pointed at the scorpion.

"What have we here?" Ravenna said tightly, looking down at Bill Chadwell. "A goddamn scorpion in such a fine establishment?"

With that she stepped forward and rammed her left boot straight down, smashing Bill Chadwell under her copper-spurred heel. The scorpion crumpled under the red boot, blood and goo oozing out around the heel and staining the floor.

"She's a witch!" James Younger squealed, pointing at Ravenna with one hand and snagging one of the two Schofield pistols he wore in shoulder holsters inside his long denim jacket.

The piano fell silent once again, as did the crowd. All heads turned toward the commotion. James Younger whipped the Schofield up, raking the hammer back, and fired. Only his target was no longer before him. Younger's slug hammered into the side of the head of a bearded bounty hunter sitting at a table in Younger's line of fire.

As the man's head snapped sideways wildly, blood flying out his opposite ear to paint the two men sitting to the wounded bounty hunter's left, Younger gave another horrified yell and glanced down at the rangy mountain lion snarling and curling its tail in the same spot in which Ravenna had been standing only a second before.

Several startled bellows rose, the men sitting nearest the wildcat leaping to their feet and jumping back as

Ravenna's angry cry swept through the room, and she leaped off her back feet. She was a tan blur to most of the gents in the room as she rammed her lithe, dun, white-bellied body into James Younger, who trigger his pistol into the floor as Ravenna dug her fangs into the young border tough's throat, jerking her head from side to side, ripping and tearing. The young man's carotid arteries jetted hot, scarlet blood in all directions as the snarling lion rode him straight back to the floor with a reverberating thud, causing the floor to lurch violently.

Thunder pealed as every man in the room not already standing bounded out of his chair and slapped leather, shouting. Charlie Hondo loosed his own version of a Rebel yell as he and his three partners kicked their own chairs back and filled their fists with wood and iron, crouching as their pistols leaped and roared, flames stabbing toward the James-Younger table.

The James-Youngers were caught unawares, as they'd all trained their pistols on the mountain lion, who, in the ten seconds that had elapsed since it killed James Younger, had bounded onto the back of Clell Miller, driving him into the floor beneath the James table.

Charlie Hondo's first shot blew Cole Younger's right earlobe off. Having bolted out of his chair and now aiming his Peacemaker and a short-barreled Remington toward the mountain lion killing Clell Miller under his table, Jesse James flinched and swung around toward Charlie. Hondo's second bullet slammed through Jesse's shoulder and punched him back into the table behind him.

As the mountain lion bounded out from under the James-Younger table, someone from another table triggered two shots at it, plunking one bullet into Frank James's knee while the other shattered the Missouri gorilla fighter's beer schooner, spraying glass and beer in all directions. James bent over, yowling and shooting the short, derby-hatted ghoul hunter who'd pinked his knee.

More pandemonium followed, the ghoul hunters shooting one another in the confusion while the mountain lion swept the room, dodging bullets and grabbing men's legs or arms and pulling them to the floor to rip their throats out beneath tables. The ghoul hunters were so confused as to whom exactly they *should* be shooting at, aside from the lion, that Charlie and the boys had a fairly easy time drilling one ghoul hunter after another, after making fast work of the James-Younger bunch, all of whom lay in bloody piles among overturned tables and chairs and blood-splattered cards and spilled ashtrays.

When most of the other men in the room were down and powder smoke hung in an almost impenetrable haze from the rafters, Charlie started making his way to the front of the room, reloading one of his pistols quickly. "Come on, boys—I reckon we done wore out our welcome in the Rincon Beer Parlor!"

Lucky was down on one knee behind the bullet-shaped stove in the room's center, having just reloaded his own pistols, and was rolling the cylinder of one across his forearm, looking around in sparkle-eyed delight. He echoed Charlie's Rebel yell and shot a wounded man climbing to his knees on the room's right side, then ran after the others, following Charlie to the front of the room and out the batwings.

"Come on, darlin'!" Charlie shouted back into the room from over the doors. "You cleaned up right well. Yessiree, indeed you did!"

He laughed as Ravenna bounded toward him, leaping sleekly over the only three tables still standing upright, and followed Charlie on out of the saloon. Only it wasn't the mountain lion leaping across the front gallery but the lovely black-haired witch herself, cursing shrilly in Spanish as the end of her red sash trailed out behind her.

"Mierda!"

"Best you learn to control that bean-eater temper, darlin'!"

"I think you're right, *mi amor*. But I have to admit to enjoying myself back there!"

"You still want that bath?" Charlie asked her as he untied his horse and swung into the leather.

"*Sí*, but I guess a creek will have to do!"

She leaped into the saddle of her own mount and jerked her gelding away from the hitchrack. Boot scrapes sounded from across the gallery. The jovial barman, no longer looking so jovial covered in blood, pushed through the batwings wielding a double-barreled shotgun.

"Monster bast-*arrrds*!"

He leveled the shotgun. Holding their horses' reins taut in their left hands, Charlie and Ravenna fired the pistols in their right hands. The bloody barman screamed as he triggered both barrels of his shotgun into the gallery's roof and danced back into the saloon where he fell with a thud.

Charlie and the boys and Ravenna looked around warily. Men were moving toward them from up and down the street, crouched over rifles or extending pistols.

"Which way, *chiquita*?" Charlie said. "I'm feelin' a mite crowded."

Ravenna looked around, saw a gap between two buildings behind her. "South!"

Her gelding whinnied as she wheeled it around and shot it through the gap, the others galloping behind her, Lucky and One-Eye triggering a couple of rounds at men cautiously approaching along the main street. They thundered down the gap, weaved around several stock pens and piles of stacked mesquite wood, and hammered off into the saguaro- and greasewood-stippled desert, their hoof thuds dwindling behind them.

Back at the Rincon Beer Parlor, gun smoke sifted out over the still batwings and across the gallery, as though a fire smoldered inside. A face appeared in the smoke over the doors. Two pale blue eyes shone against ridged, sandy brows beneath a domed, windburned forehead. The man was hatless, his thin, light brown hair sitting close against his bony skull.

Jesse James staggered through the batwings. Holding himself tensely, bleeding from a shoulder wound and a leg wound and several grazes, he stumbled out to the edge of the gallery. His knees buckled, and he slammed onto the gallery floor. Kneeling there, bleeding, his face bleached and bland except for one eye twitching, he stared through the gap between buildings through which the gang of ghouls that had cut down his gang had disappeared.

"You got a reckonin' comin', ghouls," he muttered, gritting his teeth till his jaws cracked. "You . . . you ain't seen the last o' Jesse Woodson James!"

25

THE LITTLE MAN IN THE BONEYARD

"GODDAMN, you green-livered cur—drop that boot! Drop it this instant, you hear?"

The enraged admonition rumbled inside a shed on the left side of Tucson's crooked main drag. Hearing it, Uriah Zane reined General Lee to a halt before the long, disjointed, mud-brick and wood-frame building of which the side shed was a part. A shingle identified the sprawling dump as H.A. DEROSSO'S CABINET MAKING AND UNDERTAKING, with a smaller sign below that read: *No Injuns Served Here. See Miro Estacado at the Blacksmith Shop.*

The voice inside the shed cursed sharply just as a yellow-and-brown mutt hurled itself through the one-foot gap in the shed's sliding door. The dog gave a little cry as the boot caught on the door and slipped from the cur's jaws to lie in the dust just outside the shed. Undeterred, the cur picked up the boot and, as a potbellied, stoop-shouldered older man in a shabby canvas hat poked his head out the gap in the door, the thieving beast took off at a dead sprint past Zane, Angel, and Al Hathaway, heading at a slant across the main drag.

The potbellied man, in his late sixties though he could have been older, sucked in his gut, shuffled sideways out the door, and shook his fist toward the cur, shouting, "That's Cole Younger's boot, you son of a bitch! You bring it back here pronto and I maybe won't fill your ass full o' double-ought buck!"

The cur didn't slow its step but ran beneath a ranch supply wagon parked in front of a general merchandise store. He ran out the other side of the wagon and cut into a break between the general store and a tonsorial parlor, disappearing down the gap, leaving only a smear of sun-coppered dust behind him.

"God-damn!" cried the potbellied oldster, whose face was nearly as black as the cur's stolen boot, though he was obviously a white man. He wore a red-and-black-checked shirt under a greasy deerskin vest that hung down to his bony knees. "Where'm I gonna find another boot to match the other'n?"

Angel studied the oldster. "Did you say that was Cole Younger's boot?"

"That's what I said, all right." The old man stared after the cur, his eyes still sharp with fury. "Got him all laid out inside, all dressed up and ready for plantin' in the suit Jesse picked out his ownself—*minus one fucking boot!*"

He cut his tan, fury-bright eyes to Angel and flushed with chagrin. "Sorry, there, young lady. Please pardon my blue tongue."

"Ah, it ain't nothing I haven't heard before when a cur was caught stealin' a dead man's boot. Under similar circumstances, I'd probably indulge in an epithet or two, myself."

The old man's eyes spoked as he stared fondly up at the redhead. "I'm Hank DeRosso, owner of this fine establishment behind me. Some call me an artisan. Soon to be a dog killer." His shoulders jerked as he wheezed a short laugh. "Who might you be, young lady, and any chance you're lookin' to settle down here in Tucson? Maybe git yourself hitched? I never been married, but . . ." He winked. "I reckon it ain't never too late to give her a shot!"

Angel laughed. "I'm Angel Coffin. These two polecats are Uriah Zane and Al Hathaway. Unfortunately, we're here on business, Mr. DeRosso. Otherwise, I could do worse than hitch my star to a man with his own business."

Uriah was staring up the street, toward the Rincon Dance Hall and Beer Parlor, against the front gallery of which several open coffins leaned. The watering hole was a block away, but the coffins appeared to have dead men inside, some with placards hanging around their necks. "What was that old train robber Cole Younger doin' in Tucson?"

"Him and Jesse and the boys come out to hunt wolves up in the White Tanks. There's an especially large bounty on 'em since a railroad's surveyin' track through that range into California, and the track layers and rock breakers been droppin' like june bugs on a goose pond."

"And likely runnin' from the law," Angel added. "The bounties on those fellas' heads is as big as that on the wolves they hunt."

"All I can tell you," said Hank DeRosso, "is we need all the ghoul hunters we can get. Especially after what happened day before yesterday to Cole and Frank James and nearly the whole damn James-Younger gang, 'ceptin' Jesse hisself. And half a dozen other ghoul hunters and two deputy town marshals." He shook his head, baffled. "How Jesse ever survived them wounds o' his, I'll never know. Reckon he must have some ghoul in him his ownself."

Hathaway spat chaw on a rock in the street and gave the man a pointed look as he ran the back of his buckskin glove across his mouth. "Charlie Hondo leave his callin' card, did he?"

"Charlie Hondo?"

"Four men ride into town day before yesterday?" Zane

asked, studying the coffins tilted against the Rincon House. "With a pretty Mex gal?"

"Shit," the oldster said. "How'd you know?"

"I'm clairvoyant." Zane gigged General Lee ahead, starting up the street. The others fell in behind him, and they angled over toward where the coffins were lined up against the Rincon House.

There were five open coffins, each containing a woeful-looking dead man. All five of the men were naked. Bullet holes showed in their chests and bellies and elsewhere, like round, gray discs. The blood had been cleaned away. Likely, their clothes had been too torn and bloody to bury them in. One had had an eye shot out. Another had two bullet holes in his forehead. A placard hung around the first man slouched in a coffin nearest the beer parlor's front steps.

The placard read: *Do you know these men?* An arrow pointed to the right, indicating the four others.

A living, breathing man sat on the steps of the Rincon House, holding a frothy beer schooner on his lone knee. His other leg was wooden, and it ended in a peg where his foot should have been. He was middle-aged, and he wore an eye patch. He was drawing deep on a long, black cigar as he eyed the three newcomers sitting their horses near the coffins.

"Them's the five we can't identify. Unknown ghoul hunters in these parts. Probably here to hunt the White Tanks, just like Cole and Jesse James was."

Zane said, "How many others killed?"

"Shit, damn near fifteen men. Including Nevada Lewis, owner of the Rincon. Half-breed's runnin' it now. He's one of only three who survived the maulin' and shootin', 'cause he was smart and kept his head down behind the bar. The others probably won't make it."

"What do you mean mawlin'?" Angel inquired.

"That Mex bitch turned herself into a wildcat. Went

wild as hell with the fires stoked." The one-legged man drew deep on the cigar and let the smoke out his nostrils, running a grimy thumbnail down the several-days' growth of beard on his pale cheeks. "The men with her opened up with their six-shooters. Coulda heard the din as far away as Phoenix or Fort Bowie."

"Did the men change?" Zane asked, looking past the Rincon Beer Parlor across the street to a cemetery flanking the church. There were several men digging graves among the titled gravestones and sage, while another man sat in a wheelchair in the minimal shade cast by a large saguaro.

"No, they didn't change. What—you think they were ghouls, too? This was day before yesterday, not *night* before yesterday. Won't be a full moon again for four nights, praise Jesus and Jezebel."

Zane glanced at Angel. "Well, they're still not changin'," she said. "That's good." She turned to the one-legged man. "Which way did they head?"

He pointed his cigar toward the gap between buildings on the south side of the main street. "Through there. A passel of hunters went out after 'em yesterday, led up by Sheriff McQueen his ownself. The town marshal lost both his deputies, who were also his sons, in the bloodbath. Pretty broke up about it. He took a couple bottles and two old Civil War pistols, and lit out for the Santa Catalinas. Doubt we'll ever see ole Carney again . . . poor bastard. If he don't drink himself on over the divide, he'll likely blow his brains out. Them boys was all he had."

Zane cast his gaze back behind the old Catholic church. "Is that Jesse out at the cemetery?"

The one-legged man turned to look, then turned forward again, nodding and taking another drag off his cigar. "Poor bastard's overseein' the buryin' of his brother, Frank. He don't normally drink, but he took a couple beers with him."

"Didn't know the Jameses were Catholic," Angel said dryly.

The one-legged man only shrugged. "Only cemetery we got."

Zane glanced at Angel and Hathaway, then swung down from General Lee's back. He tossed his reins to the scout. "You wanna stable our mounts? I'm gonna go powwow with Jesse."

"Sure thing," Hathaway said.

Zane slid his rifle from his saddle sheath, set it on his shoulder, and walked on around the corner of the Rincon toward the cemetery. He walked on past the half-ruined adobe wall that surrounded the old Spanish church that had likely been erected a hundred years ago, and began striding up the hill over which the boneyard sprawled among greasewood, bleached rocks, and Spanish bayonet. Some of the stones had been carved in the 1700s, and their edges had been weathered by time. Some of the names and years had eroded away completely, leaving flat faces of gray rock.

Zane walked up toward the crest of the hill, where two men were digging a grave with their shirts off. Their shovels clattered and scraped against the rocky earth. They were breathing hard and sweating, hat brims shading their faces.

Jesse James sat up the hill about fifteen feet, near the saguaro, though now its shade had angled away from him. Even with his left arm in a sling and a bandage around his right thigh, he was a tough-looking little man in a gray Stetson with a braided rawhide band. The hat appeared almost too big for his head. His face looked carefully chiseled from granite with its grave, deep-set eyes, delicate nose, and long, jutting jaws. The lines were clean and hard and gave the man an air of knotted-up power and barely bridled rage.

He had an open beer bottle clamped between his

thighs. Another beer bottle, unopened, was wedged between his right leg and the arm of his wheelchair. Between his thin lips smoldered a quirley emanating the sweet smell of marijuana. His chin was dipped downward, eyes on the lined pad on which he was writing in pencil.

Zane walked up on his left side and, glancing at the pad, saw that the tough-nut gorilla border dog had a fine cursive hand. Almost girlishly slanted and looping.

Zane was six feet away from the chair when, not turning his head toward the newcomer, Jesse said quietly as though speaking to himself, "Uriah Zane."

Zane stopped, looked at the two men digging the grave, then at the sealed coffin sitting beside the mounded, red-brown dirt. "Sorry to hear about your loss, Jesse. Frank was a good hunter. One of the best."

"A good bank robber, too." Jesse turned to smirk at Zane towering over him. His pale blue eyes were rheumy and red from the beer and Mexican marijuana. "Wouldn't you say, Uriah?"

"I reckon he was, at that. Leastways, he earned a fancy price on his head."

"You was too good for all o' that, weren't you?" Jesse's eyes turned accusing though somehow they did not lose their bemused cast as well. "No train robbin' for you . . . even if it was Yankee money you was stealin'."

"I didn't come here to discuss our differences, Jesse. After the War, some of us who survived went one way, others another. You're a good ghoul hunter, as Frank was, and while I wish you'd concentrate more on the ghouls and less on robbing innocent folks of their hard-earned savings, I wish you all the best." Zane pinched his hat brim, and started to turn away.

"Innocent folks?"

Zane glanced over his shoulder at the little man in the wheelchair. "It was the government that turned those ghouls loose on the South, Jesse. Not the citizens. Lincoln's dead. Grant's wallowing around inside a bottle somewhere in Tennessee."

"The government is its citizens, Uriah—don't you know that?"

"Like I said, sorry for your loss."

Zane had walked a good ten feet back down the hill, his Henry rifle resting on his shoulder, when Jesse said, "They was Hell's Angels, weren't they? And that *puta* bitch . . . she was that witch from Chihuahua, Ravenna somethin' or other."

Zane kept walking.

"I'll be ridin' with you, Uriah, when you set out after them ghouls."

"No, you won't."

Zane kept walking, the tough soles of his high-topped moccasins crunching gravel and brushing against shrubs.

Behind him, Jesse sighed. "I'm gonna change your mind, Uriah."

"Doubt it."

Zane kept walking as Jesse chuckled softly beneath the *snick*s of the shovels digging Frank's grave.

26

THE BEAST IN THE CELLAR

ZANE DINED ON HOT, spicy Mexican food in a little, no-name eatery in an adobe shack near the flophouse he always threw down in when he visited Tucson and where he and Angel and Hathaway had each taken a room after stabling their mounts. The trio of ghoul hunters ate without speaking, fatigued from the long pull down from Colorado.

Afterward, they left gold coins on the table and headed on back to the Santa Catalina Inn, where they muttered their intentions of rising at dawn and heading out before sunrise. Zane went into his musty room furnished simply with a few sticks of crude furniture and a crucifix over the lumpy bed with its corn-shuck mattress and moisture-stained pillow.

He opened a shutter to the cool, desert air, taking a deep breath of the sage and the perfume-like fragrance of burning piñon pine and mesquite. Standing at the window, hearing the mournful strains of a mandolin twanging in some smoky cantina and the love moans of a soiled dove in the whorehouse that slumped on the other side of this dark side street, its shaded windows showing pink lamp-light, Zane kicked out of his boots and stripped down to his balbriggans, which stretched across his broad-shouldered frame like buckskin soaked in a creek, then dried and shrunk in the hot sun.

He took another lungful of the fortifying desert air, lifting his chest so that the long underwear top drew even tighter against his shoulders. Then he turned the sheet and quilt back and eased into the bed, resting his head against the pillow and drawing the covers up to his chin.

He leaned over and blew out the candle on the bedside table. He closed his eyes, drew another slow, deep breath, and released it. He beckoned sleep, called for it, finally gritted his teeth and ordered it to come.

Like a rotten cur, it ran in the opposite direction.

For some reason, every muscle in his body leaped and writhed beneath his skin. His mind was a restless, twisted tangle of random, half-formed images flashing like the sun off a looking glass.

Finally, he threw the bedcovers back, dropped his feet to the floor. He'd go out and have a few drinks in the first watering hole he came to, maybe goose a few whores, and get his mind settled down. Then he'd return to the Santa Catalina, get a few hours of restful sleep, and be ready to ride at first light.

He dressed, left his rifle in his room with his other gear, and strode off down the hall lit by a single, smoky bracket lamp. Behind the doors off both sides of the corridor, he could hear men snoring, one whimpering childlike. He stole down the creaky, uncarpeted stairs with their rickety railing, walked past the hotel's middle-aged proprietor sleeping behind his desk with a *Policeman's Gazette* spread open across his chest, gold spectacles hanging down his nose, and headed out into the night.

Several pockets of lamplight shone up and down the main street, casting saddled horses tied to hitchracks in ghostly silhouette. The air was still and cool, the sky alive with stars, the desert around the ancient pueblo so quiet that Zane could hear coyotes calling from miles away.

He walked east along the street, following its meandering, widening, and narrowing course between the desert-blistered buildings. After thirty or forty yards, following the mandolin strains, he stopped and drew a lungful of air. The breath spread his ribs, opened his chest and belly, loosened the knotted muscles along his spine.

Maybe he didn't need a drink, after all. Maybe he just needed a walk to limber his legs and more of this light, cool, desert-perfumed air to nudge him off toward sleep.

He swung around and headed in the opposite direction, intending to walk a ways out of town where it was especially quiet and he could calm his racing thoughts in solitude. He passed the church that hulked up darkly against the shimmering stars that appeared as close as the many small crystals in a chandelier he'd once seen hanging in a Leadville opera house.

He came to the shaggy end of town and kept walking along the road that shone violet under the sky that as yet had no moon. The shrubs and rocks stood out in silhouette, the edges of the branches bathed in a deep purple luminescence. Zane stretched his stride, breathing deeply, the oxygen making him feel lighter, calmer. The blood flowed warm, loosening his muscles. His mood lightened.

He was beginning to enjoy the night, all the sounds he could hear, the brief blaze of a shooting star arcing across the northwestern horizon, shedding sparks before it disappeared behind a jagged-edged sierra. A coyote howled in the far distance. Nearer, he could hear a small pack snorting around an arroyo.

As he continued walking, he swung his head from left to right, scanning the terrain before him. As far as he could tell, the desert nearby was scored with no arroyo. It was dishpan flat all around him for a good half mile, before a low rise lifted like rumpled velvet in the north and began the swell of the foothills climbing toward the Santa Catalinas and the high, triangle-topped bulge of Mount Lemmon.

Zane stopped.

The coyotes continued to yip and snarl. There was a low, frantic peeping. They'd brought a deer down, and the deer was in its death throes while the coyotes finished it and fought among themselves over the warm blood and fresh, hot meat.

But where in the hell were they?

A dark, shaggy line shone to the west and slightly left of the wagon trail he was following. Could that be the arroyo? It had to be a half mile away.

No. His heart chugged softly in his ears as he stared at the mesquites and willows lining the distant wash. The cut was a good mile away. It appeared nearer only because he could see it so well, clearly enough to pick out the silhouette of the mountain lion stalking belly down amid the brush lining the wash. He could see the whiplike curl of its tail as it stole up on the coyotes.

Suddenly, the cat gave a shrill, snarling cry. The echoes rolled menacingly. Brush crackled raucously. Several coyotes yipped. Their padded feet thudded off down the arroyo, abandoning the now-dead deer to the more formidable stalker.

The wildcat disappeared in the darkness of the cut, but one last snarl sliced across the silent night, chasing its own diminishing echoes.

Zane felt his lower jaw drop. Fear pricked at him like a chill hand under his collar. His senses were alive as snakes in a den. He could not only hear the howl of a wolf on Mount Lemmon now, but he realized that the soft snicking sound he'd been hearing for the past few minutes was a snake slithering along the ground to the north, maybe fifty yards away, maybe heading for a pack rat's den it had checked out earlier that day and had marked as a good place for a meal.

He looked up. The stars throbbed and glowed as though on the other end of a sharp lens. They were so clear that seeing them now made Zane's head ache, as though someone were flashing a railroad lantern in his face.

As though chained deep in a cold, dark cellar, the wolf in the ghoul hunter stirred. It paced to the end of the chain and back, sniffing and snorting at the crack under the door, growling and mewling deep in its throat. Angry. Frustrated.

Wanting more than anything to be free to hunt, stalk, and kill . . .

Zane had chained the beast and locked the cellar door. But for how long could he keep it in there? What would happen during the next full moon, or the next, or the one after that? Would it finally break its chain and burst through the door?

Would he become like Charlie Hondo and the rest of the Hell's Angels he'd come west all those years ago to hunt?

Closing his eyes against the magnified vision, clamping his hands over his ears to quell the night sounds of predators and prey—the tearing and frantic screaming and the salty smell of blood—he wheeled and began striding back toward Tucson. He opened his eyes. The dim lights spilling out of the cantinas and saloons beckoned him. His heart beat faster but more hopefully now.

He'd get a drink and try to distract himself from the keenness of his savage senses, the barely contained will to unleash them, to follow them, and turn himself loose upon the night.

He dropped his hands to his sides, ground his teeth against the sounds that began slithering into his brain once more, making him feel dizzy and overloaded and causing his knees to grow spongy, his heart to beat faster and faster, his breath to grow shallow and weak.

His hands sweated in the chill air. His feet burned in his moccasins.

For a moment, he thought he'd pass out.

He kept walking.

As he passed the church, the padding of many canine feet sounded. He glanced down the side street between the church and the Rincon Beer Parlor that was dark now in the wake of the massacre.

Up the hill on which the cemetery sprawled, he heard frantic panting and scratching and saw the silhouettes of several shaggy wolves scrambling around the boneyard while one hunkered forward and dug, tearing at the soil with its front paws. It stopped digging, ran around, mewled and whined in frustration, then resumed digging once more.

Zane's nostrils filled with the sweet, wild scent of the carrion-stalking pack. The fetor struck his belly like pig slop, and his stomach turned, nearly heaving up its contents.

If a full moon had been rising, would he have been able to keep his wolf in its cellar?

No, somehow he had to kill it. He had to find a way to kill the beast or surely it would free itself, and it would be Uriah Zane forever chained and locked in that cellar while a madman ran loose upon the frontier.

He quickened his pace, stopped at the first cantina he came to, no more than a long, low adobe box with PULQUERIA scrawled in black paint over its deep casement door, above which a bead curtain hung, clicking and clacking in a slight breeze that had risen, bringing even more scents—so many it was hard to identify a single one—to the ghoul hunter's nostrils.

He bulled through the curtain, the beads clattering back into place behind him, loud as the thudding of shod hooves in his ears. His knees and hands shaking, he moved forward, sagged into an empty chair that sat back against the cracked adobe wall. A small, square table of half-cut cottonwood logs sat to the left of the chair. He rested an elbow on the table and entwined his hands together, mashing their heels against each other to steady himself.

He'd thought he'd been through all this months ago, during the first several full moons after he'd first been bit. It was happening again with nearly as much force as it had happened then.

He knew why.

It was happening because he'd become keenly conscious of the wolf inside him—maybe partly because of the savagery he'd seen in the Hell's Angels, maybe partly because of what they'd done here in Tucson day before yesterday—and he was steeling himself against it.

What he needed to do—and he did not know where the realization suddenly came from—was to ignore it. To ride it out. To not fight the sensations. He hadn't been fighting them before. He'd merely used the heightened senses to his best advantage. Now he was fighting them again in the same way he'd first fought them until he'd learned the key: to let go and distract himself, to have enough confidence in his own humanness to keep the wolf under lock and key without an overwhelming effort.

Without dwelling on the temptation he felt to turn the wolf loose . . .

The strains of the mandolin flooded Zane's senses. He welcomed the distracting music and looked around until he saw the player—a plump Mexican girl in an ornate Mexican basque. She was round-faced and sleepy-eyed, and she sat in a chair beside the bar made of crude cottonwood planks and resting on beer kegs. Two large crock jugs stood atop the bar, and Zane could smell the pulque inside one—a milky liquor made from the fermented juice of the century plant. In the other was *bacanora*, brewed from the agave plant, and a form of mezcal.

"Bacanora," he told the big-eared, thin-haired barman staring over the plank board at him, while the girl continued strumming the mandolin. While the barman was old and craggy, Zane could see the hint of his features in the girl, probably his daughter.

The barman, dressed in a white shirt, filthy apron, baggy green slacks, and rope-soled sandals, reached for the dipper handle poking up from the *bacanora* crock. Zane looked around the room, which spun and tilted slightly, and saw a milky-eyed man with close-cropped gray hair sitting at a table just beyond Zane's, staring blindly toward Zane and grinning toothlessly. His small brown hands with nails thick as seashells were wrapped around a wooden cup.

Three men played craps on the floor toward the back of the cantina, and two other, younger men dressed in the gaudy attire of vaqueros sprawled in chairs near a smoky charcoal brazier. They smiled shiny-eyed at the opposite wall, one waving a hand lazily to the strains of the mandolin.

Beneath the girl's hide-bottom chair, only partly visible behind the pleats and folds of her black, gold-embroidered crinoline dress, the cur that had stolen Cole Younger's boot lay curled, nose to tail, sound asleep.

The barman limped out from behind the bar and set a stone mug on the table before Zane. With a shaky right hand, the ghoul hunter lifted the cup to his lips and drank the glass down in four deep swallows, the powerful hooch that tasted a little like skimmed milk and grapefruit juice searing his tonsils and lighting a welcome fire in his chest and belly.

The heat rose from his gut and flooded into his face, and he felt suddenly as though he were ensconced in warm wool during a raging blizzard.

"Another."

The barman turned from the bar, arching one thin, dark brow dubiously. The man lifted a shoulder, retrieved Zane's mug, and refilled it from the same crock as before. He set it on Zane's table and watched while the ghoul hunter took a sip. Zane set the cup down on the table and smiled up at the man.

"Nectar of the fucking gods, eh, amigo?"

He fished some coins out of his shirt pocket, placed them one by one in the man's open palm, and waved him away.

He sat back in his chair and welcomed the warmth that washed through him—up and down and sideways, reaching as far up as his hair ends, as far down as his toes.

The girl began to sing an old Spanish ballad, "*Había hace tiempo un muchacho para mí en Chihihuaha,*" and the ghoul hunter sagged farther back in his chair, setting his hat on the table and letting his head rest against the wall.

He sighed.

A warm, relieved smile stretched his mouth. Bittersweet tears filled his eyes as he listened to the lonesome song of unrequited love in Mexico, of a girl who drowned herself in a well because the boy she loved had eyes only for her more beautiful sister, and he indulged himself without feeling foolish.

He probably looked foolish, lounging there, teary-eyed, but he didn't feel anything but sorrow for the poor girl who'd drowned herself.

He listened to the ballad and then to two more, his soul dangling from every note. He'd never felt more alone—even during those long nights he'd first started fighting the wolf inside him—but the strong Mexican hooch filed off the edges of the loneliness. He finished the pungent but deadening brew, then heaved himself unsteadily to his feet. He shambled over to the girl with the mandolin and dropped a copper dollar into the coffee tin sitting beside her atop the bar.

She gave him a cordial nod as she strummed and sang.

He bowed lavishly, doffing his hat and sweeping it down before him. *"Muchas gracias, senorita. Para uno tan joven, usted canta maravillosamente sobre angustia." For one so young, you sing beautifully of heartbreak.*

He set his hat on his head, turned, and staggered out of the cantina, retracing his steps back to the second floor of the Santa Catalina Inn. He glanced at Angel's door directly across from his own.

No sounds in there. At least, none that he could hear. She was likely asleep. His heart started to tighten, and he floated away from it. Vaguely, behind the curtain of drunkenness that had dropped down over his senses, numbing them, he made a mental note to remind the marshal that if they were still riding together during the next full moon, she'd need to keep her guns filled with silver, and a watchful eye on her partner.

He chuckled. Angel wouldn't need reminding.

He went into his own room and was finally drifting off into a welcome slumber when someone rapped loudly on his door.

"Zane! Zane! You in there, Zane?"

The ghoul hunter jerked his head up from his pillow and reached for the LeMat. He flicked the hammer over the shotgun shell and aimed the piece at the door. "Holy Christ! Who the fuck is it?"

"It's Jesse. Open up! We gotta talk, Zane!"

27

JESSE'S DREAM

IN HIS BALBRIGGANS and still holding his heavy, cocked LeMat, Zane threw the door open and stood barefoot, staring down at the wheelchair-bound, wiry little creature in the too-big hat, pale blue eyes still sparkling crazily, as they had been earlier in the day.

The outlaw/ghoul hunter was no longer drinking or smoking, but he hadn't quit long ago. He reeked of both alcohol and marijuana. He was dressed in a long, gray duster, and pistols jutted up from holsters on his hips. He held a Spencer repeater across his bony knees with his good hand, the left one still in a sling.

"We done talked at the boneyard, Jesse," Zane said, voice raspy from the sleep he'd been drifting into.

"Hear me, damn you," Jesse said, narrowing his eyes menacingly, his delicate face flushing, veins bulging in his temples. "You're gonna need me when you go after them ghouls."

"I doubt it."

"I know where they're headed, Uriah." Jesse's lips shaped a slow smile. He let that sink in, and then he added, "Seen the place in a dream last night. And it's still right here."

He lifted his right hand from the carbine's breech and set a long, slender index finger against his right temple. "You don't got time to track 'em, 'cause they're racin' the full moon, four nights away. And now they'll be coverin' their trail. Won't take no chances."

He lifted his chin to glance out the window behind Zane, where the milky wash of a three-quarter moon was brushing Tucson's rooftops. "You need me to lead you to where they're goin'."

"Bullshit." Zane started to close the door.

Jesse wheeled himself forward and stuck a boot out to stop it. "Don't you do me that way. I know where they're headed, goddamnit, and you need me to show you. My men are dead, and I need you Uriah, though I'll likely rue this night for sayin' it. But you need me, too."

"I won't ride with you, Jesse."

Zane had been invited to join the James-Younger gang years ago, just after the War, when they'd all found themselves together in Kansas. Zane had declined then, because the gang was a pack of angry killers led by a demented, kill-crazy hillbilly in Jesse James. The War had given him a good excuse to kill and rob banks, but even without the War, his severe visage would be adorning wanted dodgers throughout the West. That was just who Jesse was. It was also Cole Younger and even Jesse's late brother, Frank, to some extent, though Frank might not have been as het up without the War and the Hell's Angels giving him a cause.

"Don't be a fool, Uriah. You an' me fought on the same side. We're still fightin' on the same side." Jesse made his red-rimmed eyes bulge crazily. "And I got the gift. Handed down by my grandmammy. Second sight." His eyes danced as though there were lights behind them. "And I seen where them killers o' Frank and our Confederate brethren are headed, Uriah."

He cackled like an old woman, sitting there shaking in his chair. Just then Zane smelled cigar smoke and saw one of the men who'd been digging Frank's grave standing in the shadows near the end of the hall, near the stairs. He stood with one hand against the wall behind him, smoking desultorily, waiting to take his crazy benefactor back down the stairs.

Across the hall, Angel's door opened. The marshal stepped out in a striped nightshirt that hung to her bare knees. She had a pistol in her hand, and as she moved out into the hall, she aimed it at the back of Jesse's head, loudly ratcheting the hammer back.

The Missourian had heard the door latch click and the hinges squawk, and now he turned to see the redhead bearing down on him, and he grinned. "Well, if it ain't the lovely Marshal Coffin."

"Sorry for your losses, Jesse, but I reckon I'll be lockin' you up in the local hoosegow. Pick you up on my way back to Denver. Several rail lines will be very happy to see you hanged."

Zane sighed in frustration. "Forget it, Angel."

She furled a skeptical brow. "How's that?"

"The crazy bastard's pullin' out with us tomorrow."

Zane stepped back into his room and closed the door.

The next day, at high noon, the hunting party, including Jesse James, riding his black-socked buckskin, was angling southwest of Tucson, the direction in which the outlaw from Missouri said they were heading. The tracks made by both the Hell's Angels and the posse that had followed them out from town bore this out.

It was a cool, sunny day, though high, thin clouds moving in from California threatened rain later. Al Hathaway, who was riding ahead, checked his mule down suddenly and rose in his stirrups to inspect the trail, swinging his head slowly from left to right and back again.

"What is it?" Zane asked.

Hathaway said nothing. He swung heavily down from the mule's back, dropped the reins, and walked ahead a ways, where the trail narrowed between two piles of cracked and sun-bleached granite heaved up from the earth's volcanic bowels eons ago. Chin dipped, he swerved off the trail's left side where a thin corridor in the rocks rose up a low shoulder along an outcropping. He walked forty yards to the top of the shoulder, then turned to stare back down where Zane, Angel, and Jesse James waited astride their horses.

"They came this way, swingin' back east. The posse from town was still followin' 'em."

"Nope." Jesse shook his head.

He no longer wore the sling but kept his left arm sort of hanging gingerly at his side, gloved hand resting on his thigh. He'd changed the bandage on his right thigh that morning before they'd left, and so far no blood spotted it. A tough little Missouri devil, Zane silently opined.

"What do you mean, 'no'?" Hathaway asked, indignant. "I got eyes; I can see their trail."

"They mighta gone that way for a time, but they would have swung back west. They were just tryin' to shake the posse and anyone else trailin' 'em—includin' us. I told you fellas . . . and ladies . . . I know where they're goin'. There's no need to waste time scourin' for sign!"

He booted his buckskin ahead between the scarps and disappeared behind a bend in the trail, his dust sifting behind him.

Sitting to Zane's right, hands crossed on her saddle horn, Angel gave the ghoul hunter a pointed look. "How can you be so sure he really does know where the Angels are heading? He's crazier'n a tree full of owls, Uriah."

"That's sorta how I know." More to the point, the wolf in Zane sensed the medium in Jesse. Saw it in his eyes. He'd seen it before in the Southern hill folk, many of whom practiced the art of clairvoyance and witch doctoring and all manner of magic, black and otherwise. Besides, Jesse hadn't been studying the trail at all, but he seemed very confident about the path he'd chosen south of Tucson.

When Hathaway had stepped into his saddle, he gave Zane a skeptical glance before shuttling it to Angel, who shrugged. With a grunt, Hathaway touched heels to his mule's flanks, and Zane and Angel followed the scout on up the trail a half mile before they spotted Jesse squatting atop a hill to the right side of the trail. His buckskin lazily foraged short, green grass spiking among the black rocks.

Jesse looked at the trio below him and jerked his head, beckoning. "Take a look, friends."

Zane dismounted, dropped his reins, and started up the hill. Angel and Hathaway glanced at each other dubiously once more, then stepped down out of their saddles. They followed Zane up the hill to where Jesse knelt, staring off toward the southwest. He pointed toward a series of rocky, sun-blasted sierras rearing up against the western horizon—long, toothy-tipped ranges that appeared as dark and forbidden as the mountains on the moon.

"See that second range there, a little higher than the first with that high peak in the middle?"

Zane tipped his hat brim down a notch and squinted, following Jesse's finger. "I see it."

"That's the Lobo Negros. From a different angle—from the angle I saw in my dream of two nights ago—that high peak there looks like the head of a giant, snarling wolf, both ears sticking straight up in the air."

"And that's where you think the Angels are headed?" Angel said.

Jesse nodded.

"Since you know so much about where they're headed from this dream of yourn," Hathaway said, "you must have some idea why they're headed thataway."

"Nope, can't help you there, Mr. Hathaway. I got the powers of seein'. Not readin' what's in a man's—or, most 'specially, a wolf's—heart. But that's where they're headed, and if they keep movin' as fast as they was through here, they'll be in the heart of them mountains in three nights."

"The night of the full moon," Angel said, staring pensively off at the dark, volcanic range dappled in sunlight and shadows cast by the high clouds. She glanced quickly at Zane and away again.

A hunting hawk screeched in the far distance, though in Zane's ears it sounded no farther away than their horses.

"Let's shake a leg," he said, and walked back down the rise.

The others followed, approaching their mounts.

Angel turned to Jesse. She had her rifle on her shoulder. "James, you an' me need to get somethin' straight, because it's been gallin' me ever since we left Tucson."

The Missouri outlaw turned to her with that lascivious grin he reserved especially for the buxom, redheaded deputy marshal. "How can I help, Miss Coffin?"

Her hands and arms moving in a blur, she swept her rifle off her shoulder and rammed the butt hard into the outlaw's belly. Jesse gave a great, pained *whoosh* of expelled air and dropped to his knees, kicking up a dust cloud.

"What . . . in Christ . . . ?" he grunted, making a face while pressing the heels of both his hands to his battered midsection.

"That ain't much, but that's for all the trains you robbed and all the people, including badge toters, you killed over these years since the War. And that's my promise to you that when our mission here is over, you'll be accompanyin' me back to Denver in cuffs and shackles."

She spat into the trail beside the grunting, panting Jesse, gave his dislodged hat a kick, and turned toward her horse.

"Feel better?" Zane inquired.

"I do."

As Angel mounted her horse and Hathaway shook his

head, choking back snickers, Zane crouched over the damaged outlaw and grabbed one of his arms. "You all right, there, Jesse?"

He helped the man to his feet and gave him his hat.

"Law, law," Jesse said, shaking his head as if to clear the cobwebs, limping over to his horse, "she is a caution!"

They camped that night about seventy miles southwest of Tucson, having made good time and seeing enough of the Hell's Angels' sign as well as that of the posse behind them to convince them all, including Angel, that the outlaw was indeed leading them in the right direction—pretty much on a cross-country beeline toward the Lobo Negros.

They rose well before dawn and traveled by the light of the large moon still high in the western sky and shedding nearly as much light as the dawn sun would. They followed arroyos and shallow canyons, crossed two low jogs of dun-brown hills, and found a bowl in the hills where Apaches had once camped, the jacales still standing and waiting for the wandering hunters and warriors to return. Five horses had been picketed nearby, and there was a pile of fresh ashes in the middle of the camp.

Without a doubt, Hondo's group had camped here.

The posse from Tucson had followed about three hours later but did not camp. As it turned out, they would never camp again, for as Zane's party headed into a deep, narrow canyon between two shelving escarpments of cracked sandstone boulders, they found seven of the nine posse riders and their horses lying smashed to bloody pulps beneath the rocks and boulders that had been loosed from one of the ridges.

The killings had occurred about a day ago, judging by the state of the carcasses after the carrion eaters had been at them. They were still at them. The canyon was aswarm with quarreling buzzards and coyotes that pranced among the rocks on the sides of the ridges, tongues hanging, eyes bright with the feeding frenzy. They'd likely been hard at work in the canyon bottom, fighting with the buzzards, before they'd heard the approach of the four riders and scrambled away.

The buzzards were more persistent. Some refused to leave the bodies, flapping their ragged, dusty black wings in challenge, or flying awkwardly onto boulders nearby to bark and curse the interlopers, their proprietary eyes sharp and wicked.

No one said anything as they weaved their horses around the dead men and their dead mounts and the boulders now nearly jamming the canyon. Zane's casket-carrying coffin scraped against the rocks, occasionally getting hung up until Zane clucked to General Lee and nudged it free. He was riding point, the others riding Indian-file behind him, when he jerked back on the palomino's reins, slid his cross-draw pistol from its holster, and raised the piece, clicking back the hammer.

He loosened his trigger finger. A man sat atop a flat-topped boulder with his back to the scarp behind him. His legs were stretched straight out before him, the badly worn, pointed toes of his boots tipped slightly to each side. He was dressed in dusty denims and a canvas coat.

His head had been hacked off of his shoulders.

The head was now resting in his lap, cradled in his arms as though its owner was afraid he might lose it.

28

THE WINGED DEMON RETURNS

THE EYES of the disembodied head, still wide in horror, stared out over Zane as though at the dead man's own killers among the rocks on the other side of the canyon. The head's thick, chapped lips were stretched back from scraggly teeth. He was missing one eyetooth. He wore a three-day growth of black beard and a deep gash below his left eye.

He also wore a dusty, faded-yellow Stetson with the front brim pinned to the crown. Several buzzards and a lone hawk circled above the corpse. One buzzard was perched atop the man's shoulders, probing the gap where the man's head had been and where now only blood and viscera shone. The bird turned its ugly eyes on Zane and gave a challenging squawk, splaying one wing and shifting its weight from one foot to the other.

"Mother of God," Hathaway said behind Zane.

"No, it's Day Summerville," said Jesse. "Ghoul hunter from over Nevada way." He clucked fatefully. "Told me as he was leavin' the Rincon just before that *puta* bitch came in and turned into a mountain lion that he was fixin' to settle down, go back home to Winnemucca, and get himself hitched to a half-Mojave gal with big, pillowy teats."

The Missourian spat a runny quid against the face of the boulder on which Day Summerville sat.

Zane nudged General Lee ahead, and they rode down the twisting corridor and up a steep grade where the walls drew back and they were suddenly out on a broad flat once more, heading for the cut in the mountain range that would take them to the next valley and the Lobo Negros beyond.

They came to an old lava field with what appeared to be an ancient Indian trail cut through it, angling toward the Negros rearing blackly and jaggedly in the west. It appeared the only route through the field of sharp-edged and jumbled boulders that had likely spewed from the top of the Negros millions of years ago, when the volcanic cones had blown their proverbial stacks. Zane put General Lee onto the trail, looking around cautiously, caressing the trigger of his Henry repeater that he held across his saddlebows. His crossbow and quivers hung from lanyards down his saddle skirt.

When they approached a keyhole-like notch in a low ridge, Zane checked General Lee down again sharply and grimaced. The others rode up around him, following his gaze to the man tied to a gnarled paloverde along the right side of the trail, just before the trail entered the tunnel-like canyon.

The man was naked and sun-seared a bright, blazing pink. His hands were tied behind the tree, as were his ankles. He'd been cut up bad—long, deep, torturous slices. It was hard to tell for all the blood, but he appeared to be missing his privates, and he'd been gutted.

"Well, well, well—what have we here?" Angel said grimly. "Another warning to anyone dusting those killers' trail?"

"Looks that way, sweet Marshal," Jesse said. "If you

need comforting, I'd like to be the first to volunteer my services."

"Shut up, James."

"Hold on." Zane swung down from General Lee's back

"What is it?" Hathaway said.

"Thought I seen him move."

The big ghoul hunter tramped up the steep, short trail to the ledge of sand and rocks upon which the paloverde grew, its thin, slender leaves flashing silver in the breeze, which also blew the tied man's straw-yellow, coarse blond hair about his forehead, his chin tipped to his thin, bloody chest.

Zane stood before the man, whose age it was impossible to tell. He reeked heavily of blood and viscera and urine. He'd been cut up bad, but most of the cuts except the one that had disemboweled him were only an inch or so deep. He was about five and a half feet tall, and Zane could see chin whiskers a shade darker than his hair, though he couldn't see much else about his face until he reached up with his right hand and used his index finger to shove the man's head back against the tree.

The head jerked. The skinny, blood-matted chest rose slightly. The eyes fluttered, opened to slits. They were cobalt blue and dark and pain-racked.

"Pl . . . please," he rasped, barely loudly enough for Zane to hear. "Kill me . . . !"

Zane grimaced and took one involuntary step back. He turned to Angel, who sat her paint beside General Lee. "Crossbow!" A gunshot would have been heard for miles around.

She reached over and grabbed his bow, knocked an arrow to it, and tossed the weapon up to Zane. He grabbed it one-handed, aimed, and drilled the silver-tipped shaft through the man's chest and into the tree behind him. The missile crunched through the man's breastbone. The fletched tip quivered.

The man's head shook as though he'd caught a sudden chill, coarse hair sliding this way and that across his eyes. His chin dipped one last time to his chest.

"Those fucking killers," said Hathaway. "I sure can't wait to drill some forty-four slugs through those bastards' cold, black hearts." He cast his molasses-eyed gaze at Zane. "What was the point of that? Huh? Will you tell me? I know 'Paches do it, but . . ." He let his voice trail off in bitter frustration.

"They did it for the same reason the Apaches do it," Zane said, long-striding down the slope and lashing the crossbow to his saddle. "To scare the hell out of us, make us think hard about following. Which means," he added, peering through the keyhole notch, "that we must be damn close to the Angels' destination. Best proceed with extra caution."

He swung back into the leather and nudged General Lee ahead once more, Angel falling in behind the bouncing, rattling casket, Hathaway behind her, and Jesse bringing up the rear. As the Missouri outlaw entered the keyhole notch, he lifted his Spencer's barrel to scratch his cheeks, his pale eyes bright with eager anticipation. To Zane glancing back at him, he almost looked as though he were about to break out in hysterical laughter.

Zane turned his head forward again as General Lee carried him out the other side of the keyhole and they found themselves in another canyon cut into the side of a steep slope rising to the left and straight ahead, on the canyon's other side. A narrow trail hugged the side of the slope to Zane's left. The trail followed the rim of the canyon to the other side, then switchbacked up the far side to the edge of a massive block of steeply shelving sandstone crowning the ridge crest.

Zane gigged the Appy on into the broad canyon, saw several steep, rocky hills around him, between him and the mountain's far side. Another trail snaked off across the canyon floor to Zane's right, rising and falling out of sight for a time before reappearing in the far-northeastern distance, curling around the base of the steep ridge and disappearing around its side.

Nearby, a roadrunner made a red flash as it darted out from behind a low, rocky knoll covered in greasewood, and crossed the trail before disappearing into a patch of Spanish bayonet and rocks on the other side.

Zane swung down from General Lee's back. Hathaway dismounted his mule, and the two strode around, looking for sign. Hathaway crouched, grabbed a chunk of horse dung, and sniffed it.

"Rained last night here, likely compromised the Angels' sign. Musta come through here, though, as I found a couple horse apples like this one along our backtrail a ways."

"Split up," Zane said, remounting and turning General Lee down the canyon floor to the right.

Hathaway followed him. Angel turned to follow the trail hugging the slope and switchbacking up the far ridge, and Jesse reluctantly followed the marshal. "Don't see why I have to follow her," he groused, "when she could so easily shoot me out of my saddle and say I was beggin' for it."

"Wouldn't put it past her," Zane agreed.

"What the hell's that?" Hathaway said behind him.

Zane had heard it, too—a heavy *whoosh*ing that sounded all too familiar, and which caused a cold hand to reach into Zane's belly and twist his stomach hard. He looked up. A winged creature, little larger than a golden eagle from this distance, curved around the far-right side of the ridge crest and began descending. Quickly, it grew larger, its large wings flapping slowly, heavily, long tail curling out behind it like a rudder.

"Ah, no," Zane complained as the dragon rushed toward them.

He glanced behind him at Angel and Jesse following

the trail along the side of the canyon. "Take cover! Our winged friend is back!" As Angel and Jesse looked toward where the big ghoul hunter had been pointing, Zane pointed down canyon ahead of him and to his right, where a pile of cabin-sized boulders all jumbled together offered the only cover for him and Hathaway.

"Come on, Al—let's head for them rocks!"

Hathaway glanced once more at the dragon that was now within two hundred yards and winging toward him and Zane fast, eyes blazing like sunlit gold. "I'll race ye!"

Zane pulled General Lee off the trail and down the grade toward the boulders. Hathaway's mule brayed indignantly and thumped along toward Zane on the ghoul hunter's left. They gained the rocks at nearly the same time, leaping down from their saddles. Quickly, they led their mounts into a narrow notch between the boulders and the southern ridge, tying them both to spindly shrubs.

Zane ran back and grabbed his Gatling gun and a cartridge belt out of the casket. Hathaway was climbing up the rocks, breathing hard and hauling himself up one boulder at a time.

Zane climbed frantically up behind him. The *whoosh*ing was growing louder. The big beast's wings were creaking and flapping like giant flags.

As Zane scrambled up into the rocks that afforded plenty of niches to hide from the dragon's flames, he saw the beast itself as it bore down on the escarpment, its gold eyes blinking slowly, fiercely, flames beginning to spiral out of its mouth and nostrils. Zane shoved Hathaway into a notch between two of the stacked boulders. As he threw himself into the same notch, he felt the rush of heat behind him, heard the beast's enraged bugling. Belly down in the gravel between two slab-sided boulders, his Gatling beside him, he saw the orange burst of flames hammering just outside his and Hathaway's hiding place.

Fifty feet below, General Lee whinnied shrilly though

the horse was likely safe in his and the mule's deep, well-protected gap. The mule brayed raucously.

Outside the notch, flames leaped and coiled. Tendrils licked a couple of feet into the gap, like living things trying to reach Zane and the Army scout. They disappeared as suddenly as they'd appeared, leaving only smoke and the heavy smell of charred rock and foliage.

Zane looked at Hathaway. The scout's eyes were large as he stared back out of the notch. He'd lost his hat, and sweat trickled down his dark forehead and bearded cheeks. "That hydrophobic polecat with wings nearly cooked us like spitted jackrabbits!"

Zane grabbed the Gatling gun. He caught a glimpse of the bandolier he'd slung around his neck and shoulder, and cursed. He'd meant to grab a bandolier of silver, but in his haste he'd grabbed one of the lead slugs. What the hell, he thought. Dragons weren't his trade. He had no idea if any kind of slug would kill one.

Sliding the big gun behind him, he scrambled back out of the notch.

"Best stay in here!" Hathaway warned. "You ain't never gonna kill it even with that bullet belcher!"

Outside of the notch, Zane rose to his knees and perused the sky. The dragon was just then winging over the southern ridge, over and beyond the keyhole through which he and the others had entered the canyon. A second later, it disappeared on the ridge's other side.

Most likely, it would be back.

Zane shouldered the Gatling gun and began crawling up the boulders above him, grabbing the edges of the rocks and hoisting himself, grunting and groaning and using his legs to push, his arms to pull. Finally, he gained the top rock that was slightly slanted but that offered a good view of the canyon and the ridges all around.

He glanced to his left, saw the dragon banking steeply in the southwest, to his left, and begin winging back toward him. He couldn't see either Angel or Jesse. A limestone knob jutted out of the western ridge, with towers and parapets of wind-sculpted rock. Likely they'd holed up in there.

Quickly, keeping an eye on the fast-approaching dragon, Zane set up the tripod, spreading the wooden legs and mounting the gun atop the platform. He twisted the locking nut in place and rammed a cartridge belt into the cylinder, hearing the satisfying, hollow click of the first cartridge slipping neatly into the breech.

Zane swung the gun to the west and crouched low, aiming over the barrel. Gatling guns sacrificed distance and accuracy for the volume of shots and power they expelled in a short amount of time. He had to wait for the critter to get in close enough to do some damage, but not so close it would turn Zane into a roasted coffee bean before he could kill it.

If bullets of any kind could even kill such a hellish monstrosity . . .

The dragon winged toward him, black smoke curling from its nostrils. The wings flapped, making their sinewy sounds, like unoiled door hinges. A bugling cry rose from the long, down-canted snout, and the gold eyes pulsated, drilling straight across the hundred-yard gap now between itself and its quarry.

"Ugliest damn bird I ever seen," Zane muttered through gritted teeth as he began turning the wooden crank furiously.

29

DRAGON SLAYER

THE GATLING FAIRLY EXPLODED, leaping on its legs as the roaring canister spit smoke and fire at the great beast closing on it fast. Echoes hammered off the surrounding peaks.

Bam-bam-bam-bam-bam-bam-bam-bam-bam!

Zane cursed as the beast kept coming. The bullets seemed to bounce off its nose and forehead and even the two golden eyes. Determined, Zane kept cranking as the dragon winged in, dangerously close.

Bam-bam-bam-bam-bam-bam-bam-bam-bam!

"Get down!" Hathaway shouted from below, the scout's voice barely audible above the beast's angry wails and the whoosh of its giant wings. As it drew within thirty yards, the smoke curling from its nostrils, there was an orange flash and then fire began jetting from its nose and mouth. Zane had already grabbed the Gatling gun and fairly hurled himself over the side of the crag, his boot slipping on a stone ledge below. As the fire leaped like an orange blanket onto the slanted rock he'd just vacated, he rolled off the ledge and hit the boulder below it hard on his left shoulder, the Gatling crashing down beside him.

The air left the ghoul hunter's lungs in one massive grunt. He blinked rapidly.

As his vision cleared, he saw the dragon sort of twist and pivot in the air. Unsteadily? Hard to tell. Now it banked sharply left, heading toward the tall northern ridge mantled far above the beast with the sandstone caprock. The dragon continued to bank, still rising and then gradually dropping as it turned away from the ridge and careened toward the limestone knob where Zane figured Angel and Jesse were hunkered.

Apparently, the beast was going to make another try for Zane.

The ghoul hunter, buoyed by the possibility he'd done some damage to the winged ghoul and wanting to give it another shot, shouldered the battered gun and heaved himself back up the rocks to the slanted, scorched boulder at the crag's top. The rock beneath his moccasin souls was hot. He could feel the heat through his buckskins as he knelt and spread the tripod's legs once more.

He turned the canister toward the west, where the winged beast was just now banking against the lower edge of the northern ridge's caprock, and sinking back down toward the canyon.

"Come on, you devil," Zane said. "Let's do-si-do around the old oak tree one more time! *Whaddaya say!*"

The dragon dropped down over an edge of the limestone knob. As it dropped lower, one wing brushing the side of a stone parapet, a slender figure appeared suddenly atop that same rock formation. Just as suddenly, the figure kicked out away from the rock, scissoring its legs, its hat tumbling down its back, and leaped onto the dragon's back and dropped belly down against the scaly hide.

The sun flashed off bloodred hair streaming out in the wind.

Zane lifted his head from the Gatling's canister, and blinked, awestruck. "Crazy bitch!"

As the dragon angled toward Zane, the winged beast tipped to one side and then the other, its golden eyes not looking as bright as before. If a dragon could look confused, this one looked that way, as if detecting a weight on its back but unable to comprehend what it was or where it had come from. The dragon, in its confusion, tipped northward and slightly off Zane's course. As it did, the ghoul hunter watched in horror as the redhead atop the beast's back climbed up behind the massive, green head.

"Angel, for Christ's sakes," Zane shouted, lunging to his feet and cupping his hands around his mouth. "Get down from there, you cork-headed fool!"

Balancing on her knees, red hair streaming out in the wind, Angel unsheathed her long, silver Spanish sword from the scabbard hanging down her right, leather-clad leg, just behind one of her holstered six-guns. The beast was still angling slightly away from Zane, between him and the northern cliff wall.

As it came within fifty yards, he watched, lower jaw hanging, as Angel rose up on her knees and raised the down-angled sword in both her gloved hands. She and the dragon were so close to him now, the dragon suddenly seeming oblivious to him, that he saw Angel's green eyes open wide in determination and her fine jaws draw taut as she thrust downward with both hands.

The sword plunged into a ring of what appeared relatively soft tissue between the beast's head and neck. Angel threw herself down and forward, heaving with all her weight on the handle and burying the blade nearly hilt deep. As she did, and as she and the winged beast flew past Zane, whom the strong wind of the massive wings blew back on his butt, the dragon threw his head back and grimaced and loosed a high-pitched, snarling wail that bounced like thunder off the near rims.

Beneath the wail and the rush of the wind, Zane could hear Angel screaming, "Die, you son of a bitch! *Die!*"

Her scream as well as the dragon's wail dwindled as the beast flew off to Zane's right and pitched steeply groundward. For a few seconds, it looked as though the dragon would plunge headfirst into the canyon bottom.

Zane's heart was like a turnip in his throat.

The beast tipped slightly to one side of a low pile of boulders from which several cedars grew, then gave another defiant wail and, with a violent thrash of his tail, righted himself and hammered the air with his wings.

He gained altitude. Because of the distance and the shadows on that side of the canyon, Zane could no longer see Angel as the dragon climbed, launching himself north toward the steep ridge looming there. High and higher he climbed, growing smaller and smaller against the runneled and crenellated side of the sandstone cliff pocked here and there with talus slides.

Gradually, he closed on the cliff, rising toward the bulging sandstone cap.

That he wasn't going to make it became clear as Zane saw the ridge fairly swallow the giant beast a half second before the dragon crashed headlong into the sheer rock wall. Where the giant's body once had been, now a great burst of orange flames roiled outward from the cliff, consuming the still-flicking, green-and-yellow tail.

A second after the beast had smashed into the cliff, the thunder of what sounded like a barrel of dynamite detonating reached the ghoul hunter's ears. At the same time, through the roiling flames bursting outward and down from the side of the cliff, Zane saw bits and pieces of the body, including its wings free-falling toward the canyon bottom. He couldn't help watching for a slender figure clad in leather and with long, red hair. . . .

As the torn hulk of the dead beast continued falling and burning and smoking, Zane left the Gatling gun where it was and, wheeling, began climbing, half leaping and half falling down the side of the escarpment. He was halfway down when he saw Hathaway standing on a ledge of rock and leaning outward to stare toward the north cliff face. The scout looked at Zane, his eyes and mouth big as he said, "What the hell happened?"

"Fool girl killed herself," was all Zane could say, breathless, as he continued dropping down the escarpment, skipping from one boulder to another.

Ten feet from the ground, he leaped the rest of the way, landing flat-footed, spreading his arms for balance, and took off running around the side of the scarp, lifting his knees and arms high, moccasins crunching brush and gravel and pummeling sage and low cedars. He didn't know where he was running exactly—generally, toward the dragon, but as he ran he turned his head this way and that, hoping to find Angel alive somewhere among the rocks and brush littering the canyon floor.

But the brunt of his attention was fixed upslope, where the great burning hulk of the dragon was just now tumbling in pieces both large and small to the base of the cliff face, burning among the strewn boulders. He ran hard, mindless of his aching lungs and burning chest. A big chunk of the dragon teetered at the base of the cliff, then tumbled toward him, and as it burned and rolled awkwardly down the slope, he could see that it was one of the demon's wings. Rolling and burning behind the wing was the tip of the tail.

He ran to his right, avoiding the burning appendages by several yards. The scorching heat of the burning carcass growing intensely before him, like that of a vast blacksmith's forge, and knowing he could go no farther without being burned himself, he stopped suddenly, fifty yards from the cliff. He leaned forward, hands to his thighs, wheezing as he sucked breaths into his aching lungs and stared in horror at the several leaping fires.

"Red," he said, managing only a raking whisper. "For Christ's sake, Red, why in the hell'd you make such a dunderheaded play?"

Brush crackled behind him. He froze, staring straight ahead, pricking his ears.

"Damn," a familiar voice said among the crackling weeds and crunching gravel. "Anyone got a drink? This dragon-slayin' is a mite hard on a girl."

Zane wheeled, wide-eyed.

Angel stood about thirty yards downslope from him, her hair a dusty, weed- and seed-flecked mess about her bare shoulders. Her leather vest was twisted low and to one side, causing one large breast to bulge up farther than the other. Generally, she was dirty and disheveled, and her scarred face was scraped and bruised, as were her long, bare arms, the knees of her leather pants torn. But she was all in one piece.

And she was alive.

With a great burst of raw energy mixed with overwhelming emotion, Zane cursed and ran down the slope to her. He wrapped his big arms around her in a savage bear hug, lifted her two feet off the ground, and swung her in a complete circle before setting her back down. "Goddamn, you crazy redhead, I thought for sure you'd bought the ranch and the whole damn remuda!"

He wrapped his arms around her neck, and planted a hard kiss on her cheek. He placed his hands on her shoulders and held her away from him, looking her up and down to make sure she was all right.

"How in the hell did you make it out of that? You a cat or somethin'?"

Pale and exhausted, Angel blew a strand of hair out of her face and hooked a thumb over her right shoulder. "I sorta rolled off the side of that critter when I figured it was about to crash. Skidded down a few of the trees sticking out from that scarp yonder, and landed in a patch of buckbrush."

She wrinkled her nose and looked up the slope toward where the dragon continued to burn. "Contrary to the fairy tales we all read as sprouts, those dragons are repugnant damn critters. Close up, they smell like rotten fish."

She spat in disgust and ran the back of a gloved hand across her mouth.

Zane wrapped an arm around her shoulders from behind, and turned her around. Hathaway was leading both General Lee and his mule toward Angel and the ghoul hunter. From across the canyon, Jesse James was galloping atop his buckskin while leading Angel's paint, pumping a fist in the air and howling madly.

"Come on," Zane said. "I'll buy ya a drink."

"I could use one."

They walked several yards along the canyon bottom.

"Look at that," Angel said, glancing at the sky over the southern ridge. "Damn near a full moon."

Zane looked at the big, pale orb, large as a watch face in the sky fading toward a dusky gray green, and nearly full except for a loss of definition along its lower left side. Like the edge of an old, worn nickel. In twenty-four hours, that blurred edge would be clearly defined.

"Well, look at that," Zane said, dropping his arm away from the redhead's shoulder. "I do believe you're right, Red."

30

FULL MOON RISING

HATHAWAY'S resonant voice was close in Zane's ear. "Dawn, Uriah. Rise and shine."

Zane opened his eyes as the scout went over and crouched beside Angel's still form on the other side of the campfire that was a low mound of umber coals. The ghoul hunter perused the sky touched with periwinkle blue between the jutting, black velvet peaks in the east. No sign of the moon, of course.

That damn moon.

He shook the thought from his mind. He'd beaten the wolf. The only reason he felt it stirring inside him again was because he'd started doubting himself after being so repulsed by the Hell's Angels. He'd beaten it back for nearly a year, and he'd even almost stopped thinking about it. He couldn't think about it today, either. He had plenty of other problems on his mind, the biggest being the need to run down the Hell's Angels and their Mexican witch guide before they accomplished whatever hellish task they intended here in the Lobo Negros.

What Elaina Baranova had told Zane made him think that the stakes were higher than he could ever imagine. . . .

He yawned, sat up, ran his hands back through his

tangled mane of black hair, and looked around at the horses picketed nearby. Zane's party had set up camp near the scarp from which the ghoul hunter had fired on the dragon, as it had been too late to continue their trek. Besides, Angel needed rest after her ordeal, which she'd worn well despite her scrapes and bruises.

To his right, Hathaway crouched over the figure of Jesse James lying curled on his side, head resting on the elbow bent beneath him, softly snoring beneath his two wool Army blankets. Cautiously, Hathaway clamped a foot down on the gun and holster lying near Jesse, then nudged the Missourian's shoulder with the butt of his Winchester.

As expected, the outlaw jerked with a start, throwing one hand out toward the six-shooter jutting from the holster around which the cartridge belt was coiled. His hand grabbed the top of Hathaway's low-heeled cavalry boot. He froze, looked up slowly, a little chagrined, to see the dark face peering down at him.

Jesse smiled sheepishly.

"That's the lurch of a wanted man," Angel observed as she knelt, rolling up her blankets. "Don't worry, James—you won't be wanted much longer."

"Oh, I'll always be wanted, Marshal. By good-lookin' women, 'specially. Always have been."

"You flatter yourself."

"Someone has to." Jesse yawned and stretched.

Zane rolled his own blankets quickly and tied the roll closed with rawhide straps he'd sewn into the wool. He glanced at Jesse, who'd crawled toward the fire with his empty cup and used a leather swatch to lift the coffeepot from a flat rock in the coals, and shake it.

"Well, you got us to the Lobo Negros, Jesse," Zane said with reluctant gratitude. "You got some vision about where we trail from here?"

Jesse poured the scorched, smoking brew into his tin cup, then sat back on his butt, looking over the cup's rim toward the northern ridge where the dead dragon had finally stopped smoldering though the rotten-fish stench remained. "Hell, I ain't no witch. Now, my granny could lead you right to where the Hell's Angels are right now. Me—I didn't get that much of the gift. I just seen the wolf's head cappin' that peak there." He lifted his chin to inspect the ridge towering over them, capped in weathered sandstone.

Zane followed Jesse's gaze. "I don't see the head."

"It's back farther. Can't see it from this angle. Juts up from the other side of this here ridge, forms a ridge all its own. I been keepin' a watch on it as we approached the range."

Jesse blew on his coffee, sipped, and shook his head. "Them killers is gonna rue the day they killed my brother, Frank . . . Cole . . . all the others." Tears of rage and grief glistened in the outlaw's pale eyes. "Them's all the family I have except a few stashed here and there in the hills back home—all beaten an' broken by the massacre o' Lincoln's"—he gritted his teeth—"mercenaries."

"Well, you'll get your chance at what's left of those mercenaries," Zane said, donning his hat and adding a few chunks of piñon to the fire. "Just don't forget who your enemies are. Might cause me to make the same mistake."

"I scouted north last night, before good dark." Hathaway had emptied the coffeepot and was adding fresh water from his canteen. "Found a coupla piles of horse apples them spooks didn't bother to hide."

"Probably figured the dragon would keep their backtrail clear of shadowers," Angel said, tossing a pouch of Arbuckles to the scout, who caught it against his chest.

"I 'spect we won't have much trouble followin' 'em. From what I seen, just north of here there ain't too many trail options. Rough country, all up and down, steep ridges of sandstone and granite. Not much water, neither. Just a few trails between narrow canyons. Devil's playground kind of place."

"Well, hell," Zane said, grabbing his rifle and blanket roll and walking toward their picketed mounts. "No reason to burn daylight here, then."

"There ain't much daylight to speak of, Uriah." Angel sat back against her saddle, watching him.

Zane glanced toward the lilac sky showing between black ridges in the east, then continued striding toward the horses, casting a look in the direction the full moon would rise. "There's enough."

Behind him, Hathaway glanced at Angel and shrugged. As he began pouring the coffee water back into his canteen, he sighed. "I reckon we can brew a pot later, when we stop to rest the hosses."

"What's his hurry?" Jesse wanted to know as he sipped the last of the brewed coffee without chagrin, glancing over his shoulder as Zane walked away. "Might have poor luck, trailin' in the dark."

Angel kicked dirt on the fire, then lifted one of her six-guns from its holster. "I reckon Uriah's got it right," she said, also casting an uneasy glance toward where the full moon would rise. "There'll be light enough soon." She rolled the cylinder across her forearm, imagining each of the silver slugs nestled in their chambers, then sheathed the piece, grabbed her rifle, saddlebags, and bedroll, and strode off toward the horses.

Only a few hours' ride ahead rode the Hell's Angels and Ravenna Gonzalez-Vara. At midmorning, riding along a narrow, crooked, steep-walled canyon, Ravenna glanced at the sky.

"Chico, where are you, damnit?" She noted the wary tone in her voice and didn't like it.

Riding to her left, the other three riding single-file behind, Charlie said, "What's the matter, *chiquita*?"

"Chico. I haven't seen him since just after I managed to

conjure him again finally. And I had a dark dream last night."

"About the dragon?"

"*Sí.* I think so. I don't like it that he's not near."

"Thought he was supposed to be out interceptin' folks who might be shadowin' us."

"*Sí, sí.* But I should see him. I conjured him. I can call him back when I have the power. I have the power now, and I called him back this morning, after my dream. To reassure myself that . . ."

The horses' shod hooves clacked on the stony canyon floor. A hawk sat on a small thumb of rock protruding from the two-thousand-foot cliff on the right side of the canyon, the raptor's head turning slowly, tracking the four men and the black-haired woman walking their horses along the rocky trail partly shaded by the eastern ridge blocking the climbing sun.

"To reassure yourself what?" She offered Charlie a cockeyed grin. "You think somethin' might have happened to that winged demon? I don't think so, *chiquita*. When you conjured him, you outdone yourself and any witch I ever known here or in the Old Country."

Ravenna lowered her glance from the rims of the canyon walls and turned her head forward once more. She frowned darkly, not a customary expression for her. It worried Charlie a little, and he laughed to cover it. "Come on, *chiquita*. Chico's fine. Maybe he's taking siesta."

"*Sí.*" Ravenna rode along, brooding, worried. "That's probably it, Charlie." She cast her anxious glance to the right, where an old, massive rockslide formed a jagged hill against the north wall of the canyon, starting just below a great gap in the wall, where an earthquake had likely caused the cliff to bulge and drop.

"Whoa."

Ravenna stopped her gelding and threw up a hand for the others to follow suit as she perused the massive slide, pulling her nickering horse's head up, the bit clacking in its teeth.

"Now what is it?" Charlie was impatient, edgy. "God-damn, girl, you're startin' to make me nervous, and I don't *get* nervous."

"I saw a flash up there in those rocks. Might have been a rifle."

The others turned to follow her stricken gaze.

"You sure?" Charlie asked.

"Of course I'm sure. You think I'm seeing things?"

"I don't know," Charlie said. "You're worried about a fucking dragon it'd take a whole ton of dynamite to put a dent in. . . ."

"Fuck you, Charlie!"

Snarling, she rammed the dull points of her spurs into her gelding's flanks, and galloped thirty yards to the base of the canyon's north wall. She leaped off the horse's back while the mount was still moving and onto one of the boulders comprising the rockslide. Cocking her Winchester one-handed, swinging the barrel up and down, she leaped like a mountain goat up the slide, picking her way quickly, black hair dancing across her shoulders and flashing in the golden sunlight flooding that side of the canyon.

She climbed a hundred feet up the slide, leaped onto a high, narrow boulder and down the other side, into a niche among the rocks. She dropped to a knee and scoured the niche's floor.

Recent boot tracks scored the floury dirt. There was something else. Ravenna reached down, picked up the half-smoked cigar butt, and held it up to her face. She rolled it between her fingers.

Still warm. And store-bought.

Ravenna dropped the butt, rose, and, unholstered her ivory-gripped Remington. She followed the prints back down the canyon along the slide, until they disappeared among the tumbled boulders. She stared out over the side of the slide, seeing nothing but more rock. Whoever had been here a few minutes ago was gone.

She holstered the pistol and retraced her steps back down the slide to the canyon floor. As she walked out to where her horse stood, ground-tied, she glanced over at Charlie, Lucky, One-Eye, and Curly Joe. They were all staring tensely up canyon, all unsheathing their rifles, except Curly Joe. Now Curly Joe unsheathed his saddle-ring carbine, and whistled softly through his crooked teeth.

Ravenna swung up onto her gelding's back and neck-reined the horse around to face up canyon. She stiffened in her saddle, that recent dark expression returning as she saw the six riders approaching from fifty yards away, angling out away from the a bend in the north canyon wall. They were little, dark men with long, black hair in breech-clouts and deerskin vests and high-topped deerskin moccasins. They were like living shadows astride horses.

They carried knocked bows in their wiry, muscular arms, holding them out flat in front of them while also holding their mounts' braided hide reins. Swords of what appeared to be gold dangled from beaded sashes encircling their waists.

The riders were so incredibly tattooed it was hard to distinguish anything else about their features. All their horses—rugged, short-legged mustangs—were also marked with tribal designs, with painted rings around their eyes and talisman designs unfamiliar to Ravenna etched across their breasts.

The witch was vaguely confused. Whoever had left the cigar stub in the rocks had not been one of the natives approaching her group now. These men wouldn't buy their tobacco in any store. Were she and Charlie being stalked by a white man as well as by these natives?

Charlie glanced wryly at Ravenna. "You didn't say

there'd be 'Paches out here, *chiquita*." His voice echoed loudly off the stone walls.

"Those aren't Apaches, Charlie." Ravenna's voice was pitched low with alarm. Fire flared in her veins as dream visions flashed behind her eyes.

She jerked a savage look at the wolf pack leader. "We must kill them now, Charlie," she screamed. *"Kill them now!"*

31

THE LOST TRIBE AND A VOICE ON THE WIND

A CHILL WIND blew from down canyon against Zane's back, blowing his sombrero forward. Clamping the hat down low on his head, he turned to squint behind him along the narrow, steep-walled corridor of striated granite, basalt, and sandstone, the jagged-edged rim poking like gnarled witch's fingers at a sky tan with windblown dust. The dust swirled toward him along the canyon floor.

"Lousy luck," he said. "This wind's gonna rub out the Angels' sign."

"Don't need it."

Zane turned to Hathaway, who was staring off the canyon's right side. The short, stocky man dismounted and led his mule over to a boulder leaning against the canyon's southern wall. He squatted beside the boulder and placed his gloved right hand against the side of the rock.

"What is it?" Angel asked, lifting her voice above the wind keening.

"Wolf's head carved in this rock!"

Zane and Angel both swung down from their saddles and walked over to stand near Hathaway. Jesse did not dismount, as his leg was hurting, but he gigged his buckskin over. The scout was running his right index finger along a crude wolf's head about the size of a man's open palm chiseled into the lower-middle section of the boulder. "I seen one a while back, figured it was just some kind o' rock painting like you see all over the Southwest. But now I reckon it was somethin' more."

"Prospectors often use such signs to lead the way back to a remote digging," Zane said. "In case they can't remember where it is exactly, or they lose their maps."

"Sorta like Hansel and Gretel layin' out breadcrumbs," Jesse said.

"You think that's what this is?" Angel asked. "A prospector's signpost?"

Hathaway straightened, pulled his hat brim down snug on his head. "I reckon we'll know if we keep heading down this canyon and find another one."

They mounted up and continued along the canyon, the building wind blowing their horses' tails between their hind legs and keeping a nearly constant curtain of grit and tumbleweeds ensconcing the riders. Where the canyon corridor forked, the three riders scrutinized the cliff walls.

"There," Zane said, reining General Lee toward the north canyon wall, nearest the right fork in the corridor.

Another wolf's head had been chiseled into the granite and limestone. It was fainter than the other one but still recognizable—a definite signpost. Zane gigged General Lee along the right corridor, the others falling in behind him, Angel riding to his left. Riding to Hathaway's right, Jesse yelled, "Anyone else feel like someone's watchin' us?"

Zane glanced back at the Missourian riding crouched in his saddle and tightening his jaws against the gale.

"You see somethin', Jesse?"

"In your head or elsewhere?" Angel added with a faintly wry note.

"Nah." Jesse glanced over his left shoulder, then swung his head forward again. "I just got a creepy-crawly feelin' between my shoulders, like someone's starin' a bull's-eye on it." He managed to turn it into a joke, grinning at Angel. "Used to think it was one Marshal James Coffin. Couldn't be him now, though, could it? Not in the daylight!" He stretched his lips wider, showing his small, yellow teeth.

Zane glanced at Angel. Even through the windblown grit, and even though she tried hard to hide it, he could see the injured look in her eyes. And the rage. He felt it himself, and before he fully realized what he was doing, he'd drawn the Colt Navy from his cross-draw holster. The click of the hammer was nearly drowned by the wind.

He aimed the pistol at Jesse's face. "I do believe you've outworn your welcome, James. Time to ride on over the divide with Cole and Frank an' the boys."

"Hold on!" Angel rode over and nudged Zane's right arm down. "I'll fight my own battles, mister. And we're going to need all the guns we have against the Angels. If he makes it through the battle, I want the pleasure of watching him hang."

She reined Cisco around and gigged him on up the right-forking canyon. Hathaway cast his white-ringed gaze between Zane and Jesse. "Boys, boys, boys . . ."

Zane depressed the Colt's hammer and slid it back into its holster. As Hathaway gigged his mule after Angel, Zane held his hard gaze on that of Jesse James, whose pale eyes had grown uncustomarily apprehensive when he'd seen the big pistol bearing down on him.

"You keep riding her," the ghoul hunter warned the Missouri outlaw, "and not even she's gonna be able to save your worthless hide."

Jesse frowned, tipped his head to one side. "You an' her . . . ?"

"She goes her way; I go mine." Zane nudged his hat brim down once more, reined General Lee around, and put the big palomino into a trot along the right-forking canyon trail.

Not far ahead, Angel's and Hathway's mounts stood

riderless in the middle of the corridor. Angel and the scout were crouched over what looked like rubble from a collapsed cutbank littering the canyon's right side.

Zane rode over, was about to ask what had caught their interest, when he saw a bloody, brown, tattooed arm sticking out of the rubble. Beyond, a brown eyebrow peered up from its bed of loose, red dust and clay. Hathaway was looking into a horseshoe-shaped alcove cut into the canyon wall just beyond the collapsed cutbank.

He wandered around for a time, Angel following him, her red hair blowing wildly in the wind. Zane walked into the alcove, saw a few more bodies hastily tossed among the boulders that littered the alcove's floor.

"Three more," Angel said. "With the four someone tried to bury under the bank there, that makes six."

"Six who?" Zane crouched over one of the bodies—a young man wedged between two boulders, where he likely wouldn't be easily seen by someone passing through the main canyon. He wore crude deerskins with dyed designs that Zane had never seen. On the top of each of the young man's moccasins was a red wolf's head about as big around as a gold eagle coin.

"I was gonna say 'Paches," Hathaway said. "But I ain't never seen Apaches painted so." He stood over Zane, fists on his hips, and shook his head slowly. "I seen several of them wolf heads. One over there had it tattooed on his chest. Never heard of no 'Pache, Pima, Papago, Navajo, or Yaquis tribe with such a totem as that—just like the wolf heads we seen in the canyon yonder."

"Whoever they are," Zane said, "I see no firearms of any kind on 'em. Some bows and arrows." He brushed dust away from the leg of the young brave before him, uncovering a long, slender sheath with an engraved gold handle jutting up against the youth's sharp hip bone. He wrapped his hand around the handle and drew the sword, staring in wide-eyed awe at the solid gold, razor-edged blade.

All up and down the length of the blade had been etched the figures of wolves engaged in hunting or mauling various creatures—rabbits, deer, mountain lions, bears, and, most fascinating of all, faintly comical caricatures of fleeing humans.

"Here's another one," Angel said, holding the blade she'd found in both hands, staring down at it in wonder.

Jesse had dismounted when he'd seen the gold and was pulling up another sword from the dirt and gravel of the collapsed cutbank, grunting against the pain in his wounded thigh. He ran his hands down the blade he'd found, his eyes fairly dancing as he scrubbed away the grit and saw the pure, glistening gold beneath.

He shook his head and laughed. "Frank, this breaks my heart." Tears beaded in his eye corners. "It purely breaks my heart, brother, that you and Cole and the boys ain't here to see this."

Zane lowered the golden sword, and willed himself to let it drop back down where he'd found it. Even at such a dire time, gold had an intoxicating effect. One sword would probably be worth as much bounty money as he'd earned in the past five years.

"Leave 'em." He slapped his hands together. "We got more important work ahead of us."

"Leave gold?" Jesse laughed, tears now streaking the dust on his cheeks. "I don't think so! I'm gonna take me one of these here pigstickers in case we don't make it back this way. You know how much this is worth?"

"Think about Frank and Cole, Jesse," Angel said, knowing the way to the emotional Confederate's heart. "How would they feel—you droolin' over gold when their killers are still pounding the trail?"

Jesse looked at her, blinked the tears away, squinting against the dust blowing in under his hat brim. Angrily, he held the blade out before him in both hands. "You got a nasty side, Marshal." He dropped the sword, swung away as though it caused him great pain, and grabbed his buckskin's reins.

He'd just swung up into the leather when Zane, also walking toward his mount, Angel and Hathaway behind him, saw the outlaw flinch. In the grit haze kicked up by the wind, he thought he saw something sticking out of Jesse's back, just below his right shoulder. Jesse stiffened and lifted his chin, gritting his teeth.

"Gnah!"

His cry was obscured by the wind.

Zane froze. It saved his life. An arrow whistled through the air about six inches in front of his face and clattered against the rocks to his right. He jerked a look to his left where several horseback riders were galloping up the canyon toward him—five dark little men with long, black hair, all triggering arrows expertly as they rode. More arrows clattered among the rocks, while another slammed into the side of Hathaway's mule. The beast immediately began pitching and braying indignantly, though Zane had seen the arrow bounce off its stirrup and clatter onto the canyon floor.

"Company!" Zane shouted, palming both his Colt Navies, dropping to one knee, and beginning to trigger each pistol in turn.

He dropped one of the Indians with his first shot, as the brave leaped off his galloping mount—a lucky shot that sent the warrior spinning and cartwheeling to the ground, whooping wildly. The others commenced yowling then, as well, and Zane dropped another just as the man triggered an arrow that sliced just past the ghoul hunter's left cheek.

His bullet plunked through the brave's upper arm. As he reached for it with his other hand, dropping his bow, either Angel's or Hathaway's bullet plowed into the side of his head, blowing him back off his heels and laying him out, quivering. The fusillade of bullets was too much for the natives. The two survivors of the attack ran back down the canyon, one pausing only to trigger one more arrow before wheeling and sprinting off after the others and their fleeing, buck-kicking mustangs.

Zane holstered both his empty pistols and ran over to grab Jesse as the outlaw sagged dangerously backward and sideways over his skitter-stepping buckskin's right hip. Wrapping both arms around the outlaw, he pulled him easily out of the saddle; the wiry Missourian couldn't have weighed much more than a slightly hefty woman.

As Hathaway walked a ways down canyon to make sure their attackers were gone, Zane set Jesse down against the cliff wall, the outlaw grunting against the pain of the arrow fletched with brown and black hawk feathers protruding from his right shoulder, the stone point sticking out his back. Blood stained his denim jacket and duster.

"Leave it to a goddamn redskin to fill me with misery!" Jesse cried, kicking against the pain. "Pull the goddamn thing out, Zane! Pull it out!"

"If you'll hold still, I will."

Zane shoved one of the man's fumbling, flailing hands down, then with his own hand grabbed the six inches of arrow protruding out the man's back. With his other hand, he grabbed the front to hold it steady, then broke off the back part with a dull crack.

"Ahh!" Jesse kicked his legs and tightened every muscle. "Christ, could you give me some warnin'? We might have our differences, Uriah, but we're brothers of the Confederacy, fer cryin' out loud!"

Zane kept a firm hold on the front of the arrow and jerked it forward. It slid out smoothly, blood dribbling out from the hole it left in the outlaw's shoulder. Crouched on the other side of Jesse, Angel immediately stuffed the outlaw's own neckerchief into the hole, clamping it down hard.

Jesse said, "Oh, mercy!" His eyes closed, and his head sagged to one side as he lost consciousness.

A voice rose on the wind. "Confederates?"

There was a pause during which Zane thought the voice must have been a trick of the wind itself. He and Angel looked around, frowning.

The disembodied shout came again, louder this time, as though its owner was moving nearer from the opposite wall of the canyon. It was a man's voice, shrill with exasperation.

"Did you say Confederates?"

32

JERICHO TURNIPSEED

ZANE STRAIGHTENED TENSELY, quickly thumbing cartridges from his shell belt into one of his Colts. A figure appeared on the fire side of the canyon, materializing out of the blowing grit as he ran a sort of shambling, stumbling run, open fur coat slipping down his shoulders.

He held an old, rusted trapdoor Springfield carbine in one hand, barrel up. The gun was held together with wire and rawhide. He was tall and thin, and at first Zane thought he had no hat, but then he saw it dangling down between the man's shoulders, blowing in the wind.

Zane flipped his Colt's loading gate closed and spun the cylinder, holding the pistol halfway out from his belly, half threatening. "Hold it there!"

The man stopped about ten feet away. He had a long face and a bulging forehead. Thin, curly brown hair lay sparsely atop his head, blowing wildly. His eyes were yellow brown, incredulous. He held the rifle and his other hand out to each side in supplication. "I'm friendly if you folks are. I got me a good set of ears, and I thought someone mentioned Confederates!"

"Some of us are." Zane glanced at Angel, who stood a few feet to his left, caressing the .45 on her right hip with one hand, squinting into the grit at the raggedly clad stranger. A prospector, Zane thought. Desert rat. There was a bright, crazy cast to his brown eyes. No sane man would approach a party of strangers this far out in the high and rocky without considerably more caution than this gent had showed.

The man grinned and, ignoring Zane's uncocked Colt aimed at his belly, walked slowly forward. "Uriah Zane!"

Zane scowled, trying to place the man. A name came to him, swirling up from the gale of his distant past. "Jericho?"

The man laughed and clamped a hand thick and hairy as a bear's paw on the ghoul hunter's shoulder. "You remember after all these years!"

"For Christ's sakes—I figured you and your boys were all dead in the War."

"We'll talk later." Jericho looked both ways along the canyon, glanced from Zane to Angel and then to Jesse sitting unconscious, head to his shoulder, against the canyon wall. He gave a start when he saw Al Hathaway walk out of the windblown grit and hesitate, raising his rifle in both his hands and studying the stranger uncertainly.

"He's one of us," Zane said.

"Come on, then. Bring your injured friend there and you're horses. Ain't much time. There's more guardians where those there came from." He glanced out to where the dead Indian lay sprawled as though dropped from the sky. "And they'll be some piss-burned when they see how many they done lost in the past couple hours. They ain't a large tribe to begin with!"

In the corner of his left eye, Zane saw Angel glance at him apprehensively. He had to admit that while he'd grown up knowing Jericho Turnipseed as a good, God-fearing Carolinian who'd sharecropped on Zane's family's plantation before the War in which Jericho and his three sons had proudly enlisted, he hadn't seen the man since 'sixty-one, nearly fifteen years ago.

Men changed in less time than that, and the years had not been kind to his old friend, whose shoulders were stooped, legs skinny and bowed, eyes a little foggy. But Zane didn't see that he had much choice in the matter.

"It's all right," Zane told Angel, then swung around and hauled the unconscious Jesse James up and over his shoulder.

While Angel and Hathaway hurried out to grab the reins of their horses, the scout holding the bridle of Jesse's mount while Zane eased the unconscious Missourian over the buckskin's saddle, Jericho walked out into the canyon, holding his rifle up high across his chest as he shuttled his gaze up canyon and down, on the lookout for more—what had he'd called the dark-skinned warriors?

Guardians?

When Zane had Jesse secured, he led both the Missourian's horse and General Lee behind Jericho, who hop-skipped to the opposite canyon wall. Zane was ten feet from the wall when he saw that the wall was not solid. A crescent of thick rock jutted out from one side. Jericho beckoned to Zane and the others, then disappeared behind the crescent.

Zane stopped, frowning.

Jericho poked his head out behind the seven-foot-high wing of crenellated sandstone. "It's all right. Wide enough for your horses. I bring mine and a wagon through here all the time!"

He pulled his head back behind the rock again, and Zane looked behind it to see that there was a crooked corridor back there, twisting into the side of the cliff wall, wide enough for a couple of horses. He pulled the skittish General Lee around through the half-open door of sorts, having to throw a shoulder into the casket-carrying

Gatling gun to position it correctly to slip through without catching its wheels.

When General Lee was inside and moving freely, the wheels clattering behind him, Zane led Jesse's buckskin in behind him. Angel and Hathaway both followed, leading their own mounts, the mule braying raucously at the foreignness of this inner sanctum.

"Hold on," Jericho called from ahead, unseen in the darkness.

There was a scraping sound, the clatter of what sounded like a lantern mantle. A light grew slowly until Zane could make out the bull's-eye lantern in Jericho's waving hand, see the dusky silhouette of the Southerner below and beside it. "Everyone all right?"

"Now that we have some light," Angel said, her tone nonplussed.

Jericho laughed as though at a joke. "Yeah, it's dark in here. Lighter farther in, but we'll stop when it's widened out a little. I call that my smoking parlor!"

Jericho laughed again, turned, and continued limping forward along the twelve-foot-wide corridor. There were rocks along both sides, and Zane stumbled over them, unable to see much but deadheading on the lantern swinging high before General Lee, whom the ghoul hunter kept moving with frequent slaps to the palomino's behind.

When the corridor turned abruptly, Jericho waited until the others behind him could see the lantern before he continued forward, swinging the lamp from side to side like a signaling brakeman. More light ebbed into the chasm from chutes and funnels that opened onto the sky far above the mountain they were apparently inside. The sandstone and limestone seemed to glow the same soft red as Jericho's lamp.

They'd walked maybe fifty yards into the mountain when the right side of the corridor drew back and formed a room of sorts about twenty feet wide by fifteen feet deep and lit from above by two cracks in the ceiling. There was a fire ring in which low flames licked and a coffeepot chugged and gurgled. A rickety ladder-back chair sat near the fire ring, and a dried and cracked cartridge belt hung from the chair back, its Army-issue holster containing an old cap-and-ball pistol, the walnut grips cracked and worn.

There was an old farm wagon here, as well. Its end faced the far wall, tongue drooping forward. It was half filled with sweet-smelling hay recently cured. Near the wagon, a stocky, cream-and-brown burro was grazing on a pile of hay mounded between its forefeet and the wagon.

A wooden bucket of water sat beside the hay mound. General Lee snorted when he saw the burro. The burro switched its trail in greeting. As Hathaway pulled his mule into the room, the mule lifted a shrill, angry bray as it studied the burro gravely, twitching its ears and stomping a front hoof.

"That's Jeff Davis." Jericho stepped aside to let the men, woman, horses, and mule pass into the room. "He won't hurt you, mule. He likes company whenever he can get it, and he don't get it much around here. That's a good thing."

Zane was helping Jesse, who was coming around now and grunting through gritted teeth, down from his buckskin. As Zane led the outlaw over to the chair, he glanced at Jericho. "Those Injuns outside," he said. "Who . . . ?"

"They wasn't no Injuns like those you ever seen, Uriah. They're an old tribe, far as I can tell. Maybe an ancestor race of the Yaqui or Apache. I been here for fifteen years, and I never seen a single one stray more than five miles from this mountain range. They stay here in these mountains and canyons—some of the biggest, emptiest country in the Southwest—to guard this here mountain. Against what, I don't know. I'm the only white man I seen here in twelve years!"

He chuckled.

"Why do they need to guard a mountain?" Angel asked as she unbuckled her paint's latigo strap.

"I can't answer that question just yet."

"Why not?" asked Hathaway, who was also unbuckling his mule's belly strap.

All four were dusty and sweaty, as though they'd soaked in an alkali hole, then rolled in the dirt. Their faces were sun- and windburned, with pale circles around their eyes where their brows and hat brims offered shade. Zane's and Hathaway's beards were adobe-colored. As a group they looked like desert nomads, and they were all slouched slightly under the weight of their fatigue.

" 'Cause I don't know you well enough." Jericho squatted down beside his fire, dug a fat cigar out of his coat pocket, and looked at Jesse. "He don't look so good."

"I been better," Jesse said, his chest rising and falling sharply as he breathed. "Been worse, too. You didn't happen to see five renegades out there in the canyon, didja? That's who we're after. You can have your damn mountain."

"I seen 'em," Jericho said, scraping a stove match to life on his thumbnail. His voice was low and brooding. "They're trouble—I saw that. They picked up the wolf trail. First white men I ever seen in these mountains—leastways since I come here nigh on ten years ago now. You folks are the second bunch. When I heard you was Confederates, I decided I might have to trust you to help me keep them others away. Then I seen Uriah"—his face brightened as he glanced at the big ghoul hunter kneeling beside the fire and passing a blade of one of his bowie knives over the flames—"and my heart grew light."

Uriah looked at his old friend. "Where's that trail of wolf heads lead, Jericho?"

"It . . ." Turnipseed looked at the others, all of whom had turned to him now with keen interest. "It leads to treasure."

Uriah looked at the glowing blade in his hand. "I sorta figured. What kind of treasure? If you have a mine, Jericho, we ain't interested."

"You trust all these folks, Uriah?"

"All?" Zane set the knife down, slipped another bone-handled bowie from a sheath tucked inside his left moccasin top, and began cutting Jesse's shirt away from his shoulder, tearing the material as he sawed through it. "I reckon you could say that."

Jesse looked up at him and grinned.

Zane exchanged the unheated knife for the glowing one and pressed it against the entrance wound in the Missourian's breast. The knife sputtered as it seared the bloody, torn skin. Fetid smoke wafted. Jesse screamed, tipped his head back, and his eyes fluttered closed. Out again. Angel came over and held the outlaw up in his chair while Uriah cauterized the exit wound.

"Clean through," the ghoul hunter said. "That oughta do him. It's hard to kill a snake."

"Him a Confederate?" Jericho asked.

"He calls himself one."

"What about the Negro?"

Jericho glanced at Hathaway, who stood back near his burro, fists on his hips, looking skeptically back at the desert rat. "I notice he's wearing a Yankee hat. What I have to say, the deal I have to make, Uriah, is not one I take lightly. I've been sitting on it for a long time, waiting . . . wondering what I oughta do. Wondering how I can get the treasure to the Southern folks who need it most, so we can rebuild our country, make it better and more beautiful and gallant than before."

Zane cleaned the burned blood from his knife on Jesse's shirt, sheathed it, then dropped to his butt and wrapped his arms around his knees. Angel sat on the other side of Jesse from Uriah and began reloading one of her pistols.

Zane said, "Like I said, Jericho, we ain't interested in treasure. We're interested in those four men and that Mexican woman who rode into that canyon ahead of us. They're ghouls—the leaders of the very same pack of wolves who attacked our soldiers at Gettysburg. The Hell's Angels. Their leader is Charlie Hondo. I don't know why they're here, but we have to catch 'em and kill 'em. We'll need to get back after 'em soon."

"No point in goin' back out there." Jericho jerked his head in the direction they'd come through the cavern.

Angel said, "You mean because of the guardians?"

"No." Jerich removed the stogie from his long, yellow teeth, blew a wobbly smoke ring, and stared at it cross-eyed. "Them you're after will be in *here* soon enough."

33

CITY OF THE WEREWOLVES

ZANE, Angel, and Hathaway stared at Turnipseed, expressionless. Jesse groaned in his sleep.

Hathaway stepped forward slowly, scowling, closing one hand over the Colt Army .44 holstered on his right hip. "Excuse me, there, Mr. Turnipseed, but did you say them ghouls'll be *here* soon?" With his other hand he pointed at the floor.

"Well, not right here. But they'll be in the city soon. Them wolf pictures'll take 'em to the main entrance, on the other side of the canyon."

"City?" said Angel, arching a brow as though she were beginning to think the old desert rat might be a little touched.

Turnipseed puffed his cigar. "I done sat on the secret long enough, I reckon. Just couldn't bring myself to tell no one about it. Oh, I brought out a little of the gold now and then—bits and pieces of a wall or the shavings from a bell. Just to keep myself in hooch and see-gars and dry goods and the like."

They all continued to stare at him. He shuttled his rheumy gaze around at his dubious visitors and laughed.

He shook his head. "You've never seen the like. I'll

show you . . . as long as y'all swear to keep it a secret till we can figure out a way to use that treasure to build up the Confederate Army once more. See, there's enough gold down there"—he jerked the cigar over his shoulder—"to rebuild the South bigger and stronger than it ever was. Leave the so-called Union once and for all, squash that high-an'-mighty President Sherman like the damn bug that he is, and leave the North in burnin' ruin!"

Zane felt a twinge of unease. And sadness.

Turnipseed had been out here living in these mountains alone since the end of the War—the massacre that had claimed his entire family. But the seclusion hadn't healed his wounds, only made them fester. Like so much of the rest of the South, he was living in a dream world built on the desire for revenge. Zane didn't agree with that desire. The only way the country could heal was if all of its citizens drew their horns in and vowed to learn from the mistakes of the past—including the gigantic mistake made by Abraham Lincoln and his cabinet.

"For the last time, we don't care about the gold," Angel told him. "The gold is all yours to do with as you see fit, Mr. Turnipseed. We just want the Hell's Angels."

Turnipseed slid his glance around skeptically. Gradually, his expression changed to one of deep incredulity. "You just wait till you see what I'm talkin' about, young lady."

With that, he used his thumbnail to file the coal off his cigar, letting the ashes roll into the crackling fire, then heaved himself to his feet, his stiff knees popping. He grabbed his Springfield carbine, slung it over his shoulder, glanced once more at Zane, then walked out of this broad place in the cavern.

Zane touched his pistols, including the LeMat in its shoulder holster. He decided to leave his crossbow with General Lee, then slid his Henry from its saddle boot. He'd leave the Gatling gun here, as well, since they were after only five ghouls and the sidearms and rifle should suffice. He opened the casket's lid, however, and grabbed a bandolier filled with the silver he'd found at Padre Alejandro's.

Angel and Hathaway had already followed Turnipseed out of the room. He could hear their boots clacking on the stone floor. Zane hooked the bandolier over his shoulder and started after them.

"Hold on." Jesse's voice echoed behind him.

Zane turned. The Missouri outlaw was heaving himself up from his chair. "Stay there, Jesse. You're in no shape to tangle with Charlie Hondo. I'll bring you the bastard's head."

Jesse winced, gave up the struggle, and sagged back once more in the creaky chair. He gave a ragged sigh. Zane headed on out of the room and strode down a broad corridor that presumably led deeper into the mountain. The floor angled downward. The corridor was lit dully by occasional shafts of light dribbling down natural flues in the ceiling.

He caught up with Angel, who was walking behind Turnipseed and Hathaway. Without looking at him, she said, "What time is it?"

Zane started to reach for his pocket watch, then stopped and looked at her. She stared straight ahead, her face expressionless. "Don't worry. I'm well aware of the lunar cycle."

They walked several yards, following Turnipseed and Hathaway, the floor continuing to slant downward, the walls gradually falling back to each side, widening the corridor.

"If it should happen," Zane said just loudly enough for Angel to hear, "I not only expect you to cap a silver bullet in me, but I'll want you to."

"Not when you've changed, you won't," she said.

"You might not see it in me." He grabbed her arm,

stopped her, and jerked her around to face him. "But I will, Red."

She looked at him bitterly but with a sadness in her eyes, as well. "Glad to help, Uriah."

She jerked her arm free and continued striding along the corridor.

The floor leveled but the walls continued to slide away to each side. Light grew ahead of them, as though the cave were opening up to the world outside, falling away behind them. It did, in a manner of speaking. What lay beyond the cave was a broad canyon with walls nearly two thousand feet high in places. Lush grass and palm trees and sycamores and shrubs grew along the canyon bottom, across the bottom of which a stream threaded.

Zane was only peripherally aware of the growth and the stream.

He and the others had exited the cave onto a rocky slope some thirty or forty feet above the canyon, and now they all stood there staring aghast at the veritable city that sprawled before them—as large as or larger than Denver. But no dusty cow town, this.

Zane's heart fluttered as his eyes tried to convince his brain that what he was seeing—a city made almost entirely of giant, gold-domed buildings set upon cobbled streets—was real and not just a figment of his fatigued imagination.

The wind made a distant rushing sound above the canyon. Threads of it made it to the canyon floor, but it was only a breeze down here, stirring the mineral smell of the stream with the lush smell of the flora. Palms lined the stream as it came in from Zane's right near the other side of the canyon and disappeared behind the buildings. The palm trees fluttered in the breeze, occasional dead leaves tumbling lazily.

Zane noted with dread that the light angling down the canyon wall was striated and pink and orange—the light of late afternoon or early evening. The full moon would be up early, just after sunset. They didn't have much time.

"I'll be damned," Angel said, staring at the towering, turreted, many-tiered structures. She pointed to a near dome of a building set behind a vast wall. "Is that what it looks like?"

"If it looks like gold," said Turnipseed.

As Angel, Zane, and Hathaway followed the man down what appeared an old wagon trail, wheels ruts still scoring the rock of the canyon floor, Zane's eyes swept the terrain around him. Nearly everywhere were ruins of one type or another. Whatever structures they once had been—probably barns and stables, maybe some supply sheds—they'd been constructed of stone or brick, and now they were overgrown with brush including greasewood and sagebrush and green patches of grama and galetta grass.

Zane stopped at the wall surrounding the giant, domed building nearest the canyon's south wall. He used his gloved hand to scrape the thick dust and grime from the bricks and blinked in surprise. What lay beneath the dust was more gold. Gold bricks.

Even the walls of this giant fortress had been constructed of gold!

As he looked around at the other near buildings—there must have been more than a hundred such structures lined up along several cobbled streets—he saw that the sand, dust, grime, and bird shit of centuries covered the walls, lay piled along the foundations. A thought occurred to him, making his head light, and he turned to Turnipseed, who stood grinning at the amazed expressions on his visitors' faces.

"Are all these buildings built of gold?" Zane asked, unable to wrap his mind around the idea of nearly an entire city constructed of one gold brick after another, making up thousands of such bricks, maybe hundreds of thousands.

"As far as I can tell," Turnipseed said. "In some places, even the streets are paved in gold. They're just buried under centuries' worth of dust."

"How'd you find this place, Mistuh Turnipseed," Hathaway asked, his eyes wide, jaw slack, in his dark brown face.

Turnipseed chuckled. "I was out prospectin' with a supply wagon and mule when I found the range. Wandered into it by the same route you folks did, and started followin' them wolf heads. When the guardians attacked me, I run down that very corridor we just took . . . and found . . . all this."

"Who built it?" Angel was walking around, looking up in hushed awe.

"Don't know. There ain't nothin' here that tells—leastways, nothin' that I've ever found. And I've been through every building, over every inch of this canyon. I can tell you one thing, though. They were mighty keen on the wolf. They have statues of wolves. Even temples to wolves, and pictures etched in gold."

A chill rippled through Zane. As it did, a realization rolled through him, as well, though he was reluctant to put words to it. There was a whisper in the back of his mind, so soft that he probably wouldn't have heard it had he not been listening for it.

Eurico.

Demon offspring of Elyhann.

Eurico, *the Lord of Darkness.*

"What do you suppose Charlie Hondo hopes to find here?" Hathaway was down on his knees, staring at a patch of gold in the wall before him, caressing the shiny, unadulterated surface with the tip of his right index finger. "You think it's the gold? Like maybe that witch leadin' him an' the others found a map or some such?"

"Not sure," Zane said, though he was sure but somehow reluctant to voice it, as if voicing his suspicion would give it more credence. "But we'd best split up and start looking for him. It'll be dark soon."

Eurico. They were searching for the grave of Eurico, the Lord of Darkness. Long-dead apple of the demon-god Elyhann's eye.

And they'd better not find it. . . .

"It will at that," Angel said, following his glance toward the rim of the canyon, where the sky was beginning to turn green, the sunlight angling over the ridges now touched with saffron and copper. Shadows bled down the funnels and talus slides of the steep western slope.

Zane turned to Jericho. "The guardians ever venture in here?"

"Not since I've been here. Figure it must be against their religion or somethin'. Maybe it's off-limits to them. They're only here to protect it."

"They must know about you."

"Oh, they do, but they won't come in here after me. I live in the canyon, mostly. I mostly leave here at night to hunt, 'ceptin' when I'm checkin' my rattlesnake traps. That's what I was doin' when I spied them Angels and that Mex gal, saw 'em throw down on the guardians."

Turnipseed wrinkled his nose and raked a glance around the surrounding ridges. "I travel to Tucson for supplies couple times a year. Always come and go at night, and the guardians don't do much at night. Hole up purty tight in their little brush-hut villages scattered around the mountains. Almost like they're afraid of the dark."

To Angel and Hathaway, Zane said, "Let's start looking around. Be careful. If you see Charlie's bunch, fire a shot or two. I'll do the same. No one tries to take 'em down alone." Zane set his rifle on his shoulder. "Why don't you stay here, Jericho? Fire a shot if you see anything. Don't confront 'em. Remember, they're the worst of the ghouls."

"Will do, Uriah." The old desert rat smiled weakly.

"Sure is good to see ya again. Awful about . . . back home . . . ain't it?"

"Yeah."

Zane swung away and began heading toward the stream that seemed to bisect the city from west to east. Angel and Hathaway drifted off among the towering buildings, their eyes still amazed at the city they'd found here.

Looking beyond the rooftops toward the ridges, Zane saw that while the city itself was large and extravagantly constructed, the canyon was vast. And likely nearly totally sealed off from the outside world—both naturally sealed, and sealed by the lost race of Stone Age warriors who might have lived here through the ages, one generation after another, fed by admonishment through legend and religion that it was their duty to protect this sacred place.

Eurico's home.

The home of his race of werewolves who had likely ruled the continent. And now, most likely, the home of Eurico's final resting place.

No one had ever found this one until Jericho had stumbled upon it by accident.

Zane followed the stream into the heart of the city. It was hard to watch for Charlie and the other Angels and Ravenna. The magnificent buildings seemed to whisper to him from down the centuries. They towered over him, still and dusty with the silence of expired eons. Window casements and doors gaped at him like the eye sockets and empty mouths of grinning skulls.

The only sound was the distant whine of the wind combing the cliff tops and the faint crackling of occasional tumbleweeds or breeze-ruffled palm fronds. Pigeons cooed and warbled, perched along roof edges and window ledges. Here and there in the dust covering the cobbles were Jericho's hobnailed boot prints and the tracks of small, scurrying animals—pack rats, rabbits, mice, and quail. Near a low, squat structure, he saw the week-old tracks of a hunting bobcat.

Uriah strode slowly down the broad main thoroughfare, the façades of what must have been shops, saloons, and brothels on his left and beyond the verdant, trickling stream on his right. The buildings were of all shapes and sizes, all made of gold. Occasionally, he stopped to peer in an empty window, but the buildings, so extravagant on the outsides, were as hollow as caves within.

Once in a while, he saw a golden statue of a wolf or the figures of wolves in all states of being—hunting, sleeping, fornicating—etched into walls. An anxiousness bit at him. It was like electricity from a near lightning storm leaching into his bones, plucking his nerves. As if from another world, he could hear a howling in his ears. Half-formed visions of werewolves flashed behind his retinas—dark nights of slaughter. Even bright days of slaughter during certain seasons. And then the return to this canyon, this city of gold.

Their home.

Where they lived with their living god who allowed them to shapeshift even during the day.

His pulse beat faster and faster. He pressed his hand to a gold casement. The gold fairly vibrated beneath his flesh. Silver had made them sick. But gold had given them strength. That was why they'd built an entire city of it.

The gold in the city was giving Zane strength, as well. The wolf in him stirred. He cast a wary eye at the sky and drew back from the window casement.

Something ripped his hat from his head and pinged loudly off the gold casement to his left.

A rifle screeched shrilly.

A man laughed and howled. "Uriah Zane!" The booming voice echoed madly. "Fancy meetin' you here, pard!"

34

STREET FIGHT

Zane jerked around and pressed his back to the front of the building he'd been looking in. In a window across the stream-bisected street, a man stood aiming a Winchester at him.

Smoke and flames stabbed from the rifle's maw. At the same time that Zane flung himself forward and the bullet slammed into the front of the building behind him, ricocheting wildly, the rifle's hammering report reached his ears.

Zane rolled off his right shoulder and, staying low, sprinted into the palms and willows lining the creek.

Dust blew up in front of him, and the rifle roared twice, sounding hollow inside the building from which the Hell's Angel was shooting. Zane pressed his shoulder against the front of the palm he was crouched behind, swung his rifle around the tree, and aimed hastily toward the window as the shooter drew back away from it.

Zane fired three silver rounds quickly, the ejected casings winging back over his shoulder and pinging onto the gravel. He racked another cartridge into the Henry's breech, glad more than ever that the Henry firearms company had had the wherewithal to design a sixteen-shot long gun, and sprang out from behind the palm. He ran into the stream, splashing over the sandy, gravelly bed, the gold-colored water flying up against his thighs and knees.

Gaining the opposite bank, he sprinted up it, through a heavy line of willows, stopped, and fired three more shots toward the large, square window in the building beyond.

One bullet ricocheted off the gold façade. Two more screeched on through the window and hammered off the walls or support pillars beyond.

Racking another cartridge, Zane bounded off his heels and began sprinting once more. He looked around carefully, knowing he could be running into a trap. Seeing no other Hell's Angels around him, or the venomous witch who had guided them, herself led by Elyhann, he slammed his back against the building's grimed front, and slid a cautious glance through the window.

He caught a brief glimpse of a man with a long, yellow ponytail leaping out a window on the other side of the hall-like structure. Zane snaked the Henry through his own window and fired a single round that merely blew grit and grime from the foot-thick casing. The shooter disappeared, running toward the building's rear.

Behind Zane, water splashed. He whipped around, cocking the Henry and extending it straight out from his right hip. He eased the tension on his trigger finger when he saw Angel and Hathaway running across the stream behind him, about ten yards apart.

"Be careful!" the ghoul hunter yelled. "Might be a trap." He gestured for the two to head on up the fast-darkening street, then slipped around the side of the building and strode quickly down the gap between it and other hulking structure, toward the rear.

When he reached the back of the building from which the man with the ponytail had ambushed him, Zane slowed. He stepped out into the open behind the buildings on either side of him. Something hot ripped into his right cheek, just beneath his eye, then hammered the corner of the building to his right. Zane lunged forward and dove into a stone trough of some kind—probably part of some elaborate sewer or freshwater system—as at least three rifles thundered before him. The slugs tore into the lip of the stone trough and into the shrubs lining it, throwing torn sage and rabbit brush branches every which way, spitting rocks.

When the shooting died, Zane lifted his head to see one shooter standing crouched atop a ruined rock wall about thirty yards ahead and to his left. One more was crouched at the base of the wall the first man was shooting from, while another stood atop a boulder perched on a low ridge straight ahead of Zane.

As the rifles exploded once more, all three shooters howling and yipping devilishly, Zane ducked his head behind the lip of the stone trough, gritting his teeth as the bullets hammered into the ground above, spitting more dust, branches, and rocks into the trough.

When the shooting tapered off, Zane whipped his rifle up but held fire. He looked toward where the ghoul whom he'd recognized as One-Eye Langtry had been standing atop the boulder. The ghoul had disappeared. The others had disappeared as well.

To Zane's left and up the rocky, ruin-stippled slope, spurs chinged. He heard the thudding clacks of boots running on stone, and saw the three bushwhacking ghouls dashing along the base of the far ridge as they ran deeper into the canyon.

Rifles barked to Zane's hard left and from about twenty and thirty yards away. Angel and Hathaway were both down on their knees behind a ruined wall overgrown with ancient vines, firing toward the base of the ridge as they slid their rifles left, tracking the fleeing wolves.

Zane scrambled out of the draw and ran over to where

both Hathaway and Angel knelt behind the wall, reloading.

"Only three," Zane said. "Must've been looking for us."

He knelt down near Angel, pressed his back to the ruined wall, and slipped the loading tube up from beneath the Henry's barrel. Quickly, automatically, while gazing through the ruins and the brush between him and the base of the ridge, he slid silver cartridges from his bandolier and punched them down into the loading tube.

Angel gave an angry grunt as she racked a shell into her Winchester's breech. "Ravenna must've missed her dragon, figured she had someone behind her."

Hathaway said, "Or maybe they heard our shots when we threw down on them guardians, as Turnipseed calls 'em."

"Well," Zane said, "they know we're here . . . and don't like it."

"Where do you suppose Charlie and the witch are?"

"Lookin' for what they came here for. That's why only the lesser three in the pack came after us. They'll likely try another bushwack so's we don't interrupt Charlie and his sweet Mexican darlin'. I got a feelin' they're hearin' ole Eurico's howl."

Angel frowned at Zane, genuinely puzzled, more than a little worried. "Who's Eurico?"

"I'll tell you later." Zane shook his head and rose a little higher to stare off through the ruins. "But that they're here now and the moon's full is no coincidence."

"The moon'll be up in an hour or so," Hathaway said, "if I got the calendar right, an' I usually do. Somethin' big's gonna happen here, tonight, with that moon on the rise. I can feel it in my blood."

Zane shuttled his glance between Hathaway and Angel. "The other three haven't given up—they'll try to circle around us. I'm gonna head up this slope a ways, try to cut their sign, stay behind 'em. You two split up again and gradually move down canyon. We'll likely run into 'em again soon. We have to get those three out of our way, cause they'll do everything in their power to keep us from getting to Charlie and Ravenna."

Zane broke away from the others, running at a crouch up the slope, weaving among the ruined outbuildings and cisterns where the city had probably stored its water during the dry months. He walked a hundred yards, following the clear sign of the three running ghouls until they split up, one angling straight back into the city, one angling up canyon, the other continuing along the base of the slope.

Zane glanced at the sky. The light was almost gone. Heavy shadows plunged down the canyon walls, and the air was growing cold. Zane's heartbeat quickened. He squeezed his rifle in his hands as, on one knee where the tracks of the three ghouls had split up, he gazed off over the darkening city.

Where would Charlie and Ravenna find Eurico?

He crossed the stream and headed back into the city, where he promptly lost the tracks of the ghoul he'd been following. The man must have followed the stream either up or down canyon. Zane didn't want to take the time to backtrack and look for him. He had to concentrate on Charlie and Ravenna. The moon would be up soon, and it was those two he needed to kill first.

A half hour later, as he prowled a back alley and silently willed the moon to slow its ascent, there was the spatter of belching rifles. He broke into a run, leaving the alley and finding himself in a broad street between more golden ruins that were dark gray now in the thickening darkness. The rifles crashed from up the dusty, cobbled street down which a breeze now kicked up tumbleweeds and brought the dank odors of the canyon.

Three rifles flashed above street level on the right side, while an answering gun barked in a shaded portico on the left. Just then a man screamed and dove forward out of a balcony on the right. Zane made out a black eye patch as One-Eye turned a somersault and dropped his rifle as his body thudded to the street, kicking up dust.

The other two ghouls, one firing from a rooftop, the other triggering lead from a third-floor window, stopped firing. In the street, One-Eye arched his back and groaned. A rifle flashed and barked from the shaded portico, and One-Eye's head jerked sharply to one side, dark blood jetting into the street.

Zane sprinted to the street's left side. The other two shooters opened up once more, hammering the building fronts around Zane. The ghoul hunter felt the burn of a bullet across his right thigh as he threw himself into the shaded portico behind four gold pillars, the base of each suspended on a long-clawed wolf's paw.

Zane flung himself back against the front of a building, saw Hathaway lying on his side a few feet away, one bloody leg stretched out before him, the knee bent slightly. The man's left hand was clamped over the bloody wound just above the knee. His other hand held his rifle.

"How bad?" Zane asked, edging a look around one of the support columns toward the rooftops on the other side of the street.

"Just pinched me but I can't straighten my leg."

"Where's Red?"

"She was up the street when they bushwhacked us. Last I seen she ducked back into an alley." Hathaway looked at Zane gravely. "She might be hit."

As two bullets smashed into the cobbles around him, Zane dashed up to one of the support columns and snaked his Henry around the side. He triggered two shots at the shooter to the left, who gave a yelp and dropped flat atop the opposite roof. His hat poked up from the level of the roof, and Zane triggered another shot.

The hat flipped up off the Angel's head and disappeared.

The ghoul gave an angry howl. "For that, amigo," he shouted tightly, belly down against the roof, "I'll be takin' your hat just as soon as you have no more use for it! Won't be long."

Meanwhile, the other Angel, to the right of the first, was continuing to pound Zane and Hathaway's position with lead. The slug barked against the front of Zane's column as well as the one covering the scout.

Zane turned his body and slid a glance out around his column's right side. He saw the silhouette of the shooter and the man's rifle in the second-story window. Orange flames jabbed from the Winchester's barrel, and Zane drew his head back behind the column. The shooter's slug hammered the side of the column, ricocheting against the building behind him and Hathaway. The screech of the slug was deafening.

There was another shot. This one sounded more like a *crack* than the thundering rifle shots—a pistol shot. A man screamed hollowly. The scream echoed inside the building across the street.

A familiar voice added its shouted echo to that of the scream. "That's for Frank and Cole, you mangy, yellow-livered coyote!"

Lines cut across Zane's forehead. "Jesse, that you?"

Zane looked around the pillar, saw Curly Joe slouched beside the empty window, one arm slung over the broad gold ledge. His hat was off, and he was facing toward Zane's right, where a figure just now leaped through a window between the joined buildings and into the same building as Curly Joe was crouched.

The new figure, Jesse James, aiming two pistols out in front of him, stumbled in front of another window. Jesse's pistols cracked and leaped in his hands. Curly Joe's head snapped back, and he dropped down beneath the window.

Jesse walked over to Curly Joe's window, looking down before turning his head toward Zane. He threw an arm out in a wave, then slumped forward and to one side with the effort, grabbing the shoulder that the guardian's arrow had pierced. "At least I got one of the spineless damn killers!" he bellowed. "I got one of 'em, by God, and Frank's smilin' in his Catholic grave!"

Zane saw movement on the roof to the left of the building Jesse was in. He raised his Henry, trying to draw a bead on the figure running from the building's rear toward the front, taking long, leaping strides. The ghoul gave a shrill cry and bounded off his heels, throwing his rifle out to one side as he launched himself over the street.

Zane lunged out from behind the pillar, desperately trying to plant a bead on the airborne wolf. He triggered the Henry, but the ghoul arced up and over the street and disappeared above the roofline of the building behind Zane and Hathaway.

In a pain-pinched voice, the scout said, "Did he do what I thought he just done?"

"Yep."

The ghoul had felt the gold—probably also the full moon—as Zane was feeling the otherworldly influences himself. It made him light-headed and electric, fairly bursting with energy.

"I'll be back, Al!" Zane leaned his rifle against the side of the pillar and ran around the corner of the building and down the side about twenty feet, until he saw a second-story window directly above him.

He did not hesitate, but set his heels, bent his knees, and sprang straight up off his feet. He gave a great groan as he closed his hands over the gold, grime-encrusted ledge, and was surprised that he could so easily hoist himself up with his arms and swing his feet over the ledge and through the window.

He got his feet beneath him and landed at a crouch.

The ghoul before him, who'd been heading toward a stairway toward the back of the empty, pillared room, likely intending to get behind Zane and Hathaway, was as surprised by Zane's burst of strength as Zane was himself.

He swung around with an exasperated grunt, the flaps of his yellow duster winging out to his sides, and pressed the stock of his Winchester against his hip. The gun roared, flashing in the nearly night-dark room. The slug hammered the wall behind Zane as the ghoul hunter flung himself forward and dug his LeMat out of its shoulder holster. Rolling up off his shoulder, he aimed the revolver quickly and pulled the trigger, detonating the twelve-gauge shotgun cartridge beneath the main barrel.

The fierce hogleg thundered and leaped in the ghoul hunter's hand. The wad of silver dimes he'd filled the cartridge with tore through Lucky's chest, lifting the ghoul a foot in the air and punching him six feet straight back before he hit the floor hard and lay, limbs akimbo, snarling and quivering. Zane flipped the latch-like switch on the side of the versatile weapon and fired two silver .45 rounds through the dying ghoul's forehead, putting him away for all eternity.

Zane turned to a front window and barked a curse. The full moon was up. As large as a dinner plate, it fairly throbbed with pearl light. With anxious eyes, Zane followed the trail it would take across the city. His gaze held on a high, cylindrical tower about two hundred yards away and capped with a snarling wolf's head mounted at the edge of the domed ceiling and limned in the milky lunar wash.

From the direction of the tower, a woman's terrified scream rolled over the hulking buildings.

Zane's spine tensed as he stared across the night. He ground his fingers into the window ledge. *"Red!"*

35

WOLF MOON

A HALF HOUR before Zane blew Lucky Snodgrass to hell with his LeMat, Angel stepped through the low, arched door at the base of the cylindrical tower with the wolf's head perched atop its dome several hundred feet in the air.

She'd seen the tower just as she and Hathaway had been ambushed in the street. Somehow realizing that Charlie Hondo and Ravenna were in the tower, Angel traced a circuitous route to the bizarre structure. She'd known Al had been hit—she'd taken a graze to her upper right arm, herself—but saw that he'd been able to pull himself to relative safety in the alcove.

The moon was climbing, and Angel knew she had precious little time to stop the wolf leader and the witch before they attained whatever dark power they were after. She had to abandon Al for now and go after them.

Now she stared into the dank dimness before her, where stone steps spiraled up the tower into musty darkness. She pricked her ears to listen, but there was only a ringing silence in the cavernous cylinder punctuated by the increased shooting along the street behind her.

She knew that Charlie and Ravenna were in here. When she'd first set eyes on the building with that snarling wolf's head capping it, she'd known it had to be the place they'd been heading for. The three other ghouls had placed themselves on the rooftops nearby to keep the hunting party away from it.

She started up the steps, and immediately the darkness and the close confines, the chipped stone steps rising steeply before and behind her, made her feel as though a giant fist were closing around her. Claustrophobia tugged against her, making her legs stiff. When she'd climbed what she'd figured to be about sixty feet, however, the light from the full moon pushed through small, diamond-shaped notches carved into the walls about two feet apart from one another. The stairs appeared in the milky half-light, forever rising, forever falling away behind her.

Gradually as she climbed, voices emanated from somewhere above. At first they sounded like little more than a vibration in the golden walls. Little by little, however, the vibrations separated, became two distinct sounds, and as she continued to climb she could make out a man's voice and a woman's voice. Mostly the woman's. Ravenna seemed to be doing most of the talking.

"Chatty bitch," Angel muttered to herself—a lame attempt at dulling the myriad fears clinging to her like thorns.

It was soon only Ravenna's voice that Angel was hearing. The witch was chanting loudly, her voice growing louder and louder so that Angel could plainly hear the echoes now. She was speaking in Spanish, and Angel could hear only bits and pieces of what the witch was chanting—something about many years passing, the full moon, a new age beginning for the wolf people.

Angel quickened her pace. She stopped when the moonlight revealed the steps opening onto a flat surface, the walls falling away. Lifting her Winchester fully loaded with silver, Angel continued up the steps, walking slowly now on the balls of her boots, and stepped onto the floor above. She found herself in a vast circular room lit via the diamond-shaped ports in the walls by moonlight.

Two torches flared, fixed in brackets against the walls on the other side of the room, which was three steps below Angel, who remained hidden in the shadows against the wall behind her, near the stairs. Angel squinted to see more clearly in the dawn-like light, and then she frowned.

On the far side of the circular room sat a giant, golden chair. It was a throne with two golden wolf's heads rising from the back, two giant wolf feet serving as front legs. Sitting in the chair was Charlie Hondo. The ghoul was tense and stiff, arms resting on the chair arms, and he stared straight ahead, expressionless, eyes wide, as though he were in a trance. The gold hoop rings dangling from his ears shone like silver in the angling moonlight.

He looked pale and wiry, sitting there in that big chair in his cavalry blues that were a size too tight for him, the pants too short. He looked ridiculous, his long hair mussed, several days of beard growth darkening his jaw, the two blasphemous tattoos on his sunburned cheeks. The man—or god—for whom the throne had been built must have been three times Charlie Hondo's size.

Behind him and a little to his right stood Ravenna de Onis y Gonzalez-Vara in black leather, with red boots and a red sash blowing out away from her in a breeze that Angel could not feel. The witch held what appeared an eight-sided amulet above her head. It, too, was made of gold. She had her eyes raised toward a round hole in the domed roof filled with the blue black of the moonlit sky. Through the diamond-shaped ports in the dome, Angel could see the moon rising on an interception course with that hole in the dome.

Angel stepped forward to the edge of the wall shadows, and raised her Winchester, drawing the hammer back. Her hands inside her gloves were hot and sweaty. Her heart thudded. Drawing a deep, slow breath, she planted the carbine's sights on Charlie's chest.

Something peeped sharply nearby. Startled, Angel lowered the rifle a few inches, and looked down. A rat stood on the sunken main floor, staring up at Angel, twitching its whiskers and wiry tail.

Ravenna broke off her chanting, and raised her voice more loudly as she said in English, "You don't think I know you're there?" She laughed wickedly, still holding the amulet above her head.

Angel pressed her cheek against the Winchester's stock, narrowing one eye as she slid the sights over Charlie's chest, the ghoul staring at her now, eyes sharp but his face otherwise still expressionless. Again, Ravenna laughed, making Angel's hands jerk as she tried to slide the bead at the end of the carbine's barrel into the V-notch above the breech.

A cat wailed sharply, the snarling cry filling Angel's ears. Her hands jerked, and she nudged the rifle up, the gun exploding and the slug slamming into one of the wolf heads rising above Charlie Hondo's pale, bony shoulders.

The cat—it couldn't be a cat!—wailed again. Angel saw something large move toward her from where the rat had been standing a few feet before and below her. The gray, yellow-eyed mountain lion lunged up the three steps, showing its long, curved fangs, and began to leap toward Angel as the marshal stepped back and swung around, ejecting the spent cartridge and throwing a fresh one into the chamber.

The cat was a gray blur bounding up off its springlike hind feet. Angel screamed as she lowered the carbine's barrel, pressing it hard against the cat's chest and squeezing the trigger, the explosion muffled by the great feline's powerful body.

The cat slammed into Angel, pinned her arms down to her sides. She dropped the Winchester, heard it clatter to the gold-cobbled floor a half second before she hit the floor on her back and shoulders, slamming her head down so hard that everything went black and silent. The slap of bare feet grew in her ears, and she opened her eyes to see the great cat staring glassily down at her, its forehead pressed against hers.

Its glassy, dark brown eyes rolled around a little in their sockets, and the jaws spasmed. Angel felt the hot blood spilling out of the hole she'd drilled in the beast's chest, soaking her vest and running down between her breasts to her belly.

Ravenna reached down, grabbed the back of the dying cat's neck, and pulled it off of Angel, who drew a deep breath and closed her right hand over one of her pistols.

"Did you kill my dragon, too, you fucking bitch?" Ravenna's shrill voice echoed sharply off the gold walls and the dome, the round hole in which was growing brighter and brighter. "It was you, wasn't it? I know it was you. I just now saw it! Dragons do not materialize out of thin air without some effort on the part of the conjurer, you know!"

"Here," Angel said, flicking the keeper thong free from her Colt's hammer, and sliding the piece out of its holster. "Let me make it up to you."

She jerked the gun up and began clicking the hammer back, but she did not get the barrel leveled on Ravenna before the witch slammed her bare foot hard against the underside of Angel's wrist. The pistol flew up out of Angel's hand, hit the floor behind her with a sharp thud, and slid back into the shadows.

Ravenna leveled an ivory-gripped Remington at Angel's head, and cocked it, smiling. "Get up. You're interrupting us and the Lord of Darkness, who stirs even as I speak, and you're piss-burning me bad!"

Angel lifted her head, wincing, and looked around the witch toward Charlie, who sat as before, stiff and tense, trancelike. He was staring toward Angel, the moonlight sharp in his otherwise flat eyes.

"But I won't kill you," Ravenna said, reaching down and pulling Angel's other pistol from its holster and tossing it away with the other one. She removed the ivory-gripped stiletto strapped to the marshal's right calf, tossed it away, then ripped two whang strings from Angel's leather pants. "No, I am going to make you watch the transformation. If you do not die of fright, you will die by Eurico's fangs and claws!"

She kicked Angel onto her belly and drove a knee into the base of her back, pinning her to the floor. The witch was stronger than she looked, and the braining Angel had taken made it impossible for her to fight. Her limbs were weak, and she was seeing double, her ears ringing madly. As Ravenna tied Angel's wrists behind her back with the whang strings, the witch leaned down and whispered sensuously into Angel's right ear.

"Or maybe we should make you one of us, eh? A girl such as you would be a formidable wolf in Eurico's pack. He and I might be honored to have you running along beside us in our war against the quivering mortals!"

"Don't bet on it!"

Angel gave a clipped cry as Ravenna grabbed her hair and jerked her to her feet. Angel got her boots beneath her and kept them moving as Ravenna pulled her savagely across the floor by her hair. Angel watched with keen frustration as her rifle faded into the distance behind her. Only vaguely did she notice that the dead wildcat was gone and that in its place lay the rat, nearly torn in half by Angel's silver bullet.

She fought at the leather ties to no avail. She couldn't move her hands at all, and she felt the numbness as the blood flow was pinched.

Ravenna dropped her about fifteen yards in front of Charlie, still seated in the large golden throne. Angel sprawled belly down, grunting and cursing, then lifted her head and sank back against her heels, struggling in vain against the leather ties cutting into her wrists.

"Now, watch and quake, you miserable, mortal slut! Elyhann promised that if I brought Charlie here and replaced his soul with Eurico's, I'd share his Lord of Darkness powers." Ravenna laughed heartily. "I guess that would make me the Queen of Darkness, wouldn't it?" Ravenna, chuckling, set down her gun, picked up the amulet, and resumed her position flanking Charlie, who now stood grinning drunkenly, wolfishly, down at Angel.

Ravenna resumed chanting, thrusting her tan breasts out from behind her revealing leather vest and raising her eyes once more toward the ever-brightening ceiling. After several minutes, a circular gold dais rose up out of the floor with a hollowing scraping sound. In the middle of the dais lay what appeared an oblong, light blue vase.

A giant red heart lay inside the vase, throbbing.

With each throb, the organ grew redder and redder until it fairly glowed. It seemed to be growing, as well, threatening to burst out of the vase.

"The immortal heart of the Lord of Darkness!" Ravenna squealed, staring down brightly at the ever-brightening heart. "Oh, Charlie!"

Angel cast her horrified gaze at the hole in the dome. The huge moon had edged inside the hole. Angel wasn't sure if it was only her battered brain registering things that weren't there, but the moon appeared to throb with each beat of the red heart on the pedestal between her and Charlie Hondo.

Charlie's eyes also rose toward the moon.

His chest began to expand, as though he were drawing a deep breath. The leer faded from his lips, and now an expression of magisterial awe and wonder shaped itself there. A similar expression brushed across Ravenna's regal features, and slowly, holding the amulet in front of her breasts, she dropped down to her knees beside Charlie. She placed her right hand on his thigh and held her gaze on the hole in the ceiling quickly filling with the pulsating moon.

"Oh . . ." Ravenna wheezed in hushed awe. ". . . *Charlie . . . !*"

Angel felt her own heart beating with every throb of the heart in the blue vase. She continued to struggle fiercely against the leather stays, until she finally tore her right hand free, scraping off a good bit of skin in the process. She glanced up again at the ceiling, and a cold sweat oozed from every pore.

She was too late.

The hole in the dome was completely white.

Before her, the heart in the vase was gone.

Charlie's chest was red, and it throbbed. Ravenna's chest was also red and throbbing.

Both of them were growing larger and larger as thick brown hair began sprouting on their suddenly naked bodies, their hands and feet broadening and extending into paws. Their skulls thickened, ears rising, eyes sinking, noses enlarging and extending. In seconds, they were both more wolf than human, and Angel was scuttling back on her rump, digging into the pouches sewn inside her cartridge belt with quaking hands.

Ravenna's eyes glowed as red as her chest. Charlie's eyes glowed even brighter.

Ravenna opened her mouth and showed her white fangs, stepping toward Angel on her four paws, what could only be a smile shaping itself on her mouth, in her glowing eyes.

"Son of a *bitch!*" Angel's fingers closed over the silver shuriken nestling in the pouch. Quelling her fear, she gave herself over to her training, and whipped her arm back behind her before flinging it forward and loosing the five-pointed silver star.

Ravenna howled miserably as the disc thumped into her chest, burying itself so deep that the tip of only one point showed through the thick matting of dark brown fur. Blood oozed out around it. The she-wolf snarled and yipped and clawed at her chest with both paws, running in circles.

At the same time, the wolf that had been Charlie Hondo only fifteen seconds before tipped his head back and loosed a howl that filled the cavernous, round room like the yowls of a thousand wolf demons at once. The tooth-gnashing din slammed against both sides of Angel's head like giant fists.

The room shook before her, the floor bounding beneath her.

Charlie bounded up out of the chair, stood on his hind feet for a half second before diving forward, hackles raised, knifelike fangs bared, front paws with their terrible black claws swiping at the air. Something moved behind Angel, and then she felt a hot rush of air across the back of her neck as the thing leaped over her from behind and crashed headlong into Charlie Hondo.

36

THE WRATH OF ELYHANN

THE WOLF that had leaped over Angel hammered Charlie Hondo backward onto the dais, knocking the vase onto the floor where it did not break, and sunk its teeth in Hondo's neck, the enraged growls and slathering snarls of the second beast joining with Hondo's own screams to set up a shrill ringing in Angel's ears.

The din as well as the appearance out of nowhere of the second beast sent her into further shock, and it wasn't before the two wolves had rolled off the dais and had risen onto their back feet, snarling and digging at each other's necks with their fangs, that she realized the second wolf was Uriah. Only the hazel eyes were his. The rest of the wolf was long and rangy and humpbacked and nearly the same black and charcoal color of Hondo.

But whereas Hondo fought with a savage defensiveness, Uriah fought with a dominant, mindless rage, his hazel eyes turning yellow red and throbbing with primal fury. Hondo had the strength some awakened black god had given him, and it was enough to withstand Uriah's ferocious, selfless attack.

The two fought entangled and leaping around the large, round room for a long time, without sign of either tiring, until at least a bucketful of blood had washed across the golden floor. Angel looked at her rifle, but it was too far away, and the two were fighting between her and the Winchester. Besides, even if she could reach the gun, there was a chance she'd hit Uriah with one of her silver bullets.

Frustrated sobs racked her, and she pressed her hands to her temples as if to clear the horrible vision of the two fighting beasts from her head, and the horrifying yips and snarls and tearing growls from her ears. Finally, after fifteen minutes of savage fighting, the wolves separated, facing each other, breathing hard, their hot breath frosting in the air above their heads. Their eyes pulsated.

The moon had angled away from the circle in the domed ceiling, and its liquid white light angled onto the two beasts as if to isolate them in an otherworldly incandescence.

Their dark bodies were massive, their fur standing on end across their humped necks. The moonlight limned the ends of their fur coats like bristles. Blood black as ink pooled beneath them on the gold-cobbled floor. Their bellies sagged, shoulders slumped.

Finally, the wolf with the pulsating hazel eyes glanced at Angel, then drew a deep breath, gave a terrific howl that seemed to nearly implode the tower, and leaped off its back legs. It dugs its teeth into Hondo's already bloody neck, drove the ghoul to the floor, and, with one last decisive slash with its razor-edged fangs, tore the rest of Hondo's throat out.

It tore the entire neck out.

Whipping his head up, Uriah cast the ghoul's large, hairy skull high and far across the room to land in the dim reaches, bounce, roll, and thump against an unseen wall. Blood geysered from the gaping hole between Charlie's shoulders.

The wolf that was Uriah Zane stared into the darkness of the room. Finally, his head and shoulders sagged. He slumped to the floor with a ragged sigh, and rolled onto his side. His blood-matted side rose and fell heavily.

Angel stood and walked over to him, dropped to her knees by his side. In the time it had taken her to make the short trek, he'd assumed his human form once more, his clothes torn, blood leaking from a dozen different deep wounds. His chest rose and fell shallowly, and his eyes were closed.

Angel placed a hand on his shoulder. "Uriah."

He didn't move.

"Uriah," she said, clearing the phlegm from her throat and jerking his shoulder. "Heal yourself, Uriah. You have the power."

Zane's eyes opened. He stared blindly for a time, and then he turned his head to her, and rolled onto his back. He swallowed, licked his lips. "Finish me."

Angel shook her head. "No."

"Go ahead."

"You saved me. Now heal yourself, you bastard."

Zane shook his head. "Leave me, then."

Beneath Angel's knees, the floor vibrated. The vibration grew into a rumbling quiver. She looked up. Dust sifted down from the domed ceiling. The rumbling grew gradually from all across the night-cloaked, moon-bathed city.

"Get out of here," Zane told her.

"No." Again, she shook her head, tears rolling down her cheeks. She grabbed the collar of his buckskin shirt in her fists, and jerked his head up off the floor. "Not without you, goddamnit."

Zane closed his eyes. His body lay absolutely still for a time, and Angel thought he was dead. She placed a hand on his chest, felt the insistent beat of his heart. She ran her eyes across his body.

His clothes were still torn, but the bleeding appeared to have stopped. After several more minutes, during which the vibrations grew louder and more violent, Zane opened his eyes and stared up at Angel. “Sure wish you’d make up your mind,” he rasped. “First you wanna drill me with a silver bullet; then you refuse.”

“Get your ass up,” she said. “I think we’ve made someone angry.”

“Wouldn’t be the first time.”

She looked around, blinking dust from her lashes as it sifted down from the ceiling. Now chunks of gold were beginning to fall, as well, hitting the floor with loud crashes.

She grabbed his hand in both of hers, and, rising, pulled. “Can you stand?”

“Think so.”

He let her help him to his feet and wrap his right arm around her neck. Together, Angel crouching beneath his considerable weight, feeling the weak trembling in his own spent body, they made their way toward the stairs, Angel pausing only to grab her Winchester.

By the time they’d reached the bottom of the tower, Zane was strong enough to walk on his own. He saw the others—Jesse James, Al Hathaway, and Jericho Turnipseed—milling around outside the tower, the wounded James and Hathaway leaning on their rifles. They all looked shocked and miserable, glancing around at the slowly crumbling city, the pillars cracking and crashing and golden objects tumbling from roofs.

“What the hell happened up there?” Jericho shouted above the din.

“All hell broke loose,” Angel said. “But I think we got the gates closed. For now.”

Tenderly, Zane limped forward and beckoned to the stunned crowd behind him. “Best pull our picket pins, fog it out of this place.”

“The gold!” Jericho shouted, turning slow, shambling circles, his eyes on the crumbling roofs.

Leaning on his rifle, Hathaway gave the prospector a shove toward Zane, who was limping the way back the way they'd come. "Come on, fool, or you're gonna be buried with your precious gold!"

"It's all Zane's fault," said Jesse James, looking around and shaking his head. "You can't take that no-account Carolinan nowhere he won't cause trouble!"

"My gold!" the prospector continued to scream in disbelief, face tipped to the moonlit sky against which the city slowly shook loose and fell. "I waited so long!" He bawled like a baby as he stumbled after the others, hands raised as if to hold the domed city of gold in place. "Oh, merciful Jesus, *noooo!*"

They managed to retrieve their gear and horses and hightail it out the cavern before the brunt of the earthquake struck.

They couldn't see the effects as they galloped their rested mounts back the way they'd come, back past the dead guardians and finally out onto the western flats. But they could hear the loud rumbling and crashing, like enormous, distant cannons, of the canyon walls caving in on the city.

By the time they were miles away, the light from the sagging moon shone only a pale, dusty streak in the sky where the mountain shaped like a wolf's head had once been. The streak resembled stardust wafting from a damned, destroyed world. No one spoke for the rest of the night as they continued to ride northwest and away from the tantrum of Elyhann, who had been waiting for Charlie Hondo only to watch him die in the god's temple, the demon's hope for a master race of werewolves snuffed for the present.

At dawn, they made camp and slept at the base of a low escarpment near which a tiny spring trickled. At midmorning, they saddled their horses, filled their canteens, mounted up, and continued riding, swinging northward toward Tucson where they'd seek medical help for their wounded. As they left the escarpment, Zane glanced back at the mountain. Dust continued to waft, forming a thin cloud over the vanished peak and lower ridges around it. Nearer, a line of dark riders threaded toward him through the chaparral on small, rangy ponies.

Zane told the others to go on ahead, and gigged General Lee up a hillock near the old Spanish trading trail the others were following. He positioned the wheeled coffin in a gap in the rocks crowning the hill. Quickly, he set up the Gatling gun on its tripod, and squatted behind it in the open coffin.

When the dozen or so guardians rode into view around another outcropping and galloped to within fifty yards of Zane, the ghoul hunter triggered the Gatling gun, shattering the midmorning silence with the machine's staccato bellow. The slugs blew up a line of dust in the sand in front of the riders, who reined their ponies to sudden stops, jerking back on the rawhide reins and looking around wildly, dark eyes frightened.

The lead, tattooed rider turned his head toward Zane and the smoking Gatling gun. He yelled something in his guttural tongue, and he and the other riders reined their ponies around and galloped back in the direction from which they'd come. Their dust rose, sifting slowly. Gradually, their hoof thuds dwindled.

Nearby, a shod hoof rang off a stone, and Zane turned to see Angel riding up behind him, staring after the fading line of natives from beneath the crown of her dark brown Stetson.

"Can't help feeling sorry for them," she said. "A whole race born to protect a city. Now the city's gone. No wonder they're angry."

Zane sighed and leaped out of the Gatling's casket. He returned the gun to its bed among the silver and other ghoul-hunting paraphernalia, and closed the lid. He swung up onto General Lee's back and booted the gold stallion down the hill, stopping beside Angel. She was looking at him obliquely.

"You all right?" she asked.

Zane lifted his hat, ran a hand back through his long, black, sweat-damp hair. He stared after Turnipseed, Hathaway, and Jesse James continuing to ride northward along the faint trail angling through the chaparral.

"Damn dangerous—don't you think?" he asked.

"What?"

"Doin' what you did. Or *not* doin' it. Might only be makin' more trouble for yourself later." Zane tilted a glance at the bright, brassy sky. "Next full moon . . ."

Angel leaned toward him, wrapped an arm around his neck, and kissed him. "I reckon I'll take my chances." She kissed him again. "Come on. I'll race you to Tucson and a long bath in a tubful of whiskey!"

She reined her paint around and booted the horse into a ground-eating gallop. Zane glanced once more behind him at the thinning dust cloud over the vanished mountain, then gigged General Lee into a lunging lope behind the marshal as she smiled back over her shoulder at him, through a wave of wine-red hair.

CANYON OF A THOUSAND EYES

PROLOGUE

West of Camp Hawkins, Colorado Territory

FOURTEEN-YEAR-OLD HARLEY COOPER, prospecting for gold with his family deep in Poudre Canyon, turned to his father and yelled, "Hey, Pa—think I found somethin'!"

Calvin Cooper was twenty feet away, prying up boulders with a long, iron rod. "Well, dig it out and pan it, boy!"

Harley had set his tools down and, belly down on the ground, was digging in the soft sand beneath a large, flat rock. Less than six feet to his left, the Cache la Poudre River gurgled between rocky, pine-studded banks.

"It's...bones or somethin'," said Harley, probing the sand with his gloved hands.

Removing his right hand from the hole, he snugged his left shoulder up closer to the rock, and shoved that hand farther into the gap between the rock and the ground. His canvas hat tipped back on his head, a lock of dark-red hair licking over his forehead, he winced as, straining, he got his hand around something and pulled.

The object slipped suddenly from its resting place. Harley pulled it out where he could see it, then gave a girlish screech, and dropped it. He scrambled back on his butt, all the blood draining out of his face.

"Ah... *Jesus!*"

The dirt-encrusted human skull, with sand caked in its eye sockets and mouth, and thin strands of grizzled hair clinging to it, bounced off the rock Harley was kneeling on, and rolled back toward its resting place. It rested up to the edge of the flat rock bordering the hole it came from, and laid still, its sandy face grinning grotesquely up at Harley.

A thick angleworm flicked its tail along the drooping right jaw and buried its head in the jaw hinge. Several more worms and spiders clung to the hair.

Harley's older brother, Web, chuckled on the other side of the river. "What'd you find—a dead man?"

"Yeah," Harley said.

"What?" asked his sister, Beth, working on her hands and knees to Harley's right, farther up the riverbank.

Harley sniffed and stared down at the skull. "It's a head."

Calvin Cooper paused in his work with the iron rod. He leaned his tall, stooped frame against it, resting. Long, gray hair hung down from his billed wool hat, brushing across his shoulders. Holes in his blue-plaid shirt revealed the wash-worn underwear beneath. "Take it down to the water, and pan it out. Might have some flecks in it. "Anything else in that hole?"

Regarding the skull and the hole with his lips stretched back from his teeth, Harley said, "I don't know."

"I'll have a look," said Beth.

Holding her trowel and short-handled broom in one hand, the thirteen-year-old girl, who had long hair the same dark-red as her brothers and clad in blue overalls and high-topped, lace-up boots, skipped down the rocks toward Harley.

Web crossed the river on a fallen pine, holding his

arms out for balance, his eyes bright with expectation. He was seventeen, his face as pimply as a frog's back.

Harley stood and probed the skull with his booted toe. "I don't want to touch the thing."

"It's just a bone, like any other," Beth said casually, stooping to retrieve the skull. She set it carefully in Harley's tin pan.

"It ain't like any other," Harley said, leaning down to peer beneath the flat rock. "It's human, for chrissakes."

"Get away, sissy," Web said, bounding off a boulder upstream from Harley. He shoved his younger brother aside and dropped onto his knees to peer into the hole. "Last year, I came upon an old grave, and it had several good-sized nuggets lodged inside the leg joints. It's as good a place for gold to wash as any." He glanced up at Harley. "Hand me that other pan, tinhorn."

"Shut-up, Web." Harley kicked the pan down to his brother.

Web chuckled and mimicked the screech Harley had loosed when he realized he'd been holding a skull in his hands.

"I said shut-up!"

Chuckling, Web reached into the hole, fished around for a second then gently removed his hand. Between his thumb and index finger was a small, slender finger bone sheathed in patches of withered skin and mud. A long, purple fingernail protruded from the mud.

"Christ," Harley muttered as Web set the finger gently into the pan then stuck his left hand back inside the hole.

He rummaged around for several more minutes, producing more small bones and four long ones. He set the small bones inside the pan, the long ones, on a large rock to his left, careful so the dirt which might bear the precious gold flecks was not scraped away.

Web had both hands inside the crevice when he stopped fishing around, and frowned. Slowly, he pulled his arms out of the hole. In his calloused hands was a thick, gray hide clinging to a large, snarling wolf's head. The head and the hide were perfectly preserved, as if they'd been buried only a month ago.

"Jumpin' Jehosaphat, Pa!" Web said. "Look what else was in there!"

Web set the skull atop his shaggy, red curls and danced around, hopping from foot-to-foot, and whooping like a painted Injun.

"Quit your nonsense and let me see that," said Calvin Cooper.

He'd put down his bar and was moving stiffly over the rocks, scowling. He spat a tobacco quid, rubbed his mouth and grabbed the wolf's skull and hide from Web. Examining it closely, he ran his gloved hands over the dirt-flecked hair.

"I'll be damned. It had to have been in that hole as long as the carcass, but it still looks like new."

"They must've preserved it somehow," Webb said.

"Can I keep it, Pa?" asked Harley.

Webb snapped a look at him. "I'm the one who fished it outta there."

"I'm the one who found the grave."

"You can keep the head," Web jeered.

"Hey, look what I found!" Beth yelled from the river. She stood knee-deep in the tea-brown water, holding the pan and the skull in one hand. In the other, she held up a small, gold nugget about the size of a kid's marble.

"Mercy sakes, girl," said her father, stumbling down the bank to the water's edge, his sons following close on his heels. "Mercy sakes, let me see that."

Cooper quickly removed his gloves, tossed them down, and plucked the nugget from the girl's palm. He held it up and examined it closely against the sky. His chest rising and falling sharply, he stuck the nugget between his jaws and clamped down on it.

"That ain't pyrite. No sir. That's gold!" Cooper whooped, his gaunt, haggard face coming alive. "Boys, Beth, you get your butts over there and dig up that whole grave. Chip away the rock. Dig up every bone you find and then keep working the crack as far back as it goes."

Cooper tossed the nugget in the air, then closed his fist around it and strode upriver, stumbling over rocks. "This here's more gold than we found the past two whole weeks. I'm gonna stow it back in the cabin."

"You got it, Pa!" said Beth, setting down her pan and hurrying back to the grave with the boys.

Near dark, when they'd pried all the rocks away from the grave and scooped out all the bones, dirt, and sand as far down as the bedrock, they went to work panning it all out in the river. They'd found several more flakes but no more significant nuggets when, sifting through the dirt they mounded beside the grave, Beth found a stone disk about the size of a dinner plate.

A strip of rawhide, still in good shape, had been attached to two knobs at the eleven o'clock and one o'clock positions on the disk. When Beth brushed the stone clean in a pan, she found that the disk had been polished smooth as marble, with a hunk of turquoise embedded in the middle.

Around the turquoise were small etchings of animals —a wolf and a bear on one side, a hawk and a mountain lion on the other. At the top was a weasel, at the bottom, a skunk.

"Can I keep it, Pa?" she asked her father, having showed it to him around their supper fire later that night. A haunch of venison roasted on the spit, owls cooed in the pines.

Nearby, Webb and Harley were splitting wood, Webb still riding Harley about his girlish exclamation when he'd found the skull. The older brother had mounted the skull on the front of their cabin, with the deer and elk antlers and the skull of the bear Webb had shot last fall.

"I reckon," Cooper grunted as he splashed whiskey into his coffee cup. "Ain't worth anymore than the turquoise anyhow."

Beth looped the rawhide over her head and settled the disk against her chest. "I'll wear it for good luck."

It had been a big day for the Coopers. Tired from the excitement of finding that much gold in one place in one day, and eager to get a fresh start again in the morning, they were all in bed before the moon rose above the Sleeping Elephant rock on the canyon's south side.

Sometime in the early hours, Beth's bladder woke her. Amidst her father's snores and Harley's unconscious mutterings, she slid out of bed, drew a blanket around her shoulders, crept outside, and strode around back to the privy.

She was sitting on the privy, half-asleep, when the stone disk around her neck suddenly grew warm against her chest. It seemed to vibrate slightly, as if coming alive. A chill wind smelling of rot seeped through the cracks in the privy door. She knew deep in her bones it was not only a foul wind, but a bad, bad wind.

Outside, the thunder of galloping hooves rose sharply above the wind's howl. The ground beneath the privy shifted and shuddered, and a horn blew—a loud, shrill, raucous sound that seemed to drop straight down from the stars. Beth winced and covered her ears.

The thudding stopped nearby.

There was a wooden crash, like a door kicked in. Lowered, groggy voices.

Beth heard her father's voice, shrill with exasperation, "What the *hell...?*"

Harley screamed.

"Webb, grab the rifle!"

"Pa...*oh...!*"

The sound of tearing and slicing, of breaking bones, rose from the cabin. There were grunts and thuds and whimpers. The wind picked up, the fetor of rot so strong through the privy door that Beth leaned forward, gagging.

Her father's terrified voice sounded, "What *are* you?"

A shotgun roared, two quick blasts.

"Christ, Pa, it won't go dow—" A scream, then a wooden thump, like a body hitting the floor.

Beth stood before the privy door—frozen—eyes wide, staring through a crack between the boards, the amulet around her neck beating like a heart.

The cabin was silent except for the muffled thuds hooves on the split pine floor. After a few minutes, an animal snorted. The horn blew—a deafening roar—then the pounding thuds once again as the beast tore off into the night.

Silence.

The amulet cooled and stilled.

Beth stood for a long time, staring at the privy door, seeing nothing but darkness, listening intently, her heart pounding. She could hear little but the blood surging in her ears.

Finally, she pulled the blanket around her shoulders and opened the door. She stood silently for a moment before stepping down to the ground.

She stole slowly around the cabin to the front door.

There was the smell of blood, so thick it took her breath away. And just beneath it, the sickly sweet smell of a wild animal and the heavy fetor of burned hair and powder smoke.

Somewhere above, a magpie screeched.

Beth took one more step to the door before a hoarse cry rose in her ears. The ground pitched like a wind-whipped lake. She dropped to her knees, and everything went black.

1

Seven years later...

CLAY CARMODY RODE in the driver's box of his beat-up covered wagon, past the sprawling cottonwoods lining the west bank of Crow Creek. To his left, the brassy autumn sun dropped toward the Front Range of the Rocky Mountains. Carmody had tipped his hat to shield his eyes from the sharp arrows of fiery light.

All at once, the sun was gone, silhouetting the flame-shaped Long's Peak and the other toothy ridges around it, and splashing a painter's palette of bright color into the sky behind it.

Thick shadows leaned out from the trees. The breeze acquired a definite edge, chilling the sweat along Clay's broad back and chest. Out of habit, he cast a glance over his left shoulder. No horseback riders appeared on his backtrail. He hadn't thought there would be, but he couldn't be too careful. He glanced at the darkening mountains again.

Ah, to be snugged away in one of those canyons where no one could find him—just him and Nathan with their picks and shovels, chipping away at the rock, looking for the pot of gold at the end of their rainbows.

As badly as he wanted to get to Camp Hawkins, pick up Nathan and head into Poudre Canyon with a wagon load of fresh supplies, he still had another good day's ride ahead. He swung the wagon off the trail and into the tall brush under the cottonwoods.

A half hour later he'd staked his horses in thick broom grass near water, built a fire, and was brewing coffee while he sliced salt pork into a heavy iron skillet. The cottonwoods' low-hanging branches scraped against the patched, ribbed canvas of his wagon that had, over the dusty miles between here and the Chugwater Rocks, turned the color of Southwestern adobe.

A man's voice broke the night's quiet. Hooves kicked stones and splashed through water.

Carmody turned to the creek on his right, saw three inky shadows moving toward him from the other bank. He set the pan beside the fire, slid the knife into the sheath on his left hip, then stood and picked up his Winchester Yellow Boy repeater. Jacking a fresh shell into the breech, he backed away from the fire to stand between the wagon and a thick cottonwood, holding the Winchester down near his right hip, barrel straight out toward the creek.

"Hello-o the camp!" one of the riders yelled above the splashing hooves.

Carmody turned a look behind him, toward the trail he'd ridden earlier. Seeing no sign of anyone trying to flank him, he turned his head back to the river. "Come on in slow."

One of the riders said something Carmody couldn't hear. The horses slowed but kept coming. As all three mounted the creek bank and thrashed through the brush, Carmody stepped forward, staying wide of the campfire and keeping the Yellow Boy aimed straight out from his hip.

The riders entered the edge of the firelight's guttering sphere, their horses blowing with exhaustion, hides glistening with river water and sweat lather. All three riders were so dusty it was hard to distinguish their features.

"No need for the long gun, amigo," said the one on the far right—a blond, little coyote with a bear coat much too large for him, and a shabby bowler hat with a spray of dead flowers pinned to the crown. "We're peaceable."

Carmody didn't say anything.

The middle rider had a thick accent that Carmody detected as Australian, having know a few Australian punchers. "Name's Bill Wayne. These two blokes ride for my spread. We're chasing cattle rustlers. You haven't seen any riders come through here in the past couple hours, have ye, mate?"

"No riders this way."

"Well, damnit," said the dark, slender man on the far left, running a hand over his two-day growth of beard. "Maybe we been followin' the wrong tracks all along, boss."

"Could be," Wayne allowed, his eyes sliding around as he thought it through. He tipped his sugarloaf sombrero back off his sunburned forehead and cast his glance to Carmody. "Mind if we share your fire tonight, mate? We have our own food and coffee. Don't mind sharin', if you're short."

Carmody studied him without expression, the fire's glow sliding along the hard planes of his broad, dark face.

"We'll be out of your hair and back on the trail of those long-loopers first thing in the morning," Wayne assured him.

"How many were there?" Carmody asked.

"Four," said Wayne. "We shot one out of his saddle. He was ridin' double with one of the others. I thought maybe they'd spotted you and tried to steal one of your horses."

"How many head they get?"

Wayne returned his stare with a level one of his own. He was a stocky gent of middle age and medium height, with a blonde, handlebar mustache and red neck scarf with white polka dots showing above the fur-trimmed lapels of his buckskin coat. His horse was a handsome dun with two white stockings. The saddle was hand-tooled, the rifle in the boot well cared-for.

He grinned knowingly at Carmody. "Fifteen. We got the beef back. It's the men we're after. They've hit me before. Don't want 'em hitting me again."

Carmody kept his rifle leveled at the three strangers as he glanced into the darkness behind the wagon and the cottonwoods, listening. Hearing and seeing nothing suspicious, he turned back to Wayne. "Rustlers can be bad for a man's business."

"Ain't that the gospel?" said the scrawny coyote in the over-large bear coat.

"I got plenty of side pork and beans," said Carmody, depressing the Winchester's hammer and raising the barrel. "You can stake your horses with mine in the weeds yonder, as long as they ain't scrappy."

"Obliged, mate," said Wayne.

As he and the other two reined their horses upstream toward Carmody's pair of hitch-broke piebalds, Carmody dropped his rifle low to his side and moved toward the fire. He'd taken two steps when an explosion sounded from the western darkness. What felt like a Plains Indian arrow tore through his left temple, picked him straight up off the ground, and flung him back to where he'd been standing when he first faced the newcomers.

He lay belly-down in the grass, his hat and rifle lying several feet away. Thick, red blood seeped from his left temple.

Wayne and the other two men reined their horses back toward the fire and stared down at Carmody.

"Nice shootin', Eb!" yelled the scrawny coyote. "Head shot—sure as a whore's cheatin' heart!"

Soft footfalls thudded in the brush west of the wagon. Presently, a short hombre with a shaggy beard, low-crowned sombrero, and long stringy hair appeared, a Sharps Big Fifty resting over his right shoulder, a lit quirley dangling from his mouth. He wore high-topped boots and a duster that dragged along the ground behind him.

"Easy as shootin' a bull buff wallowed in river mud."

Wayne had dismounted and was heading for the campfire. "Lucius, you and Heck unsaddle our horses and stake them out with his. I'm gonna have some coffee."

Wayne squatted beside the fire and, with his gloved right hand, lifted the chugging coffee pot from the coals. He glanced at the marksman, Eb, who was standing up on his tip-toes to peer into the end of Carmody's covered wagon. "You better put another bullet in our friend there. Make sure he's good and dead."

"Don't tell me my job, Wayne," Eb said. "I been turnin' folks toe down since before you robbed your first bank."

Wayne sent Eb a cold, level look, the coffee pot in his left hand, his right hand resting on his thigh, just below his tied down holster from which the last two inches of a silver-plated, seven-inch barrel protruded. "I thought we came to an understanding, Eb. Back at The Forks."

Standing at the back of the wagon, one hand holding the canvas pucker open, Eb glared back at Wayne. Cursing under his breath, he released the pucker and walked around the wagon toward Carmody lying belly-down in the brush.

Seeing no reason to waste a cartridge, he shucked his big Bowie from his belt sheath and hunkered down beside the body. Before he could make the swipe across the jugular vein, Carmody turned suddenly, knocked the man's knife away from his neck with his own left wrist and, with his right hand, brought up his Russian .44, thumbing the hammer back.

Eb's eyes snapped wide, and his jaws dropped as Carmody's big .44 leveled on his head and roared, blowing a silver-dollar sized hole through the broad dome of his forehead, two inches up from his nose.

Dropping the knife and the rifle, Eb hit the brush on his back, his legs kicking spasmodically.

Carmody rose to a knee, thumbed the Russian's hammer back, and turned toward the fire.

Wayne was crouched on the fire's west side, his silver-plated hogleg held straight out from his shoulder, squinting his eyes to peer into the darkness. The Colt barked, geysering smoke and fire. The slug sliced the air over Carmody's right shoulder.

Carmody triggered a slug through Wayne's lower left side, just above his hip. As the ambusher stumbled back, cursing, Carmody again triggered the .44, the second slug drilling Wayne through the chest and punching him off his feet, straight back in the dust.

The Australian landed with a hard thud and a heavy groan, triggering his own revolver and barking a wayward slug off a rock in the fire ring, spraying blue sparks.

The sound of running feet rose from the trees where Carmody had staked his horses. Turning that way, he saw the silhouettes of the young coyote and the tall scarecrow bolting out of the cottonwoods, their gun iron flashing in the starlight. Carmody pivoted right as he threw himself forward and down, rolling off his right shoulder and coming up behind a thick stand of serviceberry.

Crouching, holding the .44 barrel-up in his right hand, he peered around the left side of the thicket as the two men ran into the campsite and stopped just beyond the edge of the firelight. Sharply raking air in and out of their lungs, the men waved their pistols around the campsite, pivoting from left to right.

The scarecrow had turned back toward the fire when Carmody extended his pistol toward him. "Over here."

The man whipped around, guns reflecting the fire's umber glow. Carmody quickly shot him through the heart. Before the blond coyote could get his .45s lowered, Carmody shot him in the belly.

The kid grunted sharply and stumbled two steps back, dropping both pistols at his sides. His knees buckled, but before he started going down, he raised the pistol in his right fist.

Carmody shot him through that arm, breaking the bone, the forearm dropping instantly, the gun popping and drilling a hole through the kid's right foot. He howled and fell hard on his ass.

"Drop the other gun!" Carmody yelled.

The kid didn't think twice. He dropped the gun like a glowing horseshoe and slapped his left hand over his bleeding belly.

Carmody moved toward him across the campsite, glancing at the dead sharp-shooter and the man called Wayne staring glassy-eyed straight up at the dark sky on the other side of the fire. The scarecrow lay unmoving.

Carmody angrily brushed at the blood dripping down the side of his face, from the open gash across his left temple. "What the hell you think you're doin', boy?"

"Shit!" the kid shrieked, crouched over his gushing middle. "My first d-damn bank job. We outrun the posse and then—*Shit!*—we run into *you!*"

"You after my horses?"

The kid sobbed and nodded dully, stretching his lips back from his teeth as the pain spasms racked him. Carmody snarled at him and brought his leg back for a kick, but set his foot back down beside the other.

"What bank did you hit?"

"Cheyenne."

Carmody stared down at the blond coyote and shook

his head. "Well, you're dead, kid. Dead as a can of corned beef, and I can't say I'm sorry." He swiped at the blood still dribbling down his face, then lowered the .44 to the kid's left temple, and pulled the trigger.

Carmody lowered the gun to his side, sighed, and swiped once more at the blood on his face. It was just a graze, but if that Big Fifty had been aimed a fraction more to the left, his brains would have dribbled out his ear. He slid the .44 into its holster then reached down, grabbed the back of the kid's coat collar, and dragged him over to the rocks along the river's edge, a good thirty yards from the fire.

When he'd dragged the scarecrow, Eb, and Wayne out to the rocks, he checked on the horses. The kid had unsaddled two but only loosened the cinch on the third. Carmody finished unsaddling the mount and was tossing down the blanket when he saw the leather satchel leaned up against a slender willow.

As the horses munched grass or snorted up water behind him, he picked up the satchel, took it over to the fire, opened it, and reached inside, dipping up a fat wad of greenbacks secured with paper bands band. He looked into the satchel, where two more wads snuggled together at the bottom like two prairie dogs deep in their holes.

Carmody whistled softly.

For a moment, while studying the money, he heard mariachi music, smelled garlic and tequila, and the perfume of brown-eyed senoritas in short skirts and skimpy cotton blouses. He smelled the faint salt tang of the sea, felt the ropes of an old hammock beneath his ass, the sun on his face...

He sniffed the leathery, inky, parchment odor of the greenbacks, dropped them back inside with a curse. He buckled the straps and tossed the case down with the outlaws' tack, halfway hoping someone would snatch the money while he slept. He wanted nothing to do with it.

He stomped back to the fire, squatted down, and picked up the coffee pot. It was surprisingly light. Frowning, he held it up for a closer look. A neat round hole shone in the speckled black tin, two inches up from the bottom.

"Ah, shit." He rose to his feet and chucked the pot in the general direction of the dead outlaws. It hit the ground with a tinny clatter. "You bastards ruined my coffee pot!"

2

CARMODY DIDN'T SLEEP well that night. The money and the visions of the Mexican senoritas plagued him. He woke well before dawn and wondered what he should do with the dead men and the loot.

Keeping the money was out of the question. Carmody was many things, but a thief was not one of them. Besides, his likeness already graced one set of wanted dodgers; he needed more trouble like a bad case of the pony drip.

He could leave the loot and the men here for a posse to pick up, but from what the outlaws had said, the posse had turned back. The money might end up in the wrong hands. If he turned the money over to a lawman, however, he'd better turn the dead men over, as well. The bodies would explain his having the money in the first place and might forestall a necktie party.

Grumbling, he crawled out from under his blankets, stomped into his boots, built up his fire for coffee, and walked out to where the dead men lay in the rocks, under a sky streaked with the first reds and blues of dawn. Shadows moved amongst the bodies. There was a guttural snort and the clicking of toenails on the rocks, a brief flash of feral eyes.

Carmody shucked his Russian and triggered a shot into the scuttling shadows. A coyote yipped. With raking breaths and clattering feet, the shadows scattered up and down the shore, one splashing water along the creek.

Carmody slid the .44 back down in its holster. "Damn bone-pickers."

After a quick breakfast of coffee, corn cakes, and side pork, he led the dead men's horses up from the brush, trussed the blanket-shrouded bodies belly down over their saddles, then tied the horses on a long lead line to the wagon's tailgate. He wedged the outlaws' satchel between two picks and a sluice box in the back of the wagon, just behind the seat, then backed his team to the hitch.

A warm morning breeze rustled the foxtails as he turned the piebalds onto the southern trail snaking across the high-desert prairie, the cedar-studded foothills rising on his right, the higher ridges painted salmon by the rising sun. The gaps between the high western peaks, bespeaking shaded canyons through which icy snowmelt rivers curved, beckoned to him with their quiet isolation and hard, gold-hunting labor. There he could hide out till the bounty hunters had forgotten him or gone on to other men with higher prices on their heads.

The voice in his memory, high-pitched and screechy with youthful passion, shouted, "You can't say you wasn't warned, Carmody!"

Then the blast from the .45 and an icy burn along's Carmody's left hip. Carmody's .44 returned fire—three shots triggered in quick succession followed by shattering glass, a shocked grunt, and the thud of a body hitting a roof. Then another thud and crack as, rolling off the roof, the body landed in a buckboard wagon sitting on the night-cloaked street below.

Now, Carmody blinked and ran a big hand down his face to clear his head. Bad luck, sure enough. And bad luck tended to follow on a short lead. The big drifter looked around warily then shook the ribbons over the piebalds' backs.

"Step it up there, boys. These carcasses are gonna start stinkin' like the devil's supper real soon!"

The late-summer sun rose high, and the bodies began stinking even sooner than Carmody anticipated. The northwest breeze shepherded the sickly-sweet smell up from behind the wagon. The neckerchief over Carmody's face, behind which he'd tucked aromatic sage sprigs and juniper berries, helped only a little.

By two o'clock in the afternoon, a small flock of turkey buzzards swirled twenty feet above the dead men's horses, the boldest of the bunch swooping low for the occasional quick peck. One must have made off with something juicy; the scraggly, black beast flapped down behind a large sage tuft to dine unharassed by the others.

Carmody winced behind his red neckerchief and remembered the wisdom voiced by an old stage driver he'd once ridden shotgun for: *For proof of the devil, look no farther than mustachioed women and turkey buzzards.*

Carmody couldn't have been more pleased to see, three hours later, the small Cavalry outpost of Camp Hawkins and, two miles farther south and west, the little town named after it. Wanting nothing to do with soldiers, he skirted the outpost and followed the Poudre River into the sun-baked little settlement nestled in the sage and cottonwoods along the river's south bank.

"P-U, son—you're a might whiffy on the lee side!" complained a one-legged old gent in a battered Confederate kepi. The old soldier lounged under the brush arbor of the three-story, mud-brick, mercantile store. He squinted over the smoking bowl of his corncob pipe, his wizened face pinched up as he stared at Carmody's makeshift caravan.

Carmody continued down the quiet street and reined up before a peeled-log, blacksmith shop so recently constructed that it still emanated pine resin. The leather-aproned blacksmith—middle-aged, with wildly curling gray hair, hawkish nose, and round-shoulders—stood between the open double-doors, a half-eaten sandwich in one broad hand, a half-smoked cigarette in the other.

He wrinkled his nose as he scrutinized the dead men. Buzzards had pecked through the blankets in several places, and blood and meat glistened in the afternoon sun.

"You smell like hell on house-cleanin' day," the old blacksmith rasped at Carmody, an ironic grin tugging at his bushy cinnamon beard. "Who you got there?"

"Four sidewinders needin' a hole powerful bad. But first I need to talk to the sheriff." Carmody glanced around the dozen or so buildings rising above the sage and rabbit brush. "I hope like hell you have one."

Taking a bite off his sandwich and staring at the sun-seasoned carcasses behind Carmody's wagon, the blacksmith said, "The Poudre, over yonder."

Carmody followed the man's glance to a tall, unpainted building about half a block away, with a second-story balcony and a high false front announcing, THE POUDRE RIVER SALOON, in large green letters. Before its broad, roofed front gallery, half a dozen saddle horses stood tied to the hitch racks, flies buzzing about their hanging heads.

Carmody set the brake and wrapped the reins around the handle. "Will you watch my rig for a minute?"

"Who you think's gonna take it?"

Stiffly crossing the sun-blasted street and beating dust from his pants with his hat, Carmody stepped between two tied horses and mounted the porch. He pushed through the batwings and squinted into the cool shadows smelling the stale beer and sawdust.

There were seven or eight men in the long, narrow room, most involved in a single poker game. Carmody saw no one wearing a badge. He stepped up to the bar where the apron stood, hands spread wide on the bar top, eyes glued to the poker game across the room.

"I'm lookin' for the sheriff," Carmody said.

The stocky gent with black-Irish eyes and hair, and wearing faded Cavalry blues beneath a grimy apron, didn't seem to hear. When he kept staring intently at the poker game, Carmody cleared his throat.

The barman winced and shook his head, annoyed. He grabbed a glass and a bottle, and, not taking his eyes from the game, quickly filled the glass and shoved it in front of Carmody, then craned his head to see around him.

Puzzled, Carmody turned to regard the players gathered around the table on the far side of the room, about mid-way between the front and the back. They were a dusty, unshaven crew, wearing chaps and six-shooters. A rangy man with his back to Carmody had long, cinnamon hair swirling down the back of a brown leather vest, a long cigar in the ash tray near his right forearm.

The players huddled intently over the pasteboards fanned out in their hands, calling and raising in hushed voices, thick tobacco smoke rising above their heads and glowing in the brassy light angling through the front windows. Chips clattered and shot glasses were set down with glassy thuds. Smoke was exhaled through raspy sighs.

Carmody saw nothing special about the men or the game, but the barman was obviously entranced. Maybe the stakes were high.

Grudgingly, he stepped aside and sipped his drink. He'd wait the barman out. After the long ride with four, smelly, dead men, he could use a quiet drink. Aside from the need to get the carcasses underground, he was in no real hurry. Nathan wouldn't be here for another two or three days.

When he finished his drink, he set the glass on the scratched pine counter and turned to the barman, who was still regarding the card game as he absently polished a beer mug.

"All right, fella," Carmody said. "I hate to—" He stopped and stared at the barman. The man's face had gained a sickly pallor, and his hands stopped working on the mug as he cast his wary gaze at the table.

Behind Carmody, one of the card players barked, "I don't think so, Sheriff. I seen that card you slipped out of your sleeve!"

The man no sooner finished the sentence than a chair scraped back from the table. Carmody turned to see a bearded gent, with a green bandana worn like a cap, bound out of his chair clawing a worn Remington from his low-slung holster.

As he brought the pistol up, the slender, long-haired hombre, his back to Carmody, stood abruptly, his chair bounding straight out behind him and falling to the floor with a loud clap. He drew his own pistol so quickly all Carmody saw was a blur of movement, then the smoke and fire stabbing from the Peacemaker's maw.

The man with the bandanna grunted and stumbled back, firing his snub-nosed Remy into the floor, both explosions rocking the building.

"Ah, Jesus!" groaned the barman, jerking with a start and ducking down behind the counter.

The slender, long-haired gent—the sheriff, Carmody assumed—spread his legs and crouched as he swung his Peacemaker left, and shot the gent two gents down from the first attacker. The man's pistol exploded into the ceiling as he flew straight back off his feet, his head striking the plank wall with a thunderous crack.

He hadn't hit the floor before the man to his left brought up his right hand, a double-barreled derringer rearing up from the slide under his sleeve like a wicked little prairie dog poking its head out of its hole. Standing and yelling incoherently, his pea shooter extended straight out from his shoulder, squinting against the wafting powder smoke, the man tripped one of the two triggers and watched the slug tear nap from the vest at the sheriff's right shoulder.

The lawman stumbled stiffly back, turning slightly toward Carmody before dropping to one knee and turning back toward the table.

As the sheriff returned fire at the man with the pea-shooter, a man bolted out of the shadows at the room's rear. He was a big, thin-bearded gent with a broad-brimmed hat and high-topped boots. Marching swiftly toward the lawman, he raised a sawed-off, double-barreled shotgun to his belt buckle, raging, "You're done fer now, ye damned, badge-totin' *whore!*"

Before Carmody knew what he was doing, he'd picked up a nearby chair and swung it one-handed toward the man with the shotgun. It slammed into the man's left shoulder, throwing off his aim. As he stumbled right, the shotgun discharged with a volcanic explosion, the buck-shot peppering the two hombres remaining at the table exchanging gunfire with the sheriff.

As both men screamed and stumbled back toward the wall, clawing at their bloody faces, the sheriff shot the man with the pea-shooter. The man with the shotgun, now down on one knee, turned his outraged gaze toward Carmody. "You'll pay for that—!"

Crouching, Carmody clawed his .44 from its holster and fired twice. As the slugs punched through the man's chest, he discharged the shotgun's second barrel, and the five-gallon jar of pig's feet on the bar exploded, showering brine.

Spying movement to his right, back in the room's shadows, Carmody dropped to both knees as two guns flashed and popped. The slugs plunked into the bar on both sides of him, another smashing into the back bar's mirror.

Behind the counter, the barman loosed a muffled

lament, drowned out by Carmody's big Russian sending three quick shots toward the room's rear. One of the remaining two gunmen cursed loudly and fell to a shoulder. The other bolted out from behind an overturned table, a stocky, hatted shadow bolting toward Carmody.

Clay leveled the .44 at him. The man crouched behind the piano at the middle of the room, snugged up to a square-hewn, center post from which a bull's eye lantern hung. Knowing he had only one more pill in the wheel, Carmody held the shot but kept the .44 leveled at the piano.

The man poked his head out from behind the post and the lantern. Carmody fired. The bullet shattered the unlit lamp.

The gunman screamed and stumbled out from behind the post, his face a bloody mess of glass-and-bullet-shredded meat. He dropped his pistol and hit the floor howling and kicking, beating his boots against the floor.

Carmody dropped to his butt and pressed his back against the bar. As he automatically began replacing the spent brass from the .44's cylinder, he glanced left, where the smoke hung thick over the overturned gambling table. Blood-splattered chips and playing cards were scattered across the floor. The man who'd produced the derringer lay limp over an overturned chair, bleeding from several wounds. Carmody caught only glimpses of the other gunmen lying in twisted heaps against the far wall.

The sheriff sat with his back to an overturned table, knees raised toward his chest. The lawman was fumbling with the gun in his lap, reloading from his cartridge belt. He was having a hard time, as his right arm was shaking, apparently from the graze to that shoulder. His face was hidden by the flat brim of his snuff-brown hat.

Carmody got up and walked over to the sheriff, his ears ringing, eyes stinging from the smoke. As he stopped before the man and opened his mouth to speak, the man snapped the Peacemaker's loading gate closed and jerked his head up suddenly. The pistol shot straight out from the man's chest, the barrel aimed squarely at Carmody's heart.

Carmody's gaze flitted from the revolver to the face of the most beautiful woman he'd ever seen.

3

"*Damn*," Carmody muttered. He stumbled back but held the cold, suspicious gaze delivered by two eyes green as polished jade. "You're the sheriff?"

"Who the hell are you?" the woman growled, squinting one of those agates as she stared down her Peacemaker's barrel.

"Easy." Carmody raised his hands, grasping his .44 around the cylinder. "I'm peaceable."

"Answer the question, friend."

"Carmody." He gave a half-smile, cheek nubs warming as the woman's beauty penetrated his loins. "You can call me Clay... Sheriff."

She studied him for another stretched moment, then peered past him to the room's rear, where the man Carmody had shot still thrashed on the floor like a gut-shot dog. Her gaze didn't soften so much as turn more speculative. She lowered her gun and pushed herself to her feet.

"Nice shooting," she muttered, turning to inspect the four men she'd taken down.

"Same to you."

Carmody turned to watch her walk across the room to

the wounded man, her fringed chaps flapping against her slender, nicely rounded thighs.

The wounded gent lay flat on his back still beating his hands and feet against the floor.

She stared down at him. "Irvin Fry, you're hit bad," she said matter-of-factly. "I can send for the doc, but he's probably soused by now. I doubt you'd live through the night, anyway. You've lost both eyes and a lot of blood."

The man gurgled as he thrashed, managing one coherent word, "*Bitch!*"

She turned to the barman, who stood behind the bar looking warily back at her, both fists again mounted on the brine-covered bartop. "Vern, will you sign an affidavit attesting to the fact that this man elected to be put out of his misery?"

"Shoot the bastard, Claudine."

Casually, she turned back to the wounded man, sighted down the barrel of her Peacemaker, and squeezed the trigger. The gun popped and smoked.

The wounded gent gave a guttural grunt and relaxed.

She turned and walked back to the overturned table, then stooped down and picked through the chips and greenbacks. "Vern, I'm taking my winnings. The rest is yours."

The barman shook his head and ran a hand down his face with a heavy exhalation. "'Preciate that."

Still standing where he'd been when he first learned the sheriff of Camp Hawkins was a buxom brunette with a rosebud mouth and the cold-steel talent of Wes Hardin, Carmody watched her move toward the batwings over which several surprised faces peered from the porch. It took him so long to gather his thoughts and to remember what he'd come here for that she was almost through the doors when he said, "Uh... Sheriff?"

She stopped and, holding one door wide, tipped her hat back from her forehead as she turned her heart-shaped, strong-jawed face to him. The light from outside illuminated those green eyes like the early morning sun on a high-country lake. "Yes, Mr. Carmody?"

"When I walked into your little bailiwick here, I'd come to talk business with you."

"Business?" She arched an eyebrow and looked him up and down. "What business do you have with the law, Mr. Carmody? Dogs tree your cat?"

The barman chuckled, as did several other townsmen standing on the porch. Blushing, Carmody holstered his .44 and hitched his cartridge belt on his hips. "My cat's just fine. It's those men yonder, tied over their saddles, I come to palaver about."

She turned her head to gaze across the street, frowning, still holding the single batwing open. Finally, she quietly ordered a couple of townsmen to bury the men she and Clay had shot, then stepped away from the doors, the left one shuddering behind her.

As three burly men moved into the saloon, casting timid, puzzled glances toward Carmody, Clay moved past them through the doors. He descended the porch steps and angled across the street toward the wagon sitting before the blacksmith shop. The sheriff was already moving along beside the horses, lifting the dead men's heads by their hair to inspect their sallow visages.

When she finished, she ran the back of her hand across her nose and strode back toward Carmody, who stood beside the wagon's right rear wheel, casually rolling a cigarette.

"How do you like my handiwork, Sheriff?" he asked, deftly rolling the cylinder closed.

"Nice." Stopping before him, she drew her Peacemaker in one butter-smooth motion, keeping the pistol, barrel forward, down by her right hip. "Why don't you hand over that .44 nice and slow, butt-first?"

"Ah, don't get your neck in a hump." Carmody stuck

the quirley in his mouth, turned, moved toward the front of the wagon, and reached through a gap in the canvas.

"Hold it, Mister," the woman warned sharply.

Carmody turned toward her and held up his left hand, palm out, keeping his right hand in the wagon. He met her sharp gaze with an ironic smile as he slowly pulled his right hand out of the wagon box and held up the satchel by two fingers.

She reached out with her left hand to grab it away from him. Keeping the Peacemaker trained on his belly, she wedged the satchel under her left arm, opened it, glanced inside, and then frowned up at him.

He lit the quirley. Blowing smoke and waving out the match, he said, "They stole it off a bank in Cheyenne. I confiscated it when they rode into my camp last night and tried to *confiscate* my horses."

The sheriff glanced at the bloody bandanna wrapped around his forehead, beneath his tan hat. Closing the satchel, she tapped her fingers on it musingly. "My, an honest man." She holstered the Peacemaker and gave him that cool up and down glance again.

She could stand there and look at him all day, because he couldn't think of anything more fun than standing here, feasting his eyes on the way she filled out that striped, collarless shirt beneath the brown leather vest. How her hips flared slightly beneath the black cartridge belt, the black denim jeans and fringed batwing chaps clinging to her long, slender legs like they couldn't think of a better place they'd rather be, either.

He lifted his gaze back to her face, the green eyes shaded by her snuff-brown hat brim. Those plump, red lips had to be more fun to kiss than ripe river plums were to eat.

He canted his head to the side and squinted one eye. "How in the hell did a woman get to be sheriff of Camp Hawkins?"

"No one else wanted the job after my father, the sitting sheriff, was shot out of his chair in his own office." She extended her hand. "I'm Claudine Bridger, Mr. Carmody."

Carmody shook her hand. Fine-boned but lightly calloused and firm-gripped, the appendage bespoke a woman of the outdoors as opposed to the piano parlor. As if her cold-steel work back inside The Poudre hadn't been proof enough. The feel of her hand in his made him tingle down deep in his loins.

"Pleased to make your acquaintance."

"If you'll walk over to my office with me, I'll have you fill out a report for the sheriff in Cheyenne. There might be a reward for the men and the money."

Carmody needed no reward beyond Claudine Bridger's very presence. She was indeed a sight for the sore eyes of a man who'd seen *no* woman for at least a month. He wasn't going to fall all over himself, however. She hadn't even thanked him for helping her out in the saloon, when he'd tossed the chair into the hombre wielding the barn-blaster. If it hadn't been for Carmody's intervention, she'd be plastered against the saloon's front window about now, not looking half so enticing.

"Mr. Faraday," she said, turning toward the blacksmith working at his forge, a shapeless hat shoved back on his gray curls. "Tell your nephews that if they plant these bodies in the boneyard, I'll furnish their first bottle of busthead tonight in The Poudre."

The blacksmith brought the hammer down with a ringing clank, and nodded. "They might stir themselves for that, all right."

As the blacksmith bellowed for Ted and Ernest, still tonging the andiron in his forge, Sheriff Bridger and Carmody headed back across the main street. They skirted the saloon, through the batwings of which one of the dead men was being carted by three grim townsmen, and headed north along a cross street.

As they approached the low-slung, brown-adobe jailhouse with a brush arbor over the front door, Carmody turned to the woman taking long strides to his left. "This may be none of my business, but did you really pull a fast one on those boys back there?"

"You mean, did I really have a card up my sleeve?" The sheriff chuffed. "I don't have to cheat to win at blackjack."

"They wanted you dead powerful bad."

"They were cattle rustlers, but I couldn't prove it. With my deputies looking into trouble in Poudre Canyon, I didn't have enough firepower to run them out of town, but I made a deal with those border roughs. If I could beat them at blackjack, they had to leave the county. For good."

"They didn't much care for that idea."

"I didn't think they would. I was just stalling until my deputies returned to back my play. The long-loopers had a good operation here." She mounted the boardwalk before the jailhouse and placed a hand on the doorknob, but didn't turn it. "And they under-estimated my ability to collect on the bet."

"Well, they won't make the same mistake again."

She poked her hat brim back and looked up at Carmody, who stood a full foot taller and who shaded her with his broad-shouldered bulk. "I may be a woman, Mr. Carmody, but I am first and foremost the Sheriff of Crow Dog County. Those who underestimate my abilities do so at their own peril."

Carmody threw up his hands. "I saw that, ma'am."

She pushed through the door and stepped into the dark room rife with the smell of adobe, dirt, and coal oil.

Carmody followed her inside, leaving the door open. Despite the two small windows on either side of it, the room would have been dusk-like dark with it closed.

He stood just inside the threshold as she set the valise on a spool-back chair beside a gun rack on the left wall, then dropped with a sigh into the swivel chair behind her cluttered, flat-topped desk. Opening a drawer, she produced a lined tablet and a pencil, and tossed both onto the blotter, the draft blowing wanted dodgers and scribbled notes to one side.

She doffed her hat, shook out her rich, cinnamon curls, and picked up the pencil. "Okay," she said, "tell me what happened."

"What do you mean?"

"I'm going to transcribe your story, and you can put your mark on it when I'm done. I'll witness it for you."

"You think I can't write?"

Crouched over the tablet, she stared up at him skeptically.

"My ma was a schoolteacher, and she didn't raise no dummy." Carmody grabbed a chair from the left wall, positioned it before the desk, and sat down across from Sheriff Bridger. He pulled the tablet toward him and plucked the pencil from her fingers. "I'll write it down for myself and *sign* it. How'd that be?"

An amused smile tugged at the corners of her plum-ripe mouth. She reached into another drawer, produced a bottle and two water glasses. She set the bottle and the glasses on the desktop between her and Carmody. "Drink?"

"Why not?" he said, taking a drag off his quirley then touching the pencil to his tongue and hunkering over the tablet.

As he began writing, the sheriff splashed whiskey into each glass, then set the bottle on the desk and corked it. She leaned back in the chair and crossed her boots on the deskstop. She lit a long, thin cigar and, smoking and sipping the whiskey, watched the big man across from her bemusedly as he scratched the pencil across the tablet, frowning with concentration.

Carmody threw back half his drink, sighed, cracked his

knuckles, took another drag off the cigarette, and resumed writing.

Claudine Bridger felt a strange warmth grow into a slight burn in the pit of her stomach. She sipped her drink, took a drag off the cigar and blew the smoke out to the side. A handsome man, this Carmody, with strength, kindness, and intelligence in those gray-blue eyes—a rare combination in these parts. Backed up by a raw power in those thick hands and arms.

In her mind's eye, Claudine saw herself reaching out with both hands and pressing her palms to the twin slabs of his chest straining the weather-worn, calico tunic. Brown, sweat-damp hair swirled close to the suntanned skin between the first two, open, bone buttons below his neck.

As if from the bottom of a deep well, she heard his voice. "Ma'am?"

She lifted her eyes to his, staring back at her expectantly, his forehead wrinkled with mild amusement. She jumped, knocking cigar ash onto her lap and nearly nudging her boots off the desk. "What?"

He tossed the pencil onto the tablet he'd pushed across the desk. "I said, that's pretty much what happened. I've signed it. Your turn."

Her face was warm as fresh-baked adobe and her hands shook slightly as, frowning to cover her chagrin, she lifted the tablet, read what he'd written, then threw back the last of her whiskey, and signed the statement. She tossed the tablet onto the desk.

"Thanks, Carmody."

Carmody stood. "Ma'am."

"Where can I find you, if I need you?" She hurried to add, flushing all over again, "I mean, if there's a reward to be issued."

"Maybe you can tell me. I'll need a hotel for two or three days, till my prospecting partner hits town."

"The Canyon Inn would be my choice. In fact"—she nonchalantly took another drag off the cigar and blew smoke at the low ceiling—"I keep a room there myself."

"Is that so? You bathe there, too?"

She coughed, bouncing slightly in her chair and waving the smoke around her face. "They have a bath-house out back."

Carmody nodded. He didn't say anything for a moment as he studied the cluttered desktop. "Pardon me for pryin', Sheriff, but is there a *Mister* Bridger?"

She boldly held his gaze. "Why do you ask, Mr. Carmody?"

Carmody's own eyes didn't waver from hers, her heart-shaped face framed by the delicious swirls of thick, cinnamon hair. He spread his hand in supplication. "Now, don't go getting' your back in another hump. I'm just snoopy's all."

She let the question hang there for a moment, as if deciding whether or not to answer it. "There is no *Mister* Bridger. I reckon you could say I'm hitched to my job."

Carmody nodded and hitched up his cartridge belt then reached across the desk to shake her hand, which was warmer now than before, the palms slightly moist. "Much obliged for the information, Sheriff. Maybe we'll run into each other over at the hotel." He chuckled. "Or, hell, maybe in the bath house!"

Trying to maintain a haughty expression, she stubbed the cigar out in the ashtray on her desk. "Oh, I doubt that, Mr. Carmody. The hotel has two bath houses--one for men, and one for women." She smiled blandly up at him, trying hard to ignore the burn in her belly that seemed to be inching toward her thighs.

"Well, that makes sense, I reckon." Carmody offered another self-effacing grin, then pinched his hat brim, turned, and left the jailhouse.

Behind him, Claudine Bridger stared at the closed door, sucked her upper lip into her mouth, and chewed it.

CARMODY PARKED his wagon in the town's single livery and feed barn, where he also stabled his horses. After paying the liveryman two day's advance stabling and tending of the horses and wagon, he secured a room at the Canyon Inn on the west edge of town, facing a fir-stippled, sand-colored rimrock. Then he had a hot, soothing bath in the men's bathhouse behind the place, soaking out the trail dust and death stench that seemed to have seeped clean into his bones.

The bath house was tended by an affable, bib-bearded Chinaman who kept the water hot, sent his customer's dirty clothes out for laundering, shaved him, and even scrubbed Carmody's back with a horsehair brush. The scrubbing felt so good it raised goose pimples over every inch of Carmody's bulky frame.

He was just finishing up the bath, feeling like a hundred and eighty pounds of jelly, when thunder-heads broiled over the mountains and began pummeling Camp Hawkins with rain-drops the size of silver dollars. He ate a steak and had a few drinks in the hotel's restaurant, then went back to his room. By the light of a single lamp, he stripped down to his clean balbriggans and lay on the soft feather-bed, watching the lightning flash in the rain-streaked window...waiting.

Around ten-thirty, someone knocked on his door.

Carmody smiled. "It's open."

Sheriff Claudine Bridger walked into the room.

Silhouetted by the dim hall light behind her, she wore a bulky bear robe that came down to only her knees, and her snuff-brown hat. She was barefoot. Her rich, cinnamon hair flowed loose about her shoulders, framing her oval face and cool, green eyes.

In her left hand she clutched a brandy bottle by the neck. In her right hand she held one of her long, slim, black cigars. She kicked the door closed and moved to the bed, where Carmody lay with his hands laced behind his head, ankles crossed.

"For your help in the saloon earlier," she said huskily, popping the cork from the bottle and handing it to him.

Carmody took a pull from the bottle and gave it back to her.

She took a pull then set the bottle on the dresser beside the bed. Sticking the cigar between her teeth, she opened the robe then let it fall to the floor.

Before him, she stood in all her naked loveliness, wearing only the hat, puffing the cigar.

4

"Take off the hat," Carmody said.

She put a hand on her hip and turned her head slightly. "You're giving the orders?"

"That's right."

Thunder cracked like two boulders crashing together on the other side of town. Lightning flashed blue through the rain-streaked window, for a moment silhouetting the woman's slender, curvaceous figure against a pane.

Claudine set her cigar in an ashtray on the dresser, in which Carmody had stubbed out several quirleys. Then she removed her hat, tossed it onto a chair, and shook her hair out around her porcelain shoulders and large, full breasts. Her nipples were hard little thimbles jutting toward him, as if reaching for him.

He laid there, hands behind his head, watching her, giving himself a good eyeful of this cold-steel Goddess with her hard, round breasts, taut belly, and gently flaring hips tapering to thighs alluringly shaped from riding.

"Like what you see?" she whispered down to him, running her eyes down his broad torso straining the top of the long-underwear shirt, to his crotch causing a bulge in his underwear's buttoned fly, and from which the swollen brown head of his penis was beginning to protrude.

"Just so's ya know, I don't normally do this sort of thing." She climbed onto the bed and straddled him on her hands and knees, her hair brushing his chest. "In fact, I haven't..." She stopped, as if uncertain how to continue, and placed both hands over the twin slabs of his upper chest.

His voice was a low, raspy growl. "You haven't had a tumble in a while?"

"When you're the sheriff, you have certain...rules."

"I'd imagine gettin' your womanly satisfaction would be a might on the tricky side."

She was crabbing down the length of his body, toward his feet, running her hair and her hands down his torso. "You have...no idea...."

Hooking her ankles snugly around his, she lowered her head to his crotch, pressed her nose to his member jutting up from the fly.

He'd never felt anything quite so exhilarating, such powerful shock waves radiating up from his belly, pinched off his wind. She nuzzled his hardening shaft for nearly a minute, then extended her pink, wet tongue, which he could see between waves of her richly falling hair, and licked the purpling tip.

The warm, moist sensation set his loins on fire. He grunted.

She licked the jutting rod for another minute then closed her mouth over it, taking it all the way to her throat. She lifted her head, crabbed back up to his chest and smiled down at him between the twin cascades of cinnamon hair swirls.

"This must be absolutely *secreto. Comprende, amigo?"*

"Si." Carmody lifted his hands and swept her hair back from her face. "If the God-fearin' citizens got wind of their unmarried sheriff coupling with drifters, you might not get reelected."

She leaned down, licked his lips, nibbled his chin, and kissed him hungrily. "And then I might not get a second chance at finding my father's killer." She kissed him again then lifted her head and ground her groin against his.

"Your father's—?"

"Shh." Arching her head back even farther, she settled down over his member and gently pressed her right palm to his mouth, clamped her knees against his hips, and shuddered.

Outside, thunder rumbled and lightning flashed.

Leaning down hard on her outstretched arms, hands on Carmody's shoulders, she worked away on top of him for several minutes. The draft from the window caused the lamp to smoke and sputter before finally snuffing it out.

Blue lightning lit up the room as Carmody, pushed nearly to the edge of his passion, rose up suddenly with a bear-like groan, and tossed Claudine onto her back.

She hit the pillow with a sudden, surprised cry then followed it up with an excited laugh as he sank between her spread legs and went to work in a passionate fervor of unfettered lust and need.

She groaned and cried and ground her heels into the drifter's arched, pistoning back. Thunder exploded, rocking the building and rattling the windows.

Lightning flashed through the rain-splattered panes. Carmody lifted his head with surging relief and a long, rising groan of bittersweet release. He remained frozen there, face to the dark wall, for several minutes until he lowered his head to her breasts and suckled each erect nipple in turn.

He slid down her lithe, sweat-damp body, rested his cheek against her belly. She gently pulled at his sandy hair then released it slowly, leaving her open hands on his head, and relaxed against her pillow.

They slept, awakened a half hour later by an especially violent thunder-clap and made love again, more gently and leisurely this time. Then the two conversed groggily for a few minutes before again falling asleep in each other's arms.

CARMODY DIDN'T KNOW what time it was, but it was still storming when he heard a voice shouting in the street.

Claudine woke, as well, and lifted her head from his chest. She looked toward the window. Lightning flashed in the western distance, illuminating every raindrop on the window.

"Claw-*deene!*" rose the voice again—a man's voice pinched and trembling with fear and desperation. It was followed by a single pistol shot and another yell.

Claudine scrambled off the bed and strode naked to the window facing the side street.

Behind her, Carmody pulled his Russian from the holster coiled over the bedpost, then got up and moved to the window. Peering over her shoulder, he saw two blurry horseback figures riding up and down the street before the building. They peered at a window on the opposite end of the same floor Carmody's room was on.

"My deputies," Claudine said.

On the street one of the men called her name again and fired another shot into the air above his head. "Sheriff —!" His jittery mount turned around just then, muffling his cry. The other man's horse also turned suddenly. The man lost his grip on the horn and fell down the mount's right side. He hit the soggy street, splashing mud and dung, but he clung to the horse's reins.

"What in God's name?" Claudine grabbed her bear robe off the floor, threw it around her shoulders, and scrambled out of the room. She ran down the dark hall, opened the outside door, and stepped out onto the stairway leading down the cross street side of the building.

Holding the robe closed at her throat, she blinked against the spitting rain, waved her arm out, and yelled, "I'll be right down!"

When she ran back into the hotel, Carmody waited in the hall, in the balbriggans he'd hastily donned, holding his pistol down by his thigh. "What's goin' on?"

"Those are two of my three overdue deputies." Claudine brushed past Carmody and moved quickly into the room. "I figured they'd just run into some prospector with extra sour mash. Looks like they ran into trouble. I hope to God Henry isn't dead. His mother'll kill me."

Carmody grabbed his jeans and sat on the bed to pull them on.

Claudine grabbed her hat off the dresser and looked at him. "What're you doin'?"

"Those boys look as riled up as mules in a hailstorm. I'll come with you."

She leaned down, grabbed his head in both her hands and kissed him hard on the lips. "Thanks for the evening, lover. Happy trails to you."

With that she swung around and left the room, drawing the door closed behind her. Carmody sat on the bed, stunned, and listened to her pad off down the hall to her own quarters.

Claudine dressed quickly in the room at the other end of the hall, grateful the two Civil War veterans who lived around her hadn't awakened from their slumbers and seen her running half-naked from Carmody's room.

When she'd wrapped her cartridge belt around her waist and donned her India-rubber rain slicker and hat, she left the room and descended the dark stairs to the lobby. The wizened, arthritic ex-trapper who ran the place with his Cheyenne wife and half-wit granddaughter, stood near a side-street window, wearing a tattered robe and nightcap and holding a candle in his right hand.

He turned to Claudine with a concerned expression. "Sheriff, you hear your deputies out there...?"

"I hear 'em, Mr. Bardoul. Go on back to bed. Everything's under control."

"They look like they seen a whole tree-full o' the devil's owls!"

Claudine walked outside and descended the broad porch to the street, the rain now only a fine, breeze-blown mist. Lights were on over several stores along both the side-street and Main, the deputies' shots having awakened half the village.

"Keith, what the hell is goin' on?" she asked one of the two men sitting his enervated horse at the corner of the Main Street intersection, peering west with his Spencer carbine raised high in one hand.

The other man, Grits Tatum, had gained his feet after falling from his horse. He stood now beside the mount, staring westward. Neither man wore his rain slicker, and their wet clothes clung to their skin. The pounding rain had turned the brim of Keith Boley's cream Stetson straight down, so that the rain dribbled onto his mud-splattered face and shoulders.

"Don't know how to explain it, Claudine," Boley said with a shudder.

"Where's Henry?"

"It got him!" yelled Grits Tatum, wheeling his short, bulky frame toward Claudine.

By the vagrant light reflecting off the puddles dotting the street, she saw the fear in his wide eyes and drawn cheeks, beneath the brim of his sodden bowler.

The fear in both men was an almost palpable entity. Claudine's skin turned cold from the inside out. She studied both men for a time, then reached out and grabbed the bridle of Boley's dun mare.

The horse gave a start and whinnied loudly, pulling free of Claudine's grip. It took two awkward steps to the right before its front legs bent and, with a shrill whinny, hit the street on its belly. Keith Boley leapt heavily from the saddle as the horse rolled onto its side, like a fishing boat turning over in a heavy gale.

"Christ!" Claudine said, turning to the animal. Its snout and neck were basted with foamy blood. Glancing at the deputy scrambling onto his knees in the muddy street, she said, sharply accusing, "You've blown her plum out, Keith!"

The blond, fair-featured Boley pushed himself to his feet, regarded the horse with frustration, then cast a guilty glance at the sheriff. "Y-you didn't see what we saw, Claudine."

Sheriff Bridger cursed again, drew her revolver, planted the barrel behind the mare's right ear, and put the spent beast out of her misery with a single shot. "Come on," she ordered both men, heading east down the sodden street, her boots splashing through the mud and dung.

Halfway to the end of the block, she glanced over her right shoulder. The two deputies moved heavy-footed toward the boardwalk, Grits Tatum leading his own, hang-headed pony a good twenty yards behind Boley. Behind them both, the dead mare was a broad, black hump in the middle of the street.

Claudine opened the jailhouse door with her key and went inside, leaving the door standing open. She lit the bracket lamp on the peg beside the door, then the hurricane lamp on her desk. She was stuffing paper and tinder into the tin stove when Boley stumbled into the jailhouse, followed a moment later by the short, stocky Tatum in his sodden bowler, holding his Spencer repeater beneath his right arm.

Claudine shoved some kindling onto the growing

blaze, then, leaving the stove door open, sat down in her chair and produced the bottle and two glasses from a drawer. She set the glasses on the other side of the desk and popped the cork on the bottle.

"Pull up a chair and sit down," she ordered, splashing two inches of whiskey into each glass.

Boley sat in the chair Carmody had left before the desk. Tatum pulled up the spool-back from the opposite wall, sat heavily, grabbed one of the glasses in his trembling hand, and threw back half the whiskey in one shot. He set the glass on the desk, ran a hairy-backed hand up his forehead, nudging off his hat, which rolled off his left shoulder to the earthen floor. Tatum ran his hand back through his thin, brown hair then down the back of his head to his neck, squeezing as if to distract himself from troubled thoughts.

Boley sat to Tatum's left, slumped in his chair, his down-turned hat brim still dribbling droplets onto his face and shoulders. He just stared at the desk, eyes bright with fear and confusion.

Leaning toward both men, her elbows digging into the desktop, Claudine said slowly, enunciating each word clearly, "Now, tell me what happened. Where is Henry Acres?"

"Dead," said Grits Tatum, wincing as if from a pain spasm. He set both elbows on the edge of the desk and kneaded his temples with his fingers. "Ah, sweet Jesus—Henry's dead!—An' I wish I was dead, too, after what I seen!"

5

"HAPPY *TRAILS* TO YOU?" Carmody said in the dark of his room, still sitting on the edge of his bed, one leg stuffed down in his pants, the other out. "Is *that* what she said?"

Men were supposed to say that to *women* they'd slept with—excepting whores, of course, who merely pocketed their earnings and began looking for more. Women were supposed to stare after departing men much the way Carmody was staring at his closed door, with shock, surprise, and more than a touch of injury.

He looked at the bottle on the dresser. At least she left him that. He grabbed it, took a long swallow, then another. Only after the liquor had soothed his pride did he remember the crazed deputies shooting their sidearms in the street, and began wondering again what the trouble was about.

Well, the haughty sheriff hadn't wanted his help, so he'd be damned if he was going to worry about it. He'd saved her life once, and entertained her in the old mattress sack. Apparently, that was all she needed him for.

He'd been dismissed.

To hell with her. He was going to sleep.

He took one more pull off the near-empty bottle, set it

on the dresser, kicked out of his jeans, lay down, and drew the blankets up. He sniffed. The sheet and quilts smelled like her—like honeysuckle and lilacs and musky, female need.

He took a deep breath, feeling the hurt and anger grow once more, like a little flame behind his heart. Mentally swatting it aside, he turned his thoughts instead to Nathan's imminent arrival and to heading into the mountains. To the prospect of getting rich off Poudre Canyon gold then trekking to San Francisco, rich as robber barons, to break some tender hearts of his own.

He slept.

THE NEXT MORNING, he dressed and gave himself a whore's bath as the crisp morning sunlight angled through the room's two windows. He shaved in the warped mirror over the washstand, again trying to get his mind off the bewitching hours he'd spent wrestling naked with Camp Hawkins's beguiling law woman.

He'd just dipped his bone-handled razor in the basin, remembering the exquisite feel of her hard-nippled breasts in his hands, when a man's shrill scream rose through the wooden floor beneath his bare feet.

Carmody froze and cocked his head to listen.

Again the man screamed. Loud thumps and scrapes followed. A woman shouted in a guttural Native tongue while the man went on yelling, "Oh...oh, Christ... Look out, Wynnie!"

"Gun!" the woman screamed.

Carmody dropped the razor in the sudsy basin and was turning toward the door when a pistol exploded twice, then a third time. Amidst the sound of stomping feet and the thuds and booms of an indistinguishable origin,

Carmody grabbed his pistol belt and wrapped it around his waist as he headed toward the door.

He was descending the stairs when the gun popped again.

"There!" yelled the Indian woman.

"He's under the table," the man raged. "Get back!"

Hearing several other guests descending the stairs behind him, muttering puzzled exclamations, Carmody hit the lobby on the run. He turned left around the front desk, entering the hotel's small restaurant area consisting of a half-dozen wooden chairs and tables and a bar of pine planks stretched across whiskey kegs.

A trapdoor had been drawn up from the floor, revealing a small rectangular hole. Around the hole scrambled the hotel's bald, gray-bearded proprietor named Chester Bardoul and his stocky Indian wife in a threadbare cotton dress and apron. Winnie was beating the floor with a broom while the bull-legged Bardoul was aiming a .41-caliber Colt Lightning, tracking something moving fast toward Carmody.

"Lookout, mister!"

Carmody leapt back as the snake struck, rising as high as his knees then springing back to the floor, coiling and probing the air with its forked tongue and sliding its flat head from side-to-side, ready to strike again.

"Holy shit!" yelled another hotel guest standing in the doorway behind Carmody.

Carmody extended the Russian and fired twice, the second shot drilling the snake about six inches back from its head and sending the viper into a writhing frenzy, knocking a chair and a table with the force of a man's arm.

Bardoul's Lightning popped, and Carmody lifted his gaze to see another viper whipping around near the base of the plank bar to his right.

"Holy hounds of hell!" another guest exclaimed. "The room's full of 'em!"

Through his own powder smoke, Carmody raked his eyes across the room, where nearly a dozen rattlesnakes were slithering across the floorboards, crisscrossing each other in their haste to escape the bullets and the woman's thrashing broom. One was trying to climb the far wall, clinging to the wainscoting as if to take a gander out the window above.

Carmody shot it, shot the one below it, shot another twisting up a table leg.

"Look out!" wheezed one of the oldsters behind him.

In the middle of the room now, his Russian smoking in his fist, Carmody wheeled sharply right as one of the vipers struck at him, sinking its fangs into his right jeans cuff. Carmody squeezed off a shot. Kicking the dead snake free of his leg, he turned to see two more snakes slithering up from the hole.

"Close the damn door!" he shouted to Bardoul.

The Indian woman screamed as a striking snake caught its teeth in her apron. She stumbled back, falling against a chair, which fell onto its side and the wailing woman on top of it. Bardoul raised his gun to shoot the snake, thought better of it, dropped the gun, and fell to one knee, grabbing the striking snake in both hands and flinging it across the room.

The writhing snake flew toward Carmody. He ducked as the viper glanced off his right shoulder and hit the floor near the bar, coiling, lifting its head, and regarding the drifter with flat devil's eyes.

Carmody extended the Russian and squeezed the trigger. The hammer clicked on an empty chamber. As the snake struck, Clay leapt back, tripped over a chair, and hit the floor on his butt.

The snake slithered toward him, head raised. A thunderous explosion filled the room, making the walls shudder. The snake's head disappeared in a spray of pink vapor. Jerking his head sharply right, Carmody saw a one armed, old, gray-hair with a thick dragoon mustache holding a double-barreled shotgun in his left hand.

"There, Mike!" yelled another old man behind him, pointing.

Mike swung the shotgun around and fired again, and another snake became a pile of meat on the floor near the bar's right whiskey keg.

His skin crawling and heart pumping, Carmody scrambled onto his knees, jerking wild looks around him, looking for the next snake. The only living diamondback was pulling its rattles into the crack between two puncheons. Carmody relaxed, lowered his empty pistol to his right thigh.

Bardoul was helping his wife to her feet.

"She bit?" Carmody asked.

Bardoul looked at him and shook his head. The Indian woman was porcelain-pale beneath her natural tan. She stepped back from her husband and pushed against the wall between the dining room and the lobby. Her hair had come loose from its bun, and she clutched the broom before her defensively, the apron torn where the snake's teeth had caught.

"Hey!" old Mike shouted, pointing at the open hole in the floor from which another viper's head appeared, sticking its tongue out.

Bardoul bolted forward, heaved the door up to drop it over the hole with a shotgun-like bang, blowing dust, and turning the snake's head to mush.

Carmody, the old men, Bardoul, and the Indian woman fell silent, casting cautious, wide-eyed glances around the room. Carmody reloaded the Russian and snapped the loading gate closed.

Loud footfalls sounded, and he turned toward the door. Faraday, the blacksmith, stepped into the room, pushing between the two oldsters. The big man looked around, lips stretched back from his teeth, his adze-sized right fist clutching a three-foot tongs.

"What the hell?" he muttered, using the tongs to shove his hat back on his steel-gray curls.

"A little snake problem," Carmody said, his pulse finally slowing as he pushed himself to his feet.

"Same damn thing happened to me last week," grumbled the blacksmith, staring at the dead snakes on the floor.

"Happened over at the school the week before," said Mike, the one-armed oldster now holding his barn-blaster straight down toward the floor. He had a walnut-wrinkled face, broad, pitted nose, and long silver hair. His threadbare, serge, suit coat hung off his spindly shoulders. "I was haulin' wood for Miss Cooper, found her fightin' off a whole passel of 'em slitherin' out from the privy. Kids yellin' and screamin' all over the playground."

No one said anything for several seconds as they digested the information.

"Looks like the whole town has a snake problem," Carmody said finally, holstering his .44 then walking slowly out of the room.

His heart still fluttering and his skin still crawling, he walked through the lobby and outside. He'd never seen that many snakes in one place, not even in his worst nightmares. He stood on the porch and took several deep breaths of the air—fresh after the storm, the dawn sky clear. He looked across the muddy street. A young woman stood on the opposite boardwalk, outside a drug emporium wedged in between a harness shop and a millinery store.

She was a tall, slender young woman with dark-red hair pulled up beneath a feathered, velvet hat. She wore a conservative, lemon-yellow muslin dress with white lace flounces, white shirtwaist, and a vest of light-brown wool. A small, leather reticule dangled from a lanyard around her left wrist; under her right hand she clutched a thick portfolio secured with string.

Standing at the very edge of the boardwalk, giving her full attention to the hotel, she wore a worried expression on her pretty, oval face. She'd heard the commotion, no doubt. Carmody raised his hand to her, to signal all was well, but he froze when a breeze lifted on his right.

He turned to see a dust-devil swirl toward him down the middle of the street. The funnel whistled softly as it came abreast of the hotel. Carmody felt a sudden, icy chill in the wind, which blew his hair and buffeted his jeans cuffs, pressing his undershirt against his chest.

Wincing against the chill and the flecks of blown grit, he tracked the funnel moving at a fast walking pace straight north along the side-street, patchy with early-morning shadows. The street was deserted except for a single horseback rider moving toward Carmody from the north.

The man—a raisin-faced, old Indian in an overlarge calico shirt, deerskin leggings, and knee-high mocassins—rode through the dust devil atop a paint horse with one white eye. The Indian squinted against the dancing dust and hay, his silver-streaked, shoulder-length hair blowing about his face. The cayuse lowered its head and flicked its ears with annoyance but continued plodding through the mud.

The old man stared straight ahead, singing or chanting in a dull monotone relieved only when he took a deep breath and tipped his head slightly back on his shoulders, closing his eyes and throwing the notes up toward the false facades like an offering. He passed to Carmody's right, turned down the main street, and disappeared around the general store.

Carmody blinked. The dust devil was gone, but the chill stayed with him. He looked down to make sure no snakes had followed him out of the hotel. First, vipers crawling up out of the earth, then an old Indian chanting like some evil wizard riding through an abnormally chilly dust devil.

What the hell kind of crazy place was this, anyway?

Remembering the girl, he cast his glance across the street. The boardwalk she'd been standing on was vacant.

Puzzled by her sudden disappearance, Carmody looked both ways along the street. No sign of her. Scratching the back of his head, he turned and walked inside the hotel, past the dining room where Bardoul and his wife were scraping the bloody, snake carcasses off the floor with butcher knifes and shovels, and up the stairs to his room.

The chill followed him, as did the woman's image, the Indian's, and that of the snakes.

6

When Carmody had finished shaving and dressing, the hotel's dining room was still in no condition for serving food. He walked over to a cramped little cabin on the east end of Main whose big shingle jutting over the muddy street proudly proclaimed, THE MERFYN FRYCH CAFE.

The smoke gushing from the tin chimney pipe smelled like pine, spiced meat, coffee, and pancake syrup. Stepping over the shaggy, burr-laden mutt snoring on the front step, Carmody went inside and invited the thick Welshman, who took orders while he cooked, to fill his trough.

When he'd stuffed himself on the Welshman's sausage, pancakes, eggs, and potatoes—all cooked to perfection—he flipped a silver dollar on the table, grabbed his hat, and rose to leave. He was halfway to the door when, glancing around the room, his eyes landed on a familiar face. He froze, staring at the young woman who'd been standing on the boardwalk. She sat now at a table against the opposite wall, crouched over strewn papers.

She had a pen in her left hand and sipped coffee with her right, her attention glued to one of the papers upon which someone had scrawled in heavy pencil. Her hat lay on the chair beside her.

Except for the Welshman and a couple of trail riders nursing hangovers with strong black mud near the front, she and Carmody were the only ones in the room. As the Welshman scraped his stove with a wire brush, Carmody sidled past several chairs, making his way to her table, his hat in his hands.

"Snakes."

She lifted her gaze from the pencil-scrawled paper to regard him with slightly arched, dark-red brows. She was younger than he'd judged by the conservative dress—maybe nineteen, but no older than twenty. Her hair, piled and secured in a bun behind her head, was a shade lighter than her brows. She was more pretty than beautiful, with a slender, coltish frame, several light freckles on her cheek nubs, and brown, precocious eyes. "I beg your pardon?"

"That's what all the ruckus at the hotel was about."

"I figured that."

"Oh?"

The corners of her mouth drew down and her face paled. "I had the same problem over at the school recently. Diamondbacks pouring out of the privy. I still have students who would rather"—she glanced around furtively—"do their business in the bushes."

"Oh, you're the teacher."

She set her coffee cup on the table and extended her right hand. "Beth Cooper."

"Clay Carmody."

"Ah, yes," Miss Cooper said, a wistful light in her eyes. "The man who assisted our sheriff in the saloon yesterday." A bemused smile jerked at her mouth corners. "She's beautiful, isn't she?"

"Haven't noticed."

She studied him for a moment, a quick, involuntary up and down movement of her eyes. "Have you moved to the area, Mr. Carmody, or just passing through?"

"Waiting on a friend. We're gonna prospect up Poudre

Canyon." He smiled with irony, lifted a shoulder. "We hear it's the El Dorado of Colorado, and still pretty quiet."

"There's a little color up there, if you know where to find it. The problem is finding it."

"Done a little prospecting your ownself, Miss Cooper?"

"My father and brothers chipped a little rock in the canyon." Her eyes gained a pensive cast as they dropped to the table. "You're right—word hasn't gotten out yet about the canyon's showings, but it's not all that quiet, I'm afraid. You'll want to watch yourself, Mr. Carmody."

A voice came from behind him. "Now, Miss Cooper, you're not trying to frighten off visitors to our fair area, are you?"

Carmody turned.

Two men had just entered the Merfyn Frych—both dressed in three-piece suits and crisp beaver hats. The man who'd spoken was tall and wiry, with stringy white hair, round, silver-rimmed spectacles, and a blond mustache with curled, upswept ends. He wore a wolf-skin cape and black, calf-skin gloves.

Wielding a cherry-wood, ivory-headed walking stick, he sidled up to Carmody, smiling anemically as he removed a glove and held out his right hand. "Bruno Kitchener, Mr. Carmody. I heard about the help you lent our high sheriff and wanted to thank you personally. I assure you, however, Miss Bridger seldom needs anyone's assistance."

"I don't doubt it."

Miss Cooper said with little enthusiasm, "Mr. Kitchener is Camp Hawkins's mayor, Mr. Carmody."

Kitchener turned to the shorter, older man standing slightly behind him and left—a round-faced gent with a sharply receding hairline, close-set eyes, and a double-chin boasting several large, brown moles. He stared up at Carmody with a witless, perpetually befuddled expression, as though the brawny prospector were a particularly formidable tree in need of trimming.

"This is one of Camp Hawkins's more prominent businessmen—Mr. Irving Windsor. Irv, Carmody here is a prospector."

"Oh, oh, oh," Windsor stammered eagerly, his hand feeling like a damp leaf in Carmody's grip. "You'll want to visit Windsor's Mercantile, young man. It's the only general store in town, of course. My son and I have ample supplies for every prospecting need. Screens and boxes to hand trowels and flannel shirts." The man clutched his own shoulders and gave a mock shiver. "Gets cold up there, even in summer!"

"And don't forget Amos White's Gun Shop for pistols, rifles, and even knives," added Kitchener with a booster's zealous glee. "Finest weapons in the Territory, if I do say so for myself. Amos being my brother-in-law." The mayor laughed phonily, letting it die when he saw that Carmody wasn't smiling.

Carmody glanced at the young woman staring up at him and the other two men, chewing her upper lip, a mocking light in her eyes. Her gaze landed on Carmody as she twirled her pen in her left hand. "You can always stop by the school...if you need to brush up on your penmanship before heading out to dig gold...."

"Much obliged, Miss Cooper," Carmody said, setting his hat on his head.

Although he'd like to have continued his conversation with the schoolteacher about the trouble she'd alluded to in Poudre Canyon, he turned to the two men flanking him. How could there be more trouble out there than what he'd seen right here in town?

"Mayor, Mr. Windsor, pleased to meet you both. I'll try to drop as much of my jingle as possible in your fair city, though, until my partner gets here, I'm afraid most of it will be concentrated in the whores' cribs an' saloons." He pinched his hat brim at both men, winked at the young school teacher, and left the café.

He didn't realize he'd been heading for the sheriff's small jailhouse until he was nearing the stoop now bathed in bright, high-desert sunlight, the breeze smelling like sage and mud. He had no intention of going in and making a pest of himself; he was just curious about what last night's trouble had been about and if the lovely vixen of a sheriff weathered it all right.

Carmody chewed the quirley in his teeth as he read the note nailed to the door. "Sheriff Bridger and her deputies will be out of town on business until further notice." It was signed, Sheriff Claudine Bridger, in a bold, flowing hand.

Carmody sucked the quirley and let the rich smoke out slowly as he considered.

It had to be important business for a sheriff not to leave even one deputy in town to man the office. The image of the two sodden deputies rose behind Carmody's eyes, shooting revolvers into the night sky above their prancing mounts, whipping their heads around to look behind them, as if the hounds of hell were on their heels.

They were peering west, Carmody remembered. Back toward Poudre Canyon.

Vaguely nettled, Carmody dropped his quirley in the mud, stepped it out with his boot toe, then turned and headed for the saloon, which was where he spent most of the next two days, whiling away the time before Nathan arrived.

It was a quiet two days, with no more snakes spilling out of dung holes or cellars, or men riding frantically into town, shooting pistols into the air. Playing cards with trail riders or other prospectors in the Poudre River Saloon, Carmody had nearly forgotten his unease when, late in the afternoon of his third day in town, he folded his cards and headed out back to use the privy.

He was standing there, trying not to imagine snakes pouring out of the hole he was pissing into, when a chill, menacing wind seeped through the privy's plank walls. It chilled him the same way the wind from the dust devil had chilled him three days ago.

Goose bumps rose between his shoulder blades and, though he was nowhere near finished after all the beer and bourbon he'd consumed, his piss stream pinched down to a trickle. He winced, shifted his weight from foot to foot, trying to relax and get flowing again. The chill wind stopped blowing, but as it faded, something scraped the roof over Carmody's head.

He jerked with a start, his piss stream stopping altogether.

Lifting his gaze toward the ceiling, he saw, through the cracks between the wall planks, a magpie beating its white-tipped black wings just below the roofline of the left wall. The wings made a windy, thrashing noise against the boards. A stubby beak probed a crack between the planks.

Again, the bad wind rose, slipped between the planks and pressed against Carmody like water from a snowmelt stream. It whistled like a deep breath sucked through teeth.

Clay quickly buttoned his fly, grabbed his Russian .44 from its holster, and turned to the door. He peered through the crack between the door and the frame.

A figure in a tan hat and black frock coat stood six feet beyond the door. The man wasn't moving, just standing there, waiting, one hand held chest high.

Caution tapped a slow tattoo against Carmody's chest. Breathing slowly and regularly, he reached out with his left hand, gently lifted the door's nail lock from the steel hook in the frame, and lowered it quietly against the door. He stepped back against the privy seat, drew a deep breath, thumbed the .44's hammer back, lifted his right foot, and smashed his heel against the door.

As the door slammed against the privy's front wall with a sharp crack, Carmody bolted forward, extending the gun straight out from his right shoulder, sighting down the barrel.

Before him stood one of the two young drifters, a stocky kid with tight curly hair, with whom he'd been playing blackjack. Carrot-Top wasn't holding a gun; he was just standing hipshot along the stone path absently inspecting his fingernails. Seeing Carmody bolt from the privy like a bull from a chute, his eyes snapped wide and his jaw dropped as he stumbled backwards, raising both hands defensively.

"Hey, hey, hey!" he shouted, his tightly funneled hat tumbling off his head. "Hold on, there!"

Carmody jabbed the .44 toward the kid's suet-colored face. "Why the hell are you lurkin' around the privy?"

"I'm waitin' to take a piss!" The kid—freckled with pale features and a small, upturned nose—took another step straight back. "If you ain't finished, hell, I ain't tryin' to rush ya none!"

Carmody studied him, chagrin setting in. Feeling his face warm with embarrassment, he lowered the pistol. Carrot-Top's own six-shooter was snugged down in its holster, the keeper thong secured across the hammer. "Sorry, kid."

Seeing those snakes and that Indian and feeling that chill breeze in late-August had frazzled his nerves.

"Whew," the kid said indignantly, still flushed with fear and exasperation.

"Here." Carmody flipped him a nickel, which the kid caught as he stooped to retrieve his hat. "Next beer's on me."

Carmody holstered his pistol. As he started forward toward the saloon's back door, he glanced at the kid, whose periwinkle-blue eyes landed on something or someone just behind Carmody's left shoulder, brightening with devilish glee.

The kid's jaw hardened. "Hit him, Nestor! Damnit, hit him *hard!*"

7

Something hard glanced off the back of Carmody's head and smacked the nub of his left shoulder, driving him down to his left knee as that ear rang like goat bells in a twister.

"Harder, Nester, damnit!" Carrot-Top railed. "Hit him harder!"

Carmody set his left hand on the stone walk to steady himself as the ground slanted this way and that. From the corner of his vision, he saw the man behind him stoop down toward him, drawing his right arm back.

Rallying his faculties, Carmody bolted up and forward as the man behind him landed another glancing blow across his back, grunting loudly. Carmody continued forward, grabbing Carrot-Top's drawn six-shooter and nudging it wide as he threw himself into the kid's chest.

Crying out, Carrot-Top stumbled straight back and sprawled across the stone walk, Carmody on top of him, holding the kid's right hand down while smashing his left fist into the kid's stubby chin.

Ripping the gun from the kid's hand, Carmody rolled onto his right shoulder as the tall, blade-nosed youngster behind him fired a long-barreled Smith & Wesson.

Carrot-Top wailed as the bullet ripped into his side. "Nestor, you damn, stupid, son of a bitch!"

Carmody raised the kid's pistol as Nestor recocked his own weapon extended in both hands, shuffling his feet, his yellow eyes snapping nervously as his tongue moistened the left corner of his mouth.

Carmody's six-gun popped.

The tall kid grunted and stumbled back against the privy, wincing and lowering his head toward the wound in his lower right shoulder. As he sank down, he extended the pistol one-handed and, stretching his lips back from blue-black gums and crooked, yellow teeth, pulled the trigger.

The slug sailed an inch wide of Carmody's right earlobe.

As Carmody leveled the six-shooter on Nestor's chest, Carrot-Top yelled and kicked his left leg out, connecting with Carmody's side, throwing his bullet into the privy door, a full foot wide of his target.

Nestor gave a startled, hollow cry as he bolted up and ran crouching into the yard left of the privy. His legs were so long that, running sideways, he stumbled over his own feet, dropping to one knee as he squeezed off another shot at Carmody.

Clay leapt to his feet, tossed off Carrot-Top's six-shooter, grabbed his own Russian from his holster, tracked the stork-like Nestor across the yard, and fired. Howling, Nestor grabbed his left leg, spun in a complete circle, and fell. He gave another howl and raised his pistol, but Carmody drilled a .44 pill through his chest, between the lapels of his shabby wool coat.

Nestor screeched and flapped around on the ground like a landed fish for several seconds before he died.

Hearing the thuds of running boots, Carmody turned sharply right. Carrot-Top was running across the empty lot beside the saloon, heading for the backs of several stores lining Main.

Carmody cursed and strode across the lot, tracking Carrot-Top while flipping open the Russian's loading gate and extracting the spent shell. Why in the hell were these two owlhoots after him? He doubted the kid and his pal, Nestor, had been out to rob him.

During their card game, they'd seen the modest roll of greenbacks Carmody had produced from his jeans pocket. If they were going to rob anyone, it would have been the old prospector who'd sat to Carmody's left and who bragged about the dust he'd taken out of one of the canyons near Idaho Springs, west of Denver. The man had proved his success via a fat pouch of gold coins.

No, these younkers must have learned Carmody had a price on his head. That's why Clay had to track down Carrot-Top and kill him, lest he be looking over his shoulder for the rest of his stay in Camp Hawkins...

The kid stopped abruptly when two men in cheap suits and derby hats appeared between two sporting cribs flanking a run-down, canvas and timber saloon appropriately called, THE ARMAGEDDON. One of the men was smoking a cigar and wrapping an arm around the slender, naked shoulders of a small, black-haired girl, who wore only a tattered, cream-colored skirt.

"What the hell's goin' on?" asked the man who was not holding the girl, shifting his gaze between Carrot-Top and Carmody. Both men swayed drunkenly.

The kid stared at the men and the girl, then bolted toward them, grabbed the pistol out of the holster of the man holding the bare-breasted girl, then wheeled and headed north through the sage and rabbit brush.

"Hey, now...!" the man protested, releasing the girl, and pointing at Carrot-Top, as if that alone would stop him.

As the kid ran, clutching his bullet-burned side and

leaping sage and buck brush, he snapped off two wild shots at Carmody.

Clay stopped running near one of the sporting cribs and sidled up to a dead mule deer hanging from a cottonwood tree. Extending the Russian and trying to suppress the pain in his head, he squeezed off two shots. Both slugs only blew up dust and stones near the kid's running feet.

The kid stopped near a small fir tree and swung his gun toward Carmody. Clay squeezed off another shot, this one drilling the kid through the belly. Carrot-Top grunted and stumbled back, bowing his head and buckling his knees.

Holding the Russian straight out from his shoulder, Carmody walked through the brush and stood looking down at the kid. He sat on his splayed knees, head sagging to his chest. His hat was off, his pistol still in his right hand. He was too weak to raise it.

Staring down at the top of the kid's cap of tight, red curls, Carmody reached out with his free hand, and pulled a folded paper from the breast pocket of the kid's black wool jacket. Carmody flipped the paper open, saw his own likeness inked in the middle of the page, below the large, blocked letters forming the words, WANTED: DEAD OR ALIVE, and above the reward amount: $1,000.

"Wasn't really worth it, was it?"

The kid's shoulders rose and fell sharply as he breathed. "Shoulda backshot ye...taken ye in dead."

"You know I'm gonna have to kill you, don't you?"

The kid raised his head, eyes bright with angry fire. "You go to hell, you no-good, bastard of a sow's son of a bitch!"

Carmody thumbed back the Russian's hammer and punched a round hole through the bridge of the kid's pale, freckled nose. The kid's eyes crossed as his head fell back on his shoulders then sank slowly into the sage, as though reclining on a soft feather bed for an afternoon nap.

His lips were still stretched angrily back from his teeth after the light in his eyes dulled and his chest had fallen still.

Carmody holstered his .44 and ripped the wanted dodger into a hundred tiny pieces, which he let the wind cascade about Carrot-Top's bloody carcass.

"Who's that?"

Carmody turned.

The two men and the girl stood behind him. The young Indian girl, standing between the two men, was still bare-chested, but she didn't seem to mind. Her dull, brown eyes had an opium glaze, her full lips drawn up at the corners in a celestial half-smile, as if all were right with the world albeit a little confusing. Her cherry-red breasts were small as tea-cups, the nipples jutting proudly from her chest.

Carmody could smell the paint-thinner stench of cheap hooch on all three.

It made him want another drink himself.

"Just another gold digger." Turning and heading back toward the saloon, Carmody said, without turning around, "Don't forget your gun."

Ahead of him, a scraggly magpie swooped low then rose to his right, raucously cawing. Carmody stopped and regarded the bird as it dipped behind the cottonwoods lining the river.

Feeling another fleeting chill on a vagrant breeze, he spat and hurried on.

If only Nathan would get here, he could light a shuck out of this hole.

HE SPENT the rest of the day chomping at the bit and sitting in the saloon's front window, minding his own business, trying to stay out of trouble, and watching for

Nathan. When the sun went down and Nathan still hadn't shown, Carmody had a steak in the hotel's dining room then headed back to his room with a Camp Hawkins *Bugle* and a bottle of rye.

The next day, saying to hell with Nathan, he bought trail supplies on credit and packed the stores in his wagon. Leaving a note for Nathan with Mr. Windsor at the mercantile, Carmody took one last constitutional in the hotel's privy before heading up the canyon.

He was sitting in the smelly two-holer, half-listening for snakes as he read the last page of the newspaper, when something scratched the boards high on the toilet's west wall.

Not again.

Carmody looked up. Sure enough—it was that damn bird again, or one just like it, probing the crack between the boards with its claws and beak.

Why in the hell were magpies so damned fascinated by the privies in this town?

The thought had no sooner passed through his mind when what sounded like something big rustled the brush directly behind him. Grass crackled as though beneath moving feet.

Ah, hell. Beth Cooper's pupils had the right idea—he was going to start crapping in the woods.

Carmody stood quickly, but quietly, drew his pants up, wrapped his gunbelt around his waist, and drew the Russian. Gently, he opened and closed his fingers around the stock then froze before the door, straining his ears to listen.

Something ticked against the outside wall to his left, then the rustling and crackling sounded again. Whipping his head around, Carmody saw a shadow pass beyond the cracks between the boards.

If nothing else strange had happened in this town, he'd have passed the rustling off as that of a curious deer or maybe a bear cub looking for kitchen scraps. But after what he'd seen and experienced, he wasn't taking any chances.

He unlocked the door, kicked it open, and bolted outside, swinging his pistol from left to right and back again, whipping his head around. Seeing nothing, he moved to his left, swung his pistol around the privy's east corner.

Nothing there, either.

The rustling rose again, on the far side of the outhouse.

Heart hammering, anger burning up from the base of his spine, clutching the Russian firmly in his right hand, Carmody strode forward, turned the corner, and strode along the privy's back wall.

A loud clap rose behind him, as though someone had slammed an axe handle against the outhouse planks. Heart leaping, he spun around to stare back the way he'd come, expecting to see another hard-case younker bearing down on him.

Nothing but brush on the left and the privy's unpainted plank wall on the right. Ahead, more brush rose to a chicken coop and a wood shed about fifty yards away.

Carmody's heart hammered. Cold sweat dribbled down his cheeks. Gritting his teeth, imagining what he was going to do to the man or men jerking his ground stake, he moved forward. He'd taken one long stride when thick, black arms snaked around his waist from behind, squeezing the air from his lungs in one short exhalation—"*Uunghahhh!*"—and lifting him straight up in the air.

Carmody brought the pistol barrel down to shoot the man in the foot. As though reading his mind, the man behind him wrapped an enormous, bear-like paw around the cocked pistol, and wrenched it from Carmody's grip with little more effort than a grown man plucking a sucker away from a toddler.

Grunting, trying to suck air back into his lungs before he passed out, Carmody heard a loud bellow erupting behind his ear. The familiar smell of applejack and jerky wafted against his face, mixing with the rancid sweat fetor already there.

The man's iron grip slipped. Carmody hit the ground on his feet, stumbled forward, and fell over a spindly sage plant. On his hands and knees, he drew deep draughts of air into his chest, his sweat-glistening face as red as a Concord coach.

Behind him, the bear-like man bellowed loudly, great guffaws booming like a howitzer. Carmody would have recognized that laugh anywhere, but the man's putrid breath had already given him away.

"That's real damn funny, Nate..."

8

Clay's voice pinched out as he continued sucking air. "One of these times, your practical jokes are gonna get you a new blowhole bored."

"I've been trailing fer days, *mon ami.*" Nathan Laroque chuckled. "When I saw you go into the privy, I couldn't resist the temptation to have a little fun."

Still on his hands and knees, Carmody glanced up at the big mulatto standing before him in baggy, sun-faded denims, suspenders, deerskin leggings, and a blue cotton tunic dark with dust and trail sweat.

Nathan Laroque stood well over six-feet-tall—a towering giant of a cherry-skinned man with tufts of gray-streaked black hair poking out from under his shapeless black hat. Trimming the hat's crown were bear claws, wolf teeth, and beads in star patterns. A skunk's tail hung from the left brim, dangling over the big man's shoulder. These were Apache talismans. Laroque's father had been a French mulatto outlaw from Louisiana, who'd married a Chiricahua girl in Arizona.

Small and black as dried plums, the ears of the four bounty hunters who'd killed Laroque's father, mother, and two sisters hung from a sinew string around his neck.

"You're a blue-whistlin' bastard, Laroque."

Carmody climbed to his feet, retrieved his pistol, and turned to his partner with a menacing cast to his gaze. When he jerked his hands up, Laroque winced and stepped back, startled.

Carmody pinched the big man's fleshy cheeks between the thumbs and index fingers of both hands. As he rose up on the balls of his feet to stare into Laroque's wary, plum-colored eyes, he shook the man's head from side-to-side.

"And I couldn't be happier to see you if you was Fannie Brown buck naked on a faintin' couch!" He swatted Laroque's chest with the back of his hand as he turned to stride away. "Come on—let's fog it on out of here!"

"Check your damn mules," Laroque called behind him. "I just got here!"

"You don't want any grass growin' under your feet in this town. I got the wagon already supplied and hitched."

Laroque was following Carmody across the hotel's backyard, jogging every third or four step to catch up. He threw his arms out from his sides. "I'm tired and thirsty. Clay, my horse is blown. What's the hurry?"

Carmody wheeled to the bigger man and clutched Laroque's sweat-soaked shirt in both fists, staring up at him, his jaws taut, his eyes on fire. "You don't understand, Nathan. This place is crazy. It's bad medicine. You wouldn't believe all that's happened since I got here. Snakes. Injuns. Bounty hunters. A damn magpie..." He glanced at the privy roof, but the bird was gone. "I can't spend another night in this backwater. Not another minute!"

Laroque stared down at Carmody. "Easy, *mon ami.* You're gonna give yourself a seizure."

Carmody turned and hit the street at a near run, heading for his wagon parked before the livery barn. "We'll drive a few miles, camp along the river. I just wanna get clear of this damn town."

As Carmody continued to the wagon, Laroque, casting

befuddled glances after Clay, retrieved his sweat-lathered pinto from the hitch rack before the hotel. When the big man had tied the horse to the wagon's tailgate, he climbed into the driver's box.

Carmody unwrapped the reins from the brake, threw the handle forward, and planted his right boot against the dashboard.

Laroque studied him, fearful and fascinated. "Great Jehosaphat! I don't think I've ever seen you this hepped up."

"You ain't never seen me in this town before." Carmody whipped his reins over the backs of his piebalds. Nathan grabbed the seat as the wagon bolted forward so suddenly that he was nearly thrown backward into the box.

THEY CAMPED that night in a long horseshoe of the Cache la Poudre, only four miles from town—one or two miles from where the river pours out of the canyon. Far enough away for Carmody to let his guard down and drink whiskey from a cold tin cup, relaxing in his friend's company around a crackling fire.

He told Nathan about the men he'd been forced to kill back in Camp Hawkins, about the snakes, the Indian, and the chilly dust-devil wind. The only thing he didn't tell him about was his night with Camp Hawkins's lovely sheriff. He didn't know why he didn't tell about it. He and Nathan had always bragged openly about their exploits, sexual and otherwise.

Somehow, the topic of Claudine Bridger seemed too private to talk about, even with Nathan.

Carmody dreamed about her that night, the next, and the night after. And he wondered again what trouble had called her out of town, and how she'd weathered it—and if he'd see her again.

Meanwhile, he and Nathan wound their way westward through the rocky, pine-choked, high-walled canyon. They followed the stream banks and stopped often to fish and hunt, to swim and pan for gold, to chin with other rock breakers either camped or living permanently along the river.

Their second night on the road, they joined a prospecting family for supper, slept in their barn, and headed out early the next morning. That night they camped across the river from a formation called Elephant Rock, and dined on brook trout and fried potatoes.

Later that night, they played two-handed poker on a flat rock while smoking cigarettes rolled with freshly chopped tobacco. They sipped "six-shooter" coffee spiked with rye, and fed pine branches to their cook fire, which held at bay the inky darkness and chill air of the starry night.

The sound of a kicked stone rose, barely audible above the stream's perpetual rush. Loud enough for seasoned ears, however. Both men dropped their cards and filled their hands with iron, facing upstream.

"Stow your hog legs," called a woman's voice, slightly brittle and halting. "Our hands are empty."

Two figures materialized from the dense darkness and stopped just beyond the fire's flickering light, the taller, broader one leaning on the smaller figure to his left. Carmody slitted his eyes. The voice had rung familiar. But he couldn't quite believe that the slight, round-hipped silhouette standing before him, cinnamon hair curling onto her slender shoulders from under a man's plainsman hat was who it appeared to be.

"I said holster 'em before I draw my own and set you boys to squealin' like baby pigs!"

Yep. Had to be.

"Howdy, Sheriff," Carmody said, holstering his .44 and

watching the firelight wink off the five-pointed star on her vest.

He slid his eyes to Laroque sitting just behind him and right. The big mulatto had his own long-barreled Colt extended half-out from his chest, his brows wrinkled as he slid his eyes between Claudine and Clay.

"Leather it, Nathan. This woman's the Sheriff of Crow Dog County, and she'll turn you colder'n dead beef in January."

Laroque looked at Carmody again then slowly lowered his revolver, slipping it into the holster thonged on his right thigh. "A lady *sheriff?*"

Sheriff Bridger stepped forward, guiding the hatless man beside her, who had his right arm around her shoulders and was hanging his head like a tired old dog. He looked up from beneath sandy-blond brows, and his restless eyes were sharp and fearful. One might even say exasperated. He wasn't wearing a hat, and his straw-colored hair was matted and tufted about his head. The deputy sheriff's star dangled from the pocket of his torn, striped shirt.

"Some might argue with the lady part," Claudine said.

Carmody walked over and reached out for the deputy's other arm, intending to help.

"No!" the young man shouted, sweat dribbling down his cheeks. "Leave me!" The exclamation—half-warning, half-entreaty—echoed around the dark canyon.

Lifting his hands placatingly, Carmody stepped straight back and glanced at Nathan, who returned the look, expressionless, his befuddlement written in his wide-set shoulders, arms hanging straight down at his sides, breath puffing in the cool, thin air.

Claudine glanced across the young man's chest at Carmody. "I've got him." When she'd eased the deputy down to the ground beside the fire, she again cast her gaze to Clay. "Whiskey might settle his nerves."

Before Clay could say anything, Nathan Laroque reached down, picked up the whiskey bottle he and Carmody had been drinking from, splashed some into his own cup, and extended the cup to Claudine. She took the whiskey and knelt beside the deputy, holding the dented tin cup in front of him, as if offering it to a blind man.

"Here, Kyle. Take a sip. You'll feel better."

The young man whipped his head up at her, his eyes probing hers. "Damn, Claudine. They're out there, ain't they? They'll be out there again tonight!"

"You hush, now, and drink." Claudine shook the cup, sloshing the whiskey around.

The deputy took it in his shaking hands, dirty and crusted with dried blood from scrapes and minor cuts. He stared into the whiskey for a full ten seconds before he finally lifted the cup to his lips, and sipped.

He gave a violent shake, as though from a bone-deep chill. Holding the cup up close to his chin, he stared into the fire, transfixed.

Claudine stood with a sigh.

"What happened?" Carmody said.

"I'm not sure." She stared down at the young man staring into the fire. "At least, not beyond the fact that he was thrown from his horse, and his shoulder's separated." She paused. "And that I've lost two men..."

"Here you go, ma'am...er uh, Sheriff," Nathan said, holding out a heavy wool blanket, his dark eyes round and sympathetic. "He looks some chilled, he does."

"Obliged." Claudine shook out the blanket and draped it over the deputy's shoulders. Kyle Boley jerked with a start, then set the cup down and pulled the blanket around him like a shawl. Again he stared into the fire, giving occasional, spasmodic jerks, transfixed by the flames.

Claudine adjusted the pistol on her hip then sank down to Boley's right, giving her own eyes to the fire and absently running her hands down her arms, chilled.

Carmody fetched his own blanket, walked around behind her, and dropped it over her shoulders.

"Thanks."

He hunkered down beside her and tipped his hat back on his head. He splashed whiskey into his cup and gave it to her. "How long you two been walkin'?"

She sipped the whiskey, then set the cup down on a rock near the fire, as if to warm it, and removed her hat. She turned her head to peer into the darkness behind her—an involuntary reaction sparked by no sound or movement, as far as Carmody could tell. She turned back to the fire. Fingering the brim with both hands, her slender fingers curling it back toward the crown, she said, "Since about one o'clock this morning."

"You must be hungry," Nathan said, then immediately went to work, grabbing a pan and rummaging around in a croaker sack.

Carmody canted his head to the big mulatto. "That's Nathan Laroque, my gold-huntin' partner. Nathan, Claudine Bridger."

"Pleased to make your acquaintance, ma'am," Nathan said as he set a pan on a flat rock in the flames, then plopped a hunk of lard into the pan. The fat immediately began to melt and slide around on the hot iron. He looked at her quickly. "I mean, Sheriff."

"Claudine is fine, Mr. Laroque." Her voice owned a wan, tired timbre. Again, she sipped the whiskey, set the cup down on the rock, and clutched the blanket about her shoulders. Shunting her gaze between Carmody and Laroque, she said, "You two haven't seen or heard anything...strange...out here?"

Carmody glanced at Laroque, then turned his gaze back to Claudine. "Strange?"

She held his gaze, swallowed. "Then I guess you haven't seen a man—one of my deputies—wandering afoot out here, either."

Again, Carmody and Laroque exchanged a glance as Nathan dumped left-over pinto beans into the pan in which the side-pork sizzled. Carmody picked up his cup, sipped the whiskey, and then held it out to Claudine, who sat hunkered beneath the blanket, nervously glancing into the darkness beyond Clay and Nathan.

The fear and enervation fairly radiated from her and the deputy, who gave involuntary shakes as he sipped from the cup and stared into the fire, as if trying to scour his mind of horrifying images.

Carmody felt the hair on the back of his own neck prickle, found himself casting his own cautious gazes into the darkness. Noticing Nathan doing the same, he remembered Miss Cooper warning him about the canyon. He pressed it back from his consciousness.

When the sheriff had taken another sip of the whiskey, Carmody said quietly, "Want to tell us what happened?"

She stared at the pork and beans bubbling in the pan. Laroque stirred the food with a long, wooden spoon and regarded the young sheriff with interest.

"Kyle and my other two deputies rode out to investigate the murder of a prospector's family living near Cameron Pass." She paused, squinting her eyes as if at a sickening image in her head, then raised her gaze to Carmody. "When only two came back, I rode out the next day to find out what had become of the other one. Last night, something strange happened."

Claudine shook her head and took another sip of the whiskey. "These eyes...out of the darkness...blinking at us. Thousands of them."

"Eyes?" said Carmody.

The deputy looked up, his own eyes blood-shot and fear-sharp. "Same thing happened the night after we buried the butchered family. The screams and the rider coming...galloping...and Henry disappearing."

Claudine lifted her hand out from beneath her blanket,

rubbed Boley's back soothingly. To Carmody and Laroque, she said, "Our horses spooked, screaming like I'd never heard horses scream before. Kyle and I were thrown from our saddles. Grits Tatum's mount ran off. We haven't seen him since."

Carmody studied the woman thoughtfully, absorbing the information, trying to make sense of it. His stomach turned to cold jelly.

During the story, Nathan had stopped stirring the pan. Now, as a scorched smell wafted up from the fire to his nose, he began stirring again. "No sign of your horses come daylight?"

Claudine said without expression, "There were signs of them, all right. Kyle and I tracked them to where they leapt off a two-hundred-foot cliff."

To soothe his own nerves, Carmody dug his makings sack from his shirt pocket and began building a cigarette. Filling two bowls with pork and beans from the pan, Nathan said, "Sounds like a mountain lion."

Carmody touched a match flame to his cigarette and turned to Claudine. "This kinda thing...uh...happened before?" He didn't think he wanted to hear the answer.

Claudine nodded dully. "When my father was the sheriff, several men were murdered. Butchered. Our schoolteacher's family was murdered up here, as well. People have been disappearing up here for a long time, but it's been happening more and more frequently."

Nathan said, "Sounds like a loco shoat in the corn patch. Any notions?"

"None." Claudine accepted a bowl of the steaming food from Laroque, thanked him, and probed it half-heartedly with her fork.

When young Boley had accepted a bowl of food from Laroque and began eating with little more interest than Claudine, Nathan leaned back against his saddle and fished his own tobacco from his shirt. "Yeah, sounds like a mountain lion to me. I used to kill 'em for ranchers in Arizona and New Mexico. Horses ain't afeared o' nothin' like they're afeared o' mountain lions."

No one said anything again until Claudine and Boley had eaten half their food, and set it aside. "That all you two gonna eat?" Laroque said, incredulous.

Tipping more whiskey into her glass, Claudine regarded both him and Carmody. "If you men have two horses you can spare, I'd be obliged. I need to get Kyle home. They'll be returned to you shortly."

"Only have one spare," Carmody said. "We'll take you back to town in the wagon."

Claudine shook her head. "No need. We can double up on the horse and ride as far as Earl Kleinsasser's place, only a mile or two downstream. He's got a whole remuda. I'll have one of Earl's kids return your horse day after tomorrow."

Before Carmody could respond, she said, "Thank you both for your hospitality." She turned to the deputy sitting beside her with his chin on his chest, snoring softly. "Kyle and I best get some sleep."

When both Claudine and the deputy had curled up under the extra blankets Carmody and Laroque had provided, Nathan hunkered down beside Carmody and said in a hushed voice, "What do you think of all that?"

Carmody said, "If so much crazy business hadn't happened to me in that town, I'd have agreed with you. Mountain lions."

"That's what probably killed the prospectors, too. You get a rogue animal—why they'll...."

"What about the eyes they talked about?"

"The eyes staring out of the darkness?" Nathan chuckled and scraped a thumbnail along his jaw. "Well, Christ, this high altitude...mix that with a little fear and a thick night...you'll see more than just eyes starin' out from the darkness. You know that as well I, *mon ami.*"

Carmody lifted his gaze from the fire, little more than glowing coals now. An occasional flame licked up from a charred stick.

He listened hard, hearing only the river's perpetual rush, the rare rustle and thud of a pine cone falling and striking branches on the way to the ground.

There wasn't a breath of wind.

"Yeah," he said finally, nodding, leaning back against his saddle and drawing his blanket up. He sighed and tipped his hat over his eyes. "You're probably right."

LATER, Carmody's eyes snapped wide. The night was as dark as his closed lids had been. He lay listening. Something had awakened him.

A soft, cold hand closed over his mouth and pressed down gently. He jerked toward his gun with a start, but then a soft voice whispered in his ear.

"I'm cold."

She lifted his blankets from his body. Wrapped in her own, she lay down beside him. She drew his blankets over them both, and curved her lithe, shuddering body against his, burrowing her face into his ribs.

In a minute, she stopped shivering. Her breath grew deep and even.

Her body was warm and pliant.

It took him a long time to go back to sleep.

9

WHEN CLAY OPENED HIS EYES, the camp was awash with milky light and shadows. He turned to where Claudine had snuggled down beside him. Although the ground and the blankets were still warm where she'd lain, she was gone.

Her voice rose, barely audible above the river. He turned to where Nathan Laroque squatted over a smoky, fledgling fire. Blinking against the smoke, the big man set the coffee pot on the flat rock they'd cooked on last night. Just beyond him, Claudine was adjusting the sling holding young Boley's arm across his belly.

"You gonna sleep all mornin'?" Nathan said.

Carmody smacked his lips. He remembered the story Sheriff Bridger had told around the fire last night. The perplexity and apprehension squeezed back the memory of her warm body curved against his, the faint sage and lilac smell of her hair in his face.

He gave a disconsolate grunt and pushed himself onto his elbows. "I'd like to."

"Sleep well?"

"Fair to middlin'."

Nathan glanced over his shoulder, where Claudine was speaking quietly to the young deputy, whose face was drawn and bleached with physical and mental misery. Turning back to Carmody and shaping a grin, Laroque said, "Keep warm, *non?*"

Carmody's face warmed but he met his partner's mocking stare with a self-congratulating curl of his upper lip. "I did all right." He turned away, folding his blankets and stowing them inside the wagon, hearing Nathan's raspy chuckles behind him.

They ate a hurried breakfast of eggs, sideport, and more beans. Then, while Nathan saddled his horse for Claudine and the injured deputy, and Boley sat against a tree, staring grimly, Claudine wandered off to tend her personal business. Carmody took the two iron skillets down to the river for scrubbing.

Golden sunlight washed into the canyon, but deep-purple shadows still stretched out from the high, fir-clad walls. Birds and squirrels chattered in the trees. Moving through the brush, Carmody startled two does drinking on the opposite shore.

He stepped around some willows and stopped abruptly. Claudine stood a few feet away, at the river's edge. Her shirt and undershirt were draped together over a rock to her right. Naked from the waist up, she faced the morning-sparkling river. She was running a damp cloth along her left arm, extended slightly out from her body. Her head was turned slightly left, chin lowered toward the arm.

Peeking out from her left side was a pale half-moon of left breast, upturned and lightly sprinkled with golden sunshine.

Carmody stood rapt, appreciating the view.

Claudine's gaze locked in front of her, she froze. She swung abruptly around, dropping the cloth and raking her Peacemaker from its holster on her right hip. As her left hand lashed across her left breast to cup the right, partly covering them both, she extended the gun at Carmody.

The hammer clicked back.

"Easy," Clay said, spreading his hands and dirty skillets out to his sides. "I'm friendly."

She relaxed. Her eyes dropped to the area just beneath his cartridge belt. "I see that."

Carmody shrugged and shaped a boyish half-smile.

Claudine holstered her pistol but kept her arm across her breasts. Her thick hair wafted around her naked shoulders in the breeze. "Thanks for your help and...warmth."

"Anytime I can be of service, you let me know."

Claudine glanced away, pensive. "I know it all sounds crazy. It does even to me. I'm sure there's a rational explanation, and once I get Kyle back to town, I'm going to backtrack and find out what it is."

"You sure that's a good idea?"

"Why?" she asked sharply, hands touching her pistol butt as if to show she could handle herself as well as any man. "Because I'm a woman?"

As Carmody stood shifting his weight from one foot to the other, trying to come up with a response that wouldn't get him into anymore trouble than he was already in, she dropped her left arm and moved toward him. She rose up on her tiptoes and kissed his lips—a quick but passionate peck, pressing her naked breasts against his chest.

"Don't you know yet...how much woman I am?"

"Sorry," he grunted, staring down at her, running his gaze over every inch of naked skin, his need burning deep in the pit of his belly. "Reckon it's the altitude. Just the same, you watch your back. You need any help, me and Nathan'll most likely be holed up in the old Andros cabin on Bear Creek. We heard it was vacant."

"Looking for that ultimate stake?"

"Nuthin' else to do."

"And the canyon's a good place for a wanted man to hide out."

Carmody met her gaze, apprehension tempering his desire. The skillets were heavy in his hands, making him feel awkward, shackled, a little ridiculous.

She kissed him again. "Don't think I'd sleep with a stranger before going through my wanted dodgers first, do you?"

"It's a trumped-up charge."

"Aren't they all?" A smile quirked her full mouth, and she shook her head once, slowly. "Don't worry. You're not wanted around here." The smile tugged again at her lips. Her eyes dropped to his crotch, then roamed back up his chest. "At least, not in the *legal* sense."

His desire returned in earnest. He dropped one of the skillets and grabbed her bare arm, pulling her to him, kissing her hard, sucking her tongue into his mouth. She returned the kiss for several seconds, then pulled away.

Smiling up at him, she ran her right wrist over her mouth. But she was unable to wipe away her teasing, coquettish grin. "Better wash those pans before the crud dries."

Turning, she grabbed her undershirt off the rock, shook it out, and dropped it over her head. It caught on her ripe breasts and jutting nipples, and she had to give it a tug to bring it down to her waist. She grabbed her flannel shirt, picked up her washcloth, and brushed past him.

"See you later." Her eyes flashed, mocking. "Washer boy."

Carmody's heart thudded heavily. He picked up the pan he'd dropped and glanced at her walking back toward the camp through the trees and tall brush as she shrugged into her shirt. Her hair was ambrosia honey in the soft morning light. Her well-formed butt cheeks moved devilishly in the tight, black jeans, fringed chaps flapping against her thighs.

He had to give himself a hard mental shove to turn away and tend to his pan-washing chores.

WHEN HE RETURNED to the camp, Claudine and the deputy had already ridden off on Nathan's horse. Carmody couldn't help feeling a little hurt that she hadn't told him good-bye. Then, feeling ridiculous for feeling hurt, he busied himself with hitching the horses to the wagon.

The vision of that undershirt catching on those incredible, bulging breasts would not leave him.

When he and Laroque had struck camp and mounted the wagon, they drifted upstream, looking for a place to excavate the canyon's bedrock that hadn't already been violated by picks and shovels.

The farther they headed west up the Cache la Poudre, climbing steadily toward Cameron Pass forty miles upstream, the fewer gold-seekers they ran into, and the quieter the canyon became. They found more and more virgin rock, but a lot of it, because of the raging river as well as off-shooting cliffs and canyons, was hard to get to.

One afternoon, the scrawny Kleinsasser kid returned the piebald, and Carmody began missing Claudine all over again.

When he figured they were about thirty miles from the high, stony pass at the west end of the canyon, they found the boulder-strewn bed of Bear Creek and the forlorn Andros cabin. They shored up the walls of the trapper's old log hovel, patched the biggest holes in the roof, cleaned out the mice and porcupine shit, aired out the skunk stink, and moved in.

The next morning they rose early and went to work before the sun had even climbed over the fir-carpeted eastern ridge, clearing river wash from cracks in the creek's bedrock. Around noon, Carmody was prying up a heavy rock with a crowbar, when he suddenly felt as though someone were behind him.

He stopped maneuvering the bar, and glanced at Nathan. The big man, standing four feet to his left, had already turned to stare over the creek behind them both. Carmody followed his gaze to the opposite bank. Between two towering Douglas firs, a small, old Indian man in a long deerskin shirt and beaded headband sat a stocky paint horse.

It was the Indian Carmody had seen the other day in Camp Hawkins, riding inside the dust devil, chanting. Now the Indian sat holding the paint's rope reins in his gnarled hands, facing Clay and Nathan, the wind washing his silver-streaked black hair about his round, deeply-lined face and brightly beaded headband, his black eyes pinched like raisins.

Carmody had left his cartridge belt back at the cabin. He glanced at his Winchester leaning against a driftwood log, several yards to his left. The old Indian sat as if frozen to his saddle, watching them.

Carmody glanced at Nathan, and Nathan blinked at him in return, wrinkling his bushy brows, puzzled.

Finally the old man lifted his head slightly, his chest expanding as he inhaled. He called into the breeze sluicing down the creek bed, between him and the two prospectors. "Do you play the poker?"

Again, Carmody glanced at Nathan. Nathan chuckled, shrugged a shoulder. Turning to the Indian, he called back, "Yeah, we play poker."

The old man stared across the dark, narrow stream murmuring between low banks. His long, fringed shirt sported many designs on the yoke and chest, from dyed porcupine quills. Carmody was familiar with many tribal designs, but he didn't recognize these on the old Indian's tunic.

Slowly, the old man nodded and pursed his lips,

turning away with a speculative air. "I will return soon. If all is well, we will play the poker."

He batted his moccasin-clad heels against the paint's ribs, and drifted off through the forest. His shadow slid along the black water, swept the beaver dam thirty yards upstream, and disappeared.

Carmody watched him go, feeling imaginary bugs crawling around beneath his shirt collar. "That's the Injun I seen before, in town."

Nathan nodded, considering the information. "Weren't any braves with him, were there? No painted braves with rifles an' such?"

Carmody stared at the swaying, sunlit fir branches on the other side of the creek. "Nope."

Nathan turned around and began prying up the rock he'd been working on before. "Good."

THE NEXT DAY, they worked the same spot.

Carmody was hefting a bucketful of dirt and sand he'd dug up from between two boulders, when a sudden rushing and creaking rose on the other side of the creek. He looked up.

The wind was washing over the opposite ridge, jostling the pine tops as it moved toward Carmody. A few dead branches and pine cones tumbled from the swaying tree crowns.

As the wind approached like a beast thrashing through the forest, his sweat-damp hair swirled about his hatless head, cool air slicing against him. Icy cool—like a wind out of January. It raised goose bumps below his rolled-up shirt sleeves.

What really prickled his neck hair this time was the sound the wind carried. A woman's terrified screams swirled, at once soft and far-away, then suddenly loud and ominous.

The cries boomeranged around the canyon—first loud, then almost too quiet to be heard. A muffled scream sounded, as though the woman's heart were being ripped from her chest. The sound fragmented and swirled, as though the woman herself were being kited through the air above the canyon.

Carmody's right hand opened, releasing the bucket's wire handle. The pail fell, spilling dirt over the rocks.

He glanced over his right shoulder. Nathan moved toward him from the cabin, chewing, a half-eaten venison sandwich gripped in his hand, a look of cautious speculation in his eyes.

As he and Carmody stood gazing into the forest rising to the north-shouldering ridges, the wind dropped to a breeze. Over Carmody's left shoulder, the woman gave a weak moan. She sighed sharply above Nathan's right shoulder. Then, as if the wind had ushered her off down some other canyon to the east, her cries died altogether.

Neither Clay nor Nathan said anything for nearly a minute.

"Came from that way." Nathan pointed his hand holding the sandwich, toward the highest ridge rising on the opposite side of the creek. "Someone's in trouble over there."

When Carmody didn't say anything, Nathan said, "Reckon we better ride over and have a look."

Carmody studied the ridge, the icy chill from the wind still touching his shoulders and chest, kneading his scalp like a dead woman's fingers. Riding over that ridge where the wind had come from was the last thing he wanted to do.

But prospectors and other folks living isolated helped each other in times of trouble. They had to. They were all each other had out here.

Carmody glanced at Nathan walking away, then back at the ridge. After a minute, reluctance etched on his brows, he turned, and knowing that what they'd find would be just as crazy and inexplicable as the snakes or anything else he'd seen in this country of late, followed Nathan toward the makeshift corral in which the piebalds were stabled.

10

THEY RODE for an hour in the direction of the woman's screams. At the crest of a fir-clad ridge, they halted their horses and looked down into Poudre Canyon, through which the river snaked, white-stitched with rapids.

About a half-mile upstream, a small, gray cabin stood flanked by a lean-to stable and corral, nearly swallowed by the pines. A thin ribbon of smoke rose from the cabin's tin chimney pipe. A horse ran wildly around the stable, its neck and tail arched. Carmody saw only glimpses of it through the swaying trees. Thin, muffled whinnies rose on the wind.

With silent glances, the men gigged the pies down off the ridge crest. They followed a vague, winding trail through the evergreens and stone outcrops to the valley floor, then crossed the river at a broad curve and followed a faint wagon trace westward toward the cabin.

They'd been hearing the horse's frightened screams off and on as they'd descended the ridge, but the woman had fallen silent. Squinting straight over his own horse's bobbing head, Carmody drew back on the reins, stopping the pie along the trail's left track. To his right, Nathan stopped, too, and stiffened.

Four men rode toward them, side-by-side, on cantering horses, holding their reins up close to their chests. Carmody glanced at Nathan. The big mulatto's face had flushed and, like Carmody's, his right hand strayed to his pistol.

The four men rode toward Clay and Laroque, neither increasing nor decreasing their speed but riding ahead like they hadn't seen them. Carmody removed his hand from his .44's butt and shucked the Yellowboy repeater from his saddle sheath. He jacked a round one-handed, raising the barrel sharply then aimed up trail. He tightened his jaw while squinting his eyes.

The men continued toward him and Nathan, moving in and out of tree shadows. The light played across their features until they were close enough to distinguish. Carmody blinked, felt his blood freeze solid in his veins.

He recognized the men moving toward him. They were the same four owlhoots he had run into back at Crow Creek. They were the bank robbers he had killed on his way to Camp Hawkins.

The Australian, Bill Wayne.

The blond coyote in the oversized bear coat, Lucius.

The hawk-nosed scarecrow, Heck.

And Eb, the man who'd creased Carmody's forehead with a .50-caliber Sharps, and whose own broad, domed forehead Carmody had drilled with a .44 pill.

Carmody's stomach turned small and cold.

He couldn't feel the rifle in his hand, aimed straight out from his horse's right shoulder, at the four men moving toward him. The men didn't slow their pace. They moved ahead purposefully, with stony intensity, barely blinking their eyes.

"Hey!" called Nathan, his voice pinched with incredulity, when he saw the four riders had no intention of stopping.

Carmody's eyes stayed with the faces of the four men

he'd killed, whom the townsmen of Camp Hawkins had buried. The bank robbers should be in the town's Boot Hill cemetery. They looked as they had before Carmody first encountered them—sunburned, unshaven, dusty, *and unbloodied.*

Slack-jawed, Carmody gigged his own piebald off the left side of the trail.

He stared hard. He blinked. They couldn't be the same four men.

As they passed, all four bank robbers stared straight ahead, eyes riveted on the eastern horizon, as if Clay and Nathan weren't even here on the trail.

Carmody couldn't hear much because of the ocean-like rushing in his ears. But he was vaguely aware of Nathan, turned in his saddle toward the four dead men, and shouting, "...talkin' to you!"

Nathan glanced at Carmody then returned his frustrated, bewildered stare to the riders diminishing down the trail, slowly disappearing around a bend, the firs closing behind them.

Nathan stared angrily at the dead men's backs. Again he shouted, as though through a thick fog, "Hey!"

He turned his exasperated gaze to Carmody. "Those four have wreaked holy hell, sure as venom at a rattlesnake convention! Let's see if we can help that woman. We'll get after them later."

Carmody stared down trail, choking on his own spit. "I killed those four...before I got to Camp Hawkins."

Nathan glanced down trail again, where the riders had disappeared, pine and aspen boughs swaying in their wake. He stared intently at Clay, one eye nearly closed. "I don't savvy, my friend."

Carmody's voice was low, uncertain. "I did, Nate. I surely did kill 'em!"

"It wasn't those four. They ain't dead." His mind still fixed on the woman's screams, Laroque glanced up trail toward the cabin. "We'd best see if we can help that woman, Clay..."

"They ambushed me when I was camped along Crow Creek. They were on the run from a bank job, wanted one of the pies."

Laroque stared at Clay, his eyes wide and black beneath the brim of his floppy-brimmed hat. "Clay, don't take this wrong, but maybe the thin air's gettin' to *you.*"

Carmody nodded dully, wanting to believe that explained it. He turned to Nathan with a wan smile. "They sure ain't dead, are they?"

"No, they ain't dead," Nathan said as if speaking to a slow child. "Come on—let's see what kinda hob they raised!" He turned his horse westward and whipped him into a gallop with his rein ends.

Carmody squared his shoulders, laid the Winchester across his saddlebows, and then heeled the piebald into a gallop behind Nathan.

Five minutes later, he halted the horse and sat peering across the meadow to the cabin and stable sitting back against the trees, with long-toms, shovels, and wooden buckets strewn about the brush.

Wood smoke rose from the cabin's chimney pipe. The breeze flattened it out over the cabin's pitched roof and sent it back toward Carmody. There was something on the breeze besides the smell of pine.

The heavy, coppery smell of blood.

Peering through the smoke fog, he saw Nathan sitting the other piebald before the cabin, holding his .56 Spencer in his right hand. With his other hand, he gripped the reins of his horse, which pitched and frogged fearfully, shaking its head and whipping its brown mane.

Carmody's horse balked as he rode forward and followed Nathan's gaze to the ground near the cabin's right front corner. Between a pile of carefully stacked, unsplit logs was a smaller pile of split stove wood, and between the two lay what Carmody at first took to be a dead, bloody animal.

But it wasn't the right shape.

It was a man. Lying in bloody tatters, face up on the ground, eyes and mouth gaping, lips drawn back from his teeth. One dirty hand seemed to be reaching for a blood-splattered, splitting maul lying several feet to his left.

He appeared in his twenties, and was—had been—well over six-feet tall, with close-set eyes and blond red hair swept back from a sharp widow's peak.

It looked like someone had taken a razor-sharp scythe to the poor bastard, and hacked away until there wasn't more than a scrap of unmarred flesh and clothes. An especially deep gash had been gouged in the young man's chest, and the blood was thick, soupy, and black with swarming flies.

Smelling the fresh blood, Carmody's horse gave a half-hearted buck and crow-hopped back toward the trail. Holding the reins taut and making himself heavy in the saddle, Carmody swept his gaze from the body to the cabin.

The timbered door stood ajar, its split-rail, bark-covered boards splattered with blood.

Carmody said, "Am I seein'...?"

"The devil's work," Laroque muttered. Staring at the blood splashed in the grass around the dead man, he spread his lips with revulsion. *"Oui."*

"Let's get the horses out of here."

When they'd tied the pies to tree limbs on the other side of the trail, a good fifty yards from the cabin, they walked back into the yard, moving slowly, rifles extended in both hands.

As they approached the front door, something behind the cabin caught Carmody's eye. Something bright red in the brush.

"You check inside. I'll look around back."

Peering between the half-open door and the frame, Laroque nodded, sweat streaking his jaws, glistening in the black stubble on his big, round face. The skunk tail jostled from his hat brim. "Watch your ass."

Carmody moved along the cabin, his heart thudding, his entrails recoiling at the sickening smell of blood. Stepping through plenty of it in the sagebrush and wheat grass, he approached what he'd seen from the front.

Another body.

This one a woman's.

She'd been a blonde before the blood colored her hair. Her body, too, had been shredded as if by a hay scythe, so that not a square inch of her plain gray dress and white apron wasn't blood soaked. Her blue eyes had not been hacked, but they, too, were flecked with red as they stared, wide with horror, skyward.

Kneeling down for a closer look, Clay held his left arm over his nose. Like the dead man between the woodpiles, the woman's chest had been ripped open. Her heart had been removed. The gaping wound just under her breastbone was still pooling deep-purple blood and gore onto the apron angled low across her broad waist.

The sweet, coppery odor making his own innards heave, Carmody straightened and stumbled straight back, dropping his arm and lifting his head to suck air untainted by the viscera. He held his rifle high across his chest and let his eyes, stinging from the strong smell of the woman's butchered body, flick around the brush and shrubs lining the river.

Seeing no more bodies there, he turned to the cabin.

He froze.

Crouched against the cabin's back wall, a stocky, bearded figure held a long gun straight out from his chest.

Sucking air through his teeth, Carmody raised his rifle, squinted down the barrel, and tightened his trigger finger. Staring at the figure, he let his finger relax.

"Jesus," Carmody muttered, lowering the barrel.

The man wasn't standing crouched. The slender object angling out from his chest wasn't a long gun. It was the handle of the prospector's pick axe buried in his rib cage, pinning him like a giant spider to the cabin's back wall.

The man's hands were wrapped around the pickaxe handle, as if holding it there, his bearded chin sagging over it, as if in prayer.

Movement around the cabin's front corner evoked a grunt as Clay swung his rifle toward it. Nathan was moving toward him, the big man's own rifle held straight out from his waist. Laroque's eyes were wide, showing almost as much white as pupil. He swung his gaze right and forward, looking for the killer, as he moved along the cabin.

"Found a young woman inside." Laroque stared at the woman's body lying in the sage and buck brush before Clay, his thick nostrils expanding as he added, as if to himself, "Dead, like that one there."

The big man gave a grunt and stepped to his left, turning full around to face the bearded man pinned to the wall.

Nathan muttered some French and crossed himself. Standing with his rifle clutched before him, he also uttered what Carmody recognized as Apache, though Clay did not understand the words.

"The woman inside was big with child." Nathan glanced around the blood-splattered brush, then reached out and touched the handle of the pickaxe protruding from the bearded man's blood-dark chest.

"Blood's still fresh," Carmody said.

"The four we met on the trail."

"They didn't have any blood on 'em."

"They looked crazy enough. And whoever did this..." Laroque shook his head. *Fou dans la tete.*" Crazy in the head.

Laroque was leaning forward to peer closely at the

bearded man's chest, then removed his long skinning knife from the beaded sheath on his left hip. Probing the man's chest with the knife, he stretched his lips back from his teeth and said with a grim, speculative air, "They took this man's heart. Same with the woman inside."

Peering into the woods around the cabin, Carmody said, "And the woman over here."

"Why?" Laroque asked, drawing out the word.

"You tell me." Carmody had traveled all across the frontier, seen his share of grisly spectacles. But never anything like this.

Carmody shoved a pine bough aside with his rifle barrel. "The only men we've seen out here..." He stopped, turned to Laroque who was moving up on his right. "They didn't have any blood on 'em. Whoever did this'd be covered. And I've seen no boot prints. If they did this, they didn't do it from horseback."

Laroque looked at him sharply. His voice had a whipsaw note in it. "What do you think they were running from—a church social?"

To himself, Carmody said silently, *But they're dead!*

Carmody glanced away, lowered his rifle and rubbed his jaw. When he turned back, Nathan was already stomping off through the weeds, down-canted head swinging from side-to-side, the amulets swaying around his shabby hat crown. Carmody watched him then perused the brush and rocks along the river, across which a mining hole gaped in the canyon wall, above a pile of copper-colored tailings.

The poor bastards had been trying to chip a living out of the canyon when—what? The four men Carmody had already killed came to kill them and tear their hearts out of their chests?

Unable to work his mind around it, but deciding that no more bodies were to be found around the cabin, Carmody walked back to where he and Laroque had tied their horses. Nathan was already there, shoving his rifle down into his saddle scabbard.

"They shouldn't be hard to track if they're following the trail," Laroque said.

Carmody watched the big man toe a stirrup then heave himself into the saddle. Laroque reined his horse onto the trail then turned to Carmody with an impatient look.

"You comin'?"

Carmody stared at him, flushed and perplexed. Utterly baffled.

Finally, he poked his boot through the stirrup, grabbed the saddle horn, and pulled himself into the leather.

He knew what Laroque was thinking—anyone who knowingly let four cold-blooded killers run free in an isolated canyon was little better than the killers themselves.

Carmody had to rid himself of the fool notion he'd already killed those men. That just wasn't sane. Somewhere during his isolated travels, he'd lost his mind. That could be the only explanation.

"Yeah, yeah." He laid his Yellowboy across his saddlebows and batted his heels against the pie's ribs. "I'm comin'..."

11

THEY RODE HARD for nearly an hour, following the four riders' hoof prints, freshly gouged into the wagon tracks, before they climbed a low hill through an aspen copse, a low ridge on their right, a sandy creek on their left.

Carmody rode numbly, looking around but only half-seeing what his eyes took in, half-hearing the thuds of his and Nathan's horses on the brushy wagon track.

He remembered shooting each one. He remembered seeing the bodies by the creek the next morning, caked with dried blood. One had been pulled a few feet away from the others by the night-scavenging coyotes.

Now a rifle cracked sharply, echoing.

Ahead of him, Laroque's horse screamed and rose up on its front legs.

With surprising nimbleness for a man his size, Nathan leapt from the saddle, lashing out with his left hand to shuck his Spencer from the boot. As the pie twisted back and down, blood flying from its right shoulder, Nathan flung himself forward, off the right side of the trail and away from the horse's flailing hooves.

Jerking back on his own reins, Carmody peered at the low, gray-green scarp rising to the right. Two men squatted atop the scarp, one slightly higher than the other. Smoke puffed in the breeze near the higher man, who'd lowered his rifle to ram a fresh shell into the breech. Smoke and flames burst from the barrel of the other man's rifle.

Carmody ducked as the bullet whined over his head and thumped into an aspen trunk to his left.

As Clay's horse whinnied and bucked, Clay threw himself out of the saddle, hit the trail and rolled down a slight incline. He jacked a shell into his Yellowboy's magazine and fired, watching his slug slam into the rock two feet below the lower shooter.

Clay blinked up at the man.

Carmody was a good fifty yards away, but he could make out the small frame, light hair, and oversized bear coat of the blond coyote he'd greased only seconds after he'd killed the other three. The broad-faced Australian stood to the coyote's right and two feet higher.

It was them, all right.

"*Shit.*"

How did you kill men you'd *already* killed?

Carmody fired another shot as the Australian did the same. The Aussie's slug blew up grass and dirt two feet in front of Carmody, who hunkered lower behind the bank.

He glanced across the trail. The horses had fled in opposite directions. Laroque lay in the middle of the trail, several yards up from Carmody, cheeked up to his rifle's butt and hammering one slug after another into the woods behind Clay.

His .56 thundered like a small cannon, the brass shells arcing over his right shoulder as he worked the rifle's trigger-guard cocking mechanism.

Carmody peered into the woods, where the .56 slugs gouged bark from aspens, snapped small branches, and splashed into the creek. Two shadows moved there amongst the trees, smoke puffing as they returned fire from behind aspen boles.

Hunkering behind a trunk and staying beneath the trail, so he wouldn't get caught in the cross-fire, Carmody figured the other two near the creek must be the sharp-shooter, Eb, and the gangly scarecrow, Heck.

Two more ghosts to contend with.

He squeezed off a round at one of the shooters in the woods, the slug tearing up bark and cutting through a hat brim sticking out from the other side of a slender birch.

"*Jay-zuzz!*" the scarecrow yelled.

Carmody ejected the smoking brass and expelled air through his teeth with a raspy whistle. They're scared, anyway. Maybe that meant they could be killed.

But what did it take to make them stay that way?

Slamming the Yellowboy's cocking lever home, he turned as a shot from the scarp chewed a small sage shrub behind him. Smoke wafted from the rocks, where the blond coyote and the Aussie were crouched. Several shots hammered the ground around Laroque, who'd rolled onto a shoulder, facing Carmody, to fill the Spencer's loading tube.

"Nathan, I'm gonna circle around that scarp," Carmody yelled.

Laroque nodded, frowning distractedly, as he rammed the loading tube into the Spencer's stock and rose to his knees. Carmody ran across the trail as Nathan, triggering the Spencer, ran to the opposite side and into the woods.

Carmody bolted around the right side of the scarp, dodging several shots from above. In seconds he was in deep brush and boulders, scrambling over the rocks and pinions and serviceberry scrub as he worked his way to the opposite side.

He paused for a breather, peering up the jagged scarp and scrubbing sweat from his brow with his left sleeve. Maybe he and Nathan should just roll their tails, get the hell out of here. Why were they going after these guys, anyway, if they wouldn't stay dead?

But then, Nathan didn't know that. And Carmody had to admit a little doubt himself. They looked plenty alive, and it was hard to savvy the notion you were swapping lead with dead men, even when you were fairly sure you'd killed them yourself.

Shots sounded on the other side of the scarp's brow, spanging off rocks, plunking into trees with angry cracks.

Carmody was about to rise and continue his trek when he heard a boot scrape on the other side of the boulder he'd crouched behind. Sagging back down to his haunches, squeezing the rifle in his hands, he tensed, listening.

Footsteps. Air raked into lungs, expelled raspily through a nose. Pebbles dropped down-slope, clattering.

Carmody's heart increased its rhythm as he hauled the Yellowboy's hammer back quietly. He waited, listening intently.

When he heard the man approach his cover, he stood suddenly.

The Aussie, Bill Wayne, saw him a half-second after Carmody had gained his feet. The outlaw had been looking down-slope, but seeing Clay in the corner of his eye, he stopped abruptly, tensing, his eyes widening as he whipped his head toward Carmody.

Clay and the bank robber stood frozen, each man gazing at the other with flinty intentness. Carmody marvelled. The Aussie looked as he had the night he and his partners had ambushed Clay along Crow Creek. At least, the man had no bullet markings, no bandages, no obvious scars...

And he was alive.

Carmody was so busy staring at Wayne he almost didn't notice when Wayne's bristled, sun-burned face softened, the blue eyes acquiring a mocking light beneath his broad sombrero. Wayne whipped his rifle toward Clay and squeezed the trigger a half second after Clay, regaining his wits, had fired the Yellowboy straight out from his waist.

Wayne's shot glanced off a rock a foot to Carmody's left. Carmody's shot took him through the belly, chewing through the buckskin and the flannel lining of his coat. Dropping both hands, but still clutching the rifle, Wayne staggered back. His jaw dropped, eyes instantly darkening and looking only vaguely surprised.

Gritting his teeth, Carmody snapped the cocking lever down and up. "I killed you once. What the hell are you?"

Wayne dropped his rifle, dropped to his knees, both hands cupping his belly. A devilish smile tugged at his lips.

Carmody shot him through the head, watched him fall straight back to the ground, grinning lopsidedly skyward.

Glimpsing movement in the upper periphery of his vision, he jerked his head up to see the blond bulldog leap onto a tall boulder about fifty feet up the scarp. Screaming like a Rebel on the outskirts of Washington City, the blond kid snapped his rifle high and aimed down at Carmody.

Carmody flinched.

The kid's rifle twitched a quarter-second before it roared. The slug winged wide of Carmody, who stared up, eyes round with surprise. The boulder beneath the kid's feet had shifted, and the kid's boots came out from beneath him, as though he'd slipped on ice.

With a yelp, the kid dropped his rifle and fell hard on his rump atop the rock. The rock rolled forward and the kid tumbled head-first from the crest, landing hard with a grunt and rolling ahead of the rock and into the brush.

The boulder grumbled as it picked up speed, causing the ground beneath Carmody's boots to shudder.

Carmody lowered his rifle and stepped back.

The blond coyote, grunting and clutching his right leg, rose onto a shoulder and turned his head. Spying the boulder rolling toward him, his eyes snapped wide. He screeched, heaved himself onto his good foot, and scrambled down the slope.

Because of the trees and brush on both sides of him, he could flee only straight down the grade. He didn't get far. The cabin-sized boulder quickly overtook him, rolled him under like a heavy ore wagon smashing a rabbit. Without so much as a burp, the rock continued on down the slope and came to rest in a grassy hollow.

Behind it, dust sifted.

The blond coyote lay belly-down, flat, rumpled, and bleeding. His ankles were crossed, his head turned to one side, one arm straight out to the left, the other curled toward his right hip, as if he were only napping.

Carmody looked at the boulder again, snugged benignly down in the hollow. Running his palm across his chin, he walked over to the kid, crouched down, and turned the coyote onto his back.

Blood oozed from the kid's open mouth and eyes. It dribbled over both earlobes. Several broken ribs protruded from his shirt.

Aside from that, he didn't look especially odd, let alone like a ghost. He looked like bread dough after the first pass of a rolling pin.

"*Le Christ, j'ai que vous avez ete casse comme un boque!*"

Carmody swung around with a start, his heart hammering his ribs. Laroque was jogging toward him over the shoulder of the slope, holding his Spencer across his broad chest, worry etched in his eyes. Carmody's pulse slowed as he watched the mulatto move toward him, his brain slowly translating Laroque's exclamation. Seeing the boulder, Nathan had thought he'd been "smashed like a bug."

"Not me," Clay said, turning to the blond coyote. "Him."

Nathan followed Carmody's rifle barrel. "See there? Look at that." With a mocking smile, he thumped

Carmody's chest with the back of his hand. "One of your *ghosts* was smashed just like a man!"

"Diddle yourself."

"Such barn talk is ignoble."

"Where're the other two?"

"Fornicating with each other in hell." Nathan grinned again and patted his rifle. "My '63 Spencer, with the fifty-six shorts, is like shooting silver cartwheels with a howitzer."

"Yeah, but what do you do when that seven-shooter clicks empty?"

Nathan shrugged a shoulder. "Reload."

"Come on," Carmody said. He reached down and jerked the dead coyote up by his coat collar. "Let's get these bastards buried."

Laroque's bushy brows beetled. "Leave them for the crows!"

Carmody dragged the body down the slope, toward the grassy hollow where the digging would be easiest. Remembering that he hadn't buried these men when he'd killed them the first time, he spat, "I want them buried good and deep. Under rocks."

"*Vous etes fous!*" Nathan yelled behind him. You are crazy!

Later, once Nathan had given up trying to convince Carmody that burying such human dung beetles was a waste of time and energy, he grudgingly dragged his own two dead men down to the hollow. He and Clay spent a half hour retrieving their horses, relieved to find that Nathan's pie's shoulder had only been grazed. While Nathan cleaned the wound, packed it with manure and healing herbs, Carmody dug the grave with the folding shovel strapped to his saddlebags.

He dug quickly, working up a sweat and casting frequent glances at the four men lined up on the north side of the hole, as if expecting them all to suddenly get up again and begin wreaking more havoc. At the same time, he suspected he hadn't really killed them before, and that somewhere during his time alone in the Chugwater Rocks, his head had gotten a little soft.

Fearing the four dead men staring skyward and wondering how you retrieved your sanity once you lost it, he chipped and gouged at the rocky soil, sending up load after load of silt and clay. The mound behind the grave was four-feet high when he flipped another load over his shoulder and spied Nathan hunkered down beside the hole.

The mulatto regarded him with a gentle but half-mocking smile on his light-cherry features, his floppy hat with all its talismans pushed back on his head, a stubby cigar in his teeth. "You've dug a hole deep enough to plant these men standing up, *mon ami.* It's time to quit."

Carmody swung his head around to regard the hole he was standing in, neck deep. He sighed, tossed the shovel into the mound of fresh dirt, and extended his right hand to Nathan. Laroque helped him out. Carmody straightened slowly, working the creaks out of his bones and brushing at the dirt on his jeans.

An eerie voice rose above and behind him, chanting softly. A rattle shook with a heart-like rhythm.

The hair prickling beneath his collar, Carmody grabbed his pistol from his hip and whipped around, raking back the trigger.

It was the old, poker-playing Indian. On a grassy knoll twenty feet away, he stood, shuffling his feet, chanting, and waving a rattle. Carmody glanced at Nathan standing to his left, his own revolver extended straight out from his shoulder. Laroque shot a glance at Clay, slitting his eyes and bunching his hub-like cheeks.

"What the hell's he doing here?"

"Maybe he wants to play poker," Carmody muttered, staring incredulously up the knoll. He didn't want any more nonsense. He wanted to get these carcasses into the earth then head back to the cabin and bury the dead prospectors before the sun went down.

The Indian danced in place on the knoll's crest, bending his knees and waving his arms, his silver-streaked hair blowing. A deer hide medicine pouch and a necklace of bleached bat skulls jostled across his chest. The somberness of the man's chants was somehow emphasized by each shake of the yellow gourd rattle. Occasionally, he tilted his head back and lifted his face to the sky, as if conjuring spirits from the clouds.

Carmody frowned impatiently and lifted his voice. "Hey, listen, old-timer, we appreciate the serenade, but—"

Nathan poked his shoulder, cutting him off. Carmody turned, followed Nathan's gaze down to the dead men lying beside the grave.

His gut recoiled as he took one involuntary step backward.

The dead men were stiff and wizened, eyes bulging from dried sockets, rawhide lips stretched back from yellow teeth, skulls shrunken and bony beneath their grizzled scalps.

Old wounds appeared—the wounds Carmody had inflicted back along Crow Creek over a week ago. The blood was as black as tar.

12

As if their heads were manipulated by the same puppet string, Carmody and Laroque turned their gazes from the four bodies to the old Indian shuffling and rattling upon the knoll, their eyes round, foreheads deep-lined and flushed.

"What the hell's goin' on here?" Carmody growled.

The Indian fell silent. He dropped his gaze to the two men staring up at him, and lowered the rattle to his side.

"I am *Katchi-lo-go-we*, of the People of the Diamondback." He lowered his gaze even farther, to the four toothy, dessicated cadavers sprawled beside the grave. "These men will remain in the spirit world now. They will not return. I have dissolved the *chi-wah-hay* that led them back."

Carmody stared at the old man. As perplexed as he was by the Indian's sudden appearance and everything connected with the dead bank robbers, he felt his back muscles slacken with a slight relief.

Laroque stepped back from the cadavers. "You mean, they really were *ghosts?*"

The Indian stared back at him, his eyes crinkling at the corners, as if searching the distance for the words. "They were dead men returned to the land of the living by a *chi-*

wah-hay cast by a demon from the Land Beyond the Darkness."

"What the hell's a *chi-wah-hay?*" Carmody asked.

The Indian appeared to have trouble coming up with an explanation in English. Lines of effort spoked the corners of his eyes.

Laroque said, *"Sortilege."* He glanced at Clay. "In English, a hex or a spell. There's a similar word in the Chiricahua tongue."

The old Indian nodded slightly and fingered the bat skulls hanging down his chest.

Carmody had lowered his pistol to his side. Now he depressed the hammer and said, "You say a demon cast the spell, sending these hombres back to earth?" The words sounded so ludicrous that, if he hadn't seen what he'd seen with his own eyes, he would have laughed. "Why?"

"It's a long story," the Indian sighed. "And I have grown weary. I must rest." With that, he turned and, head bowed, disappeared down the other side of the knoll.

Clay glanced at Nathan. "Do you believe any of this crazy shit?"

Laroque nodded. "I was raised to believe it." He paused. "But I've never seen it." He looked at the dead men, well on their way to becoming skeletons. "Till now."

Carmody studied the bodies. He didn't want to touch them. "Come on," he growled, moving reluctantly forward, "Let's get 'em in the ground and get the hell out of here."

He bent down, face pinched with revulsion. The death stench was sharp and sweet. "Whew!"

"Breathe through you mouth."

"Doesn't help."

Carmody shoved his hands beneath the blond coyote's shoulders, and sucking air through his gritted teeth, lifted the kid's torso off the ground while Nathan lifted his legs. Carmody swung his end around, and he and Nathan dropped the cadaver unceremoniously into the hole. It landed with a dull thump, bits of dirt and gravel falling down the sides.

When all four bodies were in the hole, and Clay and Nathan had filled in the grave and covered it with stones, Nathan raked a sleeve across his red, watering eyes, and turned to Clay. "What about the prospectors?"

Carmody had purposely not been thinking about them. He didn't want to ride over there. Tired, weary, and skittish as a colt surrounded by slathering coyotes, he wanted to be back in his own canyon with a tin cup filled with cold whiskey.

"Reckon we best bury them, too."

"Not much light left," Nathan said, glancing at the sky. "We could come back tomorrow and do it."

"I don't want to ride back over here tomorrow." Carmody grabbed his shovel and rifle, and headed for his horse. "Let's get to it."

They mounted up and, to save Laroque's injured pie, rode slowly back toward the cabin. The sun had angled behind the ridges by the time the little, gray hovel came into view at the back of the stump-spotted clearing. Purple shadows canted out from the canyon walls and descended upon the woods.

No smoke rose from chimney pipe now. A silence punctuated by the mournful calls of sparrows and finches hung heavy over the clearing.

Carmody and Laroque tied their horses where they'd tied them before, a good distance from the yard. Carmody was shucking his rifle from its boot when a wolf sent a long, chortling call from the ridge five hundred feet above the cabin. Clay started, snapping his head up.

He gazed up at the darkening, boulder-strewn slopes, only the tops of the tallest pines still touched with copper by the quickly falling sun. In the dry air they were as clear as if seen through a high-powered telescope.

"You sure you wanna do this?" Laroque said. "Could come back tomorrow."

Clay squeezed his rifle in his hands and started walking toward the cabin concealed in the heavy shadows shouldering down from the ridge. "Come on."

As they crossed the meadow, Nathan said, "There's some picks and shovels inside."

Glancing at the dead man in the yard, Carmody followed Laroque to the cabin door. A low growl sounded inside.

"Look out!" Nathan said, shoving Clay left as Laroque himself bolted right.

Between them a gray-brown blur shot out through the cabin door.

Heart hammering, jacking a round into his rifle's chamber, Carmody turned to see the coyote land in the yard and, yodeling angrily, lope off across the clearing, its dun coat glistening in the pink light.

Puffing his cheeks out with a deep sigh, Carmody turned to Nathan. Laroque offered his own relieved chuff, lowered his rifle, peered cautiously into the cabin, then stepped slowly inside. As Nathan moved to the right rear wall, where shovels and picks hung from nails, Carmody stopped suddenly, as if an invisible hand were suddenly thrust against his chest.

Before him and left was a long table hand-hewn from pine logs. Upon the table lay the young, pregnant woman, on her back, head and arms dangling off the table's near side. Her mouth hung slack. Blackflies buzzed around her blood-flecked lips. A pair of the clearest, gray-blue eyes Carmody had ever seen stared straight up at him, as though silently beseeching him for help, or as if to say, *Look what happened here.*

Her swollen belly was a mass of jellied blood around which more flies swarmed, buzzing. The stench was thick, impenetrable. Beside her on the table lay a pat of freshly-churned butter, a strawberry and two delicate leaves stamped on top as a decoration.

Something poked Carmody's right shoulder. "Here," Nathan said.

Clay gave a slight start, turned his head. Laroque stood beside him, holding out a shovel, handle-first, regarding him expectantly.

"Let's get this grim business done and get the hell out of here."

Carmody grabbed the shovel. "I hear that." He turned, walked outside, looked around the clearing. Jerking his head toward the grassy terrain about fifty yards left of the cabin, he said, "Over there's a good place."

"Good as any," Nathan said. Hefting a pick in one hand, a shovel in the other, he headed in that direction.

The picks made the work faster, but the sun was sinking fast, lowering a chill and an ominous air, the night coming down like a burial shroud. Racing it, Carmody felt as though they were busting rocks with hand trowels. Full dark found them only half-finished digging the four graves. Nathan went into the cabin and came out with several lanterns, which he lit and placed in a semi-circle around the excavations.

The light made it easier to see their work, but harder to see into the blackness beyond the cabin. Wolves and coyotes set up their symphonies on the canyon slopes, no doubt smelling the blood. Clay figured it was his imagination, but he sensed eyes watching from the dark trees lining the river. He looked up occasionally from his work, seeing only bending tree shadows and the zig-zagging blurs of swooping bats attracted by the lanterns.

"What the hell was that?" Nathan said suddenly, knee-deep in a grave, shovel in his hands.

Clay froze and peered into the darkness. Something white bobbed up and down, about thirty yards east of the cabin. It disappeared in the dark pine wall. Soft hoof falls sounded, snapping branches and crunching grass, barely audible above the constant rush of the river.

"Deer," Carmody said, letting out his breath.

Laroque grunted.

"At least you got charms on your hat," Clay said, swinging the pick. "Imagine how I feel."

"They're Apache and Cajun, some Comanche," Nathan said. "I don't know if they'll work on the spirits in these parts."

"Just goes to show, you should always check out the local evil spirits, so you'll have the right talismans to ward 'em off."

"Now ya tell me."

When they'd dug four graves about four feet deep, Laroque stabbed his shovel in a dirt pile and swiped sweat from his forehead. "Best bring the bodies on over."

Carmody slung his own shovel into a dirt pile, his features sweat-soaked and drawn in the lanterns' glow. He glanced off into the darkness. "Why the hell didn't we do that while it was still light? We can't carry the bodies *and* the lanterns."

Nathan chuffed and shook his head. "Cause that woulda been too easy."

Deciding to bury the pregnant young woman first, they started walking toward the cabin, stepping carefully so they wouldn't trip over sage or buckbrush clumps. Halfway there, Carmody stopped suddenly and turned toward the river.

"What is it?" Laroque whispered.

"Didn't you hear it?"

Laroque cocked his head to listen. He shrugged. "Nothing."

Carmody stood frozen, staring and listening. Quietly, he said, "Sounded like a grunt. Deep-throated. Sorta like a bear or somethin'." He glanced back toward the graves lit by the three lanterns. Both his and Nathan's rifles leaned together against a slender aspen, the iron and dark wood glistening dully.

"Just your imagination," Nathan said, lightly tapping Carmody's arm and starting again toward the cabin. "Come on."

Carmody stayed where he was. "Somethin's out there, Nathan." He could sense the presence, thought he could even smell the sweet, fetid, urine-like smell of something large and primitive.

Laroque turned back to him. "There's lots of things out there, *mon ami*. Deer, coyotes, wolves. Maybe bobcats. They smell the blood. Now, come on."

Casting another glance into the trees, his shoulders tense, Carmody followed Laroque to the cabin. Nathan pushed the door wide and stepped inside, Carmody following.

They paused just over the threshold to let their eyes grow accustomed to the darkness. Violet starlight etched the hard angles of tables and cots, a hide-seated rocker and a sheet-iron cook stove. The dark, angular lump of the girl still sprawled upon the table.

Carmody peered behind the door. Nothing there but a broom and a tintype hanging crooked on the wall.

Carmody stepped up to the table, holding his breath against the blood and gut fetor. The girl lay across the table, head and arms dangling toward the floor, eyes glistening slightly in the feeble starlight.

"Shit," Carmody said.

"You take the arms," Nathan said. "I'll get her feet.

"What about blankets?"

Laroque stopped and looked at him. "Reckon they should be covered..."

"Here." Carmody turned to one of the room's two beds and removed two quilts that had been neatly tucked under the cornshuck mattress sack. From a shelf above the bed he found two more threadbare army blankets. "Good enough."

He threw the blankets over his shoulder then moved back to the table, crouched, and shoved his hands beneath the young woman's shoulders, felt the sticky slickness of the half-dried blood. When Laroque had a good hold on her legs, they each lifted his end. The girl's tattered dress stuck to the bloody wooden surface, stretched taut, then gave as they eased her up and sideways, Carmody moving backwards and feeling the skin beneath his collar tingle, out the cabin door.

Shuffling awkwardly across the meadow, tripping over sage clumps, they carried her over to the graves, eased her gently into the hole farthest from the cabin. Carmody tossed one of the blankets over her body, reached down to make sure she was covered.

"Rest easy, mama," Carmody whispered, pulling his head back out of the hole, resting for a moment on his knees, hands on his thighs. "Sure am sorry this happened to you."

He shook his head, climbed to his feet, and followed Nathan, who was already moving back toward the body before the cabin—the young lady's husband, they'd decided.

When they'd laid the young man in the grave beside the girl and covered him with a blanket, they retrieved the other woman, laid her in the hole beside the young man, and then went back for the bearded gent who'd been impaled in the cabin's rear wall.

Clay grabbed the handle and yanked. The blade was set deep in the wall.

Nathan placed his own hands on the handle, and the two men worked it back and forth several times, grunting, before the blade came free with a wooden crunching sound behind the old gent's back. With the pick still impaling the man's body but no longer attached to the log, he dropped straight down from the wall. Clay held him there with the pick. Grimacing, feeling as though his nostrils were coated with the death smell, he gently worked the blade free of the bones and gristle.

Both hands on the man's right shoulder, Nathan held the body against the wall as the bloody end of the pick rose from the man's chest, glistening in the starlight. Carmody tossed the implement into the grass, as though it had suddenly turned hot, then stooped to pick up the dead man's feet. "Let's get this poor bastard in his grave, and you and me the hell away from here!"

When they had the bearded man in his grave and covered with a blanket, it didn't take Carmody and Laroque, energized by fear, long to fill in all four graves. It took considerably longer to cover the graves with rocks from the riverbank, however, which they decided they had to do. Otherwise the predators would dig the bodies up in minutes and all their work would have been for nothing.

Carmody had made ten trips when, returning to the river for more rocks, he pushed through a pine bough and stopped suddenly.

Again, he'd heard the guttural, growl-like noise.

He turned to face downstream, straining his ears to listen above the river's metallic chortle. Nothing. Just the water and the low, sinewy whistle of a bat in the treetops. Clay was about to turn away when two dull yellow lights appeared about fifty feet downstream, on the opposite side of the river. They looked like the eyes of a big cat, a little larger than silver dollars.

They flickered, as if the eyes had blinked.

Carmody stared, feeling as though the air had been pinched out of his lungs, as the lights began moving toward him.

13

"WHAT THE HELL YOU SEE NOW?" Nathan yelled as Carmody ran toward him.

Clay was hoofing it fast toward the graves, where Laroque was planting another stone. "You wouldn't believe it if I told you, so let's just get the hell outta here!"

"What're you talkin' about? We ain't fin—"

"That's enough rocks," Carmody said, running past his partner and heading for the horses. He couldn't see them but he could hear them nickering back where they'd been tied.

Breathless and sore-footed, Carmody stopped and turned. Laroque was moving toward him, the big man striding quickly, a hatted silhouette against the dark trees. He'd blown out the lanterns. Behind him, Carmody saw no sign of the eyes, or lights, or whatever the hell they were.

But he sensed they were still there. Apparently, the horses did, as well.

"Somethin' sure put a bur under these hosses' hides," Nathan observed as he caught up with Clay.

Clay shoved his face up close to Nathan's. "It looked like a big pair of eyes. I ain't gildin' no lily. Big, damn eyes. Like cat's eyes. They moved toward me across the river."

"Cat's eyes, huh?" Nathan cooed to his horse and untied the reins from the pine branch. "Well, there ain't nothin' out there now."

"I saw 'em, I tell you." Carmody clung to his pitching horse's saddle horn and fought a boot through the stirrup. "And I think we've done decided I ain't crazy."

"Well, not *pure* loco, anyhow. Easy, horse, easy!"

They got the pies settled down enough to turn them eastward onto the trail, Nathan riding ahead, Carmody about ten yards behind. A bird shrieked in the woods on the right side of the trail. Carmody saw a crow-sized bird with a long, slender tail perched in a branch arching over the trail.

"You son of a bitch," he muttered, lifting his chin to watch the bird as he passed beneath the limb. The bird rose, shrieking like the demon's own bat.

"What's that?"

"Nothin'. Some damn magpie's got it in for me, that's all."

Laroque turned in his saddle. "I mighta spoke too soon. You're crazier'n a snakebit coyote chasin' moon shadows!"

They crossed the river and started back up the ridge toward their camp in the cross canyon, steering by starlight and the three-quarter-moon floating over Elephant Rock.

Their nerves were shot. They spoke little.

To comfort himself, Carmody conjured images of Sheriff Claudine Bridger standing topless by the river on the morning he'd last seen her, a gun in her hand, a cartridge belt wrapped around her waist. She was some woman, and the only good thing that had happened to him since he'd come here.

"Oh, yeah..."

Riding ahead on the vague trail angling sharply toward their camp, Nathan turned in his saddle. "What're you snortin' about? You seen *anything* lately to tickle your funny bone?"

"Just your face, hoss," Carmody growled. He hadn't realized he'd laughed out loud. Still, there was no law against chuckling. "I'm suppressin' a big belly laugh at this very moment!"

Laroque stopped his horse and looked at Carmody, his face expressionless beneath his hat brim. Carmody stopped and held Nathan's glare. Clay's horse shook its bridle and stomped a front hoof.

Nathan's shoulders jerked back and forth. Carmody heard the low chuckles.

Clay grinned. "You reckon we're a might nervy?"

Laroque lifted his head. *"Ohhh!* I need a long drink." With that, he reined his horse down the trail, but he hadn't taken more than two strides before he reined back sharply and raised his right hand. He grunted softly with surprise, clucked his tongue.

Carmody frowned. "What—?" Peering down the grade over Nathan's right shoulder, he cursed. Between the slightly bending pine boughs, a campfire flickered at the bottom of the canyon.

"That's our camp," Laroque said quietly. "I took a reckoning off that big dead cedar yonder."

"You invitin' folks over again without tellin' me?"

"Ain't right—movin' onto a man's claim when a man ain't home."

"I've noticed a dearth of parlor manners in this neck of the mountains."

They rode down to the canyon floor and swung down from their horses within hearing of the water's warble over dams and snags. Carmody figured they were about fifty yards downstream from their cabin.

Feeling as blown as a horse run hard over high ridges, he wasn't sure he had the energy to tussle with claim jumpers—or whoever had taken over their camp. Just the same, he shucked his rifle, jacked a round in the breech, and turned to Nathan, who was doing likewise.

"I'll head upstream then cross and come back down, sneak around the cabin."

Laroque nodded. "I'll ford here and give you a few minutes."

Carmody walked away through the trees along the moonlight-speckled stream.

Hunkering low, he followed the stream past the cabin, which sat a good thirty yards back from the opposite bank. He could see a man sitting on the other side of the fire—a single silhouette who appeared to be hunkered low in a blanket drawn around his head and shoulders, a broad-brimmed hat on his head. A rifle lay across his knees. Carmody smelled roasting meat, and his mouth watered.

He continued upstream for another thirty yards, crossed the stream on a beaver dam, and a few minutes later, his pants soaked to the ankles, scuttled up to the cabin's rear wall. He held the Winchester up close to his chest as he stole along the side of the cabin. When he came to the front right corner, he stopped.

The man sitting before the fire, his back to Carmody, held a sharpened stick in his right hand. He was picking roasted rabbit off the stick and plucking it into his mouth. Carmody could see his head move as he ate.

Carmody moved slowly toward him, setting his feet down lightly, one after the other, the rifle extended straight out from his right hip, the barrel aimed at the center of the intruder's back.

A sound rose on his left. *ZZZZZZssssssssssssssssssss!*

Carmody froze. A diamondback rattler was coiled up about four feet away, well within striking range. Its head was up and ready to do just that, its flat, coppery eyes reflecting the fire's flickering light.

Carmody pivoted, swung his rifle toward the hissing viper.

"Ko-ko!"

The admonishing voice of the man before him kept

Carmody from pulling the trigger. The snake's head pulled back slightly and dropped a fraction of an inch. Cowering?

The man turned half around. Without looking at Carmody, he extended his gnarled left hand between Carmody and the snake. He made a slow sweeping motion over the snake's head. The mahogany-colored hand was deep-lined and slashed with many knotted, white scars. The thumb was knobby and crooked, as though it had been broken and not set.

The snake's head moved back and forth several times, then dropped, turned, and slid toward a croaker sack lying nearby. The head slipped into the sack's lip and disappeared, the rest of its body following until the entire snake was inside the sack. It could have been a large wrinkle in the tattered burlap.

The old Indian turned back around to the fire. "Teach you to sneak up on an old man."

Carmody heard a familiar chuckle and lifted his gaze to see Nathan approach from the other side of the fire, his old Spencer resting on his shoulder. The encounter with the snake having done nothing to improve his already colicky disposition, Carmody stepped around to the left side of the fire, where he could see the old man's face beneath the brim of his wide-brimmed sombrero. A band of hammered silver discs decorated the low crown, shimmering copper and gold in the fire's light.

Between the old man and the rocks of the fire ring, two more unskinned cottontails lay, the snares Carmody had set the night before still looped around their necks.

"Makin' yourself at home, are ye?"

Still grinning, Nathan dropped to a knee.

The old man—face perpetually impassive—ripped meat from the stick and stuck it into his mouth, licking the grease from his fingers and chewing with his mouth open, studying the carcass with sullen interest, as if determining from where his next bite should come.

"Can I get you anything else?" Carmody asked, his sarcasm sounding more venomous than he'd intended. After all, the old man had helped him out of a heap of trouble. "Some whiskey to wash that down with, perhaps?"

The old man shook his head and glanced at Carmody's coffee pot chugging on a flat rock in the fire. A tin cup steamed beside his right knee.

Carmody looked again at Laroque and chuffed with disgust. The old man had obviously brought out Carmody's possibles bag from the cabin. It lay not far from the croaker sack containing the snake. Keeping his distance from the diamondback, Clay stabbed the possibles bag with his rifle barrel. He peered inside to make sure it hadn't become a den for another serpent, then reached in and pulled out a dented tin cup. He tossed the cup to Nathan then reached for another.

With a leather scrap, he removed the coffee pot from the rock, and filled his cup. He looked at the old man, still silently eating. When Carmody had filled his cup, he tossed the scrap leather to Nathan, who gained his knees, grabbed the pot, and filled his own cup.

The big mulatto blew ripples on the hot coffee. Looking over the rim at the old Indian, he said, "What brings you here, old one?" He nodded his head at the croaker sack. "With your snake."

Chewing and staring at the meat remaining on the stick, the old man said, "I came to say a blessing over your cabin. I ate one of your rabbits. The others are here." He picked up one of the rabbits and tossed it at Carmody's feet. He tossed the other to Nathan, who caught the rabbit in mid-air. "The meat is young and tender. The cottontails never get very old in this canyon. A family of wolves lives close."

Carmody hunkered down beside the fire, enjoyed the soothing radiance. He stared at the Indian to his right, sipped his coffee. It warmed him, calmed his nerves. He became less peeved at the old man. The Indian had sent the four outlaws back to wherever Clay himself had sent them the first time. For some reason, he found himself believing they wouldn't be back.

"What the hell's goin' on around here?" he asked the old man. "Snakes by the dozens slitherin' out of holes, dead men comin' back to life again, folks murdered, their hearts ripped out of their chests." He gave an involuntary shudder.

The old man set his cooked rabbit on a rock. He broke the thigh bone in his greasy fingers and sucked out the marrow. Smacking his lips, he said, "Ademon has been awakened. His name is *To-de-hee*, in the tongue of the ancients. He prowls this canyon, the sacred home of his people, killing and taking the hearts from those he kills and offering them to the dark God of the Magpie People, for sustenance."

He sucked marrow from the other end of the broken bone, then tossed both bones into the fire. "You should be safe here, as long as *To-de-hee's* powers remain no stronger than mine. I have blessed this cabin, these grounds. But he knows I am here. Demons act strange when they are afraid."

Carmody frowned at the oldster, who now sat, belly full, his hands resting on his crossed legs, staring into the darkness beyond the fire. Clay remembered the magpie pecking at the outhouse in Camp Hawkins. "Magpie People?"

"To-de-hee's people," the old man said. "They lived in this canyon long, long ago. Many springs and winters gone. The Magpie Spirit told them it was time to go to the land beyond the falling sun. They haven't been seen since; only the bones of their dead remain."

"This To-de-hee was one of the Magpie People?" Nathan asked.

The old man nodded. "He was a shaman, like me. I am

of the Diamondback People, descended from To-de-hee's line. In many waking dreams, I have been told this."

Laroque stared into the cup he held in both hands. "An evil sorcerer."

Slowly, the old man nodded. His voice low, barely above a whisper. "His restlessness makes me restless. I will not sleep again until he rests."

"How're you gonna make him rest?" Carmody asked.

"I am going to kill him and bury his heart with his amulet." Staring into the fire, the old Indian opened and closed his hands in his lap. "But first I need to find the amulet."

"What amulet?" Laroque said.

"The one he was buried with...back in the time of the ancients."

Carmody hiked an eyebrow. "It's still in the grave?"

The Indian shook his head. "That is the trouble. The amulet got separated from the body, setting the demon spirit once again loose on this world." He looked at Clay. "The teacher's family dug it up...seven years ago. There has been trouble since, but more now that I have been summoned. To-de-hee knows his time is short. He is fearful and angry."

"It's a big canyon," Carmody said. "Where the hell you gonna look for it."

"It's a big *territory,*" Nathan added.

The Indian closed his eyes. "I have seen it. I have not seen where it is...but I will... If I keep an eye on the spirit world. My Diamondback brothers on the other side will show me...if the magpie allows." He opened his eyes and peered into the darkness beyond the licking flames. "The magpie is an irascible messenger from their world to ours. He allows us to see and hear what he wants. Sometimes only what *To-de-hee* wants. That is why I keep Ko-ko nearby, to clarify what I see in my dreams...and to warn me of anyone sneaking up behind me. I am an old man, and my hearing could be better."

Clay said, "What about the snakes that raised a ruckus in town?"

"The magpie stirred them up...got them working for To-de-hee." The old man shook his head grimly. "The magpie Che can be a cunning liar. Only the strongest snakes, like Ko-ko, can see through his tricks."

Carmody spit into the fire. He and Laroque sat quietly for a time, trying to absorb the man's words.

Finally, Nathan poked a stick at the fire. "How you gonna kill this To-de-hee? You even know what he looks like?"

The old man shook his head. "He is a demon from the spirit world, but he lives in a body like any earthly beast. I will know him when I see him." The old man patted the stock of the trap-door Springfield he held across his lap. "And I will kill him with this."

"He's a big son of a bitch—I know that," Carmody told the oldster. "He stuck a pick through a man's chest and halfway through a stout pine log wall. I hope that old blunderbuss packs plenty of firepower."

"It packs enough," the old man said. He looked at the dead rabbits lying before Clay and Nathan. "Eat, now. You need nourishment. I sense your discontent. In the morning, you should leave here."

"Why?" Carmody said. "If you can kill him with that, we can hold him off with these." He patted his Winchester.

The old man picked a sliver of meat from between two rotten teeth and regarded Carmody blandly.

The fire cracked and snapped. Owls cooed in the woods.

"You are not ready to confront the beast," he said. "In the morning, you must go."

"But I thought you blessed our cabin here," said Laroque.

The old man nodded. “But who knows what, if anything, the magpie allowed to be heard.”

The fire popped, shooting sparks.

Carmody glanced at Nathan. “Told you that damn bird had it in for me.”

14

In bed in her small, frame house at the south edge of Camp Hawkins, the Widow Miller snapped her eyes open. Face up on her pillow, she stared at the ceiling, listening. She fumed.

A fly buzzed around her head. It whined this way and that, unseen in the darkness but loud enough in the silent room to wake the dead. The widow set her jaws and sucked air through her nose. The neighbor's amorous bitch had kept the widow awake for three hours at the beginning of the night.

Now, the fly.

Bunching her lips and swelling her nostrils with fury, the widow waited, tracking the confounding insect with her keen hearing. It flitted from the bed to the dresser and back again. It bounced off the window, caromed over the washstand. Buzzed louder as it found something of interest in the porcelain washbowl.

For a moment, silence.

She waited. The buzzing resumed, got louder. The fly landed on the thimble-sized mole lodged in the crease between the widow's nose and cheek.

Holding her body rigid, the widow slowly slid her right

hand out from under the blanket and quilt covering her muscular, barrel-shaped physique. She flung her hand toward her cheek, snapped it closed.

She held the fist before her face—a vague shape in the darkness. She couldn't feel the fly in her palm. She heard it, though, rattling against the room's single windowpane to her left.

She swore in German.

The window behind the curtain showed the beginning of a milky wash. Nearly dawn. Normally she would have slept for another half-hour, but if she went back to sleep now, it might be hours before she awoke again. Her husband, a prospector who'd eked a modest gold poke from the canyon, had been dead for three years, leaving her alone to provide for herself. She couldn't sleep in like a banker's wife. She toiled hard from sunup to sunset.

The old woman threw the covers off and heaved herself up from the creaking bed, huffing and puffing and groaning as though against an enormous weight. She quickly made the bed, brushed out her hair, pinned it up, and ambled through her bedroom's open door.

She stopped suddenly, and turned back to the room, facing the window. She raised a bony fist. "You better find a way out of here by sunset, you fly, or so help me, you'll wish you had!"

When she'd set a fire in the kitchen range, she sat down to her usual, meager breakfast of gruel and a corn muffin—plain, without butter or honey—and a single cup of tea. The sun was barely above the horizon by the time she'd fed her chickens, repaired the hole some night critter had torn in the fence, and had gotten down on hands and knees to weed her kitchen garden.

She weeded the entire garden and picked several ears of corn for canning. Heaving herself up with a grunt, she ambled into the house, pausing to scrub her heavy shoes on the hemp rug just over the threshold, and started across the kitchen toward the table.

A shrill, sibilant noise rose, giving the widow such a sudden start that, gasping, she dropped the corn and stumbled back against the door, rattling the glass in the panes.

"*Was die Holle!*"

A diamondback rattler lay coiled on the scrubbed puncheons before the parlor door, staring at the widow and rattling. Hissing. Its forked tongue probed the air.

"How in da hell did you get in here?" the widow shouted. She flung up her right hand, reaching for a hoe leaning in a nearby corner, behind some coats hanging from hooks.

Then she froze, statue-still, staring at the snake. Her eyes glazed, her sandy-gray brows meeting in the middle of her forehead. She turned her head slightly but kept her eyes on the snake.

"You want me to do what?" she said softly, in German.

The snake was no longer shaking its rattle. It remained coiled, staring at the woman intently, its forked tongue flicking in and out of its arrow-shaped head.

The widow stood frozen for several minutes, trance-like, communing with the snake.

Finally, leaving the corn scattered on the floor, she turned, opened the door, and stepped outside. Leaving the door open behind her, she ambled down the field rock walk, past the chicken coop on her right and the sprawling cottonwood on her left, and disappeared inside the old stable where her husband had once housed his horses.

A minute later, expressionless, moving stiffly but purposefully, she stepped out of the stable. In her hand was a coiled rope. As she moved toward the cottonwood, its arching branches bobbing and swaying in the mid-morning breeze, its leaves touched silver by the high-country sun, she deftly shaped a noose. Although the widow had never known a hangman or had ever shaped a noose, the perfect noose she shaped was that of a professional executioner.

She slipped it over her head, drew the slipknot taut at the back of her neck.

The widow hadn't climbed a tree in over fifty years. But when she reached up to the lowest limb, clutching it firmly in her work-toughened hands, she swung herself up into the forked trunk like any tree-climbing veteran child. Noose around her neck, coiled rope in her right hand, she monkeyed up the tree's main leader. She pulled her arms and pushed with her legs, her gray skirt drawing up to reveal her heavy stockings and cotton pantaloons.

When she'd climbed twenty feet off the ground, she crawled out to the middle of a stout branch. She tied the end of the rope to the branch with a double-knot, and yanked it firm. Without adieu, the widow glanced at the ground and leaned forward, throwing her arms out as if diving into a deep prairie lake.

When the rope drew taut, the widow's neck snapped like a pistol shot.

"What's the matter, Mary?" Beth Cooper asked one of the only two students who'd showed up for school that day.

Beth didn't expect to have more students until after the autumn harvest and roundup on the farms and ranches surrounding Camp Hawkins.

The school sat across the street from the Widow Miller's house. Mary Blanchard, eleven years old, was gazing out one of the two windows facing the widow's yard. Her lower jaw hung, her round eyes unblinking.

"Mary, what is it?" Beth asked, frowning from her desk at the head of the room, where she was grading the girls' spelling tests.

"Mary...?"

The girl turned suddenly toward Beth, twin braids flying out from her head. The girl's voice was thin, high-pitched with shock. "Mrs. Miller is hanging from her tree."

"What?"

Beth set her pen in the ink tray and slid her chair back from her desk. Standing, she stepped off the dais upon which her desk was perched, and strode quickly over to the window. Placing one hand on Mary's shoulder, she stooped to look through the glass she'd cleaned only yesterday afternoon.

She looked at the tree, the dominant feature in the widow's yard, and gasped. She stared for several seconds, until she was sure she was really seeing the stumpy widow hanging from the tree, turning gently this way and that, chin tipped to her chest.

Beth pushed the girl away from the window. "Mary, go sit down," she said, hearing the frantic trill in her voice. "Go sit down, and...and Lydia, you stay where you are."

She quickly drew the shutter closed, locking it, then hurried to the other window and closed that shutter, as well, shading the east side of the long, narrow room.

As she ran to the door, she said, "You girls keep studying those math pages I gave you," only vaguely realizing how ridiculous the instruction sounded. Mary wouldn't be able to think of anything but the widow hanging from her cottonwood tree, and Lydia Carlson would want to know what had happened.

Beth drew the schoolhouse door closed, descended the steps and, holding her skirts above the ground, ran across the street to the widow's yard, hoping that somehow she'd imagined what she'd seen from the window, or that the thing hanging from the tree was only a scarecrow or something...

It was the widow.

Standing beneath the tree, Beth stared up at the old

woman dangling from the hangman's noose around her neck, the gray skirt fluttering about her heavy legs and scuffed black shoes. Beth sobbed and stepped back, pressing her hands to her temples.

Why?

Her mind had only started working through the question when she noticed that the tree was nearly covered with magpies. The shrieks she'd been hearing were not coming from her own horrified mind, but from the birds themselves. They sounded like a dozen ungreased wagon axles. She'd never seen so many magpies in one place.

As she stared up at the tree, puzzled and horrified, shading her eyes with her arm, one flew up and started away. The others followed, rising as a flock, screaming, wings beating as they turned and flew over the small cabins and shanties toward the main street and beyond.

A hundred, small, white, indigo and black kites with long, slender tails.

A cool breeze pressed against Beth's back, chilling her deep. As she stared after the birds, she dropped her gaze to the stone house in the lot just north of the widow's. Easily the largest house in town, it belonged to the Mayor and Mrs. Kitchener. It was a three-storied affair with porches both in front and back, and two fieldstone hearths. On the front porch stood Mrs. Kitchener herself, staring toward Beth.

The woman was dressed all in black, except for an indigo-blue cape drawn taut about her shoulders. A white poke bonnet was snugged down on her auburn head.

Beth, snapping out of her shock, sucked air into her lungs and threw her left arm out, waving to get the woman's attention. "Mrs. Kitchener!"

Hoping the mayor was home, she began running around the tree, heading for the stone house. But when she'd crossed the broad lot in which transplanted trees stood amidst the sage and rabbit brush, she slowed her gait and stared at the house.

Mrs. Kitchener, dressed in the colors of the magpie, had disappeared from the porch. The front door closed with a dull thud and a click. When Beth gained the walk beneath the front steps, the white-lace curtains jostled in the window, and fell still.

"Mrs. Kitchener!" Beth ran up the steps, crossed the porch and pounded on the door. "Mrs. Kitchener, I know you're in there!"

When no one opened the door, she cursed, descended the steps to the yard and looked back toward the Widow Miller's yard. The widow hung from the tree, her back to Beth, swinging gently in the breeze. She could have been a scarecrow some farmer had hung from a tree at the edge of his cornfield.

Beth couldn't tell if the old woman had been hanged by someone else, or if she'd hanged herself. It didn't matter. The result was the same. And Beth knew that the killer—in whatever form—was the same evil presence that had conjured snakes out of the school privy a couple of weeks back, and had lured more up from the floor in the hotel.

It was the same presence, she knew, that killed her family in Poudre Canyon and had lured her back to Camp Hawkins after she'd gone to Denver, where she'd earned her teaching certificate. She'd come back to find a way to kill the demon—or whatever it was—which she and her father and brothers had unknowingly turned loose nine years ago, when they'd dug up the grave and removed the amulet.

Animosity mixing with the sorrow inside her—she'd always liked the crotchety old widow, who'd often baked apple pies for the schoolchildren —Beth turned angrily to the stone house. Yelling would do no good. Mrs. Kitchener wasn't coming out. She certainly wasn't coming out with the amulet.

One way or another, Beth would get her hands on the amulet later.

She whipped around and strode up the sparsely populated side street, her ashen cheeks streaked with tears. She walked so fast that her dark-red hair came loose from the French braid she wore while teaching. When she'd let several prospector's wagons pass on the main street, she crossed to the jailhouse, knocked once, and opened the door.

"Sheriff!"

Beth stopped, gasped. Standing before the rifle rack, Claudine Bridger was aiming a cocked pistol at Beth's face. The pretty, hard face behind the Colt relaxed, eyes rolling. The sheriff depressed the hammer and lowered the gun with a relieved sigh.

"Jesus Christ, Miss Cooper. You come barging in here like that, you're gonna get drilled!"

"Sorry, Sheriff." Beth had noticed the saddlebags slung over the sheriff's right shoulder and that the woman was stuffing cartridge boxes under the left flap. "What're you doing?"

"Heading up canyon again, to see if I can figure out what..." Claudine looked at the teacher. "What's the matter, Beth? You look like you've seen a ghost." She chuffed, exasperation flaring her nostrils. Around here, that wasn't much of a joke. "Don't tell me you have."

"Worse," Beth said. "Mrs. Miller is hanging from the cottonwood tree in her backyard. Dead."

The sheriff stared at the teacher. Claudine dropped her hands to her sides, turned, and sagged back against the gunrack. "Ah, hell."

"When I went over there, the tree was covered with magpies and Mrs. Kitchener was standing on her porch, looking very strange."

"Please, Miss Cooper. No more of that amulet hogwash." The sheriff lowered her right shoulder. The saddlebags dropped to the scarred floorboards with a thud. "I am not going to confiscate any of the mayor's wife's fireplace decorations."

"Even if it's contributing—possibly *causing*—all the bad things that have been occurring in this town and in the canyon?" After scouring the canyon and the town for the past two years, Beth had learned only last week that the amulet was resting atop Mrs. Kitchener's fireplace mantle.

Flushed with frustration, not knowing what she believed anymore, the sheriff pushed off the wall and headed for the open door.

Beth followed her outside. Once Claudine sent a passing townsman for the undertaker, she slipped her horse's reins from the hitchrack and swung up into the saddle. She extended a hand to Beth, who took it and, poking her left foot through the left stirrup, swung up behind Claudine.

When they'd ridden over to the widow's house, the widow was no longer hanging from the tree. Not even the rope was there.

The sun-washed tree rustled peacefully in the breeze.

15

"Claudine, she was hanging right there," Beth said, pointing to the branch to which the rope had been tied. "You have to believe me."

Staring at the tree, Sheriff Bridger nodded. "I do."

"Someone must've taken her down."

Beth looked around. There were only a few cabins and frame shacks on this side of town, and she saw no one outside any of them. She looked at the Kitcheners' stone house. No one out there, either. The wind rippled the wheat grass and rabbit brush in the lot separating the widow's yard from the Kitcheners'.

Beth felt the same unseasonable chill she'd felt before.

A screech rose on the breeze. Both women turned toward the house. A magpie perched on the peak of the house's low, shake roof. It returned their stares, jerking its head from side to side, flicking its long tail.

"Why don't you look around out here?" Sheriff Bridger said, unholstering her revolver. "I'll check inside the house."

"I'd better release my students," Beth said. "They must be pretty frightened." She added softly, "I know I am..."

Claudine headed for the house, holding her Peacemaker's barrel straight up in her right hand.

Beth turned and hurried across the street to the schoolhouse, where she quickly released the girls for the day, ignoring their questions about the widow and instructing them to avoid the widow's yard on their way home.

Heading back toward the yard, Beth slowed her pace when she saw the sheriff standing on the widow's back step.

Claudine beckoned to Beth then turned back into the house.

Holding her skirts above her shoes, Beth crossed the back yard and entered the house. She froze only a foot inside the door to slap a hand to her chest. "Oh!"

Claudine Bridger stood between the range and the widow's small kitchen table, in the middle of which a stone bowl of crabapples sat. The widow herself sat on the other side of the table, facing Beth.

The noose was still drawn taut around her neck, the rope coiled on the floor beneath her chair. The widow's head tipped back on her shoulders, canted slightly right. Her eyes were drawn wide, as if surprised by something on the ceiling, her lower jaw hanging so that her wrinkled mouth formed an egg shape.

"Found her," the sheriff said grimly, staring down at the dead woman.

"How...?"

Claudine looked at Beth. "You sure you left her hanging from that tree?"

"Of course," the teacher snapped. "You think I'd have forgotten climbing up the tree to cut her down then—!"

"All right, all right." Claudine cursed under her breath as she dropped to her haunches and studied the dead woman gravely. She reached out with her right hand but lowered it when the clatter of hooves and wagon wheels sounded on the road beside the house.

Outside, footsteps rose. Beth had left the door standing open behind her. A paunchy, broad-shouldered man with gray-streaked, black hair cut square across his forehead appeared in the open doorway. Lucius Danglehorne, the furniture-maker/mortician, stared past Beth at the widow then, opening his mouth to speak but getting no words out, he looked at Claudine. He blinked several times.

When he finally found his tongue, his voice was deep and stricken. "What the hell happened to Mrs. Miller?" A face closely resembling his own and belonging to his sixteen-year-old son, Horace, peered over his left shoulder. The boy's right cheek bulged. A wooden sucker stick protruded from his lips.

"Miss Cooper found her hanging from the cottonwood tree by her chicken coop," Claudine said.

"Why's she sitting here at the table?" the undertaker asked.

"That's what we'd like to know," said Beth.

Danglehorne let out a deep breath as he stepped slowly into the kitchen on his hobnailed boots, nervously running his big, brown hands down his blue denim shirt.

The boy followed him into the kitchen, staring at the dead woman, pursing his wet lips around his sucker, his eyes round.

"There's been so danged many crazy-assed things happenin' around here," the undertaker said quietly, "that sometimes I just wanna drop my head between my knees and howl."

In the seven years since her family had been murdered, Beth had witnessed several bizarre occurrences herself, but she wondered what the man was alluding to. "You mean the snakes?"

Danglehorne looked at her sharply. "I don't mean *just* the snakes. I haven't told nobody this. Last week, that Mex who died playin' the guitar in the Cattlemen's Saloon? I laid him out on the slab and went home for supper. When I come back and start unlockin' the back door, I hear someone strummin' a guitar. I go inside, and he's sitting there in my office chair, his guitar layin' across his knees. He looked up at me, and his skin was white as bakin' flour, and his eyes were black." With his index finger, Danglehorne traced slow circles around his right eye.

He shifted his gaze to Sheriff Bridger. "I done passed out. When I come to, the man's in his coffin, dead as hell. His guitar's layin' across my desk."

Trying to suppress the creepie-crawlies wriggling across her back, Claudine stared at the man. "Why didn't you report it?"

"Hell, I didn't even tell *him.*" Danglehorne canted his head at his son who regarded him wide-eyed, the sucker making his cheek bulge. "Didn't want no one to think my turnip had gone soft."

"Well, I guess if your turnip's soft, Mr. Danglehorne," Beth said tonelessly, staring at the widow, "then I and the sheriff are right pulpy, as well."

Claudine took a deep breath. "Take her away, will you, Mr. Danglehorne? I'll notify Reverend Blake."

"Good luck."

Both women looked at the undertaker.

"When you sent fer me, I was about to send fer you. Blake blew out his brains in his privy last night...after he laid open Mrs. Blake's head with a hatchet."

Horace pulled the sucker out of his mouth. His lips were wet and red as he stuttered, "B-b-birds all over the...the p-place."

The sheriff had a dazed look when she turned to Beth. "Reckon I'd better get over there."

"I'll tell you somethin' straight," said Danglehorne. "This is the last soul I'm buryin' in Camp Hawkins. Before sunset tonight, me and Horace are gettin' the hell outta town." He chuckled without mirth as, making a face, he loosened the noose at the back of the widow's neck. "And I won't be back."

"I'm with you, Pa," the boy said, staring at Widow Miller.

Claudine had already moved through the back door and was striding toward her horse tied to a low branch of the cottonwood.

Beth ran up behind her, tripping on her skirts and almost falling. Her hair, having come completely loose from its braid, swirled in coils about her shoulders. She grabbed Claudine's right arm, turned the woman toward her.

"We have to get that talisman out of the Kitchener house."

"What's so damned important about that so-called talisman?"

"It's the key to all of this. I and my brothers dug it up from an old Indian grave. That night, my brothers and father were killed while I was wearing the talisman around my neck! I've read up on ancient Indian spells and incantations, and I've consulted with a shaman. It has to be returned to the place where we found it, to put the demon back to sleep."

Claudine stared at her.

Beth said, "The strange things that have been happening to this town started happening after we dug up the disk."

"How did Mrs. Kitchener get her hands on it?"

"The night my family's cabin exploded, I dropped it and ran into the woods. Vern Applegate was prospecting up there, and he was the one who eventually found me. He also found the talisman near what was left of the cabin. For several years, unbeknownst to me, the disk hung in his saloon, as a *good-luck* charm, until Bruno Kitchener won it in a poker game and gave it to Mrs. Kitchener for Christmas."

When Bridger looked away, Beth grabbed her wrist. "I think it's turned her into a witch. After I saw it in her house, during a school fund raiser last week, I offered to buy it. She got furious. I thought she was going to stab me with her cake knife."

Bridger had turned to stare at the stone house, her hat shading her tan face with clear eyes and high, wide cheekbones. She reached for her reins. "I have to get over to the parsonage." As she swung up into the saddle, she looked at Beth pointedly. "You stay away from the Kitcheners'."

"But—"

"I mean it!" Claudine shot a hard glance over her shoulder. She touched spurs to her horse, and the animal lurched off its rear hooves, galloping across the road, heading west through the schoolyard. The sound of the horse's pounding hooves faded as the dust sifted behind it.

Hearing grunts and boot scuffs to her left, Beth turned to see the undertaker and his son carrying the widow toward their box wagon. The boy carried the old woman's thick ankles while Danglehorne gripped the body under its arms. They were in too much of a hurry to bother with a blanket. The woman's head tipped toward her right shoulder, lips pooched out grotesquely. Her arms flopped down toward the ground, fingers brushing the blond weeds of her yard.

"Yessir," the undertaker said. "We're heading back to Dakoty. Never shoulda left there in the first place!" He gave a grunt as they heaved the bulky body over the side of the wagon. "Say what you want about the winters. There, the folks *stay dead!*"

CLAUDINE BRIDGER FOUND the bodies of the Reverend and Mrs. Blake pretty much as Danglehorne described them.

The missus lay on the kitchen floor of the parsonage, a splitting maul buried in her scalp, nearly cleaving her skull in two equal halves. The Reverend sat fully clothed on the privy behind the house. The old Colt Patterson he'd used to paint the privy walls and ceiling with his blood and brains lay on the floor beneath his shiny black shoes.

It was a hell of a mess, all the worse because the undertaker had quit. Claudine enlisted the help of several burly townsmen and three pious ladies from the reverend's church congregation, and had the bodies prepared for burial by seven o'clock that evening.

By ten o'clock, she was well into a whiskey bottle in the Poudre River Saloon.

Several drovers and traveling drummers tried to get her to join their poker game, but she refused. Dark and distracted, she grabbed her bottle and headed for her room. She finished the bottle and lulled herself to sleep imagining she wasn't a sheriff, but just a woman wrapped in Clay Carmody's thickly corded arms.

The next morning, at dawn, she cantered her claybank gelding toward the Kitcheners' stone house. A horseback rider moved toward her and pulled up to the iron hitch rings before the Kitcheners' yard. Beth Cooper rode a black Morgan with a bedroll, saddlebags, and a croaker supply sack dangling from the saddle horn. A Spencer carbine jutted from a leather sheath. Beth wore a long-sleeved cotton blouse and split wool riding skirt. On her head she wore a green felt sombrero.

"I thought I told you to steer wide of this place," Claudine said as she swung in beside Beth.

"I thought on it all night," Beth said, tightening the muscles in her face. "I decided you're going to have to throw me in jail to keep me from wrestling that amulet away from Mrs. Kitchener. I've summoned a shaman. He's in the canyon, searching for the amulet. I'm going to bring him the amulet and help him kill the beast."

Swinging down from the claybank, Claudine said, "Stay here, Wild Bill Hickock. And listen to me this time or I will throw you in the skookum house."

"What are you going to do?"

"I'm going to *reason* that amulet away from Mrs. Kitchener. Then you can show me where in the canyon you and your brothers dug it up."

Claudine slip-knotted her reins to one of the rings, opened the wrought-iron gate, walked up the stone path, and mounted the porch. After glancing back at Beth still sitting her black Morgan beside Claudine's claybank, she peered through the window in the top door panel. Faint lantern light shone at the end of the main downstairs hall. She rapped the brass monkey-head knocker against the door.

She waited a few seconds then rapped again.

A figured moved in the hall, and Mrs. Kitchener opened the door. She wore only a long, red housecoat, her tight, red curls smashed flat against her skull beneath a black hair net. Bags sagged beneath her eyes. From behind her pushed the aroma of warm muffins, fried sausage, and coffee.

"Sheriff Bridger, what a surprise so early in the morning."

Claudine removed her hat and became conscious of her boots, hoping she had no shit on them. "Can I come in, Mrs. Kitchener?"

The woman stepped back. "Is there trouble? My husband is still in bed. A late night card game, I'm afraid," she added, pinching her mouth.

Claudine hesitated as the woman closed the door. "Actually, it's you I wanted to see."

"Oh?"

"It's about the amulet. The one your husband gave you for Christmas?"

The woman looked up at Claudine, as if she had no idea what the sheriff was talking about.

"The one that Vern Applegate used to hang above the back-bar at the Poudre River Saloon."

Claudine turned through a doorway opening off the foyer, crossed the elegantly furnished parlor to a field rock fireplace. On the mantle were several framed photographs and decorative gas lamps, a brass stallion, and the flat, polished stone disk with the triangular hunk of turquoise embedded in the center. Small stick animals and what looked like the letters of a foreign tongue had been carved into the disk's face. The object's rawhide thong coiled at its base.

"It's a very nice piece," said Mrs. Kitchener, sidling up to Claudine. She gazed at the amulet, one boney hand spread across her breast. "When Bruno first gave it to me, I thought it was the most ghastly thing. Obviously pagan. But then I began to see its artistic worth, and I'm afraid I'd never be able to part with it. Not in a million years."

Claudine glanced over at the woman, making sure she had no weapons, like a cake knife, in her hand. "This is going to sound loco, Mrs. Kitchener, but I think the amulet is the instrument of some ancient Indian demon. When it was dug up with the demon's bones, it set the demon's spirit free on the canyon and, obviously, on our town. I'd like to bring it back to the canyon and rebury it."

Mrs. Kitchener turned to the sheriff, but before she could open her mouth to object, Claudine said, "If it doesn't put an end to all the bizarre happenings, I'll dig it up again and return it to you."

"Certainly not! Sheriff, you're mad to think my...my...*decoration* has anything to do with all the curious events that have visited Camp Hawkins."

"Maybe..."

Claudine stepped forward and reached for the amulet. Before she could get her hands on it, Mrs. Kitchener barreled against her right shoulder, discharging a scream that sounded like a cross between a boiling teapot and a swooping raptor.

The old woman wrapped her cold, dry hands around Claudine's neck and drove against her with shocking power. Claudine stumbled sideways and hit the floor on her left shoulder and hip, the impact softened slightly by a thick woven rug.

The old woman lay sprawled across the sheriff's right side, squealing that awful squeal and, using her fingers at the back of Claudine's neck for leverage, pressed her thumbs against her throat so hard that Claudine's eyes watered as she sucked futilely for air. Bridger got her boots beneath her thighs and, rocking her pelvis to try and dislodge the woman, brought her right elbow up sharply against the woman's side.

The maneuver shook Mrs. Kitchener's grip loose for only a moment. As Claudine's back rolled flat against the floor, and she raked fresh air down her battered throat, Mrs. Kitchener renewed her grip on Claudine's neck, again pinching off her wind and slamming her head against the rug.

Amazed by the woman's incredible strength, Claudine closed her hands around the woman's wrists and pushed straight up.

The woman squealed even louder, her face a hideous red mask of abject fury. But her grip held firm. Claudine's own face went white, and her eyes dimmed from lack of oxygen. She lowered her right hand to her hip and unsnapped the keeper thong over her Peacemaker's hammer. Beth Cooper's face appeared in her field of vision, over Mrs. Kitchener's right shoulder.

The teacher held her Spencer rifle in both hands as

she stared down at the struggling pair, apparently trying to figure out what to do.

Claudine's eyes blazed up at the teacher as she silently screamed, "Hit her with the rifle!"

Beth shifted her grip on the rifle, held the butt above the woman's back, and slammed it straight down between the woman's shoulder blades. The woman jerked slightly but her grip did not waver.

Inwardly, Claudine scoffed at the teacher's tentative rap. Her eyes fluttered. She felt herself losing consciousness as she slipped her Colt from its holster and set her thumb against the hammer.

Suddenly, the widow's hands moved away from her neck. Claudine arched her spine and tipped her head back, gasping. She opened her eyes, saw Mrs. Kitchener slumped to one side, kicking her pantaloon-clad legs, opening and closing her mouth spasmodically. Beth stood over her, holding her rifle by the barrel, bringing it back from a sharp upswing. The teacher's face was flushed as she stared, terrified and repelled, at Mrs. Kitchener.

Blood shone on the rifle's brass butt plate.

The woman gurgled, choked. Her hands clawed the floor as if for purchase.

Gulping air, Claudine let her Colt fall back in its holster, then climbed to her knees, and sat back on her heels.

Beth slid her gaze from Mrs. Kitchener to the sheriff. "Are you all right?"

Claudine massaged her throat. "Who needs a wind pipe?"

"She must be incredibly strong."

"Even for a witch."

As if in response to the observations, Mrs. Kitchener sprang to her feet like a child's wind-up toy. Eyes glowing red as railroad lanterns, she loosed an ear-ringing shriek even louder than the one before. Knees to her chest, she hunkered down, arms draped over her legs, and regarded Claudine with those blazing red eyes. She sprang toward the sheriff, hands stretched toward Claudine's throat.

Beth leapt back with a start.

Still sitting back on her heels, Claudine slipped her Colt from its holster, and fired. The bullet plowed through Mrs. Kitchener's heart.

The woman gave a grunt, fell against Claudine's right shoulder, and crumpled up on the floor. Lying on her back, she pressed her hands to the floor, and began pushing herself up.

Claudine stood, extended her Colt straight out from her shoulder, and drilled a hole through the woman's cheekbone, two inches from the corner of her left eye.

"What in the name of Christ is going on?"

Claudine turned to the doorway at the opposite end of the room. Bruno Kitchener stood there, at the bottom of the carpeted stairs, clad in silk balbriggans and a shabby blue robe with frayed sleeves. His tufted hair stuck out like wires all around his head. His eyes were rheumy, red, and heavy-lidded. He was so hung-over from last night's poker game that he had to grab the doorframe to keep from falling down.

He looked from his prone wife to Bridger and back again, blinking as though he wasn't quite sure he wasn't having a nightmare.

Claudine aimed her gun at him. "Stay there. We're taking the amulet." Still holding the Peacemaker on Kitchener, she cut her eyes at Beth. "Take it!"

Beth stared at the mayor glaring at her from the door.

"Take it and go!" Claudine shouted.

Beth turned and grabbed the amulet from the mantle. She knocked over a lamp, which knocked over a brass horseshoe—a gift to the mayor from the Colorado Horsemen's Association—and both tumbled to the brick hearth.

The clatter of the shattering lamp hadn't died before the teacher disappeared through the parlor door.

The mayor stumbled into the room and dropped to his knees. Sweat beaded his face. He retched then lifted his head. *"Murdering bitches!"*

Claudine squinted at the man down the barrel of her cocked .45. "Don't come after me, Mayor. I'll explain later."

She lowered the pistol and ran outside.

"You murdering bitches!" the mayor railed behind her.

16

"PULL it out and give it to me, Clay."

Carmody grinned.

"Give it to me," Sheriff Bridger ordered in a soft, husky voice, running a finger up and down his fly, giving each button a taunting little flick. She stuck her tongue in his ear. "All of it."

Carmody snorted. "Shit."

She punched his arm.

"All right, all right."

She punched him again, harder. He opened his eyes, found himself on his cot in the old trapper's cabin.

The weathered, bearded, frowning countenance of Nathan Laroque stared down at him. The big mulatto held his rifle in one hand. He punched Clay's right shoulder again with the other.

"Wake up, Casanova. It pret' near full light and I just spied a big buck on the southern ridge. Let's take the horses and get after it."

Carmody felt as though he'd had a gallon of icy snowmelt thrown on his face. Instantly, the hard knot in his long underwear eased, but not his longing for the bewitching sheriff of Camp Hawkins.

Annoyed by the rude awakening, he flung the blankets aside and sat up at the edge of the cot. He planted his elbows on his thighs and rested his head in his hands. Laroque had leaned his rifle against the table and was pouring a cup of coffee.

"I thought we were leaving the canyon tomorrow."

Laroque turned to him sharply. "You wanna *leave? Now?*"

After their visit with the old Indian three nights ago, they'd decided to leave the canyon at the end of the week. But then yesterday afternoon Laroque found a gold nugget the size of a small Christmas ornament. It had been snugged, plain as day, against a rock at the edge of the creek, under only about five inches of water. Pink-throated trout had probably milled around it, attracted by its flash, for a hundred years.

Carmody and Laroque hadn't discussed any change in their plans last night. They'd gotten too drunk to discuss much of anything but how much the gold was worth, agreeing on a figure right around a thousand dollars.

If there was one nugget that size just lying around where anyone could stumble on it, there was bound to be more.

"What about the beast?" Carmody asked.

Laroque hiked a shoulder and sipped his coffee. "Hell, I ain't afraid of any beast. Besides, the old Injun blessed this place. And we ain't had a lick of trouble since he left." He raised his cup to his lips, muttering, "But, if you're afraid, *monsieur...*" Staring into his steaming cup, Nathan sipped his coffee.

Carmody glared at him. "You're the one wearin' all the fobs and googaws on your hat!" He got up and reached for his pants. "Go out and saddle the horses. I'll be out after I've had some of your pond sludge."

When he'd slipped into his pants and boots, Carmody downed a quick cup of coffee then grabbed his Yellowboy repeater. Thumbing cartridges into the breech, he headed outside, where Laroque waited in the gray dawn with both saddled pies.

"Where'd you see this buck?"

Nathan turned in his saddle and extended a gloved finger at the southern ridge. "To the right of that notch up yonder. I counted seven points. He had a neck like this." Nathan tossed a set of reins to Carmody and held his hands straight out from his shoulders. "You know what the Creoles say about a seven-point buck?"

"What?"

"The one shoots him, his pecker grows seven inches."

Clay swung up onto his pie and settled himself in the saddle. "You need 'em more than I do, so I'll give you the first shot. Me, I'd settle for gettin' our larder filled with fresh venison. I'm a might tired of johnny cakes and fish."

Laroque reined his horse around and put him into a fast trot south of the cabin. Clay followed, his dream of Sheriff Bridger still tingling his loins.

The tingling didn't last long. As they began climbing a game path to the southern ridge, a chill wind swooped in from the south. Whistling through the pines and whooshing against the ridge, it pushed hard against Carmody's back, raising goose bumps down his arms. His pie nickered and tossed its head. The chill was relieved only slightly when they'd climbed into the sunlight.

The horses picked their way toward the ridge crest, dipping their heads and leaning forward, digging their shod hooves into the slope. The wind died suddenly. It was like a large, cold monkey paw removed from Carmody's back.

Silence, and the sun's warmth, replaced it.

Clay didn't say anything to Laroque about it. Nathan was leaning out from his saddle, looking for the buck's tracks in the ridge's gravel and short, brown grass.

Because of the gold, Clay wanted to believe it had only

been a wind like any other, not that ominous, unseasonably cool breeze he'd first encountered in Camp Hawkins, after the rattlesnakes had slithered out of the cellar. He looked around at the sun-washed ridge. Seeing no sign of trouble, he released the concern from his mind and began helping Nathan look for sign.

Laroque found the buck's spoor a few minutes later. They followed it slowly across two ridges. On a grassy slope, Carmody reined his pie to a stop and raised his binoculars. The buck grazed at the edge of a distant clearing—a large, brown blur against the black pines behind it.

Carmody and Laroque dismounted, tied their horses in an aspen copse, shucked their rifles, and climbed to the next ridge crest. Lying just below the peak, Laroque raised Clay's glasses, trained them on a tongue-shaped bowl on the other side of the ridge.

"He's still there, not a care in the world."

"Too far away for a shot."

"I'll get above him and spook him into that draw. Since you're *arguably* the better shot, you better wait at the bottom."

They split up.

A quarter-hour later, Carmody was waiting behind the ball of an uprooted lodgepole, in the forest below the park in which the buck grazed. If Laroque spooked the buck from directly above his current position, he should head right down the draw and pass within twenty feet of Carmody's Yellowboy.

They'd be eating roasted venison for supper, washing it down with the last of the whiskey they'd brought out from town.

Carmody held his rifle across his knees and waited. He peered up the ravine, straining his ears to listen for the buck.

Nothing.

Fifteen minutes passed.

Still nothing.

Had the buck spooked in another direction? If so, how long was Nathan going to let him sit here before calling for him or firing a signal shot?

Someone screamed. It was Nathan.

The scream began deep in Laroque's throat then rose to a glass-shattering pitch. Turning brittle, it caromed down the draw like something solid, then broke apart as it rose toward the treetops and faded, echoing, as if javelins of fluid sucked out the top of an enormous bottle. It was filled with such horror and abominable physical anguish that it turned Carmody to stone.

Uncertainly, he climbed to his feet, crawled under the tree, straightened on the other side, and shouted Nathan's name.

Laroque's response was several low protesting groans which Carmody could barely hear above the pounding of his own heart, the rushing of his blood in his ears. Somewhere in the near distance, a magpie screeched.

Carmody found a game path and began running up the draw. He hurdled low shrubs and deadfalls, sucked air into his lungs as he ran. He could no longer hear Nathan's voice at the top of the draw—only the thumps and crunches of his own boots, the raspy, hoarse intakes of his own breath. He clutched his rifle in both hands across his chest, but he couldn't feel it.

Another sound rose from the top of the draw.

It was a slow, guttural barking he could hear only vaguely and intermittently. Hoof beats rose to obliterate it. Beneath his running boots, the ground shuddered. A sound like the shrill blast of a bull horn sounded once, twice, three times.

The hoof thuds stopped.

Carmody looked up the draw and stopped dead in his tracks. Above the right bank and about fifty yards ahead, a horseback rider stood amidst the close-growing lodge-poles, firs, and aspens. The horse was enormous, the color of fresh-fallen snow. Its eyes glowed red.

The man sitting atop it—if you could call him a man—was like something out of a nun's nightmare. He was huge, broad-shouldered, and fur-covered. His head was as large and round as an overgrown pumpkin, the face bone-white, eyes two enormous black disks. Inside the disks, the pupils glowed the same red as the horse's. The pink mouth was also round and pooched out like a pig's snout.

The rider must've been wearing a pillow case, like the customary barn-burning night-rider. He had to be. No man looked like that naturally.

The horse and rider stared back at Carmody.

Clay snapped the rifle to his shoulder, levered a round in the chamber, and aimed.

"What'd you do to my partner, you son of a bitch?"

The man threw his head back on his high, broad shoulders that appeared covered by a bear-hide coat. The mouth opened wide and the blast from the horn sounded again—two clipped shrieks that ricocheted amongst the trees and filled Carmody's gut with boiling bile. With each blast, vapor jetted from the rider's mouth and nostrils.

Any normal man would have felt the urge to run like hell. Carmody felt the nearly overwhelming urge himself. He steeled himself and dropped to his left knee, sighting down his Winchester's barrel. "Come and get it, you son of a bitch!"

The horse and rider had already bounded toward him, eating up the ground as fast as a charging griz. As they approached, Carmody was nearly overcome by the smell of wild, sweet, rot more overpowering than a hot barn full of fresh pig shit. It was like a sharp slap to his face. It pinched his windpipe and made his gut contract, and he breathed deeply through his mouth to keep from vomiting.

He triggered the Yellowboy. The rider didn't dodge the

bullet. Carmody knew he'd hit him, but there was no reaction.

Carmody rammed another round in the breech, fired again.

Horse and rider closed. Carmody could see both clearly now. The horse was nearly half again as large as the largest saddle horse he'd ever seen, with shoulders the size of small, chiseled boulders. The horse's eyes indeed blazed red—it was no trick of the light—as did the man's.

But the rider was no man in a pillowcase mask. It was a beast of some kind, with a hideously disfigured face the same shade as old snow, with a pink pig's snout and short brown hairs growing about its jaws. The beast's hair was like gray, coiled wires growing straight back from its face, whipped to and fro in the wind. It didn't have hands, but enormous paws and claws three or four times longer than a grizzly's.

Carmody aimed at the hairy center of the beast's chest. When the thing was twenty yards away, Carmody fired. He watched only dust puff from the dull, matted fur.

Then the horse and rider were on him, and Carmody flung his rifle away and dove sharply left. But not before the beast leaned out from the horse's back and raked its right paw across Carmody's right arm and shoulder, the claws slicing his flesh like razor-edged bowie knives.

Clay groaned as he flew off a slight ledge at the bottom of the draw and smacked his left temple against a rock. He felt his body rock and sway as though sinking through warm, black tar, his head throbbing without mercy. The ground shuddered beneath him as the beast passed to his left, the overpowering stench rushing over Carmody, filling his mouth and nose.

His gut heaved. Face down on the ground, he retched.

Then everything went black.

When he came to, he could still smell the stench but it wasn't as bad. He had the sense that only a few minutes had passed. He rolled onto his right shoulder, sleeved the vomit off his mouth and chin, and looked around.

The beast was gone. Or so it appeared.

Carmody looked around for his rifle then saw it lying over a small pine growing out of the side of the draw. As he climbed to his knees, his head felt as though someone were slamming a cast-iron skillet against it, over and over. He gritted his teeth, stood, staggered to his rifle, and stooped. His eyes dimmed. He dropped to both knees. He fought off the nausea and the rising tar of unconsciousness, and regained his feet.

Clumsily, both hands tingling from the fall, he ejected the spent shell, rammed in fresh, and looked around. The beast was nowhere to be seen. From up the draw came soft drumbeats. Carmody turned and walked toward the sound. Chants rose with the drumbeats, and Clay realized that was what he heard just before the beast pounded toward him.

The drum beat like a slow heart, intermittently accompanied by a rattle.

Carmody walked several yards before he realized he was bleeding, saw the four or five gashes across his arm and shoulder, shredding his shirt sleeve. They were deep wounds, but he didn't feel them. When he came to the clearing at the top of the draw, the draw's mouth widening and the forest pulling back on both sides, he raised his rifle and stopped.

The old Indian stood on a low scarp about fifty yards ahead. A drum hung around his neck. He beat the drum with one hand, shook a rattle with the other. His chants ripped and tore on the breeze, occasionally drowned out by the clamor of the magpies swirling above his windblown hair.

Right of the Indian and back several more yards, a man lay sprawled on his back across a flat-topped boulder.

"Nathan," Clay muttered and moved heavily forward, tripping over his boot toes. Before him, a long broad path had been marked in heavy, dark blood, leading down the draw the way the beast had ridden.

17

BRUNO KITCHENER CRAWLED across the parlor floor and stared down at his wife. His face pale, from both his hangover and the horror of watching the sheriff drill a slug through Irma's head, he reached up and dipped his index finger into the blood dribbling down her jaw.

He turned the finger toward his face, narrowed his eyes at it.

It really was blood.

She really was dead.

Kitchener raised his head to a drape-cloaked window facing the street, golden sunlight seeping around the edges. His voice brittle and screechy, he kicked his legs as he screamed, *"Murdering bitches!"*

He looked again at his wife staring glassily up at the ceiling. Not that he hadn't wanted to kill the woman himself on several occasions—no more pious, persnickety, carping woman had ever been born. But she'd been *his* wife, by God, and Sheriff Bridger and the schoolteacher had marched into *his* house and killed her!

Leaning on his right elbow, Kitchener turned to look at the fireplace, where the disk had been. A knowing light entered his eyes.

His heart pounding, his head throbbing even worse than before, he awkwardly gained his feet and stumbled across the room. At the parlor door, he stopped and looked down at his bare, white feet with thick, yellow nails curved like small clams over his toes.

Muttering oaths, he turned, retraced his steps across the parlor, and climbed the stairs to the second story. He came back down a minute later, dressed as he'd been dressed before but with low, brown slippers on his feet, his ankles flour white between the shoes and the frayed cuffs of his wash-worn underwear bottoms. The hem of his black robe with stitched purple cuffs buffeted about his calves as he scuffed across the parlor, into the foyer, and out the front door.

He stalked out of his yard and north along the rutted clay street. The mayor's face was a hard mask of fury as he swung his arms stiffly and dragged his heels over the gravel to keep his slippers on his feet.

A few minutes after leaving his house he came to the corner of the main drag and stopped. He peered up and down the street, the rising sun making a golden river between the shaded boardwalks. Hoof clomps and wheel squawks rose on his right. He turned to see Bright Dormand, foreman of the D-Dot ranch, approaching from the east. Dorman was a big man with a close-cropped, gray beard and rain-stained hat shading his eyes.

"Howdy there, Mr. Mayor," Dormand said as he passed, turning his head to keep his befuddled eyes on Kitchener. As the wagon kept moving, he twisted his body around to stare behind him, squinting. "Mr. Mayor, you ain't sleepwalkin', are ye?"

Ignoring the man, Kitchener stepped off the boardwalk and angled toward the Poudre River Saloon, meeting a mottled brown dog carrying a large rat in its jaws, the rodent's long hairless tail brushing along the street.

The Poudre River's morning apron, J.T. Lilly, was

sweeping the saloon's front stoop. He glanced up as the mayor approached him then returned his eyes to his work. He lifted them again sharply as the mayor mounted the boardwalk in his nightclothes. Lilly scowled, a fat, freshly-lit cigar protruding from his mouth. "What...in blazes...?"

"Any men in there?" the mayor asked, canting his head toward the batwings.

Lilly ran his gaze up and down the mayor once more and said with a distracted air, "Jack Davis and his boys were waitin' for me when I got here at six. They're washin' steak and eggs down with rye."

Davis and his sons, Bo and Joon, were wolfers who worked for area ranchers, though it was also believed they sold whiskey to Indians and soldiers. Nodding with grim satisfaction, Kitchener said, "Bring them and at least five other good trackers and crack-shots to my house in a half hour. I'll pay them thirty dollars a man, fifteen up front."

He turned and started back the way he'd come, stopping suddenly when another thought occurred to him. He wheeled toward the bartender, his thin, white hair sliding around his head in the rising breeze.

"Make sure none are squeamish about shooting women!"

CLAUDINE BRIDGER and Beth Cooper had ridden less than five miles up the canyon, the river running slow and wide under aspens at this lower elevation, when they heard the thunder of heavy wagons moving toward them. A man cursed loudly and cracked a whip.

Riding abreast on the shaded mining road, the two women halted their horses and peered ahead along the curving trail.

Two mules appeared, jogging around a bend, tossing their heads in the air. The wagon followed—a big Pittsburgh outfitted with heavy brakes and tires. An old man held the reins and the long blacksnake. A younger man with similar features sat beside him. In the covered box, an old woman and four girls of various ages rode propped on camping equipment and food stuffs.

Behind them, another mule-drawn wagon jogged around the bend, a middle-aged couple in the driver's box, two girls, and a young boy in the back.

They were a haggard-looking lot—tired, gaunt, and dusty. Fear shone in their staring eyes.

The wagons were approaching so quickly that Claudine and Beth reined their horses off opposite sides of the trail. The first wagon barreled up between them as the old driver hauled back on the reins shouting, "Whoa!"

The pungent smell of the lathered mules and sweaty humans hung in the air like a cloud.

As the second wagon pulled up, the driver of the first glanced at the badge on Claudine's leather vest. "Where you two ladies headed?"

"Up canyon," Claudine said. "Where are you folks headed in such a hurry?"

"Don't go up canyon," the old man urged. He had a long, thin nose with a huge mole on the right nostril, and a skinny neck with a quivering Adam's apple. "There's trouble up there, and there ain't nothin' you can do about none of it!"

"None of what?" Beth asked with quiet dread.

"The killin's," said the old woman in the wagon's box. She sat with her back to Claudine, her right arm resting on the sideboard. She held a blanket-wrapped bundle in the crook of her other elbow, as though it were a baby in swaddling clothes. A corner of the blanket had blown back to reveal the face of an old cuckoo clock.

"Everybody's turnin' crazy, killin' each other," said the bib-bearded, middle-aged man driving the second wagon.

"If the creature don't get 'em first," said the old man, holding the first team's reins.

The young man beside him didn't look right in the head, staring as he did, slack-jawed and vaguely cross-eyed, at Claudine's chest, as if mesmerized.

"Everybody's leavin' the canyon if they haven't already," the old man continued, glancing from Claudine to Beth and back again. "Some are comin' this way or headin' over Cameron Pass toward Walden. It'll be a ghost canyon soon. Just as it should be!"

The old man slapped the reins over his mules' backs and yelled, "*Gid-yaah!*"

The mules leaned into their collars, shook their heads, and trotted off down the trail, drawing the squeaking, clattering wagon behind them.

As the second wagon passed, the young woman in the driver's box twisted her torso around to keep her gaze on Claudine. She wore a soiled dress of blue gingham, small cows and horses orange-stitched into the long, ruffled skirt. A white, lace-edged bonnet hung down the back of her head. She lifted her right hand to her face, indicating her eyes with two fingers.

"The canyon has eyes," she said, drawing her lips wide, cheeks dimpling with a sharp grimace. She was thirty yards beyond now, but Claudine thought she saw tears running down the girl's dirty, sunburned cheeks. "It has a *thousand* eyes. You'll see!"

As the dust sifted between them, Claudine looked across the trail at Beth. The teacher was staring after the wagons, tears streaking her own cheeks.

"We best get a move on," Claudine said. She reined her claybank onto the trail and heeled it upstream.

After a few minutes the teacher caught up to her, and they rode silently, meeting three more wagons and two horseback riders—all prospectors hurrying out of the canyon, warning Claudine and Beth to do the same.

The two women rode until night poured into the canyon like tar into a rain barrel. They set up camp in a U-shaped curve on the north side of the river that was moving faster now, rushing over rocks and fallen trees. When they'd picketed their horses and built a fire, they sat around the fire ring, hunched in their heavy coats. They nibbled jerky, washed it down with strong, black coffee laced with whiskey.

"Those eyes that woman told us about," Claudine said, holding her steaming tin cup in both hands as she stared into the flames. "I've seen 'em. They damn near drove my deputies crazy." She paused. "Damn near drove *me* crazy."

Beth looked at her over the rim of her cup. "I've seen them, too. A long time ago."

"When your family died?"

"After they were killed, and I was running out of my head along the river."

Claudine waited.

"People who saw the cabin said we must've been attacked by a grizzly. I didn't say anything about what I'd seen and heard, because I didn't want people to think I was crazy. Heck, *I* thought I was crazy. But after I came back to Camp Hawkins and strange things started happening there and in the canyon, I realized something strange *indeed* was happening. And that it was probably caused by the demon that murdered my family."

Claudine stared across the fire at the teacher. "The demon you think digging up that amulet set loose."

Beth had been hunkered down on her haunches. Now she stood, wincing at the stiffness in her legs. She stepped back two feet and sat on a pine stump. "Those prospectors mentioned a beast," she said, taking her coffee in one hand and adjusting her skirt over her knees. "I heard it gallop up to our cabin. It sounded like thunder. The ground shook. I was in the privy. I heard a horn. Heard a big animal burst through the door and murder my father and brothers..." Her voice cracked, and she stopped.

Claudine sipped her coffee slowly, trying to quell the crawling sensations along her back. "And then?"

"I don't remember much after that. I heard a magpie. I passed out. Then I was running, seeing the eyes in the darkness. The barman, Vern Applegate, said he found me huddled in the rocks two miles from the cabin. All I remember, after the running from the eyes, is waking up several days later in town. Mrs. Laymon took me in, gave me a home till I was old enough to go off to the teacher's college in Denver."

Beth sipped her coffee, slid strands of hair back from her cheek. "I always felt compelled to come back here and find out what had *really* happened to my family." Her jaws grew hard as she narrowed her eyes at the fire. "And kill the damn thing that took them away from me."

"Where'd you find the shaman?"

"I told an old Ute medicine man about the beast. He sent me back to Camp Hawkins. Soon, Katchi-go-lo-we appeared outside the schoolhouse." Beth chuckled. "Scared my students half to death. He stayed in my carriage shed for a few days, chanting and dancing, then said he was heading up the canyon. He was very frustrated. He said he knew the amulet was near but a dark force kept him from seeing it. A few days after he left, I found the amulet on Mrs. Kitchener's mantle."

Claudine bit off a piece of jerky. She chewed, sniffed. "Sounds like your sorcerer isn't having much luck. Sounds, in fact, like the demon is working himself into a frenzy. I just hope we find your shaman before—"

She stopped and turned her head to one side.

Beth tensed, looked around. "What is it?"

Claudine spit half-chewed jerky into the fire. "Heard something behind me."

They listened.

The river gave a constant low rush. A riffle made a hollow chug as it empted into a pool along the shore. In the distance, occasional owls hooted softly.

"Maybe it's all this talk about the beast," Beth said after a while.

"Like hell," Claudine said. She stood and picked up her rifle. "Step back from the fire. Keep your rifle handy. I'm gonna go take a look around."

Beth opened her mouth to speak, but before she could get the words out, Claudine jacked a fresh round into her Winchester's chamber and disappeared in the darkness.

18

STEPPING beyond the fire's glow, Claudine squeezed her rifle in both hands, setting her feet down softly, and swinging her head slowly from left to right. Out here, the night was as black as the bottom of a well, the towering pines and looming canyon walls with their rocky crags and fir-studded pediments blocking the starlight.

She walked to the river twenty yards away and stared across the gray, rushing water. On the opposite bank, tangled shrubs and boulders were velvet splotches amidst the tree columns.

Turning right, she walked upstream for thirty yards. She stopped, paused, listened, turned, and crept back the way she'd come. She kicked a stone, stopped, and winced, looked around for figures moving toward her in the darkness.

Steeling forward again, she swung her gaze from right to left. The fire was an insignificant glow behind branches, surrounded by trees and boulders. Beth stood near the fire, holding her Spencer carbine in both hands, swinging her head around slowly. She looked small and fragile in the thin light pushing against the darkness, wearing a blanket coat over her dress, her slouch hat tipped low over her eyes by the teacher-like bun at the back of her head.

Claudine's right boot snapped a branch. She stopped, wincing, swung her gaze toward the fire. Beth had turned toward her, body tensed, rifle pointed.

Claudine muttered an oath. "It's only me," she said, loud enough to be heard above the river's rush.

Beth's shoulders relaxed. She lowered her rifle.

"Shit," Claudine muttered as she continued moving downstream, ignoring the worms wriggling around in her belly. Whoever had made the noise knew she was out here now. And something *had* made a noise. She hadn't imagined the sound. Besides, she sensed another presence, thought she could even hear someone breathing.

When she'd pushed through a chokecherry thicket and climbed through a notch in a boulder snag, she turned and walked left to the wagon trail. She made another left, completely circled the fire, and stood west of the flames. Because of trees and shrubs between her and the fire, she couldn't see the teacher.

She breathed deeply of the cool night air. She enjoyed the relaxing sensation it gave her, until she detected the faint scent of rot amidst the dewy earth and pine smells. Sniffing, she turned in the direction from which the smell came, walked toward it, stepping over fallen branches, ducking under arching boughs, and weaving around tree boles.

The fetor grew stronger. Her nostrils contracted. She parted her lips to breathe through her mouth.

A low growl sounded. Close to the ground, a shadow moved. Two red eyes shone, glowing faintly in the fire's dull light.

Heart turning somersaults, Claudine froze and raised her rifle to her shoulder. With a quivering thumb, she raked the hammer back.

Something scuttled in the brush. Twigs snapped.

There was a yip and a guttural groan. The coyote wheeled and loped off through the woods, a bobbing, diminishing shadow.

Claudine held the shot. As her heart slowed, she walked forward, keeping the rifle aimed straight out from her shoulder. She looked down, saw the vague figure of a small, dead animal—a young deer draped over the gap between a rock and a juniper thicket. Blood shone dully where the coyote had ripped into the animal's hindquarters.

Claudine looked around then turned and headed back toward the camp.

"It's me," she called when she was ten yards from the fire.

She ducked under a branch, and straightened. Beth stood where she'd been standing before, holding her Spencer across her thighs, regarding Claudine expectantly.

"Anything?" she asked.

Before Claudine could reply, Beth's eyes snapped wide. An arm snaked around Claudine's right shoulder. Her rifle was ripped from her hands, flung into the woods. At the same time, another arm shot in from her left and fastened around her waist. Something cold and round was thrust at her head, just above her right ear.

She gritted her teeth against the pain.

The revolver's hammer clicked back with a metallic rake.

Ten yards away, Beth raised her rifle and wheeled, her skirt flying around her legs. Before she could raise and cock the Spencer, an arm swung out of the darkness. The back of a hand connected with her mouth, sending her sprawling. The rifle clattered off a rock near the fire.

"Easy, Sheriff," a man cooed in Claudine's right ear, blowing his sour beer and jerky breath and ramming his cocked pistol even harder against her head. "Make one move and I'll drill a hole through your purty brain."

Beth gave a pained, angry groan and pushed up on her elbows. A stocky, powerful-looking man in a tattered, blood-stained, wolf coat stepped out of the semi-darkness where she'd been standing. The wolfer, Jack Davis, aimed a long-barreled Smithy down at Beth, freezing her there on the ground. He showed a single, yellow tooth in the far right corner of his lewd smile.

"Well, look what we have here!"

"Davis, you son of a bitch!" Claudine said. "What the hell do you think you're doing?"

The wolfer glanced at the tall, skinny kid shuffling up beside him—his youngest, son, Joon, whose bulging, wide-spaced eyes flicked darkly between Beth and Claudine. The kid held a Henry rifle straight out from his hip. His long, curly, chin beard danced against his knee-length buffalo coat.

"We come to partake of that coffee you got simmering there on the fire," Davis said, returning his randy eyes to Claudine. "And you."

The arm around Claudine's waist slid up her belly, the hand slipping into her coat and closing over her right breast. She recoiled, jerked her head right, grimaced at the gun's pressure against her skull.

A voice in her right ear said, "I'll take the sheriff, Pa. Her and me got a bill to settle."

It was Davis's older boy, Bo, who had raped a farmer's daughter around Tie Siding a year ago. His victim had been too afraid to testify against him in court, so Claudine had been forced to set him free. He was a big kid who walked with a limp, having fallen down a well when he was three. He weighed over two hundred pounds, and his limp took little from his toughness.

He pinched Claudine's nipple through the fabric of her flannel shirt and chemise.

His voice deep with lust, he nuzzled Claudine's neck and said, "She owes me one, sure 'nough."

"That bitch owes us all one," Davis said. He stood between Beth's spread legs, staring down at her. "But me—I like the teacher."

Joon spoke with his characteristic rasping wheeze. "Pa, we was s'posed to bring the women back to Mr. Kitchener's camp unharmed." He spoke as though he were just reminding his father of their orders.

"We ain't gonna harm 'em," Davis said.

"Nah," said Bo. He ran his wet, rough tongue along the side of Claudine's neck. "We're just gonna have some *fun*!"

As Tom squealed a laugh, Claudine lowered her head sharply then swung her right arm up. She slapped the big man's pistol so hard with the back of her hand that she thought she cracked a knuckle. The gun exploded, smoke wafting. Claudine's right ear rang.

"Whore!" Bo shouted a half-second before Claudine stomped down hard on his right foot.

He bellowed and hopped back.

She wheeled, grabbed the gun he was trying to aim at her. Lifting it up and shoving it back, she slammed her right knee up between his thighs, driving home with a satisfying thump.

He grunted loudly as air exploded from his lungs. But instead of bending over as most men did when their jewels had been hammered, he only stumbled back two steps, blowing spittle through his teeth. With his left hand, he grabbed a fistful of her hair and jerked her head back so hard that her hands slipped off his gun.

Giving her a taste of her own medicine, he stepped forward and slammed his right knee into her belly.

It drove so deep Claudine thought his kneecap connected with her spine. She bent forward and dropped to her knees. Blood pounded in her head. Red lights flashed before her eyes. Wheezing and choking, she fought for air. The ground tilted first one way then the other.

Scuffling sounded to her right; there was a sharp slap. Beth Cooper cried out and cursed.

In the corner of her vision, Claudine saw the teacher struggling with Jack Davis while the bib-bearded, Joon watched, holding his gun across his shoulders, shuffling around and grinning with embarrassment.

"You just stand there and hold your gun on her, Joony-bug," Jake said. "Watch how your old man does it. Ha! Watch an old pro go to work!"

"Ain't like we never seen ye before, Pa," Bo said in a tone that said he hadn't been all that impressed. He reached down and rolled Claudine onto her back. "Me, I'm gonna do this sheriff so hard she won't walk for a month!"

Claudine lifted her chin and arched her back as she sucked oxygen, making hoarse, choking sounds.

"That feel good?" Bo stared down at her with a mocking, lascivious grin. He holstered his pistol and moved his hands to the buckle of his cartridge belt.

He had fishy blue eyes that had haunted Claudine's sleep every night for the three weeks she'd had him in jail. She'd known letting him out meant turning a maniac loose on other women. She hadn't realized that she, herself, would be one of those victims, though the way he'd ogled her should have given her a clue.

Still arching her back and sucking air, she glanced right and saw Beth trying to ward off Jack Davis. Joon squatted between her and Beth, looking nervously from one to the other.

Still standing over Claudine, a boot on either side of her shoulders, Bo turned away to toss his gunbelt down. It landed eight feet away. Spying a rock, the sheriff twisted her torso left, lunged for it, and fell back.

She raised the rock to her right ear, but she'd only started swinging it forward when Bo, moving with more speed than she'd thought possible with his bum hip, dropped to his knees, straddling her. He threw his left hand up, catching the rock before she could release it.

"You bastard!" Claudine screamed through a choking gasp.

Bo laughed and backhanded her hard. He tossed the stone away and, as she kicked and squirmed beneath him, he wrestled both her arms under his knees, pinning them both to the ground. The pain made her eyes water. She kicked up with her feet but he was too far forward for her boots to reach his head.

"You're gonna enjoy this," Bo said, grinning down at her. With both hands he began unbuttoning her coat. "Just like that half-wit Hagen girl did. She was wantin' it *all along!*"

Claudine gritted her teeth and raised her head, her eyes blazing kill fury. "You're about as bred-up as a common goat, Davis."

He laughed.

"You'll never stick your wet, little noodle in me, you numb-nutted ape!"

"That's what you think," he grunted, shifting his knees on her wrists, flushed but smiling as though thoroughly enjoying the fight.

She struggled to free her right wrist, hoping she could somehow reach down and pull her stiletto from her right boot well. "Get off me, you pansy, Nancy-boy, or..."

"Or what, Sheriff?" He scooted up on his knees so he could reach the lower buttons of her coat. "Just what're you gonna do? I ain't in your jail cell no more, you bitch!"

Claudine's response was drowned out by a loud, snarling wail which rose from the woods behind Bo like the angry voice of God. He'd just opened her coat and had taken a fistful of her shirt, intending to rip it open, but the noise stopped him. He froze and turned his head to stare into the dark woods behind him.

"What the hell was that?" Jack Davis demanded.

He was crouched between Beth's legs, his pants and underwear pulled down around his knees, his jutting dong bobbing stiffly as he craned his head back.

Joon had set his rifle down and was holding Beth's arms above her head. Her skirts were bunched up around her waist, her white pantaloons pulled down to her thighs. She'd stopped struggling and canted her head to the right, to see behind her attacker.

It was as if they'd all paused for a photograph.

The wail rose again, louder. It echoed like thunder in an amphitheater.

Beth peered around Bo. She'd gotten most of her wind back, but the wail pinched it off again as she strained her ears to listen.

Whatever was out there was big and angry. And from the thrashing brush and snapping branches, it was headed straight for the camp.

19

Bo stood and turned toward the woods.

Before him, a broad, hulking figure appeared between a tall boulder and a pine. The fire shone on cinnamon fur, reflected in two eyes set close to a wedge-shaped snout. The beast rose on its back legs, to a height of at least ten feet, and threw its head back on its shoulders. The wail rose again—an insane cry of unmitigated fury, rattling Claudine's eardrums painfully.

"Griz!" Bo wheeled left and stooped over his cartridge belt. "It's a damn huge grizzly bear, Pa!"

"Jumpin' Jehosophat!" Jack Davis shouted. Forgetting that his pants were still down around his ankles, he bolted forward, tripped, and hit the ground face-first with a grunt.

Joon screamed and backed away, tripping over his rifle.

Throwing its arms out as if for a hug, the beast moved forward with surprising grace for a four-footed creature on its hind legs. Revolver in hand, Bo wheeled toward it and thumbed the Remington's hammer back. From Claudine's perspective, Bo's frame was nearly swallowed up by the mountain of dark-brown beast moving toward him.

"Pa, Joon, get your damn rifles!"

Bo's cry was barely audible above the bear's roar. He extended his pistol straight out from his shoulder and fired three shots. They sounded like twigs snapping. They didn't slow the beast a bit.

Growing even more enraged, the bruin continued moving toward Bo, swatting at the slugs plunking dust from its thickly-furred chest, as though they were only insects.

"Joon, shoot the damn thing!" Jack Davis cried as he pushed up on his elbows.

Dazed, Claudine gained her knees, glanced behind her. Joon was still backing away from the bear, his eyes round and terrified. Nearly beyond the circle of firelight, he backed into a tree, and froze.

The bear's wail became a squeal. Claudine turned back toward it, and winced. The bear had overtaken Bo. It engulfed the big man in its arms, and squeezed, snarling and squealing, lifting Bo off his feet, shaking him the way a dog shakes a rabbit.

"Help me!" Bo cried, his thrashing legs flying nearly straight out from the bear's belly. The bruin buried its snout in the man's left shoulder, evoking a clipped scream.

"Joon, damn ye!" Jack Miller shouted. He'd gained his feet and pulled his pants up to his waist. Darting horrified glances at Bo and the bear, he buckled his belt, then glanced around for a rifle.

Claudine scuttled several feet back from the bear, sitting on her butt with her back to the fire. Now, as the bear continued to give Bo the ride of his life, she looked around. Beth was on her knees on the other side of the fire, beckoning to her and yelling above the bear's wails and Jack Miller's curses: "Let's get the hell out of here!"

Claudine glanced at the bear. It released Bo suddenly, flinging him to her left. The young man hit the ground like a grain sack flung from a moving freight wagon, and laid still, blood pouring from a broad gash in his upper left chest.

"I'll teach ye, ye damn son of a bitch!" Davis shouted. He'd found his rifle and, moving toward the bear, rammed a fresh shell into the chamber. "Get away from my boy, ye damn son of a bitch!"

But the bear already had Bo's chest in its jaws, was again thrashing the man from side to side. His arms and legs hanging limp, Bo merely winced and sobbed, his blood-foamed lips forming the word, "Help."

Claudine got up and glanced behind her. Joon was sitting before the tree he'd backed into, knees and jackboots drawn up to his chest. He was shaking and staring at the bear, jaw hanging, his bib-beard brushing his belly. Claudine grabbed his Henry rifle, which he'd dropped beside the fire, and followed Beth across the camp to the very edge of the firelight. They stopped, turned their gazes back toward where the bear was mauling Bo, and dropped to their knees.

Jack Davis was moving up on the bear, rifle raised, shifting from side to side. He was trying to get a shot at the bear without hitting his son, but it was obvious to Claudine that Bo was already dead—or as good as dead. He hung limp in the bear's jaws, blood dribbling from his mouth and ears, his face a mess of scratches and bruises from where the bear had whipped him against boulders and tree trunks.

Davis extended the rifle at the bear's head, having to hold the barrel up at a forty-five-degree angle. The bear turned as if to amble off with its prey.

The rifle cracked.

The bear's head snapped to one side, as though it been slapped across its snout. Its cheek smoked where the bullet drilled through the hide and bone.

The bruin dropped its prize and turned to Davis. It

staggered slightly, looked befuddled. Davis cocked and fired again. The bear shook its head wildly, dropped to all fours, and turned away. Again shaking its head, it jogged off, heavy-hipped and rolling from side to side.

"Come back here and face me like a man, you smelly son of a bitch!"

Davis moved toward it, ejecting the spent shell, ramming another into the breech, and firing. The bear continued ambling off, cracking brush and twigs. About twenty yards from the fire, it ran into a boulder, sort of glanced off the stone, and dropped to a shoulder. Slowly, it rolled onto its side, its belly heaving, kicking one back leg.

Kneeling beside Beth, Claudine said, "Stay here."

She rose, hefting the Henry in both hands, and walked slowly up behind Davis and the bear. Jack stood over the bear and, cursing, fired three more shots into the bruin's head. The belly stopped heaving.

Holding his rifle in both hands, Davis turned and walked back to his son, knelt down beside Bo, who lay unmoving on his back—arms and legs akimbo. He was covered with dark-red blood.

Claudine stopped about fifteen feet away. She was about to say something when movement caught her eye. Joon walked slowly toward his dead brother and his father, wringing his hands together.

His voice was small. "Is... Is he dead, Pa?"

Davis's back was heaving. He lifted his head toward the boy. "No thanks to you, ya yella rat!"

Joon sniffed, his tear-wet face crumpling, his long chin whiskers shivering.

Davis bolted up, snapping the rifle to his shoulder while jacking the cocking lever. He extended the gun at Joon, and fired.

The slug plunked through Joon's cheek, jerking him straight back as he covered his face with both hands. He twisted around, dropped to his knees, and fell belly down on the ground.

"Drop the rifle, Jack," Claudine said. She brought the Henry to her shoulder, aiming down the barrel.

She didn't want him to drop the rifle. She didn't have time to haul his worthless, perverted hide back to the jailhouse, and she wasn't going to turn him loose. Davis didn't disappoint her.

Taking his rifle in one hand and giving a melodramatic sigh, he leaned to his left, as though he were about to set it on the ground. Then he wheeled toward her quickly, snapping the rifle back up to his shoulder. She shot him through his right temple. Blood sprayed out the back of his head, bits of skull ticking in the grass and brush like small bits of hail. He toppled straight back, glanced off a rock, gave an enormous fart, and lay still on his left side.

Claudine drew a deep breath then let it out slow as she turned to the bear.

Walking up behind her, her own rifle in her hands, Beth Cooper took the thoughts right out of her mouth. "That isn't any ordinary bear."

"It did seem to have an extra-large chip on its shoulder, didn't it?"

"Sort of like Mrs. Kitchener."

"Speaking of her," Claudine said, staring down at the bear, "we best get the hell out of here. The mayor might have heard the racket."

When she'd walked away, Beth turned to regard the three dead men. She fingered the bruise swelling high on her right cheek, the cut on her lower lip. "Doubt I could sleep any more tonight, anyway."

THE NEXT MORNING, Carmody woke late.

He opened his eyes. Clean, high-country sunlight flooded the cabin's open windows, dust motes sifting through the rays. Outside, birds chirped pleasantly.

Carmody blinked at the low ceiling beams, and took inventory. His head, pushing up a goose egg where he'd smacked the rock in the ravine bottom, felt like someone had laid a clothes iron across his left temple. That meant it was getting better, because yesterday morning, the morning after he and the Indian, Katchi-lo-go-we, had hauled Nathan down from the ridge and buried him near the creek, it had hurt like someone was laying that iron across Clay's temple over and over again.

He threw off his blankets, swung his legs over the side of the cot and, squinting, heaved himself to his feet. The hammering got only a little worse. That was good, but hammering or no hammering, he was hunting the critter that killed Nathan. He'd bring its head back and mount it over the cabin door.

The memory of what the beast had done to Laroque increased the pain. Carmody let it go, holding onto just enough rage to help him dress and down a cup of the six-shooter coffee the Indian had left on the stove. He set his empty cup on the table, turned toward the door, stopped, and turned back.

Ten .44 shells were lined up along the table's other end, casings down, forming a long semi-circle across the split pine planks. The Indian had camped here the past two nights. He must have left the shells. It wasn't surprising that he'd arranged them in such a curious way. Everything the old man did was curious, including spending the night outside by the fire instead of taking Laroque's bunk in the cabin.

Carmody gave a snort, shouldered his saddle and bridle, and threw open the door, staring into the brightly lit canyon alive with the creek's gurgling rush and bird song. A morning-cool breeze wafted against him, smelling like the creek's pure snowmelt, sage, and pine.

He took a deep breath, eased his hat on his head.

He took a step into the hard-packed yard. Hoof thuds rose to his left. The old Indian was approaching along the creek, dragging a makeshift travois upon which a dead deer flopped. From the massive antlers, Carmody could tell the deer was the big buck he and Nathan had been after before the Beast intervened.

The Indian angled up from the creek and stopped the paint before the cabin.

"The larder box almost empty," the Indian said tonelessly.

"I'll wrap a haunch in a croaker sack and take it with me," Clay said, turning and heading toward the makeshift stable behind the cabin.

"Where you go?"

At the cabin's corner, Carmody turned back to the Indian, whose dark face shone like old, cracked leather in the sunshine. The shaman's coarse, silver-streaked hair hung straight to his hunched shoulders.

"I'm goin' after that thing that killed my friend. Two, three days, we're gonna use its ugly head for a hat rack."

"You make big mistake."

Carmody poked his hat back, adjusted the saddle on his shoulder. "Now, how's that?"

"It must be buried with the amulet. If not, it will not stay dead."

"What if I shoot it a dozen times and chop it up in little pieces?"

"The only way to kill it is with the ten bullets I placed on the table." The Indian canted his head at the cabin. "The only way to make sure it *stays* dead is with the amulet."

"What's so special about those shells?"

"I spoke medicine over them. I blessed them." The Indian shook his head. "Only those bullets will harm him."

Cursing, Carmody tramped around the cabin. In the stable, he bridled and saddled one of the pies while the Indian tied his horse in a patch of tall grass then hung the buck from a tree limb. Carmody walked over to Nathan's grave, near a cedar south of the cabin. It was a mound of red clay and creek shale, a makeshift cross sticking up from one end. Nathan's death, the creature, the dead men rising from their graves—it all seemed so unreal that Carmody could find few words to say over Nathan's grave. Beyond promising his dead friend that he'd kill the beast.

He donned his hat and led the pie to the cabin's front door, tied it to the hitch rack, and went inside. Grabbing his sheathed Yellowboy, he glanced at the old man sitting stiffly at the table. A mug of coffee steamed before him. The bullets were still arranged on the split-pine logs of the table's scarred surface, near the old man's right elbow.

Carmody swiped the shells from the table, dropped them in his jeans pocket, and glanced at the Indian. "I'll be back in a few days."

Katch, as Carmody called the old man for short, sat staring into his coffee cup, a troubled light in his deep, dark eyes. As Carmody stood over him, the old man placed both hands on his cup and peered into the black liquid, as though spying something in the grounds.

"Something...happens," the old man said, haltingly.

Carmody's gut soured. "What?"

"I don't know."

Outside, shrill cries sounded.

Adjusting his rifle on his right shoulder, Carmody dropped the shells in his jeans pocket and stepped outside. Magpies careened over the yard, their bulky black, white, and aquamarine bodies flashing in the sunlight. Swooping, they resembled mud swallows darting about for bugs. Carmody set his teeth against the cacophony.

"What the hell's this all about?" he asked the old man without turning around, raising his voice to be heard above the din.

A bird dove a few feet in front of him, swooping low over the pie's head. The horse spooked, blowing and pulling against its reins.

Carmody turned his head. "What the hell...?"

Pistols popped on the other side of the creek. Men yelled. Hooves clomped. The thuds grew louder until two riders appeared, galloping through the narrow gap in the northern ridge, crouched low in their saddles as they cast quick glances over their shoulders.

Both were female. The one on the left—with long, cinnamon hair falling from her funnel-brimmed Stetson, bat-wing chaps flapping on her denim-clad legs—twisted around in her saddle and triggered a shot behind her.

Claudine Bridger.

The other woman was Claudine's height, with red hair gathered and fastened behind her neck. Less curvaceous than Claudine, she wore a green sombrero, a white blouse under a long, red-knit vest, and a long, green riding skirt split down the right side. She was astride a galloping black Morgan.

Carmody didn't recognize her until the horses were fording the creek thirty yards away, the water splashing like glistening jewels around their hocks. She lifted her head to cast a quick look at the cabin. The morning sun shone on the face of Beth Cooper.

Carmody poked his hat back and looked beyond the fast-approaching women. Six other riders broke out of the pinewoods and angled toward the lodge—five men forming a wedge behind a tall gent with a bowler hat and thin white-blond hair whipping behind his collar. Shouting furiously, he triggered a pistol over his horse's right ear. The horse bobbed its head, irritated by the shot, but did not break stride. The slug kicked up gravel just left of Beth, about two-dozen feet in front of Carmody.

Clay took another step forward as he shucked his Winchester from the boot with his right hand, and tossed the empty sheath back against the cabin. As the women brought their mounts to skidding stops off his right shoulder, scattering the magpies, he took the rifle in both hands.

"To what do I owe the pleasure?" he yelled above the gunfire.

He took another step forward, jacked a shell in the breech, and fired. His shot lifted dust and gravel two feet before the blond gent's speckle-gray stallion. The horse whinnied and jerked to the side, throwing its weight onto its back legs and causing a flanking rider to rein wide.

Both men cursed.

"Figured you to be good for a hot cup of mud," Claudine said as she hit the ground running.

She wheeled, slipped her rifle from its sheath, and slapped her horse's right hip as, just beyond her, Beth did likewise.

Claudine said, "Sorry about my friends. I thought we'd lost them until about ten minutes ago."

As Beth fired a shot off the cabin's east corner then scuttled through the open door, Claudine dropped to her right knee. Raising her Winchester, she snapped off four quick rounds in half that many seconds. The slugs barked and spanged off the rocks on the other side of the creek. One rider grabbed his left shoulder.

Carmody glanced at the beautiful sheriff, who was levering another round as she flung her hair back from her face then pressed her cheek against her rifle butt.

"I reckon I can brew a fresh pot," he said uncertainly, tracking a rider galloping upstream.

Claudine fired the Winchester. The slug pounded a rock behind which one of the riders, dismounting and scrambling for cover, had disappeared a quarter-second before.

"That's Mayor Kitchener and five market hunters he signed up to hunt me and Beth."

Carmody fired a shot. "I take it he doesn't like you anymore?"

"I killed his wife," Claudine said. She cursed as she rammed her cocking lever up and down, trying to clear a jam.

"That'd do it, all right."

Unable to clear the jam, Claudine cursed again, turned, and ran toward the cabin door. "Don't mind if I make myself at home, do you?"

"Just scrape your boots on the porch."

"Where's Laroque?"

"Dead."

Rifle raised, Carmody stared across the creek. The gunmen were taking cover behind the bank and pine trees. Smoke puffed from behind a low boulder. The slug kicked up gravel near Clay's right boot. Carmody responded with his own shot, then wheeled, tore the pie's reins from the hitchrack, and slapped its rump.

Snorting angrily, the animal bounded off behind Claudine and Beth's mounts, heading upstream with its reins bouncing along behind it.

As another shot pulverized shade behind him, Carmody leapt into the lodge and slammed the heavy door. Claudine crouched beside the window left of the doorframe. Behind her, Beth half-reclined on Carmody's cot, pressing her right shoulder against the wall as she peered through the window.

The old Indian was sitting at the table, where Carmody had left him. He was staring, lines cutting into the bridge of his broad nose, at the round, burlap-wrapped object resting beside the teacher's left thigh.

"Better get down," Carmody told the Indian. "Our visitors brought uninvited guests."

The Indian continued staring, transfixed, at the bundle. Gunfire popped on the other side of the creek. A bullet whined through the front window and cut so close to the Indian's head that it ruffled his hair before pinging off a cast iron skillet on the wall behind him.

Katchi-lo-go-we didn't move. He continued staring, frozen, at the bundle on the cot.

20

"KATCH!" Carmody shouted.

The old shaman's eyes widened slightly, and he turned toward Clay. Another close bullet snapped him from his daze. He stood stiffly, but quickly for a man his age, wheeled, grabbed his old Spencer carbine, and shambled over to the window on the opposite side of the cabin from the teacher.

As the explosions of the sheriff's rifle rocked the cabin, Katchi-lo-go-we slid a look out his window, then shoved the rifle through the opening and began shooting toward the creek. His and Claudine's shots brought dirt and chinking down from the rafters. Carmody looked at the bundle beside the teacher, who was hugging the wall tighter now that the attackers were hunkered down and setting up an earnest fusillade.

A bullet tore up slivers from the window casing only inches from Carmody's right shoulder. Clay turned and edged a glance around the frame. Smoke puffed between a rock and a sage shrub on the other side of the creek. A red-mustached face turned as the man jacked another cartridge into his Winchester's breech.

Carmody lifted his rifle and fired. The slug twanged off

the rock. The man winced, mouthed a curse, and ducked. As Clay recocked the Yellowboy, he spied movement in the corner of his left eye. He pulled back behind the cabin wall and peered upstream.

About fifty yards away, a man in a deerskin vest and flat-brimmed black hat forded the creek, crouching and holding his rifle out for balance as he stepped across a small beaver dam.

Carmody turned to Claudine, who fired her Winchester straight out across the creek, then muttered angrily, her jaw hard, as she ejected the smoking shell and jacked another. Several shots pounded the cabin's front wall and barked against the door, making the hinges clink.

Carmody shuttered his window, locked it, and strode quickly toward the back of the cabin. "One of 'em's tryin' to flank us."

"One on this side, too." Claudine closed and locked her own shutter, turned to Beth. "Can you two hold the cabin?"

"You bet," Beth said, triggering a shot as she kneeled atop the cot, then turned and pressed her back against the wall. "You got enough ammo over there, Katch?"

The Indian worked the Spencer's trigger guard cocking mechanism and nodded. "I have enough bullets to kill these white-eyes," he said, customarily toneless. He frowned as a bullet chunked into the top of the doorframe and smashed into the cabin's back wall, then crouched over his old carbine, and fired.

Carmody opened the short back door, peaked out, then he and Claudine stepped into the cabin's back yard, crouching between the twin stacks of wood he and Nathan had gathered. Claudine scuttled out behind him, shut the door, and then dropped to one knee beside Clay, who was edging a glance over the top of the right-hand stack.

"I'll go downstream, you go up," she said.

As she began straightening, Carmody grabbed her arm. "I'm kinda curious...why'd you kill the mayor's wife?"

"She was a witch...or something...and wouldn't give up the amulet."

"She had it?"

Claudine nodded. "And beat hell out of me when Beth and I tried to get it."

Carmody ran the heel of his left hand pensively against his chin. "Good enough for me." He shuffled his feet beneath him, stealing another look over the wood stack, ready to rise. "Be careful."

"You worried about me?"

He glanced back at her, looking up at him expectantly from under the funneled brim of her hat.

Carmody flushed but stretched a sheepish smile. He ran out from between the wood stacks and into a hackberry thicket on the cabin's upstream flank. When he'd moved upstream about twenty yards, he stopped. He'd heard a spur chink off a rock.

He crouched behind a boulder. Boots clattered quietly on shale. The spur hummed again. The man stopped. Another footfall and then a shadow appeared on the pine needles and shale to Carmody's left. Carmody pressed his back against the rock, and flipped his rifle around, grabbing the barrel with both hands.

A run-down boot and buckskin-clad leg appeared.

As the right boot sank into the shale, the spur singing softly, and as the other foot came forward, Carmody swung the rifle stock in a broad arc, about three feet off the ground, laying it soundly against the man's knees with a loud *crack!*

"*Gnah!*"

The man's knees buckled, the left cap dropping a good six inches beneath its normal position, but his momentum carried him forward several more steps. Dropping his rifle, he fell on his shoulder and twisted to reach for his left knee. His chinless, freckled face was brick-red and bunched with pain.

“Oh, you mangy, son-of-Lucifer,” he wheezed, glaring up at Carmody.

Straightening, Clay strode toward him quickly and rammed his rifle butt into the man’s forehead, laying him out cold against the rocks. He crouched and, seeing the man’s chest rising and falling slowly, stripped the man of his weapons—rifle, pistol, and an Arkansas toothpick he plucked from a calf sheath.

“One down,” Clay said, turning and wasting no time following the man’s path through the thorn apple and chokecherry.

He came to the creek bank and tossed the rifle, pistol, and knife into the shallow stream. Dropping down the bank, he stepped out onto the beaver dam and, keeping his head down and holding his arms out for balance, placed one boot in front of the other, making for the other side.

Downstream, bullet reports echoed around the canyon. Slugs thudded loudly into the cabin’s stout timbers. Judging by the sound, the teacher and old Katch were giving as good as they were getting.

Making the far side of the creek in seven quick strides, having slipped once, getting his left knee and rifle stock wet, Carmody leapt up the bank and jogged through the pines, heading downstream, keying on the gun reports rising on his side of the creek.

Fifteen yards ahead, near the stream, smoke puffed up from a rock cluster, and a rifle cracked. Carmody swerved right and dropped to a knee. He peered through a notch in the rocks. A man resting on his left hip cocked a Winchester, laid the barrel over the creek bank, and aimed toward the cabin. It was the red-mustached man whom Carmody had swapped lead with earlier from the cabin window.

“Hold it!” Carmody shouted, his Yellowboy snugged against his shoulder.

The man turned his head, eyes slitted.

Carmody pressed his cheek against his rifle stock. "Throw down the gun!"

The man hesitated, a thoughtful light flickering in his squinting, brow-shaded eyes. He swung his Winchester around suddenly, leveling the barrel at Clay, who squeezed his Yellowboy's trigger. The man was a pro. Anticipating Carmody's shot, he'd jerked right, dodging the shot while triggering his own Winchester. The slug whistled passed Carmody's shoulder and thumped into the fir trunk behind him.

Smiling savagely, sun glinting off his white teeth, the man bounded to his feet, tossing away his rifle and filling his hands with two matched Navies from the cartridge belts crossed over his fringed buckskin tunic. He leapt a rock and ran toward Clay, extending both pistols, firing the one in his right hand.

The round nipped felt from Carmody's hat as he threw himself left, rolled off that shoulder, and bounded back to his haunches. He'd cocked his rifle mid-dive, and he extended it now at the red-mustached gent with the Navies.

But the man had stopped moving toward him, about ten yards away, his back to the murmuring creek. Both Navies sagged to his sides.

Carmody held fire.

The man's mouth opened, forming a dark oval beneath his mustache. He blinked, swallowed, stumbled forward and dropped to his knees. His black hat tumbled off his right shoulder. When he hit the ground on his forehead, blood glinted at the back of his neck, spurting over his shoulder blades.

Carmody shuttled his puzzled frown toward the cabin. The old Indian was leaning out the upstream window, looking toward Clay. He took his rifle in his left hand and offered a stiff wave with the other, then pulled his head back into the cabin.

Carmody lowered his gaze to the dead man before him. "Nice shootin', old-timer."

Leaning down to scoop his hat off the ground, which he'd lost in his dive, he began moving downstream slowly. Katch and Beth had stopped shooting from the cabin, but at least two guns were still sending up smoke south of the lodge, back in the pines on this side of the creek.

CLAUDINE HAD DISPATCHED the man trying to sneak around the cabin from downstream by sneaking up on him from behind and laying her rifle butt across the back of his head. She hadn't meant to kill him, but kill him she had. Deader'n last night's venison haunch, as her father used to say.

She didn't feel too bad about it. Outfitted as the big hombre was, with three knives sheathed in plain view on his blood-stained, linsey shirt, and with three pistols on his cartridge belts, and a big Sharps buffalo gun in his hands, he surely would have killed her, given the chance.

Leaving him to the brush wolves, she crawled through a copse of brushy cedars, over a natural levee, and splashed across the creek. She climbed the opposite bank and threw her shoulder down against the eroded incline, just beneath the ridge. As she snuck a peek over the ridge's lip, a rifle barked, the slug blowing up gravel and a juniper branch a foot to her right.

She ducked, swiping the branch from her hair with the back of her right hand, spat grit from her lips.

"That you, Claudine?" Mayor Kitchener's voice rose, loud and clear above the creek's murmur. In the distance, the other guns had gone silent.

"No, it's the tooth fairy."

"You've been a very bad girl."

"I can explain why I had to kill your wife, Mayor."

"Why don't you come out, and we'll swap explanations?"

Claudine raised her eyes to a small tuft of sod extending over the brow of the creek bank, frowning. "What?"

"I'll explain why I killed your father. Then you can tell me why you killed my wife."

The man's words struck Claudine like a thrown brick. Her heart thudded, and her blood raced. She'd figured the man who'd killed her father had been some outlaw wanting to even the score for a bullet or a jail sentence.

"What are you talking about?" she yelled over the bank.

Kitchener laughed. "I figured that, with your old pa out of the way, a smart girl like yourself would come to your senses, and entertain the advances of a wealthy, powerful older man."

Claudine's chest heaved. Sweat trickled down her neck and dribbled between her breasts. With effort, she raised her voice loudly enough to be heard above the creek. "I...I told you I wanted nothing to do with you. I never gave you any reason to believe..."

"Oh, I know that, now," Kitchener laughed. "But I didn't know it then. I figured that was your irascible old father talking." He laughed again, a jeering guffaw that rose from deep in his chest. "But I guess the joke's on you, ain't it?"

The man laughed louder. Claudine lowered her head and gritted her teeth, squeezing her rifle in both hands. He was baiting her, confessing his murder of her father to try to lure her out in plain sight, where he could kill her. With Claudine dead, he'd no longer have to worry about her finding out who'd killed her father, and come gunning for him.

She put some steel into her voice. "You wanna know why I killed your wife?"

Kitchener hesitated. "Shit, half the county knows the

teacher's been looking for that amulet. She convinced you it'll stop the run of bad luck we've been having of late."

His voice faded as Claudine trotted upstream along the base of the creek bank, crouching to keep her hat from showing over the lip. Kitchener didn't say anything for a moment, but when he spoke again, Claudine was too far downstream to hear anything but the puzzled, anxious tone of his voice.

When she'd gone fifty yards, Claudine climbed up out of the creek bed and ran through the pines. She circled around Kitchener's position and ran back toward the bank. Her heart thudded and a red haze hung behind her eyes. She wanted to move more slowly but her feet wouldn't obey. She bolted on through the woods, leaping deadfalls and small boulders.

Kitchener's voice rose ahead and to her right, up a slight rise. "...just walked in and shot him in the belly. Shoulda seen the look on his face...while he crawled around that jail office, begging me to leave you alone."

Kitchener laughed.

Holding her rifle across her chest, Claudine ran toward the rise.

A rifle popped. A slug burned across her right temple, throwing her back, dropping her to one knee.

"Bastard," she grunted as the rifle popped again.

Biting down hard on the searing pain in her head, she flung herself toward the river a half instant before the slug plowed up dirt where she'd been squatting. Cursing her carelessness, she rolled onto her back, aimed the rifle straight out from her side and fired six quick rounds. Blood trickling down the right side of her face, her hair in one eye, she peered through her own powder smoke.

Kitchener lay sprawled on his back atop the rise, black frock coat spread around him like batwings. His belly rose and fell sharply.

Claudine gained her feet, brushed blood from her

cheek, and climbed the levee. She stood over Kitchener. Four shots had hit his arms and legs, two had been drilled through his lungs. His chest was a mass of gushing, bubbling blood. He still held his rifle in his right hand, thrown out from his right shoulder, the barrel pointing down the levee's sandy slope.

A cloud shadow passed over the hillock and scuttled into the quietly rushing woods.

Kitchener gritted his teeth against the spasming pain. "Didn't figure you could keep that cool head of yours...after what I told ye." He shaped a half-smile with his thin, pink lips. "Damn, you're good."

Claudine poked her rifle barrel against his belly. "Greet the devil for me, you son of a bitch."

Kitchener's eyes snapped wide in horror. "*No!*"

She pulled the trigger, then left him there, squealing and writhing and pissing his pants, his guts bleeding onto the levee.

Carmody stepped out from behind a tree, facing her. She stopped before him. Her face was pale and stony, her eyes hard.

"Did you hear?" she asked.

Clay nodded, looked down. "Figured he was all yours."

"Thanks." She brushed past him, heading for the cabin.

Carmody walked over to finish off the mayor, thought better of it, and walked away.

21

As Kitchener's wails wound down like an old clock, Carmody applied a mud and whiskey poultice to Claudine's grazed temple. Then he and the others hunted up all the horses that had scattered this way and that along the creek.

Carmody gave one of the horses to the man with the smashed knees, leaving it up to the bushwhacker himself to find a way onto its back. He unsaddled and freed the others horses. They'd no doubt head to town or join some prospector's cavy.

Not long after Kitchener's wails died, Carmody, the Indian, Claudine, and Beth set out from the cabin in the late afternoon, heading for the main canyon via the notch in the northern ridge.

"We must ride with great caution, with an ear to the wind," Katch said at the head of the single-file procession, Claudine and Beth behind him, Carmody riding drag. "The beast will know we are coming with the amulet. He will use tricks to try to prevent us from finding him."

"How does he know?" Claudine asked.

The old man stared straight ahead along the twisting mountain path, his horse trotting through patches of late-day sunlight and shade, his silver-streaked hair bouncing on his narrow shoulders. "He will know. Possibly, he *already* knows."

Claudine felt a rake of irritation at the old man's ambiguity.

Clay called over the women's heads, "What I wanna know is how do *you* know where we'll find him?"

The Indian hipped around in his saddle, meeting Clay's puzzled gaze with a darkly certain one of his own. "I am seeing him behind my eyes now, as I talk." With his right hand, he fingered the amulet he wore on a rawhide cord around his neck, and offered a rare, cunning smile before heeling the cayuse into a lope.

Claudine glanced back at Carmody, one dark-blond eyebrow arched beneath her hat brim, then turned around and heeled her own mount after the Indian. The teacher snugged her hat down tight on her head and followed suit.

Alone at the back of the line, Carmody looked around cautiously. "Handy, damn goo-gaw, that amulet." He hitched his Colt on his hip, then put the spurs to the pie.

It was well after dark when Carmody put his pie up beside the Indian's cayuse. "You know where we're headed *exactly?*"

Katch nodded. "There is a lake at the base of the pass. The white man calls it Agnes."

"How much farther?"

"An hour. Maybe more."

"You think it's wise traveling after dark? We can't see shit out here."

The old man glanced at Carmody, his face an oval shadow, his eyes glinting like black quartz beneath the brim of his broad-brimmed hat. "Why do you look for shit, Carmody? It is the beast we seek." He smiled at his joke and turned forward, gazing over his horse's twitching ears.

Carmody turned the pie off the trail and watched the Indian's back disappear in the darkness. Beth passed, shoulders slumped warily. Claudine halted her claybank on the trail beside Carmody's pie.

"Why are we traveling so late?" she asked, the bandage around her forehead showing white. "We can't see shit out here."

"Why are you looking for shit, Sheriff?" Carmody said. "It's the beast we seek."

She chuffed with disgust and gigged her buckskin into a trot.

A half hour later, Carmody was following the others around a long bend in the river when a chill wind pressed against his back, flattening his coat against his shoulders, rippling his hair across his collar.

He looked around, wincing against the chill. Ahead, Claudine twisted around, her eyes fearful. Her long hair blew across her shoulders. Clay took another glance around as the first gust died and another whispered through the pines, smelling faintly of rot.

Ignoring the prickling along the back of his neck, he spat to one side and called ahead to Claudine, "Not every breeze is—"

"There!"

She'd stopped and pointed at a dull light in the woods on the river side of the trail. The glow flickered, seemed to pulsate. It was about the same intensity as a bobcat's eyes staring from the darkness around a campfire. What looked like a lid closed down over the glow.

As the lid started up again, Carmody saw another light in the corner of his right eye. He turned to it. Sure enough...the same damn thing.

"Not this again," he grumbled, reaching down below his right thigh and shucking his Yellowboy. Holding his horse's reins taut in his left hand, he cocked the rifle with the other.

As more lights appeared in pairs all around them, the

horses began to agitate. Beth's Morgan whinnied sharply, and the teacher cursed. "Hold now... Easy....!"

Carmody was having trouble keeping his own horse from pitching, when the Indian called above the river's rush, "Ignore the eyes. They aren't real, but they feast on your fear. Release your fear and cover your horses' eyes, and soon they will fade."

Carmody and the women glanced at each other from atop their prancing, snorting mounts.

Carmody shrugged. "Why not?"

He slipped off his neckerchief and, leaning over his saddle horn, draped the cloth over the pie's eyes. The horse fought him, shaking its head. It lowered its snout, nickering angrily. But the longer Carmody was able to keep the animal's eyes covered, the calmer the pie grew until it stood hipshot in the middle of the trail, withers rippling tensely but its lungs expanding and contracting easily.

He looked around. Claudine had done the same to her claybank, breathing quietly beneath her. Standing beside the trail, Beth held her coat over her Morgan's head with one hand, holding the reins short and firm in the other. She looked around the night-cloaked woods on both sides of the trail, then turned to Clay and Claudine.

Her voice sounded as surprised as relieved. "They're gone."

"Neat trick," Carmody said.

Claudine removed her neckerchief from her claybank's eyes and leaned back in her saddle. "Wish I would have known that one about a month ago."

When Beth had swung up onto her saddle, the women and Carmody gigged their horses up the steeply angling trail, catching up with the Indian ten minutes later, still trotting his stalwart cayuse toward the pass. They rode hard for another three miles until a deep rumbling rose on their right, shaking the earth beneath their horses' hooves.

Carmody sawed back on the pie's reins and looked up at the lumpy, velvet-black scarp looming over the trail. Starlight rippled off plummeting rock. Boulders smashed like cannon fire. The commotion above loosed gravel and smaller rocks below the main slide, showering the trail with debris.

The horses whinnied and crow-hopped.

A stone hit Carmody's hat, canting the brim rakishly over his face and barking across his chin.

"Haul ass!" he shouted, not surprised that the others had already done just that, their silhouettes bounding away ahead of him as small stones peppered the trail, causing the pie to whip right and left with occasional, jarring buck-kicks.

He crouched low in the saddle as the horse galloped up trail. Beth's frightened black appeared out of the darkness, throwing its front hooves high in the air as sand and rocks showered down around it.

The young teacher was yelling at the horse, jerking back on the reins with one hand and clinging to the horn with the other. Her boots slipped from the stirrups and she sagged down toward the horse's pitching hindquarters.

Carmody slowed the pie to a brisk canter and leaned right, grabbing the teacher around the waist. "Let go!"

Beth released the saddle horn and let Carmody pull her back off her horse's bouncing rump. Taking his own reins in his teeth, he grabbed the black's reins and gave them a hard tug. As the pie galloped on past the screaming black, Carmody twisted back to set the teacher behind his cantle and continuing to jerk the bucking black along behind him.

He released the teacher too soon. Beth gave a scream as she slipped down the pie's pounding right hip. Carmody released the black's reins, tightened his arm around Beth, and pulled her up, the pie turning its head and screaming indignantly at its restless driver.

When she was secure, wrapping her arms around Carmody's belly and pressing her head against his back for protection, Clay crouched and gritted his teeth. Larger rocks arced over him—gray, spiraling masses careening through the darkness, landing on the other side of the trail with thunderous roars. Sand and small rocks peppered him, bounced off the horse's shaking head.

Beth gave a sudden, pained cry and tightened her grip around his waist. A wooden crack sounded as a full-grown tree was swept onto the trail only a few feet behind them, its branches popping and snapping as it blew up dust and wind, which smelled of pine sap. The tree narrowly missed the black lunging just off the tail of Carmody's pie, its white-ringed eyes large as dinner plates.

Turning back to face the trail, Carmody was almost surprised to see no more rocks falling before him or over him. On his right, the mountain had pulled back. Stars shone in the open sky. Ahead, Katch and Claudine faced him on their sweat-shiny, head-hung horses.

Carmody pulled up beside Claudine. For a long time they all just sat there, staring back the way they'd come, hearing the last of the boulders hammer into the canyon, thrash the trees and splash into the river. Small rocks and sand continued sifting off the cliff and ticking onto the trail. Dust rose skyward in a gauzy gray mass. The horses snorted and nickered. The black stood a ways off, looking around warily, reins dangling.

Claudine turned to Clay and Beth. "You two all right?"

"Fit as a fiddle." Clay removed his sand-caked hat and thrashed it against his thigh.

"I'm all right," Beth said behind him. "My horse is a little rattled, however." She climbed down from behind Carmody and walked over to the black, cooing to the frightened beast.

Carmody spat grit from his lips. "Sure wish that son of

a bitch would just show himself, so we could get this over with."

On the other side of Claudine, Katch was running a slow gaze from right to left across the canyon. His dark face was dust-caked, giving him a comical look. But his expression was dead serious.

"He will."

The Indian turned his horse around and gigged it up the trail.

THE OLD INDIAN led the weary, dirty procession along the roaring stream for another twenty minutes. They crossed the river on a crude bridge, doubtless erected by fur trappers, then rode through thin, rocky woods before descending a canyon abutted on three sides by toothy granite peaks steepling toward the starlit sky.

A lake nestled in the basin—a flawless sheet of lilac water reflecting the stars, with a wide, shale-covered shoreline. Bleached logs, having fallen from the surrounding ridges, and preserved by the high, dry air and sunlight, lay here and there around the lake, like ancient dinosaur bones.

Carmody guessed they'd climbed several thousand feet since leaving the cabin. Their breath jetted in the still, frigid air, and the water was cold enough to crack teeth.

When he'd stripped the meager tack from his horse, Katch drank some water, took his drum and rattle from his parfleche pouch, and wandered west along the shore. Soon, he was chanting softly, shaking the rattle and lightly tapping the drum. It was a plaintive sound. Carmody couldn't understand the words, but he figured the old Indian was summoning benevolent spirits to help hold the beast at bay...at least for tonight.

When Carmody and the women had built a small fire

and set up camp, Clay poured a cup of coffee and walked in the direction of the chanting until he found the old man standing atop a boulder half-buried in the rocks and sand, facing the glistening lake as he tapped the drum and shook the rattle.

Carmody extended the cup. "Mud?"

Chanting, the old man shook his head.

Carmody looked up at him. "How long you gonna do this?"

Katch paused long enough to say, "All night," then picked the chant up again where he'd left off.

Carmody considered that with a skeptical frown.

"Where we gonna find him?"

The Indian stopped and extended the rattle straight out from his shoulder, aiming it across the water at a tall rock column roughly resembling a castle pediment. It rose from a boulder-strewn ridge to tower a thousand feet above the lake. "His home is there. He'll be waiting with a few tricks up his sleeve. He knows we have the amulet and the bullets that can kill him. His medicine is strong, but for now, mine is stronger. He is scared."

"That mean we shouldn't hear anymore out of him tonight?"

"We shouldn't. But don't stray too far from your rifle." Katch continued chanting.

Glancing skeptically at the rock tower on the other side of the lake, Carmody walked back to the fire.

22

CARMODY WENT SOUTH along the shoreline, under a sky full of stars. He ran his gaze across the black water to his right then left along the beach, looking for any sign of trouble. A hundred yards from the camp, where the shoreline rose sharply from the water—strewn with boulders and stunted pines—he stopped.

The wool collar of his buckskin was raised against the penetrating chill. He stared into the darkness, listening, breath puffing before him.

After a time, he hefted his rifle in both gloved hands, and turned back.

It was at least his fifth trip out here. Unable to sleep, he paced and kept watch. Who knew what the beast would send down on them next?

Ahead, the campfire was a thin, flickering light, reflecting off the oily water to its left. Carmody couldn't see into the darkness beyond the flames, but he could hear the old Indian's plaintive chants. Accompanied by the regular beat of the drum and the rattle, they were constant, with an even pitch, and had become as much a part of the night as the crackling fire, occasional owl hoots, and the water gurgling softly against the shore.

There was a certain tenseness, an occasional hoarseness in the notes, however. It was the only thing which betrayed the old man's struggle with the beast.

Carmody had wandered back and forth from the fire enough times that Claudine had gotten used to his approaching footsteps. Sitting on the barkless, deadfall log about six feet back from the flames and the stack of dead branches they'd gathered and piled beside it, she merely glanced over her steaming coffee cup at him.

Lying several feet to her right, Beth started at Clay's chinging spurs. She lifted her head sharply from her saddle, on which she'd been dozing, and reached for her rifle. Seeing Carmody, she relaxed and sagged back against the saddle with a weary groan.

Clay leaned his rifle against the log and squatted before the fire, a few feet left of Claudine. He picked up a charred rawhide scrap and used it to pluck the coffee pot from a flat rock in a corner of the fire ring. He reached over and filled Claudine's cup, glancing into her face.

Her eyes plaintive, she watched the tar-black coffee stream into her cup. She did not look at Clay, only said, "Thanks," when her cup was full.

Carmody returned the pot to the flat rock, dropped the rawhide scrap, and took his own steaming cup in both hands. He blew ripples on the surface.

"Pretty big shock, I'd reckon—findin' out ole Kitchener killed your pa." He sipped the hot belly wash then swallowed.

"Because of me," Claudine said, staring into the fire.

"Well, you got him."

"Doesn't change the fact that Pa's dead... All on account of Kitchener bein' horny for his daughter." Claudine's eyes glistened. She squeezed them closed, and tears welled out from behind the lids, dribbled down her smooth, tanned, tapering cheeks. She ground a boot heel into the rocks. "Damn!"

"Hey," Carmody said, taking his cup in his right hand and extending his arm to her. She slid down the log to him, leaned against his chest as his arm wrapped around her shoulders.

She sobbed quietly for a minute, sniffed, and glanced up at him. "I wish we were alone, and all this was over."

He held her close, kissed her temple. "It will be soon."

"But will we still be alive?"

Carmody lifted his gaze to the dark sky beyond the fire. "That's the question."

When they finished their coffee, they slid down to the ground, rested their backs against the log, intending only to doze for a few minutes. But later, when Carmody's chin came off his chest with a start, and his eyes snapped wide, the false dawn had turned the darkness faintly milky, limning the eastern ridges.

Something was wrong.

Awakened by Clay's movement, Claudine lifted her head from his chest with a faint, startled gasp, and reached for her rifle. "What is it?"

Carmody looked around, listening. To his right, a few feeble flames licked at two charred logs in the fire ring, guttering in the cold breeze. Birds chirped in the sparse pines lining the lake. The water lapped softly against the rocks, sounding like someone swallowing, over and over.

"Katch ain't chanting anymore."

Carmody grabbed his Yellowboy and stood heavily, his legs and back stiff and creaky. Hearing his boots crunching gravel, Beth lifted her head sharply, slapped the Spencer rifle beside her.

Anticipating her question, Clay said, "Ain't sure."

As he strode out toward the boulder where he'd left the old Indian last night, the women followed. They stopped walking when the vague light revealed the boulder. The Indian was no longer standing on it. Carmody dropped his gaze left, where a figure sat at the base of the boulder, slumped back against the rock.

Carmody moved forward and left, dropped to a knee beside the figure. He squinted his eyes, balled his cheeks with revulsion.

Resting against the boulder was a desiccated cadaver in Katch's deerskin coat, fringed hide leggings, and fur-trimmed mocassins. Coarse, gray hair tufted from dark patches of skin across the skull. Eyes bulged grotesquely from bony sockets. Thin, purple lips stretched wide, revealing withered black gums and long, rotten teeth all the way to the roots.

On the chest lay a drum and the amulet, the cords of both encircling the bony neck. Near the gloveless left hand, curled as if to grasp, lay the rattle.

Carmody's heart raced. He looked over at Claudine, hunkered down beside him, staring with disbelief at the corpse. She didn't look at him, but kept her eyes glued on the old Indian, who looked as though he'd been dug up from a long repose in an air-tight grave.

"He lost." The voice belonged to Beth.

At once, Carmody and Bridger turned their heads to look behind and up. The teacher stood a few feet back toward the fire, staring stonily down at the body.

"He lost the fight with the beast," she said. "And went back to where he came from."

Claudine licked her lips. "Which is...?"

"Dead. Three hundred and fifty years ago." Beth stepped between them, knelt on one knee, set her rifle against the boulder, and gently removed the amulet from the Indian's neck. "He was sent here by the spirits of his ancestors, to kill the beast that my father and brothers and I awakened."

She draped the amulet around her neck, ran her hand affectionately down the Indian's fur-covered shoulder. "Now, I guess, it's our turn."

Before either Carmody or Claudine could respond, a hollow wail rose, as though from a giant bullhorn, from the other side of the lake. It echoed off the ridges. Somewhere behind them, a magpie screeched. The wind began blowing.

Carmody stood and faced the stone pediment, a looming, black outline against the lightening sky, swept by strands of wind-torn, purple fog. A fine rain began to fall, hanging like gauze over the water.

Again, the horn sounded.

Carmody opened and closed his hands around the Yellowboy's stock. "Reckon we're bein' summoned."

It didn't take them long to douse the fire and saddle their horses.

As the fire steamed behind him, Carmody mounted the pie and shucked his Winchester from the saddle scabbard. Taking the rifle in his right hand, he pulled his left glove off with his teeth, reached into his jeans pocket for the ten bullets the old Indian had blessed. He pushed the bullets through the receiver's loading door, cocked the rifle, then off-cocked the hammer and extended the other five shells to Claudine, who stood to his right, adjusting her bay's bridle.

"Load your rifle with these."

The Sheriff didn't hesitate or ask for an explanation. With a quick glance at Carmody, she accepted the five shells, shucked her rifle, and thumbed the shells through the receiver's door. She mounted up and turned to Beth, just then mounting her own black, the teacher's face red from the damp chill.

"Sure you wanna do this?" Claudine asked her.

"Of course I do," the teacher said, faintly indignant. "Besides, I have to go. Katchi-lo-go-we taught me the chant to be said over the beast's carcass. It's like a hex, helps the amulet take effect." Her voice grew hard. "It'll keep that *thing* from ever coming back and killing again."

Claudine neck-reined her horse southward, snugged her hat low on her head, and gigged the bay into a trot. "Let's go."

Glancing up at the rock monolith towering across the lake, clearly visible now through the gray mist, Carmody waited for Beth to pull out, then reined in behind the women. He'd keep an eye on their backtrail, make sure the beast didn't try to sneak up behind them.

The horses picked their way up the rocky, eastern slopes, leaving the thin, altitude-stunted forest behind and traversing the precipitous ridges and jagged cliffs like mountain goats, steadily rising toward the base of the beast's monolith shrouded in lightly falling snow.

When they'd climbed for two hours, the horn blast sounded again.

Carmody's horse whinnied. Lifting his Winchester from across his saddlebows, Clay looked around.

They were on a rocky ridge, about fifteen feet wide, spread out single-file along a game path littered with elk and bear scat. Junipers grew low against the rocks. To Carmody's right, a pica squeaked and scuttled into a burrow between two boulders. To his left, a wall of carelessly piled rocks rose about twenty feet high, damp with melted snow.

"Came from over there," he said, nodding toward the low scarp and, holding the pie's reins taut in his right hand, swung down from his saddle.

He gave his reins to Beth, sitting her black twenty feet ahead, then turned and climbed the scarp, his boots slipping on the wet rocks. It wasn't a tough climb but, unaccustomed to the altitude, he was breathing hard when he reached the crest, the vapor puffs bisected by the slanting, blowing snow.

He looked down the other side. His stomach tightened, and he raised the Winchester high before his chest. Hearing boots scraping rocks behind and right, he held his gaze on the macabre figure clinging to the scaly face of the towering crag, on the other side of a bowl-shaped, rocky gorge.

The beast stared toward him, its large black eyes peering from the round, pale skull capped with wiry black hair falling straight back over its thick, furry neck and shoulders. Its back hoofs were dug into the narrow shelf beneath the horse-sized, goat-shaped body, while its front feet were dug into the wall above its head.

"Jesus Christ—is that it?" Claudine crouched to Carmody's right, her moisture beaded Winchester in both gloved hands.

"Sad to say, it is indeed."

"Christ!"

"Pretty, ain't he?"

As they stared through the slanting snow, the beast stared back, massive puffs of breath billowing about its head. Its man-like chin rose, bottom jaw dropping, mouth forming an oval the size of a dinner plate.

The horn-like bellow sounded, shrill as a train whistle. Carmody winced against the shock to his eardrums, and raised his rifle.

"Open wide one more time, you pig faced—!" He aimed at the beast's head, squeezed the trigger. The rifle lurched and boomed, the smell of cordite mixing with the stony smell of the frigid air.

Carmody stared through the smoke. The beast had moved left as Clay squeezed the trigger, the slug slamming into the rock as the beast bounded up the rocky scales, moving with surprising fluidity for an abomination of its shape and size. In seconds, it was twenty feet above the shelf, weaving criss-cross patterns as it made for the monolith's toothy peak.

Claudine fired, drilling the rock right of the beast's pistoning right rear hoof. Carmody triggered the Yellowboy, his slug pounding wide as the beast pivoted left, making for a slotted cave opening about fifty feet down from the peak.

The creature scampered up the rocks beneath the hole and heaved itself onto the cave's lip. Turning, it faced Clay and Claudine, lifted its head, loosed another shrill, tooth-gnashing cry, then shifted and disappeared into the chasm.

Carmody stared over his rifle's barrel, not wanting to waste anymore of the old Indian's bullets. "Moves like an Apache horse drunk on tizwin."

"Looks like he's trying to lure us into that cave."

Carmody ejected the spent shell casing, staring at the steep cliff face. "Wouldn't be nice to disappoint him, but how in the hell we gonna get there?"

The drop from the top to the cave was sheer, as was the ascent from the bottom of the gorge. The prospect of trying such a climb made Carmody's oysters tingle with vertigo.

"Looks to me like the best way would be to go on up to the top. See that notch? We could leave the horses there and climb down."

"Fall down, you mean." Carmody's loins were really tingling now.

"Come on," Claudine said, tapping his shoulder, then rising and heading back toward Beth and the horses.

The teacher was sitting her black, holding her rifle across the saddlebows. Snow flecked the brim of her felt hat. "Find our friend?"

Carmody took his reins from her. "Snugged inside that cliff like a damn mountain goat."

"What does he look like?"

"Your worst nightmare." Carmody swung into the saddle and gigged the pie up past the two women, taking the lead. He kept seeing Nathan's butchered body lying atop the rock, and, in spite of his apprehension about descending the cliff face, his heart thudded with fury and the thirst for revenge.

They could ride for only a few more minutes, before the trail petered out and acquired a forty-five degree grade. Hobbling the horses, Carmody, Claudine, and Beth shucked their rifles and climbed the wagon-sized boulders to the notch in the cliff edge. Looking down, Carmody saw a dark slice, which, from this angle, bespoke the cave.

The bowl-shaped gorge fanned out a thousand feet below, gray with fog and snow. The ground beneath Carmody's boots seemed to shift like a slow ocean swell. His knees turned to putty.

Claudine glanced at him, snow in her hair and eyelashes, her cheeks damp and red from the cold and slicing wind. "You afraid of heights?"

Realizing his face must have bleached, Carmody took an involuntary step back from the ledge. "I don't know—I've never been this high before."

"You better let us go."

"Like hell."

Claudine dropped to a knee to inspect the cliff face. To her right, Beth did the same thing.

Carmody resisted the urge to pull them back.

"Nothing to it," the teacher said, loud enough to be heard above the wind. "My brothers and I used to climb grades like this all the time. It's really not as steep as it looks, and there's plenty of shelves and crevices. Just climb with your face to the cliff. You'll be fine."

With that, Beth stood and began moving quickly but carefully over the rocks, dropping into the gorge. A few yards below the ledge, she took her rifle in one hand, turned to face the cliff, and began picking foot and hand holds, dropping steadily as she angled toward the cave.

"Christ," Carmody said as the teacher disappeared behind the snow veil.

Claudine glanced at him, giving his coat sleeve a tug. "Don't look down. Just—"

"I can handle it!"

Smiling ruefully, Claudine turned and began climbing down the way Beth had gone. In seconds she was nearly consumed by the wet-dark rocks and snow.

Carmody gave the cliff face another study. The dizziness would not pass. Inside his gloves, his hands were hot and sweat-slick. Almost worse than the fear itself was the fear of the fear.

Release it, spoke a voice inside his head.

"Release it, hell," he grumbled, and, gritting his teeth willed his knees to bend.

Turning, taking his rifle in his left hand while clinging to each rock with his right as though to the very hand of God himself, Carmody cursed and started down...

23

CARMODY WISHED like hell he'd fashioned a lanyard for his rifle. It was damn hard, climbing down a steep mountain cliff using only his right hand and his feet.

Looking down, he couldn't see much of the cave except for the shelf the beast had been standing on earlier. Both women were there now; he could see their hats and rifle barrels protruding from the cliff face. He figured he was a little over halfway there.

Taking a deep breath and returning his gaze to the rocks he clung to, he hefted his rifle in the crook of his left arm, settled his weight on his boots dug into two separate fissures, then removed his right hand from the rock it had been grasping like a calf's mouth around a heifer's tit.

As he did so, his left boot slipped from its crack. Clay dropped like a loosened stone, straight down, feet first, face and knees skidding off the rocks protruding from the cliff face, his gut barreling straight up into his throat. With his right hand and both feet, refusing to give up the rifle until he had no other choice, he flailed at the cliff for purchase.

A high-pitched squeal rose inside his head as he envisioned the cosmos opening wide for him.

His right foot slammed into something ungiving. A

half-second later, his right hand grabbed an arrow-shaped rock, his gloved fingers digging in. He heard himself grunt and curse, breathing hard.

His gut slowly dropped back toward his middle. He stared at the rocks a few inches from his face, noticing every shade and pica fleck and hair-like fissure.

Snot dribbled from his nose and into his lips. He spit it away, cursed again, heard the voices of the women somewhere below. How the hell did they get down there so damn fast?

Through tear-glazed eyes, he looked down. His foot had smashed down on a petrified tree root.

"What are they—damn mountain sheep?"

Heart hammering his breast bone, he grunted, spat, cursed, saw a shelf below his left foot, and, muttering the words of a prayer he thought he'd long since forgotten, moved toward it. It didn't look solid, and he half expected it to slip out from the mountain wall.

It didn't.

He continued down, cursing under his breath. When he dropped onto the cave shelf a few minutes later, his knees quivering and his heart still hammering, Beth and Claudine each took an arm and pulled him to his feet.

"Sorry you had to see that," he groused, turning his head to spit over the side of the ledge.

"I've seen worse," Claudine said. "You all right?"

"You'll never catch me this high up in the mountains again." He took his Yellowboy in both hands, and crouched to peer into the cave's deep shadows. "Any sign of our boy yet?"

"Not yet."

Carmody jacked a shell into the Yellowboy's chamber. "Well, let's get this over with and find us a saloon somewhere. I'm real thirsty, of a sudden..."

Holding the rifle straight out before him in both hands, he ducked his head under the cave's low ceiling, putting one foot in front of the other as he entered the chasm's dank, stony-smelling interior. As he walked, Claudine on his right, Beth flanking them, he raked his gaze from left to right. There wasn't much to see but two stone walls, a low stone ceiling from which white fossil chips protruded, and a stony, uneven floor.

Carmody wished he'd brought a torch of some kind, because the light from the cave's entrance quickly thinned. He sure as hell wasn't going to try to confront that beast in the dark. *It* could probably see in the dark. That might be why it lured them in here.

That suspicion waned, however, when, as they rounded a slight bend in the corridor, dim light shone ahead, seeming to fall from above. Carmody and the women approached the gray light striping the downward-canting floor, and looked up. A deep crack, no more than a foot wide, rose from the right center of the ceiling to the top of the cliff.

The smooth, granite slabs on each side of the crack were lumpy with the nests of cliff swallows, rife with the smell of mud and bat guano. Cool, moist air bathed their faces, and they could see snow slanting against the gunmetal sky at the crack's mouth. The fissure didn't offer much light, but, casting his gaze forward, Carmody saw more such strips ahead.

They walked slowly, swinging their heads around, listening intently, their tenseness and anxiety etched in their faces. But for the slight clack of their heels on the stone floor, and the thuds of their heartbeats in their ears, there was no sound whatever.

A few feet beyond the ceiling crack, the ceiling rose a foot and a half, making it possible for Clay to walk without bending his head. As they moved slowly toward the next strip of gray light about forty yards ahead, Claudine stopped. "What's that?"

"What's what?"

“That.” The Sheriff extended her rifle barrel, canted slightly down, indicating what appeared to be a circle of stones at the near edge of the next light strip.

They approached the ring, stopped a few feet away. It was a ring of stones, all right, with small objects of various sizes, none larger than a man’s fist, arranged within. Carmody knelt to inspect them closely, made a face as Beth, who knelt between him and Claudine, made a guttural retching sound.

“God!” She covered her mouth and swallowed to keep from vomiting.

“Hearts,” Claudine said. “*Human* hearts.”

Carmody let his breath out slowly as he studied each organ, some shriveled to the size of plums. He counted twenty-eight. Most were black and rawhide-hard, having been cured like leather by the high, dry air. One was fairly fresh. Judging by its size and pinkness, only a few days old. It sat in the middle of the ring.

Nathan’s heart.

“So this is what that bastard does with ‘em.”

“It’s like an offering,” Beth said. “An evil offering—to evil spirits.” She stood and, backing away from Clay and Claudine, turned toward the right wall and vomited. A sob could be heard amidst the retching—for her own family whose wizened hearts were probably part of the beast’s macabre collection.

When she stopped, Claudine placed a hand on her arm. “You going to be all right?”

Beth nodded.

Carmody had straightened and taken a step forward when the beast’s hideous bellow sounded once more. Carmody froze, stared ahead as the echo slowly faded.

“Gettin’ impatient,” he said, his voice sounded unnaturally loud in the ensuing silence. He tried to ignore the chills crawling up the backs of his legs.

“I am, too,” Beth said angrily, clearing her throat and

hefting her rifle. She moved up beside Clay, staring straight down the corridor, lips pursed, eyes determined.

As they resumed their slow trek through the cave, Claudine brought up the rear, twisting and turning to make sure the beast didn't somehow sneak up behind them. Thirty yards beyond where they'd found the stone ring and the hearts, the cave forked, splitting into two corridors.

"Come out, come out, where ever you are," Claudine sang softly, glancing both ways.

"Best split up," Carmody said. He suggested the women explore the right fork while he check the left. "See anything, shoot first and ask questions later."

"Don't be givin' me orders, Carmody," Claudine said as she and Beth were consumed by the shadows of the corridor's right fork, their boots scuffing along the pitching floor. Claudine's voice echoed, quietly playful, but betraying her fear. "I'm the law in these parts...or haven't you...?"

Then her voice faded, and the women were gone.

Clay found himself strolling solo down the cave's left branch, moving faster now, anxiety gnawing at him, but eager to drill a couple of Katch's special slugs through the beast's ugly hide, and get the hell out of here. He'd prospected many caves in his time on the frontier, but suddenly he'd become as adverse to enclosed spaces underground as he was to high spaces above.

Something moved ahead of him, silhouetted by another skylight—this one a circular chimney running up from the left wall. Carmody stopped, muscles turning to stone. He raised the rifle slightly.

Whatever it was, it wasn't the beast. It was too small and moving too slowly. A scuffing sounded, like heeled shoes dragged across the stone floor.

Carmody waited. The thing moved toward him slowly, hugging the left wall. The scuffing grew louder.

His breath coming fast, Carmody raised the rifle to his shoulder, thumbed the hammer back. "Okay, what are you?"

The figure had a human form, hunched and scuffling toward Clay, crouched like an old lady or a hunchback. Vagrant gray light shone briefly on a forehead. A right arm jerked back and forth.

"Name yourself!" Clay ordered, staring down the Yellowboy's barrel.

The figure kept coming, the shoe scuffs growing louder. A voice pierced the cave's silence, an old lady's thin, halting voice, "S-son, that you?"

Carmody's heart stopped for several seconds.

"Clay?" the old woman said as she drew closer. It was, indeed, an old woman, Carmody saw now, the wan light trimming her decrepit form. She wore her silver hair long, falling straight down her hunched back.

"Stop right there!" Carmody ordered.

The old lady, who looked like Carmody's dead mother, Lottie Carmody, stopped in the wall shadows, regarded him sourly as she clutched one bony hand in the other. "You wouldn't shoot me, would you, son?"

Carmody didn't say anything. His heart beat irregularly and his legs were weak, but he kept the rifle snugged up against his shoulder. He stared down the slightly shaking barrel.

"You ain't my ma. She's dead."

"I've come back, Clay. Put that gun down and tell me how it was I raised you wrong."

"What?"

"What'd I do wrong?"

"What're you talkin' about?"

The old woman scuttled closer, the hem of her gray dress with crisp pleats and black buttons—her favorite Sunday picnic dress—swishing about her legs and square-healed, black shoes.

"Stop!" Carmody shouted.

She didn't stop until she was ten feet away, till he could smell the old smell of her. She smelled of lye soap, buttermilk, hot irons, firewood, wheat flour, root cellars, and that extra thing that smelled like nothing else except his mother.

His mother...dead now, these thirteen years.

"You're wanted by the law, son." It was Lottie Carmody's voice. She lifted her head at an angle, looking at him as though trying to puzzle him out. "They say you killed a man. I say, how could it be that my son killed a man? I didn't raise my children to kill."

Carmody swallowed the dry knot in his throat. A wetness formed on his cheek. Through tear-glazed eyes, he stared down the quivering rifle barrel, keeping the sights planted on his mother's chest.

"It's a trumped up charge, Momma. I didn't do it."

"You're a disappointment to me, son...one of my only two surviving boys..."

Carmody gritted his teeth and tried to steady his aim. "Damnit, my mama's dead. I planted her back in Iowa! You ain't my mama."

"Your father an' me—he's with me here, too, on the other side—we're both just so disappointed... To think we raised a son who'd go West to become an outlaw. A common killer!"

"Stay back."

Six feet away, the old woman canted her head sharply, gray eyes beseeching as she extended her gnarled hands toward Carmody. "Give me the rifle, son. You don't want to kill me—your own mother."

Carmody stepped back, stumbled over a slight rise in the floor. As he did so, he squeezed the rifle's trigger. The explosion rocked his eardrums. He brought his other foot back, raked the heel against the same rise he'd raked the other one, and stumbled backward.

The beast's wail blared like someone screaming into Carmody's ears through a bullhorn. Clay hit the ground and squinted through the powder smoke. The beast ran back the other way, down the center of the dim corridor, its hooves clacking like goat hooves. Swinging its head from side to side, it loosed one enraged wail after another. Echoing, the wails faded.

In the musty air hung a horrible fetor, like bear viscera left in the sun.

Lifting onto his elbows and wincing against the stench, Carmody looked over his shoulder, half-expecting to see or hear the women running toward him. They certainly would have heard the beast's wail if not his rifle shot. But the corridor was silent.

Looking forward again, he saw small dark splashes of blood on the floor. Torn between wondering where the women were and wanting to catch up to the beast, which he had wounded, he opted for the beast.

He jacked a fresh shell into the Winchester's breech and started forward. The chamber narrowed and widened as it zigzagged through the rock, the ceiling sometimes dropping to within five feet of the floor. There were stretches of utter darkness before another crack offered weak light from outside.

Carmody had walked nearly a hundred yards before Claudine's voice sounded ahead of him. He couldn't make out what she was saying, but it was her, all right. How did she get ahead?

Clay stopped, listened.

Eyes snapping wide, he bolted forward, his blood pounding.

"*Claudine!*"

24

Carmody ran through the stygian darkness. He barked a knee off a rock protruding from the cave wall, and fell cursing. Wheezing and clutching his knee, he hoisted himself to his feet with his rifle and continued running at half-speed, dragging the injured limb until the pain abated.

Ahead, Claudine's voice mingled with that of a man.

"Shoot the son of a bitch!" Carmody shouted, wincing as another spasm drilled his knee like a .44 slug.

Light shone ahead. Fresh air bathed his face. He rounded a thumb in the curving chasm, the cave receding, and he found himself on the exposed side of the mountain, the ceiling having either eroded or been raked off the mountain by an earthquake.

He blinked against the sudden light and pelting snow. The wind blew his hat off.

Ahead, beyond the rubble of strewn rocks and boulders, Claudine held her rifle straight out at her waist. The barrel was aimed at a short, stocky man in a long duster and a black, broad-brimmed, bullet-crowned hat. From his angle, Carmody could see only the right side of his face—brick-red and furry with gray mutton-chop whiskers.

His experience with his 'mother' and the expression on

Claudine's face told him who it was, or who it was supposed to be.

"Shoot him!"

As the old man moved slowly toward Claudine, Carmody bolted around a low boulder and began raising his rifle to his shoulder. He didn't see the hole before the ground suddenly fell away beneath him. His rifle clattered somewhere into the dark depths beneath his boots.

"Carmody!" Claudine shouted.

Grunting and wincing, Clay looked up. He'd fallen about five feet down the hole before his hands grabbed a narrow rock shelf, the near side of which knifed painfully into his wrists. He dug his fingertips in, desperately trying to maintain his hold. The time it took his rifle to hit bottom told him the pit was a good hundred feet deep.

Clay scraped his boot toes against the side of the hole, feeling for purchase. A face appeared above—the visage of a weathered old man, with blue-eyes, gray mustache and mutton-chop whiskers. A five-pointed sheriff's star clung to a brown wool vest beneath the ratty duster. The silver-tipped ends of the man's black bolo tie flipped around in the wind.

The oldster stuck a big, brown hand into the hole, his broad, handsome, sun-seasoned face flushed from exertion. "Let me give you a hand there, young man!"

Carmody shifted his hands on the ledge, scraped his boots against the side of the hole, fighting for a better purchase. "Get the hell away from me!"

The man's lips shaped a smile inside the gray mustache. His grim eyes held Carmody's.

"You don't wanna fall, do you?"

"Get away!" Claudine ordered. She appeared at the top of the hole, pointing her rifle at the old man.

Again, Carmody shifted his hands on the ledge, knocking stones and gravel loose from the sides of the hole. "Claudine, he's not your father!"

"I said get away!" Claudine screamed at the old man, waving her rifle.

"Shoot him!"

Backing away from the hole, hands raised palms out, the old man said, "I'm not the beast, honey. I'm Dad—your old man! I was sent back, just like the old Indian, to help you fight that miserable thing. He's probably chasing down the schoolteacher while we're standin' around here jawin'."

Carmody stared up the hole. He'd gotten a hold on another, slightly higher ledge and was inching toward the surface.

Claudine dropped to one knee by the pit and thrust her left hand toward Clay. "Take my hand!" She looked up as the old man edged toward her. "Stay there!"

He backed up, raising his hands higher. "Damnit, Claudine, you're as mule-headed as your mother. I can help!"

Carmody didn't want to take her hand. He knew that if he did, the beast would take advantage of the diversion, probably shove her into the hole on top of him, and they'd both fall to the bottom. Carmody reached up, rammed his fingers into a cleft, and jerked himself a few inches higher, wincing against the strain.

"Claudine, you gotta shoot him," Clay spat through gritted teeth.

She glanced down, her eyes tear-glazed. Her hat was gone, and her wind-blown hair danced about her face. Her expression betrayed genuine frustration and sorrow. "I can't!"

"Look out!"

She jerked her gaze around as the old man took two quick steps toward her, but she couldn't get the rifle aimed before, with one vicious upswing of his right foot, he kicked the rifle out of her hands. She grabbed her .45, but before she could raise it, he backhanded her, snapping her head back savagely and flinging her back away from the hole.

Rage seared Carmody. "Claudine!"

The old man canted a look down the pit, smiled with self-satisfaction. He looked around, moved away from the hole before reappearing at the edge, holding Claudine's rifle. Looking down at Carmody, he thumbed the Winchester's hammer back.

"How 'bout I drill you with one o' them bullets you think so highly of?" He grinned, showing tobacco-stained teeth through the mustache as he stared down the hole at Clay. "What do you think about *that?*"

"Bastard," Carmody grated out as he maneuvered a little higher, feeling a hard, sour knot in his gut. Determined not to look at the beast, but to focus only on climbing out of the hole, Carmody lowered his gaze to a rock six inches above his right hand.

As he reached for it, a rifle cracked. He jerked, tensed, heart thudding. He stared at his hand, continued reaching for the stone. As the hand wrapped around it, he looked up. The old man stood over him, head lifted skyward, face bunched in a painful wince. Blood spurted from a hole in his neck, just above his left shoulder.

He released the Winchester. It dropped down the hole, the barrel glancing off Carmody's right temple. The beast staggered back and away, loosing an earth-shuddering wail. There was a thud as its body hit the ground.

Another shot sounded.

Hooves clopped on the stones. The beast wailed shrilly.

Carmody pulled himself up by the stone, kicking his feet against the wall, grunting with the effort. He edged a look over the lip. Beth ran toward him from the cavern on the other side of the roofless cleft. Kneeling beside the pit, she set her smoking rifle down and wrapped both hands around Clay's upper right arm, pulling. "I was exploring another branch when I heard voices."

Carmody crawled out of the pit and sagged onto his

right shoulder. His arms were heavy and sore, his fingers bloody, sand and gravel sticking to them.

Beth looked down at him. "You okay?"

"Where is he...it?"

"I hit him, but he got away...down the side."

"Christ!" Carmody climbed heavily to his feet, limped over to the edge of the cliff. Placing his hands on a flat-topped boulder for support, he stared down the side.

The beast moved like a phantom bighorn sheep, descending the cliff in a lumbering, slightly tottering gate. It lifted its head, and as it disappeared around a shoulder of the cliff, a wail rose skyward, echoing softly in the snowy silence.

Carmody turned around. Beth crouched over Claudine, who lay between two boulders, limbs akimbo, head to one side. She blinked her eyes, shifted her feet, but did not try to stand.

Carmody ran over to the women, grabbed Claudine's hand as if to wake her. "Go after the beast," Beth said. "Finish him off!"

"Both our rifles are at the bottom of the pit!"

"Take my Spencer." The teacher picked the rifle off the ground, tossed it to Carmody, who caught it one-handed. "Katch blessed bullets for me when he first came to town. You'll have four more shots."

Carmody straightened, looked at the rifle, and then turned to Claudine.

"I'll take care of her," Beth said.

Hefting the old Spencer in both hands, Clay crossed to the edge of the cliff. He started down, stepping quickly from one boulder to the other, tracing the path the beast had taken, his vertigo gone. He was a lot lower on the mountain here, a boulder-strewn notch between two peaks only a hundred yards down the easy grade.

The biggest problem was snow and ice. He slipped twice on the slick rocks, so that by the time he made the notch, he'd torn a nasty gash on the underside of his right arm.

Looking around the boulders rising to his right, he walked slowly along the notch, holding the old Spencer up high across his chest. He spotted something on a rock and moved to it. A snow-flecked blood splotch dripped down the side of a cracked, triangular boulder. Climbing higher, he found more blood, followed the beast's path over the rise and into another, shallower notch.

He crossed a freshet of water steaming down from a hot springs up higher in the gorge, snake fog rising from its surface. As he began climbing a scarp, something moved ahead and left.

It was the beast, bounding down from a low rise spiked with several spindly firs. It wailed, the noise sounding like a steam locomotive barreling down on him.

Startled, Carmody levered the Spencer and pulled the trigger, then cursed as the precious slug spanged off a rock. He dropped to a knee as the beast approached, weaving around firs and boulders, loosing its enraged wails which echoed like thunder around the canyon.

It leapt to a slight ridge crest, giving Carmody a big target. Clay fired, cursed as the weirdly moaning wind caught another slug, sailed it wide. The beast continued lunging toward him, round eyes flashing fire, vapor jetting from its nostrils. Swinging its head and whipping its wiry hair, it disappeared into a hollow.

Carmody drew air through his teeth and aimed down the barrel, waiting for the beast to emerge. He couldn't risk wasting another shell. He'd wait until the beast was practically on top of him to trigger another shot.

Something moved above the hollow's brow. A human head.

It rose slowly, revealing hunched shoulders, scissoring arms, and the bulky, stooped torso of an old woman in a gray-black dress. At the crest, the woman sagged to her knees, holding a bony hand to the side of her bleeding neck. She stared down at Carmody, head canted to her bloody shoulder.

"Clay...?"

Carmody lowered the rifle and straightened. "You bastard."

"Clay, please... Help...."

Carmody spat to one side and walked forward, holding the rifle straight out before him. He climbed the low rise and stopped, looking down at his mother staring up at him with her round, milky eyes. Blood seeped out from the hole in her wrinkled neck, soaking the shoulder and arm of her favorite Sunday picnic dress.

"Help, me, Clay. Won't you help your poor ma?"

Carmody glanced at the old woman's eyes. He raised the rifle, thrust the Spencer's barrel into her mouth, and turned away.

"All right...*Ma.*"

Carmody pulled the trigger. Keeping his head turned to the side, he squeezed his eyes shut. The smell of cordite was swept away on the wind. A heavy, sickening fetor pushed against him, like a hot wind over a gut pile.

He opened his eyes.

The beast lay before him, sprawled on its side, its bloody head facing the ridge crest. It didn't move. The back of its head was blown out, brains and bone splashed across its thick, fur-covered shoulders. Carmody winced at the stench, turned upwind, and inhaled fresh air.

"Nice shootin', Carmody." It was Claudine's voice.

He turned quickly to see her and Beth moving up the slope behind him, snow slanting against them, the wind thrashing their coats. Claudine was pale and moving slower, but she looked all right. The women stood over the beast, wincing against the smell.

"You two okay?"

Beth nodded as she stared down at the beast without expression.

Claudine offered a wan smile. "Got anything for a headache?"

Carmody released her arm, walked upwind, and sank down on a rock, still seeing his mother's eyes looking up at him. He felt as though he'd lived a hundred years and every one had been a hard one.

He brushed dust and snow from his chin and, puffing his cheeks, blew out a deep, relieved breath.

USING THE HORSES, they dragged the beast over to a deep pit formed by a long-defunct spring, and rolled the body into the hole. Beth tossed the amulet on top of the fetid carcass then uttered the chants she'd been taught by the old Indian.

As the snow continued falling and darkness filled the chasm, she, Claudine, and Carmody caved rocks and boulders into the pit, until the beast was so buried that nothing short of an earthquake could ever exhume it.

They camped that night in the lee of a rocky ridge, surrounded by pines, and were on the trail back to the cabin before dawn the next morning.

"Well, this is where we separate," Beth said when, at three o'clock the next afternoon they approached the trail that cut over to the side canyon in which Carmody and Laroque had prospected.

Claudine rode beside her, Carmody bringing up the rear, smoking lazily in his saddle, his left leg draped over the horn. They'd left the snow back at Cameron pass. The afternoon was warm and sunny, the air spiced cinnamon, the aspens touched with the gold of mountain fall.

Claudine turned to the teacher. "What're you talking

about? We're going to rest up in the cabin before heading back to town."

"No, *you* are. I have to get back to school." Beth looked up at the sky. "There's a good three or four hours of light left. I'll ride until dark and hole up in one of the many empty cabins I'll find down canyon... Thanks to the beast. I'll get an early start in the morning and be back to town by nightfall."

Claudine shook her head. "Beth—"

"I'll be fine." The teacher turned in her saddle to glance at Carmody. Turning back to Claudine, she winked conspiratorially.

The Sheriff flushed.

Beth halted the black. She was trailing the Indian's old cayuse by its reins, and turned to Clay. "I don't know how to thank you..."

Carmody shook his head. "No need, Teacher."

"This was all my fault... Mine and my..."

"Like the man said," Claudine interrupted, "no need, Beth."

Beth nodded slightly, looking down at the black's glistening mane. "My family is resting easier. I can feel it. And so is Katchi-lo-go-we."

She leaned left and hugged Claudine tightly, then leaned the other way, hugged Carmody, and kissed his cheek. She reined the black around and gigged him up the trail. "I'll see you back in town," she said, throwing up a hand.

"Travel safe, teacher," Carmody called after her. When Beth disappeared around a trail bend, he turned to Claudine. "You in a hurry to get back to the cabin?"

She squinted one hat brim-shaded eye at him. "What do you have in mind?"

"I know where we can get a hot bath for cheap."

She blinked slowly, the corners of her mouth rising. "Lead the way."

Later, when they'd ridden up a rocky, forested ridge, and unsaddled their horses, Carmody climbed naked into a bubbling hot spring nestled deep in a fir-lined rock cleft. The water chugged and swirled as is seeped up from the ground, chickadees piping in the branches.

Clay winced as he eased into the water, his skin turning pink. Puffing a quirley, he leaned back, stretched out his feet, and regarded Claudine on the other side of the smoking pool.

The Sheriff had taken off everything but her long, men's underwear, hat, and socks. She was smoking a thin, black cigar. As she bent forward to remove her gray socks, her breasts heaved up from the underwear top, straining the buttons till they appeared about to pop.

"You know I been thinkin'," Carmody said, feeling his loins stir beneath the water's bubbling, gently churning surface. "We make a pretty good team."

"Oh?"

"Maybe we should get hitched."

She tossed her socks onto her jeans then turned to Clay,planting both hands on her gently rounded hips. "Let me see—you're wanted and you have no steady means of earning a living. Don't think my father would approve..."

Carmody squinted as he ran his gaze down from the Sheriff's smoking cigar to her full, round breasts visible through the wash-worn underwear top, flattened slightly against her chest and framed by her long, golden hair.

He chuckled. "Well, that makes us even, 'cause my ma wouldn't approve of you."

Full lips stretching an earthy smile, Sheriff Bridger raised her hands and began slowly peeling the top down her arms. "Did anyone's opinion ever stop you from doin' what you wanted?"

Carmody's breath caught in his throat as the top slid down her arms until her breasts bobbed free, standing up proudly from her chest, pink nipples jutting toward him.

She stepped out of the wash-worn garment, moved to the edge of the hot spring, and poked the tip of her right foot in the water.

"That a yes?" Carmody asked her.

She shook her head and puffed the cigar, the smoke curling up under her hat brim. "No."

Wincing slightly around the cigar, Claudine stepped into the water and, keeping her hands above the surface, moved toward him. She straddled him, wrapped her arms around his neck, plucked his cigarette from his teeth, and dropped it in the water. She opened her mouth, let the cigar drop. It sizzled and swirled away.

"This is a maybe."

She slid him into her ever so gently and clamped her mouth over his.

A LOOK AT: ROGUE LAWMAN

THE COMPLETE SERIES, VOLUME 1

THE ROGUE LAWMAN, GIDEON HAWK, CAN TURN FROM MARSHAL TO EXECUTIONER WITH THE PULL OF A TRIGGER...

Guided only by the barrel of his pistol, former deputy marshal Gideon Hawk no longer abides by conventional laws. Known as the Rogue Lawman, he serves his own brand of justice by carving his way through the West, leaving fallen criminals in his wake...

When "Three Fingers" Ned Meade kills his ten-year-old son, which results in his wife's suicide, Gideon Hawk, once a lawman of principle, embarks on a mission of vengeance against Meade--one that will make him a wanted man.

Rogue Lawman: The Complete Series, Volume 1 includes: Rogue Lawman; Deadly Prey; Cold Corpse, Hot Trail; Bullets over Bedlam and Border Snakes.

"Action-packed...for fans of traditional westerns."—**Booklist**

AVAILABLE NOW

ABOUT THE AUTHOR

Peter Brandvold grew up in the great state of North Dakota in the 1960's and '70s, when television westerns were as popular as shows about hoarders and shark tanks are now, and western paperbacks were as popular as *Game of Thrones*.

Brandvold watched every western series on television at the time. He grew up riding horses and herding cows on the farms of his grandfather and many friends who owned livestock.

Brandvold's imagination has always lived and will always live in the West. He is the author of over a hundred lightning-fast action westerns under his own name and his pen name, Frank Leslie.

Printed in Dunstable, United Kingdom

69060597R00316